he blurted out

"Wha-a-at?"

"Married. You and me." Ben sat up. "Think about it—if ever two people had good reason to get married, it's us."

She stared at him for several seconds, then shot upright, hurriedly buttoning her jeans. Her face flamed and her breath came in short spurts. "But…marriage! Ben, that's such a…huge leap. The kids—" She waved a hand feebly toward the house.

"Need a mom and a dad," he finished. "Abby, we've both admitted we need help with them."

"Yes, but…" Her tongue stumbled over her racing thoughts. Ben's cell phone rang.

He frowned as he took the call, then clicked off abruptly. "Abby, I have to go to County Hospital—an emergency. Could I leave Erin and Mollie with you?"

"Of course you can." She managed to get to her feet semigracefully, although her head still spun from his marriage proposal.

Ben went on instant doctor-autopilot. He hurried inside, spent two seconds explaining his hasty exit to the girls—then, poof, he was gone.

Desperate for something ordinary to focus on, Abby ran water to wash the dishes. A *business merger*, she told herself. That was all it had been. He'd made no mention of love. The absence of such a tiny word shouldn't bother Abby. But it did….

Dear Reader,

During the period in my life when I worked for three pediatricians, our doctors saw a lot of blended families. These *yours, mine and ours* families presented a special brand of problem for the office staff—where to file their charts. And then, where to *find* them for kids who had a different last name from the mother or dad who'd phoned for an appointment.

One year we installed a color-coded charting system. Color of folder was determined by the patient's name. Merged families suddenly became everyone's nightmare. We could have Johnstons and Smiths living with Browns, but no one wanted to decide which of the coded colors to use.

Because you can't work in medicine and not develop a good sense of humor, finding the correct patient charts for kids from blended families became a challenge and a game. Who could find them the fastest when a doctor bellowed down the hall? And heaven have mercy if the chart ended up in the insurance drawer or in a stack needing dictation.

In all those years I never really stopped to consider the daily challenges faced by the parents in these blended families. While I worried whether Johnny's file was blue or red or green, these stepmoms and dads dealt with far greater concerns.

I'm not color coding Abby Drummond and Ben Galloway's story. Their trials and tribulations with the seven kids they're doing their best to raise are laid out in black and white. I hope readers empathize with the unique problems faced by this couple, who started out in love. They lost it, and found it again.

I enjoy hearing from readers. You can reach me at P.O. Box 17480-101, Tucson, AZ 85731 or by e-mail (rdfox@worldnet.att.net).

Roz Denny Fox

Married in Haste
Roz Denny Fox

TORONTO • NEW YORK • LONDON
AMSTERDAM • PARIS • SYDNEY • HAMBURG
STOCKHOLM • ATHENS • TOKYO • MILAN • MADRID
PRAGUE • WARSAW • BUDAPEST • AUCKLAND

ISBN 0-373-71148-4

MARRIED IN HASTE

This edition published by arrangement with Harlequin Books S.A.

® and TM are trademarks of the publisher. Trademarks indicated with
® are registered in the United States Patent and Trademark Office, the
Canadian Trade Marks Office and in other countries.

Visit us at www.eHarlequin.com

Printed in U.S.A.

This story is for Adrianne, Ashley, Mandy and Morgan.
You girls are Harlequin's next generation of readers. In the
not too distant future, some of you may even be writers.

Books by Roz Denny Fox

HARLEQUIN SUPERROMANCE

Don't miss any of our special offers. Write to us at the
following address for information on our newest releases.

Harlequin Reader Service
U.S.: 3010 Walden Ave., P.O. Box 1325, Buffalo, NY 14269
Canadian: P.O. Box 609, Fort Erie, Ont. L2A 5X3

CHAPTER ONE

THE HOLLOW DISTANT RING of a telephone made Abigail Drummond fumble and drop the colored pencil she'd been using to mark second-grade state math tests. She automatically reached over to answer it. When her hand touched air, Abby remembered stuffing the phone, which normally sat on a corner of her desk, into her bottom drawer to make more room for the test packets. By the fifth ring, she managed to extract it and get the receiver to her ear. "Ms. Drummond." Abby answered in her crispest professional voice. Calls coming in after school were usually from parents complaining about homework she'd tucked into their students' backpacks. Abby tended to get defensive on that topic, as she assigned far less than did her counterparts at West Seattle's Sky Heights Elementary school. Today, the familiar masculine voice came as a pleasant surprise.

"It's Ben Galloway, Abby. Am I interrupting a teacher-parent talk or anything? If so, I'll try to phone you later at home."

A ripple of pleasure sent Abby's pulse skittering. She'd dated Ben, whom society columnists listed as one of Seattle's "most eligible bachelors," for roughly ten months. She'd met him when he attended an end-of-the-year-conference in his sister, Marlo McBride's stead. Marlo was a single mother, and her older daughter, Erin, had been Abby's top student.

"Ben...sorry if I sounded abrupt. You caught me grading our mandatory math exams.'' Abby twisted a lock of her crackling red hair around one index finger. ''I hate to say the early results look abominable. But they do. Which makes me seriously question my ability to teach.''

''Ouch. I recall you said that your principal is holding staff responsible for the overall class scores on those tests.''

''Yes. Odd that you phoned when I was wishing I could clone your niece. Or her sister. Where's Mollie when I need scores in the ninetieth percentile?''

Ben chuckled. ''You'll probably get Mollie next year. She's every bit as clever as Erin but that kid's a pistol. She's stubborn as a Missouri mule.''

''This from a pediatrician who sees our city's most advantaged kids? Don't forget, I've observed Mollie on the playground. She's a jewel.''

''Ha! Next time I get volunteered to take those little stinkers to the zoo, I'll know who to con into assisting.''

''No need to con. If I'm free, I'll be happy to help. Not that I'm bragging, but since I've made zoo field trips part of my curriculum for eight years, I have it honed to a fine science.''

''How did I miss knowing all this good stuff? Consider it stored for future reference. But Abby, I called to discuss an adult-type excursion.'' His already deep voice lowered to a sexy growl. Welcoming any diversion, she responded in kind. ''If you've got the night off and want to rescue me from these depressing tests, I'll toss in a home-cooked meal. I can be home in…say, thirty minutes.''

''Don't I wish. Sorry, I'm on call tonight. I've admitted a kid to Children's Health Hospital and I'm waiting for a lab workup.''

''Oh.'' Her one-word reply failed to cloak Abby's disappointment.

Ben cleared his throat. ''Getting back to why I called—

remember last week I said I'd like to wangle time for skiing?''

"Yes." Her racing pulse slowed appreciably. "I take it you've managed to free your schedule for a day at Stevens Pass?"

"Better. A full week. At Whistler. I've rented a condo up there."

"Zowie! I guess you did wangle time off. Well…have fun. While you're swishing through hip-deep powder, think of me here slaving away."

The open phone line hummed following Abby's statement. "Oh, if you need me to water your plants, Ben, I can easily swing past your apartment after work."

"I botched this call from the get-go, Abby. I want you to come with me. I happened to see the school calendar taped to Marlo's fridge. My week off coincides with your spring break."

Abby's skin prickled with excitement. What Ben was proposing would boost their relationship to a new level. Thus far, they'd gone to dinner, movies, concerts and an occasional school function together. In that time, Ben had spent one night at her town house and she'd slept at his apartment twice. Up to now, neither had suggested going beyond catch-as-catch-can dating. They tended to go out on the spur of the moment—if and when their busy schedules allowed. Which was why his invitation for a week-long tryst silenced Abby's tongue.

"Abby? You're not responding. Am I off base in assuming that we're seeing each other exclusively? If so, please tell me straight out."

"You're not. Off base," she said quickly, her heart tripping madly. She quickly thumbed through her desk calendar. "Yikes! Spring break is next week. I've been too busy to notice, I guess. No wonder the kids are bouncing off the walls.''

''I'll understand if you've already made other plans. The clinic wasn't something I could walk away from without a lot of finagling and appointment switching. I knew asking you this late was a long shot. And I'd like to leave Friday afternoon.''

''Four days,'' she muttered, minor panic building as she worried about finding time to dig her skis out of storage, not to mention dashing past the mall to stock up on a few necessities—like a sexy nightie and silky undies. Hers tended to be a hodgepodge of much-washed white cotton.

''To be exact, it's three days, twenty-two hours and fifty-four minutes from now. Jeez, I didn't mean—uh, don't think I was counting the minutes until I can get you into my bed,'' Ben said. ''Well, that, too,'' he added, laughing. ''What I meant, though, is that's how long I have left to deal with all my outstanding cases.''

''I knew what you meant. You said the other day you haven't had a real vacation since you and Steve opened the clinic. Ben,'' Abby murmured, ''are you positive you want me horning in on your days off?''

''Oh, yeah!'' This time there was no mistaking the implication in his seductive growl.

Abby pictured the two of them living together for seven whole days. *And nights!* Thirty-two-year-old, Benjamin Galloway, M.D., was the sort of man mothers the world over prayed their daughters would bring home for keeps. At six foot two, he honed his muscles with a daily jog. His light-brown hair, naturally streaked gold, was perpetually wind-tossed. Not only was he easy on the eyes, Ben was good to the bone. Intelligent. And articulate. He laughed easily, too. He genuinely liked people, especially kids.

For most of Abby's twenty-eight years, she'd watched

his type gravitate to her prettier, sexier girlfriends. Abby suffered no illusions about her too red hair and the freckles that went with it. In high school she'd been drab. Abby supposed that if her good friends were asked to describe her, they might note her above-average intellect. Or perhaps they'd mention that she kept a cool head in a crisis.

Big whoop! as her second graders would say. Given her meager dating history, the fact that a guy like Ben Galloway would invite her on a romantic getaway made Abby worry that he'd wake up tomorrow with second thoughts. "If you do change your mind or anything, Ben, you'll let me know?" she blurted.

He laughed. "I won't change my mind. Can you be ready Friday by five-thirty? I'll pick you up at your place. We can grab dinner somewhere between here and the Canadian border if that's all right."

"Sure. It sounds fantastic. Uh…is there any chance of your coming over for dinner tomorrow night? My offer of a home-cooked meal stands."

"Tempting as it sounds, Abby, I can't. I'm up to my eyeballs in dictation. As usual, I've put off completing paperwork far too long. The hospital records staff and my secretary are at the point of leaving death threats with my answering service. If I work my tail off all week, I might actually get to go with a clear conscience."

"Maybe I'll do up lesson plans in advance," she said. "In case I break my neck on the slopes. You do recall that I haven't skied in more than two years?"

"Ditto," Ben teased. "Last time I skied was before we opened the clinic three years ago. Or is it four? Man…let's hope we don't *both* fall. One of us has to drive home. Or maybe not," he added in that earlier suggestive tone. "Picture us stranded in a mountain chalet. The place I rented has a hot tub."

Abby fanned herself with a test packet. "Now, that's something to consider. Careful, Ben, I may shove you off a cliff and leap after you—if only to ensure that we get stranded."

His delighted laughter was interrupted by an insistent bleat. "Oops, gotta go. That's my pager. See you Friday. G'bye."

"I hope your page is nothing serious. I'm looking forward to spring break. I'd hate for anything to interfere."

"Nothing will, short of flood, famine or pestilence. Well, scratch pestilence. In my line of work that's a marked possibility. Damn! Whoever has my pager number isn't giving up. See you Friday, babe."

"Okay. Bye, Ben." Abby gripped the receiver tight even after she heard the soft click. Ben's calling her *babe* was new, too. Lordy, lordy—he was definitely turning up the flame. In spite of her shiver of anticipation, Abby was bothered by one teensy detail she hadn't brought up to him.

The Reverend Elliot Drummond.

Abby's older brother posed an obstacle for two reasons. In past years, during spring break, she'd always baby-sat for him and his wife, Blair. She'd started the annual treat as a way to repay Elliot for the numerous sacrifices he'd made after their parents died. Their folks had been volunteer counselors with a youth outing in the San Juan Islands when a sudden, violent squall struck the Strait of Juan de Fuca and capsized their rented canoe. All the canoeists were lost.

Abby never thought of that period in her life without profound sorrow. Especially as the months before the accident had been nearly perfect. Her parents had left their mission in Calcutta. John had accepted a church in West Seattle, where his wife had grown up. Elliot had just left for Oxford on a Fulbright scholarship. The whole family was proud of him. And for the first time ever, Abby would attend regular middle school. She'd been elated at the prospect. As the daughter of missionaries, she'd always felt rootless.

Bless Elliot. He'd given up his scholarship, returned home and gone to work at a grocery store to keep Abby out of foster care. Those had been tough years. Instead of making lasting friends, Abby was shut out by kids at school who blamed her parents for the disaster. As if they could control the weather.

Elliot's unswerving faith got Abby through. He attended college at night, and made her study hard as well. As a result, she earned a scholarship to Washington State University, where she earned a teaching degree. Teaching allowed her to make a difference in young lives. In Abby's classes, every child counted.

Considering everything Elliot had sacrificed for her, baby-sitting seemed a small repayment. Especially since he'd delayed his marriage to his childhood sweetheart because of his responsibilities to Abby.

She broke into a grin. Once Elliot and Blair did marry, they set to work repopulating the Drummond clan with five boys. Two sets of twins and an only. It wasn't hard to see that Blair needed a break from being a stay-at-home mom.

But who was Abby kidding? This uncomfortable feeling wasn't only a matter of not being available to baby-sit her brother's kids. Quite simply, Elliot would disapprove of her going with a man. And Elliot liked Ben well enough. Her brother would never condone sex outside of marriage; the *who* wouldn't matter. In Elliot's mind, Abby would forever be his baby sister. His responsibility.

She supported her chin on one hand and stared at the chalkboard. It hadn't been a week since he'd mentioned how many of her contemporaries' weddings he'd officiated at over the past year.

Marriage was a difficult issue for her. The forever-after vow bothered Abby. *Nothing* lasted forever. While she hated to disappoint Elliot, marriage was a subject on which they held fundamentally different views. He just didn't understand. Elliot would never bend a single one of the ten commandments. Ever. Not for any reason.

While she wasn't one to avoid confrontation, Abby decided she ought to rehearse what she'd say to Elliot and Blair. There was no one sweeter than Blair. And no one who deserved a break more.

Abby stacked her tests to take home. She'd think about it overnight and maybe something would come to her.

Nothing did. She stalled for two more days and nights.

Friday, her back was to the wall. She had no choice but to go by their house before work and 'fess up. But when she phoned to inform them of her plan, Elliot didn't have time to talk. He said he had a meeting in town. Blair was accompanying him so she could use the van later. "Sam needs shoes," Elliot said, sounding rushed. "And we have to drop the twins off at school."

Abby turned her calendar and panic set in. It was her morning to do the breakfast shift in the cafeteria. "I forgot I have morning duty. But what I have to tell you is important. I can't sit for you guys next week. I'm going skiing with Ben. We're going to Canada."

"*What?* Nonsense!"

"Sorry, Elliot. I have to dash or risk being late. Is your meeting an all-day affair, or can I call you on your cell phone during my lunch break?"

"I'll phone you at school as soon as I finish my meeting," Elliot told her sternly.

Abby wrinkled her nose at the buzzing phone as she hung up.

CHAPTER TWO

WHILE HER CAR IDLED off the morning chill, Abby was pleased to see sun chasing off the clouds. She hoped this would turn out to be a nice day. For February, Seattle enjoyed relatively mild temperatures.

Her breakfast duty started at seven. Their school had so many single moms and working parents, they'd long since instituted a hot breakfast plan five days a week. If she'd thought sooner, Abby would have offered Blair the use of her car. She wouldn't need it for a week, and Ben could as easily pick her up at school. Besides, it would be easier to talk to Blair about her plans. She was less…uncompromising than Elliot.

As she approached the school, Abby scanned the line of cars pulling through the bus lane to drop students at the cafeteria. If she saw her brother and his wife, she'd still make the offer. Unfortunately, the Drummonds' aging van wasn't among those parked in the circular drive, so Abby drove by and parked in the faculty lot.

She'd missed them, she discovered as soon as she entered the building. Her nephews were lying in wait to pounce on her. Nine-year-old Noah and Michael both had missing front teeth, which made what they said hard to understand. Ultimately Abby deduced that they were regaling her with the latest antics of their beloved boxer, Ruffian. "You know what, Aunt Abby? Ruffian chewed holes in Daddy's best tie this morning."

"Yeth," agreed one of the younger twins. At seven, Brad still lisped. He tugged Abby's jacket, wanting to be heard over Reed, his more gregarious twin. "Mama covered our ears, 'cause Daddy said bad words."

"No kidding?" Abby knew she should let remarks of that sort slide rather than draw attention to them. But it seemed so…not like Elliot. She paused to consider whether or not he might be exceptionally upset by her news. Or were things rocky at his church? She knew from past history that working with congregations wasn't always sweetness and light. Ministers were often unduly pressured by either their flocks or their governing boards. Maybe Elliot and Blair needed a break more than she'd assumed. What if they were really counting on her for next week?

Blair had been vague about their plans, but still…

Friends of the boys called to them. True to their fickle natures, her nephews abandoned Abby and hurried off to line up for chow with their pals.

Other kids circled around her. Abby rarely lacked the company of kids during her cafeteria or playground duties. Her attention wandered to a group entering the room. Ben's nieces were among them. Abby hadn't seen Erin and Mollie with the breakfast bunch before.

She worked her way in their direction, deciding to ask if there'd been a change in their mom's schedule.

"Girls, hi." Abby spoke to the girls even as her eyes strayed to a rowdy collection of fourth- and fifth-grade boys who seemed to be getting out of control at one of the tables.

"Ms. Drummond, how come you're on morning duty?" Erin exclaimed.

"All teachers rotate morning and after school, hon. I was just thinking I hadn't seen you and Mollie here before."

Mollie danced from foot to foot until Erin stilled her. "Mommy's insurance office went to flex time." The eight-year-old's elfin face grew serious behind her wire-rimmed glasses. "Mollie and I have to get up earlier now."

"I don't like it," Mollie interjected.

Erin, the more sedate of the two, placed a firm hand on her younger sister's shoulder. "We don't really mind. It means Mommy's home at two-thirty when school lets out."

"Well, that's good. So you're no longer going to Mrs. Scott's?"

"She moved to California to live with her son."

Mollie piped up again. "Mrs. Scott said her old bones don't like Seattle rain."

"Ah. Last year, I do remember her having problems with arthritis. Well, it seems your mom's new schedule came at a good time. Excuse me, girls. I need to go chat with those boys. In case I don't get back to you, have a great day."

Abby had taken maybe five steps toward the disruptive boys when, without warning, the cafeteria floor shifted under her feet and sent her reeling. Simultaneously her stomach tightened, then dropped. She lurched sideways, right, then left, as if she'd stepped on a carnival ride. A Tilt-A-Whirl. Abby grabbed for a chair only to have it bob crazily away. As she tried righting herself, another jolt threw her to her knees. All around her, kids began to scream and cry.

For a moment, an unnamed panic seized Abby. Her heart raced as she crawled across the bucking floor. She forced herself to climb to her feet.

Food trays flew off nearby tables. Chairs toppled. Kids scrambled over one another. Automatically, Abby clutched a whistle swinging from a cord around her neck. She blew two sharp blasts. Stretching out her arms, she caught a bunch of kids who hurtled past her. "It's an earthquake," she shouted, realizing what was happening. "Remember our drills! Jason Bingham, stop in your tracks. All of you! Listen to me."

This wasn't the first quake in Abby's career. Oddly, it was the noisiest and seemed to last longer than most. Her attempts to achieve order went unheeded.

The cook and cashier exploded out from their stations. Abby's counterpart, a fourth-grade teacher, began herding older kids out the back exit while yelling something Abby couldn't distinguish. A third shrill blast of her whistle failed to cut through a horrendous rumble.

As sheer pandemonium erupted and inanimate objects bounced past her, Abby's training kicked in. Two facts struck her—the rumble had turned into a roar, and the shaking, which had always faded quickly in past earthquakes, was splitting wide cracks in the tile floor. Tables slid in one direction, then the other. Some toppled. Dust billowed from the cracks, making everyone cough and choke.

"Children, line up by twos," Abby said between gagging. "We're going outside just like we've practiced. Leaders, head for the middle of the playground, away from anything that might fall from the building. Stop screaming! I know you're scared. You older kids, hold hands with someone younger." She had to shout to be heard. And her own stomach pitched as fear tried to take hold. She spat out grit.

When she lined up the children closest to her, more converged from all corners of the room. Their copious tears, frightened eyes and ashen faces added to Abby's mounting urgency. Off to her right, a row of pots fitted in a special warming table buckled, split, overturned and spread hot oatmeal, dollar pancakes and boiling syrup across the floor.

Hustling the first of her brood over the front threshold, Abby flinched and ducked to avoid wildly swinging light fixtures overhead. Any moment, she feared, one or all might crash down on the rows of students. Until right now, she'd never thought about how many kids ate breakfast at school. She began counting heads as sobbing, shivering groups exited the building.

"There's safety in being orderly," she hollered above the deafening roar. "I want everyone to get a buddy. Walk fast, but don't run. If you run, you may fall. Once you're outside, move away from the walls but not toward the street or parking lot." As she spoke, two windows on the north side of the cafeteria ruptured. The front bumper of a blue Ford that must have been parked beside the cafeteria had obviously jumped the curb. Slivers of glass rained everywhere like glittering icicles.

Ms. Fielding, another teacher, dodged a ceiling tile as she led her group of children toward an exit. Abby scooped two of the smallest kids into her arms. She set them outside, out of harms' way, and in so doing took a direct hit from the heavy door that suddenly swung shut. Terrified, she watched the metal casing crumple as if made of paper. The door splintered, sending a new wave of fear through the kids trapped inside. Bawling, they trampled over those near the front of the line.

Abby forcefully shoved them away from falling debris. "About face, everyone!" she commanded. "We'll use the side emergency exit." Herding the remaining few, ranging in age from six to twelve, the length of the cracking, groaning building was no easy feat. Inside her head a hollow voice chanted. *Why doesn't the shaking stop? Lord, please, it can't go on much longer.*

It felt as if an eternity had passed before she reached the side exit, and wrenched it open. Abby knew they'd lost power when the door sprang open without emitting the piercing squeal that told the world she'd breached security. She doubted anyone else noticed or cared. Outside, the air was filled with wailing sirens, ringing church bells, barking dogs and earsplitting car alarms. The sky was brown with floating debris.

Keening, shaking children fell to their knees, all trying to make sense of the disorder. There was confusion everywhere. Bricks tumbled from the second story, splitting the walkway circling their newly constructed gymnasium. Asphalt beneath the playground equipment seemed alive as it puckered and broke apart. A river of water zigzagged between buildings. ''Kids, stay away from that water,'' Abby shouted, veering her last charges to higher ground. ''We don't know if a water main inside the building broke, or if that's sewage from the bathrooms.''

Teachers and students, all looking shell-shocked, attempted to band together in the center of the playground. Abby began collecting her nephews and Ben's nieces. She checked each child for injuries before she allowed herself a deep, calming breath.

''Where's the sun gone?'' Erin asked in a frightened voice. Until then, Abby hadn't noticed that an ugly ecru sky had replaced the earlier blue. A thick layer of smoke or dust or both thickened the now still air. Blessedly, the horrid rumble had begun to recede, and the shaking was slowly subsiding. Disaster sirens didn't let up their howling.

Glancing at her watch, Abby couldn't believe that minutes, not hours, had passed. She tapped her watch to see if it'd stopped. But it was seven-fifteen the last time she'd looked, just before crossing the cafeteria to greet Erin and Mollie. Now her watch said twenty-three minutes after the hour. *All this chaos occurred in less than ten minutes?*

Mr. Conrad, the school principal, a slightly stoop-shouldered man who'd announced his plans to retire at the end of this school year, worked his way among his scattered staff. Usually impeccable, he looked thoroughly disheveled.

Abby had to peel Brad, Reed and Mollie away from her so she could go have a word with her boss.

"It's not good news," he said in a hushed voice. "The university seismology lab is saying this quake was 8.0 on the Richter scale. The West Seattle Bridge and parts of the viaduct along the waterfront have collapsed. No telling how many of these kids who were dropped off early have parents buried in that rubble."

Abby's heart did a double flip. Bile rose to gag her. Practically anyone headed downtown after leaving the school crossed that bridge. "What about the floating bridge into the city?" she asked, unclenching her teeth to speak.

Conrad hiked a shoulder. "I only got sketchy reports before I had to evacuate the main building. Our job, Abigail, is to calm the students until we get specific information on the whereabouts of their families." He sighed. "It might be a selfish reaction, but why couldn't this have waited until next week when school's out for spring break? Then parents would've had the responsibility that's fallen to us."

Abby thought about her plans for spring break, and a shiver rushed up her spine. Had her selfish decision brought God's wrath?

Don't be ridiculous!

She shrugged off the childish thought as fast as it popped into her head. A counselor way back when had made her see that her parents' accident was nobody's fault. She'd believed, as kids often do, that she'd been somehow to blame. The counselor had convinced her acts of God weren't caused by human deeds.

Beyond her, Mr. Conrad was saying, "No, children. We can't let you go into your classrooms. Remember our earthquake drills? We stay out in the open until the fire department gives us an all-clear." Numerous hands shot up, and the principal patiently answered each and every question. The smaller kids huddled inside their jackets looking dazed. A fifth-grader, whose teeth chattered, enquired about aftershocks.

Aftershocks. Abby wondered how many kids knew they could be as devastating as the original quake. If the aftershocks were big enough, already damaged buildings and bridges could shake apart. Secondary quakes often delayed rescue attempts, too.

Her head was a jumble of worries. She tried to focus on something that might occupy the restless students. The cell phone she wore clipped to her belt vibrated. Abby flinched until she realized it wasn't the beginning of another quake.

Fumbling the phone out of its case, she ventured a raspy, "Hello?"

"Ms. Drummond? This is Mercy General ER. Thank God I've finally gotten through to you! Some regular circuits were knocked out. The phone company said that eventually undamaged cell towers would route calls past towers that collapsed."

Abby said nothing.

"Have I reached, Abigail Drummond, sister of Elliot David Drummond?"

Spinning away from her nephews, Abby answered with a shaky, "Yes." The hole in her stomach widened. The woman on the phone identified herself as Nurse Olivia Warren. She continued in a thankfully even voice, "I understand the streets are a mess, Ms. Drummond, but Dr. Nelson thinks you should try to get here to see your brother. His injuries are…serious. Please come if you can make it through the snarled traffic."

"I…am a teacher. We have our own emergency here. Exactly what are Elliot's injuries? And…Blair. What about his wife? They were traveling together with their son, Sam. He's four.''

Abby heard paper rustle, or maybe it was static on the line. ''I can't tell you anything about his wife. But Samuel—a team's working to stabilize him now.''

''Sam, oh, no!'' Abby's voice broke. ''Listen, tell Elliot I'll do my utmost to get there. Are you at liberty to relay the nature of Sam's problem?'' Abby bit down hard on her lower lip to keep from revealing her panic.

''I believe it has to do with his legs. Dr. Nelson is trying to find a pediatric orthopedist. But…the entire medical community is on triage alert. We're not sure which hospitals have which physicians at this point. Your family arrived in one of the first ambulances.''

Ben. Ben would know how to find the best doctor for Sam. ''I have a friend. A pediatrician. Dr. Galloway. I'll see if he can recommend a doctor for Sam. And I'll do everything I can to get to the hospital. I'd appreciate it if you'd give my brother a message. Tell him his two sets of twins are safe. I have all four boys right here.''

Her hand shook so badly after she ended the call, Abby had to order herself to calm down. At first she couldn't remember Ben's number. She felt the same numbness she'd experienced when her parents died.

Taking a deep breath, she remembered that Ben's clinic and hospital pager were programmed into her phone. She tried his clinic first. After four tries, someone there told her he'd gone to the Children's Health Hospital. He picked up on Abby's fifth attempt to connect with his cell. ''Galloway. Make it short unless you're calling about blood gasses on Bobby Harris.''

''Ben, it's Abby. I'm sorry to bother you.'' Her voice sounded reedy to her ears.

''Abby?'' People were shouting in the background. ''I'm

surprised you got through,'' he said loudly. ''Are you okay? Newscasters say the city suffered widespread damage. Phone and power lines are down. In fact, our hospital's working off a generator.''

''I'm fine. I'm calling because I need a favor. Elliot and Sam are in Mercy General. I don't know any particulars, but Sam apparently needs an orthopedist. The nurse who phoned made it sound urgent. Ben, I didn't know where else to turn.'' Abby was afraid she was on the verge of hysteria.

''My father,'' Ben said flatly. ''Kirk Galloway. As a dad, he stinks, but as a bone surgeon, he's the best in the city. Hell, in the state. Mercy General? And the boy is Sam? Sam…Drummond?''

''Yes. He's only four. I appreciate this, Ben. I know you've never met the kids, only Elliot and Blair at the opera that night. But—jeez, I'm rambling. If your dad can see Sam, tell him I'll guarantee his fee. Elliot's insurance through the church probably isn't the greatest.''

''That wouldn't matter to me, but I'm sure it matters to my old man. I hate to cut you off, Abby, but I'm being paged. Let's try to connect later, okay?''

''Right. And…thanks again, Ben. Oh, before I forget— Erin and Mollie are here with me. They're regular little troopers. Tell Marlo if you talk to her. I don't know if anyone's answering our school phones. We're not allowed inside. I'm sure parents are worried sick.''

''Marlo? I forgot her agency recently changed her hours. She crosses the West Seattle Bridge, and I've heard—'' Ben's voice sank, then broke entirely. ''Abby, I need to go. I'll grab a minute to call my sister. Thanks for the info on the girls. Tell them I'll see them when this craziness settles down.''

Abby relayed Ben's message to his solemn-eyed nieces

before she went to find Mr. Conrad and explain her situation. "I have to go," she said. "I'll ask Raina Miller to take the boys home with her if I'm delayed getting back. Until I know where their mom is and how severely their dad and brother are hurt, I'd rather not worry them. I'll tell them I have a problem at my town house." Her lips almost didn't move, they were so icy cold.

"I'm sorry, Abigail." The principal eyed her sympathetically. "I'm afraid your news is only the first we can expect. You take care driving across town. I have a really bad feeling about this quake. I suppose we should be thankful more students weren't at school. But I can't help wondering if we're prepared to care for the many whose parents won't be able to get through the wreckage to pick them up." Normally a sedate man, he was all but wringing his hands.

Oddly, his unrest had the opposite effect on Abby. She began to think more clearly. "Someone should go get the student files. Most parents have cell phone numbers listed. The nurse who called me said the cell towers fared better than standard phone lines. You could designate one teacher to call parents."

"Excellent suggestion, Abby. I should have thought of it myself. It goes to show that no matter how many drills we have, nothing prepares us for the actuality."

"I'm sorry I can't stay and help. But…the nurse was insistent, even though she's aware of conditions in and around the city."

"Go. Reassure the boys and don't forget to explain that you're leaving them in Raina's care."

Abby turned away, hoping she'd be able to hide her alarm.

CHAPTER THREE

THE TWINS, especially the younger set, hung on Abby's jacket, and begged her to take them. "Aunt Abby," Noah, one of the nine-year-olds, pleaded. "Can't you drop us off at home? Ruffian will be so scared. So will Speedy and Poky, me and Mike's hamsters. And Brad and Reed's gerbil. Even Daddy's fish, I bet. What if a tank broke or something? Mommy's gone, so there's nobody home to save our pets."

Abby ruffled his wheat-blond hair. "Guys, I need you to stay here where I know you're safe. Mrs. Miller has agreed to watch you until someone in the family comes by. She might take you home with her. You boys have been to her house before, remember? I promise I'll be as quick as I can, but I want your word that you'll do exactly as she says."

"What if Mama or Daddy comes to get us first?"

Abby glanced worriedly away from Noah's direct blue eyes. "You'll go with them, of course." She hugged each boy harder than she normally would, but wasn't able to look back at their tearstained faces after she'd hurried off.

"Raina, I have no idea how long I'll be." Abby spoke in a low voice to her good friend and fellow teacher. "Maybe I can reach some neighbors, to see if the kids' home—and my apartment building—are still standing."

"Don't worry, Abby. Do whatever's necessary. I have a freezer full of hot dogs left over from our Super Bowl party.

Jerry won't be home. It was his day off, but he just phoned and said the precinct's called everyone in.''

"I hate to ask another favor, but…I called Ben Galloway to ask for an orthopedic referral for Sam. Ben's sister is Marlo McBride, and her daughters are in the breakfast bunch.'' She nodded toward the huddled girls, who sat still as mice. The older child's arms were looped tight around her younger sister. "Would you keep an eye on them, too, until Marlo or her designee arrives? Erin told me this morning that the woman who used to baby-sit them moved to California.''

"Hey, the more the merrier. Our house is so close to the school, it's not a problem. If the city streets are as messy as Jerry said when he phoned, I might be a clearing house for a whole bunch of school refugees. Abby, you take extra care, hear? The streetlights have been knocked out. Some roads have buckled and others are flooded. Maybe you shouldn't go.''

Abby rubbed at the furrows forming between her eyes. "If it were me in the hospital and Elliot at work, he'd make every effort to reach me. Outside of Blair and the boys, I'm Elliot's only relative.''

"I understand. I'll round up the twins and the McBride girls right now, and reassure them as best I can. You'll call me when you learn something for sure?''

"I will. Raina, I don't know how I'll ever repay you.''

"Don't start that, Abby Drummond. One favor does not make you indebted to me for the rest of your natural life.'' Mustering a smile, Raina offered Abby a stick of gum, which she unwrapped on her way to the parking lot. Remembering the cars that had come through the cafeteria windows, she prayed her small compact had fared better.

It had, and started on her first try.

An aftershock struck when Abby was little more than a

block from the school. It gave her an odd sensation. Her car seemed steady, but around her the sidewalks and curbs undulated. Trees dipped and swayed. It was as if she was viewing the world through a vibrating camera. Homes lining the street gyrated for a moment, dancing to silent music. Thankfully the aftershock was over quickly, and cars proceeded normally in both directions.

Abby popped out the CD she'd listened to on the way to school, and turned on her radio. The ringing of her cell phone caused her nerves to jump and her heart to speed up. "Hello," she said after groping the instrument out of its case and nearly dropping it.

"Abby?" Ben's voice, however welcome, sounded terribly strained.

"Sorry, Ben. I had a little trouble retrieving my phone. I'm in the car, headed to Mercy G. We just experienced a fair-size aftershock. I'm still shaking even though the tremor stopped."

"I wish you'd stay put, Abby. We've been bombarded by the first wave of casualties. There are so many critical injuries coming in, you'd think this was a war zone. Two things, and then I have to dash. My dad's probably examining Sam as we speak. Dad's condominium on Queen Anne is a matter of blocks from Mercy. So tell Elliot that Sam's in good hands. Since you've left school, it may not matter that I haven't been able to raise Marlo. I did get in touch with a co-worker who said the agency sent everyone home. She also said one end of their parking garage has crumbled."

Abby heard worry in his words. "Ben, I doubt Marlo got that far. I don't know the exact time she dropped the girls at school, but I saw them shortly after they arrived. In fact, I'd gone over to talk to them just before the shock hit. At the most, Marlo couldn't have been on the road ten minutes. Oh, before I forget, I asked Raina Miller, one of our teachers, to keep tabs on my nephews and your nieces. Marlo knows where the Millers live. If no one's at the school, she'll find the girls with Raina.''

''That's great, Abby. I'm up to my ears in emergencies. All the doctors are.''

''Can your mother collect Erin and Mollie?''

''My folks split a long time ago. Mom lives in Rome. I'm all the family Marlo has here. Dad—well, he and Marlo rarely speak.''

''This is the doctor you recommended for Sam?''

''Believe me, Kirk's patients get better treatment than his family ever did.''

Abby had never heard Ben speak quite so sharply. Which proved, if nothing else, that she knew relatively little about the man she'd been seeing for almost a year. And she'd planned to spend a week alone with him in the mountains? Looking at it like that, she found it easier to understand Elliot's concern.

Abby heard Ben talking to someone else, then he came on the line again, sounding rushed.

''I'm needed for an injured baby they just brought in. Thanks, Abby, for arranging for Erin and Mollie's care. If you have a number for Mrs. Miller I'll jot it down and see if maybe Dad's girlfriend will go pick them up.''

Abby had come to a street where the signals weren't operating, and crossing appeared to be in the hands of the bravest. She quickly relayed Raina's number, concentrating on traffic.

''Thanks,'' he said. ''With the bridge out, you'll have to swing south before you can cross and go north to Mercy. I'll call again when I get a chance.''

She dropped the phone in her lap and gripped the steering wheel tight. She surprised herself by making it across the intersection unscathed. But she couldn't help noticing that her palms were slick with sweat. So was her forehead. Navigating around debris spilling out in the roadway claimed her full concentration.

More than once Abby considered turning back. Love for her brother and his family kept her doggedly taking the detours that skirted the worst of the damage.

A full two hours after she'd left the school, Abby was about a quarter mile from the hospital. A policeman directing traffic at a cross-street flagged her down and motioned for her to roll down her window.

"Only ambulance and aid cars beyond this point, miss."

"But…" she sputtered, her fingers clutching the steering wheel. "The hospital contacted me. My brother and his son have been injured." She blinked back tears. "The nurse said it was urgent, and it's taken me hours to reach this point." She explained how she'd started in West Seattle and had to detour along East Marginal Way, then zigzag from street to street. "Please," she implored, panic cracking her voice.

"I'm sorry, I can't make exceptions, ma'am. But…I'll tell you what. My precinct station is a block ahead on your right. I'll write you a tag to park in our lot. From there you can walk up the hill to Mercy."

"Oh, yes, please. Thank you, officer. I'm not trying to be difficult."

He smiled wearily as he wrote out a permit. Abby rolled up her window, then swung around him in the direction he indicated, heading—she hoped—to his station. A short while later, she found it and parked. Once she'd climbed out of her car and locked it, leaving the tag visible, she took a minute to get her bearings.

Midway through her hike up a steep sidewalk that led to one of the city's oldest hospitals, she heard neighborhood dogs begin to bark and howl. Abby automatically braced for another afterquake. Sure enough, within seconds everything began to jump crazily. To her left, a flower bed of tulips rose and fell, reminding her oddly of ocean waves.

Up to now, she'd been so focused on her destination, she hadn't really absorbed the surrounding damage. An elegant old home beyond the bed of glads had once boasted mullioned windows. Now jagged, gaping holes left a living room filled with antiques open to the casual passerby. Next door, a neighbor's wraparound porch had split off the main house. A man, presumably the owner, who'd been surveying his roof from atop a six-foot ladder, scurried down it as the aftershock bared its teeth. He sought refuge under the spreading limbs of a giant fir. As with the previous aftershock, this one quickly subsided. But it made Abby wonder momentarily about the condition of her town house, and also Elliot's rambling old home that always seemed to be in some stage of reconstruction.

Feeling the first splatter of raindrops from a cluster of dark, fast-swirling clouds, Abby let her earlier concerns slip away. She zipped her windbreaker and pulled up the hood. Tucking her chin to her chest, she ran the remaining two blocks.

Thoroughly winded, she stared up at the solid old hospital, which overshadowed clusters of two- and three-story clinic complexes. Once used as apartments, many of them had been renovated into medical offices. Some had been turned into assisted living quarters for the elderly.

An ambulance screamed past Abby and screeched to a halt under the emergency room awning. She was relieved to note that visible wings of the gray brick hospital appeared to be intact.

As she entered the main lobby, Abby unzipped her jacket and shook rain from her bangs. She located a horseshoe-shaped reception desk, but was forced to wait while a gray-haired clerk fielded calls via a switchboard lit up like a Christmas tree. Abby strove for a composure she didn't feel. The aftershocks, along with constant worry over what she'd find here, left her brain addled.

Between calls the operator glanced up. "May I direct you, miss?"

"A nurse, Olivia Warren, phoned me. Earlier. Nearly three hours ago," Abby said in surprise as she checked her watch. "I, uh, need directions to my brother's room. His name is Elliot Drummond. His son, Sam, is also a patient. And maybe Elliot's wife, Blair." Abby sent up a silent prayer for her sister-in-law, and mentally crossed her fingers. Olivia hadn't found any record of Blair earlier.

The woman ran a finger down a patient index. She then leafed through a stack of cards piled beside her switchboard. The lighted board constantly went bing, bing, bing in the background. "I—oh, my." She looked up briefly. "Please take a seat in the lobby. I'll call a volunteer to assist you." Making a neat pile of the cards, the clerk again busied herself with insistent callers.

Abby realized the futility of trying to ask another question. She stepped into the teeming lobby and eventually did sit on the very edge of a chair. She called to let Raina know she'd made it, and got through after numerous attempts. Her friend still had her nephews and Marlo's girls. How long, Abby wondered after telling Raina goodbye, would the clerk's "minute" be? Her stomach was jittery, and anxiety nibbled away at her calm attitude. But of course she wasn't alone in her fear. The lobby was filled with pacing, terrified relatives.

Half an hour later, a volunteer in a pale-yellow uniform showed up. At a word from the clerk at the desk, the woman turned and sought out Abby—who rose at once.

She rushed to meet the volunteer, and repeated her request. Her guide in yellow spun on soundless white shoes, striding quickly along a bustling warren of halls. She walked so fast, Abby barely kept pace. As they sped around the turns, Abby was actually glad she'd been given an escort. After one sharp, right-angled turn down a dead-end hall, Abby's helper flung open a door and motioned Abby into a dimly lit room. Squinting, Abby stopped short the moment she realized she'd entered a chapel.

Her teeth began to chatter. She backed up, shrieking *No, no, no* inside her head. Her mind refused to accept the news she was about to receive. ''No!'' she shouted, and snatched the front of the woman's cheery uniform.

Frightened, the volunteer wrested the material from Abby's clutching hands.

Because her already wobbly knees simply gave way, Abby fell heavily onto a padded bench. Nearly blinded by tears, she stared at a wooden cross rising stark and silent at the front of the room, backlit by a pale, shimmering light. Wanting—needing—to run, but unable to make her legs function, Abby shrank from an approaching man. His kind but controlled expression, coupled with a black jacket and white clerical collar, declared him an enemy. Abby heard an awful noise gush from her throat, a scream of denial ripped from her very soul. Shivering, she shut her eyes, covered her ears and rocked to ease the pain in her heart. It thundered so loudly, she missed the name the man offered along with his hand.

''Easy, Ms. Drummond.'' Sitting beside her, he pried apart her icy hands. ''Abigail Drummond?'' he asked again, forcing Abby to open her eyes and really look at him through a veil of tears.

She nodded, even though words refused to form on her numb lips.

"According to Dr. Nelson, your brother, the Reverend Drummond, fought to hang on until you could get here. His chest injuries would have felled a lesser man at the scene of the accident. With God's help, he managed to attract the attention of a firefighter sent to assess the rubble of the bridge. I understand Elliot's only request was for the fireman to help his wife and son. Unfortunately—'' the man paused, "Mrs. Drummond succumbed in the aid car as paramedics tried desperately to stabilize her breathing."

Blair and Elliot, both gone. "No. Nooo!" Abby's lungs refused to expand and contract as she attempted to haul in air. The priest plucked several tissues from a box and thrust them into her hand. A heaviness invaded her limbs and the glowing cross receded until it was a mere pinprick of light. Then it loomed large again as her burning throat swallowed her curse against an unmerciful God.

The priest clumsily patted her bent shoulders.

"Sam?" Abby whispered at last, twisting the tissues into wet clumps. "My brother's son? How's he? Dr. Galloway…uh…the senior Dr. Galloway was to evaluate Sam."

"The boy is in surgery. Reverend Drummond gave verbal consent. That's not how the hospital normally operates, but considering this tragedy, our chief of staff accepted your brother's word. Ms. Drummond, did you come here alone? May I call someone for you? Your parents, perhaps? Or a sibling?"

"No one. They're all gone. All but me." She shook her head and tears rolled down her cheeks. "I'm all that's left of Elliot's family. And Blair's." Burying her face in her hands, Abigail gave in to the weight of anguish pressing in on her. She sobbed, great gulping sobs, denying everything this man had said. "Someone's made a horrible mistake. Elliot and Blair's identification could've been mixed up at the bridge. I'm sure—"

"There's no mistake." The priest bowed his head and began to pray aloud. The words meant to comfort Abby landed on deaf ears.

Before he'd finished his prayer—in what later would seem a true miracle—Ben Galloway stood in the door of this out-of-the-way chapel. His recognizable voice penetrated the darkness that cocooned Abby. Half rising, she cried his name. "Ben. Ben?" Disbelief warred with her abject sorrow.

Ben wedged himself past the Episcopal priest. Murmuring softly, he reached for her.

"Ben! Oh, Ben." She threw herself into his arms. "The bo…ys," she cried. "How will I ever break this terrible news? I know what it's like to lose both parents. They're so much younger than Elliot and I were when our parents died." Her voice became hysterical at the end. "How did you know to come here? Did Raina contact you?"

Tightening his hold, Ben rocked Abby from side to side. What he didn't say—couldn't bring himself to say—was that he'd have to impart the same unbelievable news to his nieces. Their mother was dead. Even though his own heart had shattered, Ben couldn't tell her about Marlo, which would only add to Abby's crushing grief.

But neither could he lie and say he'd come solely to comfort her. When the police had contacted Ben about finding Marlo's car under a broken pillar at the viaduct, his chief of staff ordered him off duty. At first he'd planned to phone his father—which was how Kirk would handle notification were the shoe on the other foot. But when Ben attempted to call him, he learned that his dad had scrubbed for Sam Drummond's surgery. He was also told about Sam's folks. The decision to drive to Mercy General was Ben's.

Devastated, he'd guessed correctly that Abby would be

doubly so. As strong a woman as she was, Ben knew instinctively that it'd be like reopening old wounds, like reliving her parents' accident. Feeling Abby shake in his arms, Ben didn't regret his spur-of-the-moment decision to make the harrowing journey between the hospitals.

The priest's pager went off. "Sorry, I'm needed elsewhere," he murmured, lightly nudging Ben's arm. "Sir, may I leave Ms. Drummond in your care?"

Ben's answer was to tighten his arms around the still-crying woman.

"Uh, if I can be of any further assistance, please leave word at the front desk. They can usually find me. Today," the priest said with a sigh, "it may take longer. Ms. Drummond, I hope you will one day take comfort in the fact your brother and his wife are reunited with their parents and their Creator."

Unable to speak, Abby buried her face in Ben's shirtfront.

"Thank you." Ben shook the priest's hand from an awkward angle. "I'm Dr. Ben Galloway, by the way. I practice mainly at Children's Health. Abby and I both live in West Seattle. Mercy was the closest triage hospital to the accident."

"I understand. Good luck to you both." He shook his head. "As prepared as everyone thought we were after the big quake four years ago, this one caught us flatfooted. It's more important than ever for us to get in step with God's larger plan. He expects those of us left behind to carry on his work. Remember he's a merciful God." Giving Abby's arm a last pat, the priest exited the chapel.

Abby stirred. She hated to leave the shelter of Ben's arms. But the priest's parting words rankled. "Elliot said almost that exact same thing to me at Mom and Dad's funeral."

She eased away from Ben, rubbing her upper arms. "His belief was a bone of contention between us for years. Now—" Abby faced Ben with wet eyes and trembling lips "—it's as if Elliot's sent a message back to me from…you know…" Shuddering, she eyed the cross, then glanced quickly away. "Perhaps Elliot's right and I'm wrong."

"Like hell, Abigail!" Uncaring that he was in a place of worship, Ben punched a fist into the air. "*You,* not God, will look Elliot's kids in the eye tonight. It's you who'll wipe their tears, chase away their nightmares and stumble around trying to find a way to explain their incomprehensible loss. Whose merciful plan is *that?*"

In all the time she'd known him, Abby had never seen Ben get so worked up. She pulled her jacket tighter, and considered the bleak truth of his statement. As always when faced with hard facts, Abby dug deep for a resolve that had never failed her yet in times of need. "Then…if I'm all those poor kids have to hang on to, Ben, I'd better pull myself together. I—uh—thank you for providing a shoulder to cry on. But I'd better let you go. I'm sure you're needed elsewhere, by other injured children."

Ben saw determination replace the gut-wrenching pain in Abby's tear-drenched eyes. Hopelessly in need of courage himself, he closed the gap between them and cupped her pale face. The freckles he loved were never more pronounced than now. He kissed the ones scattered across the bridge of her nose. Then he let his thumbs trace the blue shadows beneath her lower lashes. "I wish we had more time to spend together today. But…" He hauled in a deep, shuddering breath. "I need a word with Kirk…uh, my father, before I go back to my trauma unit. You'll want to see him, too, about your nephew."

Abby curled her fingers around Ben's solid wrist. Something she'd found immensely attractive about Ben from the outset—his masculine hands. Some doctors had effeminate hands, she'd noticed. Not Ben Galloway. She could as easily see him paddling a kayak in an open sea, or tossing a log on a burning campfire. Yet his touch was gentle the few times she'd seen him cradle a baby or wipe away an older sibling's tears.

"I'll never be able to express how much it means to me that you were here when I most needed someone, Ben. In a way, you were an answer to my prayer."

"Don't." He dropped his hands away from her face. "We can talk later. For now, it's enough to know we're both okay."

"Right. I need to see how Sam is. I can't believe I forgot to ask what kind of surgery he's having. He's so little. Oh, Ben! None of this seems real. I know it'll all crash in on me when I least expect it. Right now, I feel as if I'm operating in a fog."

He placed his hand on her back, and guided Abby out of the dim chapel. "I know where my father is operating. There's a small waiting room in the wing. If you'll take a seat, I'll go see what I can find out for you."

"Please." Abby might have said more, but her throat tightened again.

As it turned out, Ben's father had just stepped out of the surgery theater, a nurse informed Ben when he inquired. They spotted the elder Galloway, his surgical mask still dangling around his neck. He walked soundlessly toward them on blue booties. Impassive gray eyes surveyed his son. "What brings you to my neck of the woods? Aren't you the one who insists they work your butt off in munchkin land?"

"I know nothing's quite as important or glamorous as what you do with bones," Ben said edgily. "Rather than argue, let me introduce Abby Drummond. She's the aunt of the boy you had in surgery.''

"Have in surgery. We're at the halfway mark. My assistant is setting some of the minor bones.'' The doctor's demeanor changed abruptly as he paused to study Abby. Which was only fair, as she also assessed him. Any similarity between him and his son ended with the comparable height and breadth of their shoulders. What struck Abby about Kirk Galloway was that he seemed to be a man attempting to recapture his youth. His tan was far too dark, both his hair and mustache shouted salon blond.

"Ms. Drummond.'' He clasped Abby's hand between soft, perfectly groomed fingers. His professional charm clicked in automatically. "You're lucky, my dear, that Benjamin phoned me. I assume he's told you I handle only the most difficult cases. After surgery I'll give you a rundown on the new technique I'm using on Sam. It's one I developed while on tour in Vienna last year.''

Realizing he hadn't released her hand, Abby jerked hers away. "You're only half done with Sam?'' Her stomach rolled. "I'll…have to make a call. To arrange care for his brothers.''

Ben grabbed his father's elbow. "Would you excuse us a moment, please, Abby? Kirk, we need to talk privately.''

The gray eyes flashed. "Can't it wait? I've got a patient waiting. I came out to change into fresh scrubs.''

"This is important. As you said, I have work piling up back at Children's Health.''

"Very well. Walk with me.'' He spared a stiff smile for Abby. "If all goes well, I should have Sam in recovery by six o'clock.''

"I'll go make my call,'' she murmured. But she stood there a moment and watched the men walk away. Body language said a lot. Ben had jammed both hands in the pockets of his khaki slacks. His father threw back his shoulders. Ben said something and the older man whirled on his son. Abby could almost see the sparks flying during their brief exchange. Ben thrust out his chin. His dad waved his arms and kept shaking his head from side to side.

Abby wondered what they were saying. Were they discussing Sam? Her worry grew, especially as their argument came to a close and Ben slammed a fist into the wall before stalking off. Instead of coming to find her, he stiff-armed his way through the door to a stairwell and disappeared without a word.

His father continued down the hall in the opposite direction.

Abby didn't see Kirk Galloway again until almost six-thirty. She was exhausted, hungry and intermittently weepy. The noted surgeon appeared brittle and tense.

"I understand Sam has siblings?" he said without preamble.

"Yes. Four brothers," Abby murmured. "Two sets of twins, nine and seven."

Galloway processed that information. Or maybe not. Abby couldn't tell.

"Sam will be in recovery another hour. He'll be under heavy sedation most of the night. I suggest you go home and settle his brothers. Come back in the morning. I'll make rounds at six and update you at seven. Is that too early?"

"No. May I see him before I go? I imagine he's upset and frightened."

"Don't baby the boy. He needs to be tough if he's going to find the will to walk."

"You mean—he m-might not?" Abby breathed in deeply to stem a threatening expulsion of fresh tears. She wished Ben had stayed. About now, she could use less of his father's brusque manner and more of Ben's TLC.

A nurse, obviously overhearing, stepped up to them. "You'll owe Sam's ability to walk entirely to Dr. Galloway's surgical expertise."

"Nonsense." But Galloway preened. "If the boy walks, it'll be because he thinks he can. His right leg, hip and ankle were crushed by his mother's seat. I've straightened his lumbar spine. It remains to be seen if we'll need to go in later and do any fusing. I repaired the boy's right hip, knee, tarsal and metatarsal bones. What saved his life very probably is the fact that he was in a sturdy booster seat. Even though paramedics had to cut him out, his parents should be commended for adhering to the law. As robust a child as Sam is, some parents might ignore the law and declare him big enough to use a regular seat belt."

Abby did her best to follow Dr. Galloway's clipped speech. She found her mind wandering. Elliot and Blair's van, with its seat belts for seven and Sam's car seat, had obviously sustained considerable damage. Given the state law stipulating that kids had to be five years old or weigh fifty pounds to use regular seat belts—how would she manage to transport the lot of them in her midsize compact?

She sighed and rubbed her forehead.

"Am I going too fast for you, Ms. Drummond?" Dr. Galloway folded the chart, presumably Sam's, clicked his slim sliver pen closed, and fixed a smile on Abby.

"I'm sorry. I just feel overwhelmed by everything I'm facing in the days and weeks to come. None of which I need to burden you with. But…did I miss hearing you say whether or not I can visit Sam?"

"I'll authorize a brief visit. Say five minutes? I can't promise he won't be too woozy to recognize you. Which is just as well. You won't want to get into explaining about his mom and dad yet."

"No. Not today. First I'll tackle telling the other four.

Before I forget my manners altogether, thank you, Doctor. Frankly, if Ben hadn't recommended you, and if you hadn't been available…'' She let the sentence trail off. But that was okay as he cut her off with a wagging finger.

''Save your thanks until after you've seen my bill. I'll give you a courtesy discount, of course. I hear the quake played havoc with a ski trip you and my son had planned. Quite honestly, Ms. Drummond—Abby—you're not what I'd expect Ben to… Oh, never mind. I'm pleased to see the boy taking an interest in something other than that clinic of his. Of course, if he'd followed my advice, his career would've allowed him more freedom, prestige and needless to say…more money.'' Still smiling with his lips alone, Kirk Galloway, M.D. extraordinaire, left Abby in the hands of a passing nurse. One he stopped to bark orders at.

''From Dr. God's mouth to my ears,'' the young nurse muttered too low for the doctor to hear as he went on his way.

''But he is tops in his field?'' Abby said.

''Yes. *The* best. Sorry, I shouldn't have made that remark in front of you. My only excuse is that I hit the ground running at 6:00 a.m. and haven't slowed since. Which isn't your problem,'' she added with a deprecating shrug.

''I sympathize,'' Abby said. ''I hope your day hasn't been as bad as mine. After I see Sam I wonder…could you direct me to the department in the hospital that can tell me where—'' she cleared her throat ''—where, ah, a person or persons who died here might be sent?'' Her throat clogged and her eyes filled with tears. ''Funeral homes, I mean.''

The nurse broke her stride, and gave Abby a brief, spontaneous hug. ''I'm on break, but I'll wait until you visit Sammy, then I'll get you a list of the area funeral homes. The front office gave each nursing center copies of the list after we began to get figures on fatalities. Last I heard it was ninety and rising.''

"Oh, so many? I'm from West Seattle. My brother and his wife were apparently almost across the bridge when it—'' Abby swallowed hard, and ended by simply shaking her head. "I thought Taylor's. They handled my parents' funeral—a long time ago. Maybe them if they're still in business.''

"They are. I'll get them on the line while you look in on Sam.'' Abby already had her nose pressed to a window of the glassed-in room. "Sam's in the third bed. Someone's monitoring his vital signs. Go on in. I'm sure Dr. Galloway gave an order to let you see him.''

"You've been very kind.''

"I wish that I could change your circumstances.'' Gravely, the nurse, who was near Abby's age, turned and went behind the counter at the nursing station. That left Abby wretchedly alone to enter a room that was silent except for the hum of monitors.

She glanced hesitantly at a nurse working with her nephew. Sam looked pitifully tiny, swathed as he was in padded white bandages. Abby's chest constricted.

"Sam, honey, it's Aunt Abby. Can you hear me?'' Although his eyelids fluttered, they remained closed.

"He's responding subconsciously to your voice,'' the nurse whispered. "Try to speak normally.''

Abby blinked back stingingly hot tears. *Try to speak normally?* Sam's life had changed dramatically today. Hers, too. From now on, their roles would be totally different. Never again would she be Aunt Abby, a person to whom Sam and his brothers could look to get them off the hook with their folks. She, who never raised her voice to the boys and rarely meted out discipline except occasionally on the school playground, would be a parent. Starting tomorrow. Large tears leaked from her eyes and dripped on Sam's pristine sheets.

"Get better, guy," she muttered. She did her utmost to keep her voice from sounding panicky. "I'll be back in the morning, and I'll bring Raggedy Andy," she promised softly. Each of the children slept with a favorite toy. Sam's was a rag doll Blair had made for his first birthday. Andy had undergone several surgical procedures himself. Maybe Sam would be comforted by that. Because the older of the two nurses kept eyeing her watch and then Abby, she took it as a hint to leave. Smoothing Sam's mop of carrot-red curls, she dropped a kiss on the tip of his freckled nose. Abby had always been partial to this child. She understood firsthand the teasing he'd one day endure at the hands of schoolmates. Of her brother's five children, only Sam had inherited Grandfather Drummond's fiery Scots hair. The others all had strawberry-blond shades, and few freckles. Sam and Abby—kindred spirits.

With a last look at her broken nephew, Abby scrubbed at her cheeks and escaped from the room.

The nurse who'd promised to help Abby contact the funeral home appeared in her peripheral vision. "I have a representative from Taylor's on the line in the conference room. Come. I'll wait outside until you've finished making arrangements."

"Thank you—what's your name? I feel I should call you something."

The woman frowned at the left side of her uniform. "Drat. I lost another name tag. I lose one a month. It should say Olivia Warren here." Abby's helpful companion tapped a torn flap near her left shoulder.

"Olivia? Oh, you're the one who phoned me. I remember the name."

"I made a lot of calls. Too many." Pursing her lips, the

nurse continued to stroke the spot where she was missing her name badge.

''Hmm. Perhaps you should take your uniforms to one of those firms that embroider names on kids' ball shirts.'' Part of Abby couldn't conceive how she could carry on such a mundane conversation in the midst of tragedy. On the other hand, discussing inconsequential things gave her an excuse not to face the task she needed to face.

''I never thought of having my name stitched on. That's a great idea.''

''Sports King in West Seattle does it on site. Our elementary school gives them a lot of business,'' Abby said. ''I teach second grade, and I coach sixth-grade girls' soccer.'' It dawned on Abby, as she entered the conference room and saw the phone lying on the table, that, too, would probably change in the coming months. She knew how much time Blair spent shuffling the boys to soccer, baseball, karate and what-have-you. She deliberately blanked from her mind the fact that Blair's full-time job had been taking care of the house, the menagerie, the boys and...Elliot.

Picking up the phone with a damp hand, she said in a shaky voice, ''This is Abigail Drummond.'' She gave her address and mentioned that Taylor's had handled her parents' funeral. ''I need to arrange for a double, ah, burial. No. I...don't know if they had lots at Shady Glen. I understand you have to ask, but this is very...difficult for me. I'm calling to arrange for my brother and his wife. Apart from their asking if I'd serve as guardian to their sons, I'm afraid we never discussed the details of their...uh...wishes. I thought...we all thought we were planning for a remote possibility.'' Abby's voice faded.

''Uh, huh. Now I see the need, but then...sir...must I provide this information tonight? Oh, fine. I don't mean to be difficult, but—'' She burst into tears. "Sorry." She blotted her eyes on her jacket sleeve. "If you could work with the officials at Mercy General, I'll come in tomorrow and fill out the papers and give you a check."

Abby fumbled the receiver as she attempted to hang it up. She looked through her tears as Olivia Warren popped into the room.

"Hey, are you okay? Taylor's didn't give you a hard time or anything, did they?"

"I expected this to be rough, Olivia," Abby said around muffled sniffles. "I had no idea how bad. Taylor's were nice enough. I'm just so horribly ill prepared."

"Are you related to Dr. Galloway?" the woman asked as they left the room and started down the hall.

"No. What made you ask?"

"My friend said she saw you come out of the chapel with Dr. Kirk's son. She said he had an arm around you."

"We're…" Abby hesitated. She'd started to say, *friends.* But in view of their interrupted plans, she supposed they were more. Right now, she wished they were much more. Which was odd. Abby couldn't recall ever picturing herself married. If ever the vows of *for better, for worse* had meaning, this would be it.

"Ben and I met last year. I had one of his nieces in my class. We've dated. So, of course, he was my first thought when I learned Sam needed an orthopedic surgeon."

"I see. You taught Ben's niece? Then I guess you must know he lost his sister today."

"What? No. No, I didn't know anything of the kind." Abby stumbled over nothing on the tiled floor. "Surely you misunderstood. I…saw Ben. We spoke. He talked with his father." Abby waved a hand feebly.

"Yes," Olivia said with eyes gone dark. "I probably shouldn't have mentioned it, but apparently Dr. Ben and

Dr. Kirk had a difference of opinion over who should look after the little girls.''

Going back over a scene she'd witnessed from afar, Abby pictured it from a new perspective. From Ben's. They shared the same predicament, and her heart ached for him. For him and for Marlo's sweet, sweet daughters. Was there no end to the horror of this earthquake? Abby wondered how she had tears left to cry.

She went to Raina's to get her nephews, then to her own town house and finally the boys' home. Both places were cluttered with various things, shaken from shelves and walls and cupboards.

She learned that tears were nature's release valve, and over the next weeks she and the boys shed them freely, often in shared moments with friends and neighbors, many of whom suffered, too.

CHAPTER FOUR

SIX WEEKS AFTER the quake, the city began to restore order and set about rebuilding, a process the engineers expected to take a year or more.

Ben Galloway, in a slow moment at the clinic, studied a book on how to braid hair. He'd assumed the housekeeper-cook he'd hired after laying his sister to rest would be equipped to handle his nieces' ''girlie'' requirements. But after watching normally good-tempered Erin dissolve into tears for the tenth morning in a row over messy braids, Ben was at his wits' end. Hence the book. About the only thing in his life he hadn't altered or dispensed with to accommodate the girls had been his morning stop on his way to the clinic at a bookstore-coffee house.

Today, while the attendant brewed his hard-hitting double espresso, it struck him that a man with the manual dexterity to sew up cuts on little people surely ought to be able to braid hair. But he hadn't stopped with the braid book. Before he got out of the store, he'd purchased a hundred dollars' worth of current information on raising girls. Books promising confident, happy girls. Happy was what his formerly sweet niece was not. Erin had turned into a brat. Ben couldn't help thinking it was partly his fault. In spite of coauthoring a pamphlet on discipline, he was obviously missing the mark when it came to girls.

''Doctor, your next patient's in room five.'' Anita Sorenson stepped into the room. She was one of a staff of three that Ben and his partner, general practitioner Steve Thomas, shared. Marching straight to Ben's desk, Anita straightened the books spilling out of his store bag. "What's all this?" She rifled through the stack, reading titles aloud. "Is there something you haven't told us? Are you trading pediatrics for child psychology? Or are you and Steve collaborating on another parents' guide?"

Ben didn't want to tell his nurse how many times he woke in the dead of night worrying about the girls. "Anita, how did you raise six kids on your own? Is there a secret?"

The nurse tipped back her head and laughed, but she must have seen the misery in her employer's eyes, because she sobered midstream. "Gosh, I guess I never thought about it. Except I raised my kids from birth, so I set the house rules. Even then, there were months after Lorne died that I had to take it one day at a time."

"Time. That's my biggest problem. I never seem to have enough hours to spend with Erin and Mollie. On short no- tice, with half the city in chaos, I spent two weeks locating a suitable housekeeper-caretaker. But Mrs. Clark still doesn't understand that medicine isn't an eight-to-five job. She wants a regular schedule I simply can't deliver."

"According to an article in the newspaper, the quake did more damage to this side of town. Our death toll is sixty percent of the more than one hundred reported. Area schools have added crisis counselors. I don't know which elementary the girls attend, but you might want to have a chat with school staff if you're seeing behavioral changes. The article also said individual schools plan to form parent support groups."

Ben scowled. "How would that look, Anita? Half the parents at the girl's elementary school bring their kids to me. Since the quake, my patient load has doubled. Most come for direction related to tantrums and other disruptive behavior.''

''Oh, well, if you're the expert…'' Anita snorted, crossing her arms.

Ben gave her a sheepish smile. ''Sorry. That sounded more like something my old man would spout.'' At the mention of his father, and totally unexpectedly, Abby Drummond's face appeared in his mind. Ben had last seen her at Marlo's funeral. Abby looked harried, pale and drawn. Given her circumstances, it'd pleased Ben to see her there. He'd meant to call and thank her for the rosebuds she'd sent the girls. And she'd written each one a thoughtful note, too. All other expressions of sympathy had been directed to him. But he'd barely found time to scribble his name at the bottom of the gilt-edged thank-you cards his secretary provided.

That was another issue that grated. He'd suggested his father's current live-in take over thanking the friends who'd sent remembrances. Kirk threw a virtual fit. He let it be known in no uncertain terms that Millie or Lily, or whatever the hell her name was, served as arm candy and nothing more. Well—a lot more, Ben assumed. But nothing Kirk would ever discuss with him. And after the reaming out Kirk delivered when Ben proposed the blond bombshell collect the girls from Abby's friend the day of the quake, one might think Ben would have learned his lesson. If not then, certainly after Kirk made it clear that his role as grandfather—a term he disliked—was confined to gifts at birthdays and Christmas. Foolishly, Ben had thought his dad might want to have a say in who took care of his granddaughters.

Why Kirk's response had surprised him, Ben didn't know. After all, it was the way his old man had handled fatherhood—via his checkbook. Ben and Marlo had never been able to figure out why their dad went through a court battle to retain custody of them after their mom announced she was leaving. Eventually they'd decided it was a matter of pride to the great Kirk Galloway. No one left his exalted sphere except by his edict.

Which Marlo did when she married a no-account who later walked out, leaving her pregnant, and with Erin a toddler. A self-fulfilling prophesy, according to Kirk.

But Ben had dealt their father a blow when he chose a pediatric residency over the more prestigious orthopedic post he'd been offered at a hospital where Kirk pulled strings to get his son considered.

Sweeping aside old irritants and unproductive thoughts, Ben closed the book on braids. Again he wondered how Abby was getting along. Admittedly he'd put her out of his mind once it became evident that his carefree bachelor days were over. Except, dammit, they *weren't* over. The carefree part, yes. But he was still as single as single could be.

Ben snatched the chart from Anita's hand. "Would you see if Pat can get me out of here at a decent hour today? By two-fifteen. I'll phone Mrs. Clark and tell her I'm picking Erin and Mollie up from school. I'm friends with one of the teachers. I haven't wanted to bother her, knowing she's in a similar spot—worse, since she's been left to raise her brother's five boys, one of whom was injured in the quake. I should've contacted her before this. If anyone has the lowdown on support groups, it'll be Abby."

"Five boys, you say?" Anita shuddered. "The poor woman has my sympathy. I raised six of 'em. Frankly, Ben, I always thought girls would be a whole lot easier."

"From a woman's perspective, maybe. From where I stand, two tearful girls and their finicky cat present the most daunting challenge I've ever faced."

This time Anita did laugh as they departed Ben's office.

"Maybe you ought to combine forces with your friend who has the five boys. You could help with her boys, and she could advise you on dealing with emotional girls."

Ben mulled over Anita's suggestion as he greeted his next patient and her triplet daughters. If they'd been more than two months old, he might have asked her for advice. But the poor beleaguered new mother needed all the help she could get. Before she left, though, she said something profound that stuck with Ben. "Somebody missed the boat, Dr. Galloway. Every college should offer classes in parenting. At some point in life, most people become one. Yet the only people who get training are those going into early childhood education. Or maybe pediatrics," she said, tossing him a tired sigh. "I think teacher training is best. Teachers have to be in control of kids six or more hours a day. No offense, but pediatricians only see kids ten minutes at a time."

He considered her words for the rest of the day. And he recalled the ease with which Abby Drummond had handled Erin's class. She'd had twenty-two or so kids in that class. The few times Ben had dropped by at the end of the day, Abby appeared calm and unruffled. Who better to teach him the skills he needed to raise his sister's girls than a woman he already knew and admired?

"Anita!" He met up with her and traded charts. "Was Pat able to rearrange my afternoon schedule?"

"Yes, she managed to clear your afternoon. Actually, she said if you used the time to relax and quit biting off everyone's head, she'd blank out one afternoon a week."

"Ouch. Have I gotten that bad?"

"In a word—yes. But the staff can suffer through for a while. We recognize the strain you've been under these last weeks, Ben."

"I'll have to make a conscious effort to watch myself. I

meant what I said during the initial interviews before Steve and I opened the clinic. People spend more hours a day at their workplace than at home. The environment should be pleasant. It shouldn't contribute to a person's stress.''

''Yeah, but all work and no play makes guys like Ben and Steve cranky. I know it's not your fault you both had to cancel your vacations. The staff think you should reschedule those trips.''

''Wouldn't it be loverly?'' Ben quipped. ''In a way, Steve ended up being more tied down than me. Not only was his mom hurt, meaning he has to care for her and his wheelchair-bound grandfather, but her house suffered major quake damage.''

Ben had missed seeing the clinic receptionist walk up behind him. ''Excuse the interruption, Doctor.'' Pat waved a pink message slip under his nose. ''Your bank is on line one. What's this they're saying about a change of address on your checks? Did you move and not tell us?''

''Jeez, did I forget? I let the lease on my apartment go. Even though Marlo's house is small and I had to store some of my stuff, I couldn't bring myself to uproot Erin and Mollie. What really tipped the scales was that my complex didn't allow pets. Not that it wouldn't suit me to give away that damned cat, but...'' Ben heaved a sigh. ''I couldn't, of course. She sleeps on their bed, and she's one of the few constants left in their lives.''

Checking the name on the chart, Ben whisked the note from Pat's fingers. ''Anita, tell Mrs. Jensen I'll be in to see Daniel in a minute. This call shouldn't take long. My banker's a former college buddy. He probably assumes the bottom fell out of the medical profession. You watch, he'll love rubbing in how my new address is quite a comedown from the area I'm leaving.''

Pat tugged the message out of Ben's lax grip. ''Go see

Danny Jensen. I'll tell this bank buzzard to mind his own beeswax. In our books you're a good man, Dr. Galloway. A good man with a heart of pure gold.''

Was he? Ben pondered Pat's statement as he paused outside the Jensen room to collect his thoughts. He certainly hoped so. He'd hate to think he'd turned into an unfeeling bastard like his father.

BEN MANAGED to arrive at Sky Heights Elementary ten minutes before classes let out. He'd already stopped at the office to inform them he'd be picking up Erin and Mollie, which meant their teachers would pull the girls out of the bus line. It should allow him a minute to swing by Abby's classroom first. Considering what his staff had said about needing to make some time to play, Ben pictured meeting Abby later at a sports bar they both liked. Just to relax over a beer and talk like they used to.

He cupped his hands around his eyes and peered into her room. Whoa! He didn't recognize the dark-haired woman at the desk. She looked fresh out of college. Stepping back, Ben rechecked the room number.

It was the right one. He peered through the glass again. Maybe Abby had acquired an aide. Or the other woman could be a parent, though Ben had his doubts. She didn't look parental, somehow. But then, what in hell were parents supposed to look like?

The door opened fast, almost hitting his nose. Ben jumped back. Clear green eyes that were probably the result of colored contact lenses took his measure openly. ''Well, hello,'' exclaimed a breathy, high-pitched voice. ''Tell me you're lost, and that you don't have a student in my class.''

Ben tugged at his tie, recognizing a come-on when he heard one. ''Things have obviously changed since the last time I visited the school. I'm looking for Abigail Drummond. I thought this was her room.''

"Technically it is.'' The young woman with the bouncy curls extended a slender hand. "I'm Stacy Thorpe. I'm filling in for Ms. Drummond, but I intend to get the job permanently. And you are?'' she prompted, tipping her head coyly.

The bell rang announcing the end of school. Doors opened and kids poured into the hall to line up. A teacher leaving the room directly across from Ben eyed him. She crossed to where he stood. "Hi. Are you looking for Abby? You probably don't recognize me. I'm Abby's friend, Raina Miller. I watched her nephews and your nieces the day of the quake.''

He relaxed. "I should've contacted you before now, to thank you. A…friend of my dad's picked the girls up that day. So…thanks for helping me and Abby. My schedule's been crazy. I came to get Erin and Mollie today and thought I'd take the opportunity to talk to Abby.'' A small frown creased Ben's forehead, especially as the Thorpe woman crowded close, apparently keeping tabs on his and Raina Miller's conversation.

"Abby requested a two-month leave. I assumed you knew. Aren't you managing Sam's medical case?''

"Sam? Oh, uh…wrong Dr. Galloway. My father's the surgeon. So, you're saying Abby's at home caring for Sam?''

"I suppose Sam is home by now. Last time we talked she was only caring for the doubles. Er, that's the twins.''

"I had no idea. The boy must be in worse shape than I thought. I'll grab the girls and run by Abby's. I should've done that sooner.''

"She'd like that. I get the feeling she's floundering. Or

thinks she is. Good seeing you, Ben. Tell Abby hello for me.''

"I will.'' He turned away and bumped into Stacy Thorpe, who blocked his path.

Raina Miller had returned to her line of students. She turned and called across the hall. "Ben, I don't know if you're aware that Abby's not at her town house. She's moved in with the boys.''

Boy, did that scenario sound familiar to Ben. "Do you have an address? Or are you allowed to give it out?''

Raina grinned. "I think she'd say it's okay to make an exception for you. I have to walk my class to the busses. You're meeting the girls? How about if I stop at the office in ten minutes? I'll look up the address on the register and jot it down for you.''

"Hey, thanks. I'll owe you one. Shoot, I already owe you for watching Erin and Mollie. So, I'll owe you two.''

As Ben excused himself and skirted the teacher who'd taken over for Abby, he had an odd feeling Stacy Thorpe had slipped across the hall to question Raina Miller about him. Ben resisted turning around. He left dating women half his age to his dad. Ben and Marlo had found his preference for trophy girlfriends embarrassing. While it was evident Kirk would never change, Ben made a point of dating women who were smart, articulate and most of all, mature.

His youngest niece, Mollie, saw him first. "Unca Ben! Unca Ben. Erin, Unca Ben's here.'' The girl ran up to him, her eyes aglow. "Erin didn't think you'd really pick us up.''

"Well, here I am.'' He knelt and gave each girl a hug.

Erin, always more reserved than her sister, pulled away to adjust her wire-rimmed glasses. "Is Mrs. Clark sick? Do we have to find a new sitter?'' The child's somber eyes reflected her concern.

''Mrs. Clark's fine, honey. Everything's fine. And didn't I used to come and get you now and then?''

''Only when you wanted to see Abby, er—I mean, Ms. Drummond.''

Ben tweaked the lopsided bow he'd laboriously tied in Erin's long dark hair that morning. ''I think you can call her Abby. You never told me she was on leave. I thought we might run by and visit her. Would that be agreeable?''

''What's agree…ble?'' Mollie screwed up her face.

Ben swung the sturdy girl aloft and tickled her to make her laugh. ''It means, squirt, that I'm asking if visiting Abby is okay with you and your sister.''

Giggling, Mollie bumped her forehead against his. ''Sure, Unca Ben. I miss Abby. Maybe if we ask her nice, she'll come back and be my teacher next year.''

''Erin, you're awfully quiet.'' Ben glanced down at his elder niece. She wore an all too serious expression.

''Nothing's the same. Miss Abby's not ever going to come back. Just like Mommy's never coming back. I don't like how you and Mollie laugh. That's wrong! Nothing's funny anymore. Laughing makes everything worse!''

''Hey, button eyes!'' Ben set Mollie down quickly, and bent to look at Erin. He gathered her tense little body against his own. ''Baby, sometimes people need to laugh to keep from crying.''

But his words didn't penetrate Erin McBride's unhappiness. Her face crumpled and tears tracked down her cheeks. Holding her as tight as he dared, Ben worried that she'd lost weight since he'd done her last checkup.

''Goodness. Erin, did you fall and hurt yourself?'' Raina Miller rounded the corner and stopped in front of the trio.

Rising, Ben gave a warning shake of his head. And Raina

assumed an *I see* expression. No doubt she did understand. Surely those who worked with quake survivors weren't unused to mopping up tears.

Raina passed Ben a paper on which she'd written Abby's address. ''Normally I'd tell you to give Abby a hard time about leaving the rest of us to deal with the fallout. Except I suspect she has her hands full with her own fallout. So don't say a word. Just give her a big hug from me. I'll phone her over the weekend. I have a few bits of scuttlebutt she'll want to hear.''

Touching the paper to his brow in salute, Ben steered his nieces out of the building and toward his car. He settled both girls into the back, buckling Mollie into her booster seat. Afterward, he made a cursory check of Erin's buckle. The first day he'd driven the girls, Erin had thrown a fit because he'd yanked on her belt. Now Ben played it cool. She'd insisted she was eight and not a baby who needed help buckling herself in. But Ben had seen some nasty injuries to kids who weren't properly fastened in their seats. So he continued to discreetly check her buckle.

Placing Abby's new address on the dash, Ben realized he'd wrongly assumed Elliot's home would be adjacent to his church. This address was a mile or two beyond that. Beach property, unless he was way off base.

As the house numbers counted upward, he knew he was right. When at last he reached the address, he stopped and stared. The place was a rambling two-story structure built on a knoll. The backyard probably sloped to the beach. Ben imagined the view of Alki Point would be spectacular from an upper deck he could see, it extended all the way around the house. Gray shake siding, typical of homes built in the 1900s, was warped and weather-faded, but to Ben, it added to the overall charm.

"Why are we stopping here, Unca Ben?" Mollie kicked restlessly at the back of his seat.

"This is where Mrs. Miller said Abby's staying. Did you know she's caring for the Drummond boys? I think you girls know the twins."

"Noah and Michael pull my braids," Erin announced. "Why is Ms. Drummond staying with them at this old house? I like where she lived before. She had an awards party for her students there. It's nicer."

Ben was at a loss. How should he answer Erin? According to a newsletter the school had sent home to parents and guardians after the quake, Mr. Conrad had spoken to all classes about the personal losses many of their classmates had suffered. Ben himself had attended quite a few funerals. Too many. Wanting to spare the girls needless anguish, he'd gone alone to pay his respects. Now Ben wondered if he shouldn't have at least discussed Abby's situation with the girls.

"Erin, will you unbuckle Mollie?"

"They've got bicycles," Mollie said loudly. She pointed to a cluster of bikes and trikes in a detached garage whose door opened onto the street near where her uncle had parked. "Maybe the twins will let us ride, huh, Erin?"

Erin scowled. "They're boys' bikes, Mollie. We're wearing dresses."

"So?" Mollie skipped ahead toward concrete steps leading up to the house. "I'm wearing tights. So what if somebody sees my slip? It's the new one Mommy bought me before school started. That'd be okay, wouldn't it, Unca Ben?"

Ben glanced quickly around the area and determined that the sidewalk was fairly flat in spite of the hilly terrain. The neighborhood looked peacefully rural. "Sure, Mollie girl. You'll have to ask Abby first, of course."

Erin gripped her sister's shoulder, making the younger child flinch. "Mommy always said we had to change out of our school clothes before we play outside." The girl faced Ben. "We have books to read until we go home. Here, Mollie, this is your library book." Erin shoved a thin volume into her sister's hands.

Since the girls had returned to school after spring break, anything Ben allowed Mollie to do, Erin contradicted. Her every sentence of late began with *Mommy says* or *Mommy did*. Ben had no idea how to counter that. He'd hoped that, over time, Erin would grow to accept his authority. He hadn't wanted to lay down the law, but plainly he couldn't let her bossiness continue. It wasn't fair to Mollie. Furthermore, there was no need for Erin to burden herself with parenting chores. Yet this wasn't the time or place for a family showdown. *"Stellaluna."* Ben read the name on Mollie's book. "I haven't read this story, Mollie. Did your teacher help you select it?"

Nodding, Mollie shook off Erin's hand and skipped alongside her Uncle. "It's about bats. A mama and baby bat. Will you read it to me, Unca Ben?"

"Later, princess. After dinner." He smiled down at her as he reached over her head to ring the old-fashioned door bell. The bell not only didn't ring, it fell off in Ben's hand.

Erin sounded horrified. "You broke Miss Abby's door bell."

Not knowing what to do, and because he heard laughter and thumping inside, Ben set the pieces of the bell on the porch rail and knocked loudly.

A sandy-haired boy of six or seven yanked open the door and squinted at them from brilliant blue eyes.

"I'm a friend of Abigail Drummond's. Is she home?" Ben asked.

"Did you come to help with the toilet?" The boy's voice

seemed too deep for his age. "Water's running all over upstairs. Aunt Abby's mad at Mike 'cause he didn't tell her sooner that he flushed a dead fish, and the strainer, too."

The boy threw the door wide and beckoned them in. Ben herded the girls into a tiled entry. From there he had a clear view into a large living room. It boasted a sweeping staircase and vaulted ceilings. Colored fish tanks took up one whole wall, which would explain the dead fish in the toilet. A birdcage, home to a squawking cockatiel, hung in a bay window. The disorder of it all shocked Ben.

A little boy with bandaged legs occupied a huge recliner. Coloring books, crayons, toys and Tupperware containers were spread everywhere around him. Though pale, the kid seemed oblivious to the din. A TV blaring. A radio or CD playing. A raucous bird. And kids. Everywhere, kids.

Twins older than the boy who'd let Ben in, plus another—a mirror image of the first one—huddled midway up the stairs. All were high-fiving each other, and in general making too much racket to realize they had visitors.

All at once, a foot-high replica of an off-road truck, complete with oversize balloon tires, bounced and rumbled down the long expanse of stairs. At the bottom, the wheels spun a few times, then the truck careened across slick maple floors. Its bumper whacked Ben hard on his shins, and brought the truck to a halt. Not, however, before Ben glimpsed a rat—no, a gerbil, he decided—with a bottle cap tied to its head. Belted into the front seat of the motorized truck, the animal had obviously withstood the bumpy ride down all those steps and when one of the boys got him out, the gerbil seemed none the worse for wear.

Ben might have taken the cheering boys on the landing to task for their foolish stunt had he not been blindsided by a barking, slobbering brown and white dog that jumped on him and stared him straight in the eye. Were Ben any less nimble, he'd probably have been knocked off his feet, and would've been in danger of being licked half to death. As it was, he dodged and mostly managed to evade the wet, pink tongue.

Erin and Mollie screamed. Both girls dropped their books and took refuge in a corner of the massive entry as far as possible from the boisterous dog.

Above the racket, Abby's voice floated down the same stairs that had so recently served as the Indy 500 for the truck with its gerbil driver. "Boys, will you hold the noise down to a dull roar? Somebody see what's wrong with Ruffian. Please, guys, cut me some slack. If I don't get this water valve shut off, you five will be building an ark."

The boys on the stairs at least had the grace to nudge one another and clam up sheepishly for a minute. Then one of the two older kids spotted Ben. "Aunt Abby!" he yelled at the top of his lungs. "Reed let some strange guy in off the street. Do you want me and Mike to call the cops?"

Ben heard Abby yelp, followed by two loud bumps, followed by what might have been a muffled curse. By then he'd corralled the rambunctious boxer, a half-grown pup, Ben saw, seconds before a disheveled-looking Abby hove into view. She leaned over the bannister, brandishing a very large wrench. Her red hair, always hard to tame, stood in wild disarray. Her blue jeans were rolled up to her knees and showed signs of sogginess, as did the long tails of a too large man's shirt. Dirt streaked her face, hands and arms. Even with all that she managed to look appealing to Ben.

"Ben? Noah scared me! I thought Ruffian had cornered a burglar or at the least a vagrant. I'm glad to see you, but I'm afraid I can't talk at the moment. I'm kinda busy." She waggled the wrench.

"So I see. The girls and I stopped by to see how you're doing."

Bending lower, Abby zeroed in on the pale faces of the frightened girls. "Erin, Mollie, hi! Boys, you know the McBride girls. Honestly, guys, where are your manners? Put Ruffian in the laundry room until he settles down. Invite Erin and Mollie in. Find a game everyone can play. Make it an easy one for Sam, okay?" She gazed helplessly at Ben. "If you care to supervise, Ben, I just need a minute to deal with a situation. There's fruit punch in the fridge. Michael will show you where to get clean glasses. Or there's coffee in the thermos by the stove if you'd rather." She pulled back, then ducked down again to peer at Ben through the white balusters. "Better yet, I could use a man with a strong arm and a clear mind up here."

Recovering from his shock at seeing such chaos around a woman he always found to be orderly in all things, Ben dredged up a rakish grin. "Let me settle the girls, Abby, and I'll be right up."

"Uncle Ben, I don't want to stay here." Erin sidled up to her uncle. "This house is dirty, and that dog slobbered all over me."

"Erin McBride," he said sternly. "Start by apologizing to Abby and the boys. While you figure out what you need to say, I'll lend Abby a hand. Later, if you girls behave, I'll get you some juice."

Mollie's face fell. "I didn't say the house was dirty. Why can't I have juice?"

One of the boys—Michael, Ben thought—relieved his death grip on the boxer's collar. "I'm big enough to pour juice," the boy declared. "Go ahead and help my aunt. I'll take care of stuff down here." He puffed out his thin chest.

Abby, who'd heard the exchange, called over the railing,

"Wash your hands first, Mike. And while you're at it, refill Sam's glass. Sam? You doing okay, my man?"

A meek voice responded from the confines of the big chair. "I have to go potty. When's the toilet gonna be fixed?"

"Oh, sweetie. The hall bathroom works. Darn, give me a minute to take off my shoes so I don't track water downstairs. Then I'll take you."

"That chore I can handle like a pro," Ben informed her. "If it's okay with Sam, that is. Hey, guy, I don't think we've met. I'm Dr. Ben Galloway. My father, Dr. Kirk Galloway, fixed your legs."

Sam's eyes grew round and he shoved thick auburn curls off a pale forehead with a freckled hand. "'Kay. You look nicer. Dr. Kirk never smiles."

Ben lifted the boy, doing his utmost to support the right leg which was casted all the way to the boy's hip. Sam wore a short cast on his left. Ben guessed the kid wouldn't be walking anytime soon. He wondered why Abby didn't have household help. The ages of the children seemed reason enough to seek assistance. To say nothing of the sheer hours involved in maintaining this household.

No wonder Abby looked as if she'd dropped twenty pounds. Ben guessed dashing up and down stairs a hundred times a day would burn a lot of calories.

"There you go, Sam." Ben straightened after maneuvering them both into the small half bathroom. He glanced up, feeling a drop of water strike his ear. He identified a water stain on the ceiling, which seemed to grow larger as he studied it.

Jeez, Abby probably didn't know her problems weren't limited to the upstairs. The flooded commode must be directly above this one. "Hey there, Sam, let's not dally. I'd just as soon neither of us had to be treated for ceiling plaster falling on our heads.''

The child's lips quivered. ''I wish Daddy was here. Will that phone in your pocket call everywhere?''

''Pretty much,'' Ben murmured, still focusing his attention on the damaged ceiling tiles while he helped Sam tie his robe. ''Do you have a friend you'd like to call? If you tell me where I can find his number, I'll dial for you.''

Donning a serious expression, the boy waited patiently while Ben washed and dried his hands. ''I don't got the number for heaven. Maybe it's in my daddy's 'puter. Mommy said Daddy put everybody's number from church on his 'puter. And Daddy said God's the most important member of his church. So I think God's number hasta be there.''

''Oh. Oh, Sammy...'' Ben patted the sad-eyed child's back as he carried him to his recliner. ''I wish making contact with the Almighty were so simple. But...he's everywhere, you know, watching over us. Like...maybe the reason I picked today to visit your aunt is that I'm supposed to help her.'' Ben gave the four-year-old a coloring book and opened it to a picture of a partially colored ark. ''Ah...I believe your aunt was saying you guys might need one of these,'' he teased.

He needed to get out of the room before Sam asked more questions. Ben figured he was the last person able to explain why any supreme being let kids lose their moms and dads. He left the room no wiser than before.

Upstairs, he put his foot into two inches of water on the bathroom floor.

Abby was draped over a gurgling commode, mumbling at a pipe wrench that kept slipping off a valve cap. Rolling up his shirtsleeves, Ben relieved Abby of the wrench. He threw his considerable muscle into budging the solidly stuck shut-off cap.

"I think it gave a little," Abby said. "Ben, I'm sorry you walked into this mess. Oh, there…you got it. Oh, no! The valve twisted off." A gusher shot everywhere. "Ben, make it stop!"

Leaping aside, he swore roundly.

"Shh." Abby clapped a hand over his mouth. "We don't use language like that in this house."

"Apparently you don't ask for help in this house, either. Why are you just standing there watching Old Faithful? Get me a damn phone book."

"What for?"

"Something you should've done at first splat. To call a plumber." So saying, Ben whipped out the phone Sam thought he could use to call heaven. Directory assistance was close enough to heaven's hotline to suit Ben. As he was connected to a local plumber and gave the man terse directions to the house, Ben wrapped a white towel around the broken pipe to stem the geyser.

"My best Egyptian cotton towel. Ben, what are you thinking?"

"Something else I should've done when I first walked in," he growled, closing off her sputtering tirade with a kiss that drove the air from her lungs.

CHAPTER FIVE

BEN SET ABBY DOWN, then had to grab her arms to hold her upright.

A bit stunned, she did rally. "Here I thought my day had tanked. If that's your standard method of dealing with hysterical women, Dr. Galloway, I can see why your practice grows by leaps and bounds."

Laughing, Ben leaned in for another, slower, more sizzling and satisfying kiss. "This brand of superb bedside manner is reserved for an elite few, Ms. Drummond."

"You're full of it, Ben, you know that?" Casting a furtive glance over her shoulder and down the hall, Abby segued to a new subject. "How are the girls? I thought Erin looked…different. But I guess that's understandable, since everything's changed because of the quake." She shrugged. "Which may be all it is with Erin. I shouldn't forget she's by nature a serious child."

"True. But you're dead on, Abby." Ben bent again to twist the soaking white towel tighter. "Erin's not bouncing back. Not like Mollie, anyway. Erin's whole personality has nose-dived."

"With time and hugs, maybe she'll be her old self again. It's been almost two months. But it feels like forever. I still step into a room and expect to see Elliot and Blair." Her eyes were glossy, and she turned aside. "Nighttime is the hardest on the boys."

"For the girls, too." Ben's back tensed. He should be the man with answers.

Abby stroked a hand up his side. She thought how good the hard outline of his ribs felt, and wondered if men didn't need the hugs she'd spoken of.

She missed Ben's touch. Even if they'd had a casual dating style, they'd been demonstrative with each other. Whenever they saw each other, Ben had doled out a squeeze or two. Vastly different from the brief impersonal brush of their cheeks at their respective family funerals. Different, too, from the almost desperate kiss Ben had just delivered.

Would their lives ever get back to normal? The first few weeks after the quake, Abby thought Ben had disappeared from her life. On those occasions, an ache settled in her chest. And yet she'd accepted that was the way things might have to be.

Abby understood that she and Ben had obligations and responsibilities that came before any personal wants or needs. For perhaps the first time, she realized what it felt like to walk in her brother's shoes. Elliot, who'd selflessly put his life on hold until she was grown and off to college. Did she owe his children any less?

Straightening away from the valve again, Ben started to take Abby in his arms. A commotion downstairs split them apart. Although Abby had wrenched loose from his touch and taken a step back before the disturbance began. "Sorry, Ben. I'm afraid the timing here is off. Besides which, Ruffian's going crazy in the laundry room. I think the plumber's arrived."

Ben tried to reconnect with Abby's eyes, to no avail. Giving up, he said magnanimously, "I'll stay right here, if you'd care to rescue the poor man. Send him on up. Since I made this major mess, I'll do the explaining. Maybe you could spend a few minutes reassuring Sam. He's down there coloring an ark like mad. I'm afraid he's worried his home's in danger of floating away."

"Poor Sam. I only just brought him home from the hospital today when all heck broke loose. I'd checked the twins out of school early so they could ride along. We'd barely gotten home when Brad reported that Mike had scooped a dead fish out of one of the tanks. The minute he flushed it, he dropped the strainer." She rolled her eyes. "I tried the plunger. That did nothing, except maybe compound the problem. You showed up as I decided I'd better shut off the water to the toilet tank."

They heard one of the boys bellowing for Abby. "Go," Ben urged. "By the way, you maybe should also check on the status of a gerbil. The older twins had him in a remote-controlled truck. They sent him down from the second landing."

"Noah and Mike," she exclaimed, throwing up her hands. "Harry's their gerbil. Brad and Reed have hamsters. Yesterday I caught them harnessing their pets to G.I. Joe's parachutes. Luckily I caught them before they dropped them over the bannister. I don't know why Blair didn't go completely gray."

"Hmm. I wonder if that's what my nurse Anita meant when she said I should jump for joy that I have girls to raise instead of boys. You ought to meet her, Abby. She raised six boys on her own."

"And she's still sane?" Shaking her head, Abby turned and walked out. Ben heard her tripping lightly down the stairs.

It was twilight by the time the plumber finished, took the check Ben wrote out, packed up his tools and left.

"Ben, you shouldn't have paid the bill. It's my house.

Well, not mine, actually,'' she amended when the twins declared the house belonged to them.

''I broke the shut-off valve,'' Ben said by way of explanation.

''Yes, but the problem occurred before you set foot in the house. And...speaking of feet... Your Italian leather loafers are history, pal.''

Ben surveyed his soaking shoes as well as the lower edges of his slacks. ''Abby, you've got no idea what gets dripped on the shoes of a pediatrician throughout a normal workday.''

''I think I have a fair idea. You still shouldn't have to pay,'' she murmured.

''I paid the plumber because you said you'd feed this hungry mob.'' His sudden boyish grin creased his cheeks, which had begun to sport a five-o'clock shadow. ''My stomach is growling.''

''My guys missed lunch as well as dinner. Hey guys— and I'm including girls—how about I order in pizza tonight?''

Erin Drummond, who hadn't budged from one small corner of the couch since they'd first arrived, was the lone dissenter. ''I want to go home, Uncle Ben.''

Kicking off his shoes and peeling off wet socks, he walked barefoot to the couch and sat beside her. ''Hey, mouse, what gives? I know you like pizza.''

She held herself stiffly aloof. ''I don't like it here. It's noisy, and boys are dorky. Noah keeps saying he's going to turn that awful dog loose.''

Abby gasped. ''Noah David Drummond. I'm ashamed of you. What do you have to say for yourself, mister?''

The boy's square jaw lifted pugnaciously. ''Let them go home. Who wants Erin Drummond hanging around looking bug-faced?''

Mollie flew at Noah. "My sister's not bug-faced. You take that back." She punched him in the mouth and blood spurted.

Although Abby reached for the combatants, Ben moved faster. But Noah shoved Mollie hard. Her back struck the recliner, causing Sam as well as Mollie to cry out.

"Now look what you've done," Erin cried, slamming her book closed as she popped to her feet and glared at Noah. She stretched out a hand toward Mollie.

Ben's two-fingered whistle rent the air. "Time out," he snapped, his scowl sufficient to send both girls scurrying toward the door. The older twins froze in place. The younger ones dropped the Hot Wheels cars they were lining around the room's perimeter. Kneeling next to Sam, Ben softened his voice while he efficiently checked the boy's legs for possible injury. Then he examined Noah's swelling lip. Used to the sound of crying, Ben didn't realize all the other kids had joined the chorus. Not until he rose and assured Abby that Noah was okay.

"What's gotten into the ones who weren't involved?" he asked Abby.

"Perhaps we should postpone sharing pizza," she responded, circling her arms around the four boys. "It appears we've all had an eventful day. I'm sorry, Ben. We didn't have a chance to catch up." She checked her watch again, but instead of meeting Ben's confused eyes, she let her gaze stray toward the kitchen, where the dog had set up a racket again.

"Ruffian's hungry and lonesome," Noah declared, clenching his small hands as he stalked past the huddled girls. "It's not fair he can't come out 'cause of twitty girls. It's his house, too, you know."

"See, Uncle Ben," Erin squealed. "Noah's going to let that monster out."

"Ruffian's not a monster," Brad and Reed shouted in tandem.

Throwing up his hands, Ben grabbed his shoes and socks and waved his nieces toward the exit. "I give up. There's no chance of us carrying on a civilized conversation in this madhouse. Abby, I'll be in touch."

Ben missed the longing look she aimed at his retreating back. "Thanks for everything, Ben, including moral support," Abby said, trailing him to the door. "If you only knew how much I miss adult conversation. It goes without saying that I love the boys, but..."

Ben spun around, without realizing she'd crept up on him. She stood near enough so that her light, flowery perfume washed over him.

Shifting his shoes to his left hand, he raised his right and brushed the back of his scraped knuckles over Abby's chin. "We aren't saying goodbye permanently. Lord knows I need to talk to someone about what's happening with the girls. Preferably someone who understands what I'm dealing with." Worry clouded Ben's brown eyes as he silently watched his nieces climb into the back seat of his BMW.

"I don't know if I can be of any help, but I'd like us to talk, Ben. I care about Erin, and I thought she acted...well, odd today. Granted, the twins en masse can be overwhelming."

"She got off on the wrong foot with the dog. The girls have a cat who rules the roost at home. So...I know they like animals." He sighed wearily. "We've...uh...gotta go. I need to feed us, check Erin's math and supervise baths before getting the girls off to bed." As he spoke he stepped barefoot into the wet loafers.

"You're doing all that, Ben? I thought your father said you'd found a woman to look after the girls and take care of the house."

At the mention of his father, Ben's slight frown became a scowl. "Mrs. Clark only works from eight to five. I assure you, if my dad gave a damn, he'd help a little. Who knows better than him that doctors don't keep regular hours?" Just then Erin leaned out of the car and called plaintively to Ben. He blew out the breath he'd sucked in, tossed Abby a last *so long,* and trudged down the steps in his soaking shoes.

Abby stood on her brother's porch, staring after Ben until the BMW roared to life. She probably would've stood there longer, but Noah, who'd been her problem kid of late, turned Ruffian loose. The ungainly boxer scrambled around the corner of the kitchen and shot toward the opening, forcing Abby to quickly slam the screen door.

"Boys, take Ruffian out in the backyard for a run. He's been cooped up long enough. I'm not anxious to clean up another of his messes today."

"Aunty Abby, I'm starved," Reed whined.

"I know. So am I. Let me check on Sam, then I'll see what I can scrounge up."

"I thought you said we were having pizza." This from Michael.

She leaned against the door, crossing her arms and studying each child with what they called her teacher's eye. "You know, guys, when I was your age, pizza was a treat to be earned. Quite honestly, I'm disappointed in how you acted in front of guests. We're not having pizza. Maybe next time Dr. Galloway and the McBride girls come to visit, you'll think about this and be on better behavior."

"I don't want any old pizza anyhow," Noah shouted. "And I don't want that bat-nosed Erin McBride to come back here ever again."

"Yeah," chimed in his siblings, all looking and sounding fiercely loyal to their brother.

Abby had never noticed before that Noah led and his brothers followed. These past weeks, it had been an every-day occurrence. Frankly, she didn't know what to do about it. She wondered if Ben might have any suggestions. He was, after all, a trained pediatrician who probably dealt with behavior issues on a daily basis.

A FULL WEEK PASSED before Abby found an opportunity to ask. Ben phoned Thursday night. She was already in bed, but hadn't been able to settle down to sleep.

"Abby, hi. I apologize for calling so late."

"It's okay, Ben. Sam woke up a while ago with leg cramps. I'm trying to wean him off pain medication. Dr. Galloway, er…your father said I should stop the pain meds altogether. How can I if Sam cries because he hurts?" She sounded close to tears herself.

"What did Kirk say about the surgery sites? Are they healing?"

"He said slower than he'd like. Whatever that means."

"Probably exactly that. Some kids bounce back fast. Others don't. Still, you don't want Sam becoming addicted to painkillers."

"No, I don't. I just…maybe I'm not spending enough time with him. Poor little guy wants to play with the twins, but he's not mobile. Several times I've come in from doing laundry or something and found Sam on the floor trying to reach the cars. No one admits to helping him out of the recliner."

"Those casts are strong, Abby. As for the pain at night, did Kirk recommend using a kids' analgesic?"

"I'm not sure. He's so busy, I only ever get a minute to ask questions. I'm trying so hard to get a word in past his students. I miss half of what he tells me."

"Interrupt, Abby. The patient comes first and students

second. I doubt Kirk expects you to cut Sam off his pain meds cold turkey. Give him twice the number of tablets recommended on a children's analgesic bottle, four times a day. Time one dose for right before bedtime.''

"Thanks, Ben.'' She paused.

"Seems I'm always thanking you. Did you call for any particular reason? I'm sure it wasn't to talk about Sam, although I'm grateful for your insight.''

"You're welcome. I phoned to see if there's any chance of us getting together tomorrow night for a hamburger and beer at our favorite bar and grill. I have a sitter for the girls if you can find someone to watch the boys for a couple of hours.''

"You don't know how tempting that sounds, Ben. Blair occasionally hired teenage girls from the church to baby-sit. I'm sure she has a list somewhere.''

"Do I hear a but coming?''

"Yes, unfortunately. This household is a handful when everyone's well. With Sam's problems, I doubt any parents will want their teen to be responsible for him.''

"I guess that's right.'' It was impossible to miss Ben's glum tone.

"Give me a rain check? Oh, that's not fair, Ben. I honestly don't have any idea when or if my life will get back to a point where I can date. You should call someone else.''

"No. How do divorced parents manage? Based on the number of merged families Steve and I see at the clinic, I can tell you they met and dated somehow.''

His words stung, because it sounded to Abby as if he thought she wasn't as capable as those other women. "We're talking five kids, Ben. Not one or two. Besides, I have no idea what a sitter might charge to watch five. Probably more than I have to spare.''

He remained quiet for a moment. "Are you strapped for cash, Abby? If so, I'll be glad to pay your sitter."

"This conversation is deteriorating. I'd never let you pay for my sitter."

"Then the next question is, Abby, do you want to see me or not? I'd like to see you. I'm willing to do whatever it takes for us to have a night out. But I can't do it alone."

"I'd love nothing more than to go out with you." Abby felt her eyes sting. "If only the thought of getting ready to go out didn't seem so overwhelming. And I'm not talking about hair and makeup, either." The tears trickled down her cheeks.

"I'll tell you what. Since I've already booked a sitter for Friday, why don't I come over there after you put the boys to bed? I'll pick up a bottle of wine and some Chinese takeout. If the weather cooperates, we can sit on your porch and watch the ferries pull into port. We'll pretend it's a picnic."

"You'd do that instead of spending a night on the town?"

"I volunteered, didn't I?"

"Yes, you did. I'm really looking forward to Friday. Outside of talking with Raina Miller on the phone a few times, my only adult interaction has been with grocery clerks. Oh, plus your dad and his staff on the days I take Sam in for check-ups. I haven't even made it to church, which I feel guilty about."

"You shouldn't, Abby. Though I expect that's difficult for you and the kids. Sitting for an hour every week in a place that's connected with your brother—maybe you should try a different church."

"I've thought about it. But then I wonder how fair that would be to the boys. I think I just need more time."

"If I had a dime for every time I've made *that* statement

lately, I'd be well on my way to becoming rich. How much time is enough, Abby? There are a million things a day that remind the girls and me of Marlo. Every single one sends Erin into a tizzy. As a result, I try to hide my feelings. I'm not sure that's healthy, either.''

"Erin's extrasensitive. She was my best student, partly because of a drive inside her that wouldn't let her be happy in the number-two slot. Noah's my problem kid. His grades have slipped and he doesn't care. Since you introduced the subject, let me ask—should I be concerned about that? Or his temper? Sam throws temper tantrums, too. Because of his age, and since he's sick, I tend to make allowances. I consistently give Noah time-outs, but..."

"It sounds as if time-outs aren't effective with him. Instead, try taking away a privilege or adding a chore he dislikes.''

"That's a great idea. I've tried rewarding him for good behavior, which has no effect. By the way, that method always worked with Erin. Some kids thrive on positive reinforcement. Erin always wanted to please me and her other teachers.''

"This is scary, Abby. Do you suppose we've solved each other's problems as easily as that?''

Abby chuckled, she felt as though some of the weight had lifted from her shoulders. "I was going to say if your suggestion works with Noah, I'd owe you the price of an office visit. I'll certainly settle for a fair trade.''

"Abby, I'd like to talk longer. However, Mollie informed me she has no clean jeans, and her class has a field trip to a farm tomorrow. I'm afraid to open the door to the laundry room, for fear the mountain of dirty clothes will bury me. Since I'm not on call tonight, and I'd like to go out Friday with a clear conscience. I'll wash and dry everything in there if I have to stay up all night to do it.''

"You do laundry?"

"If I want to send the kids to school in clean clothes, I do."

"Boy, your housekeeper has it easy."

"Funny thing about housekeepers, Abby. They wait until you hire them and then they hand you a list of things they don't do. With Mrs. Clark, staying late was first on her list. Because my hours are so irregular, I negotiated away the laundry for her willingness to stay on the nights I'm running late."

"What do you do when you're on call?"

"Luckily Marlo had an elderly neighbor who's a night owl. She's an old-movie buff. She has a heart condition or I'd hire her full-time and fire Mrs. Clark. Anyway, this neighbor loves the girls. She's happy to earn a little extra on my call nights."

"I'm sorry to hear you're having such difficulty getting competent help. Over the summer I'll be looking for someone to stay here during the next school year. I sometimes have before- or after-school meetings. And Sam will only be in kindergarten half days. I never imagined it'd be so hard to hire someone."

"Maybe you'll get lucky. Various agencies told me that part of the problem right now is with the bridge being out. Some women don't want to add the mileage it takes to go past it and double back."

"According to the paper, it may take two years to rebuild the bridge. I can't be out of work that long. My savings are dwindling fast."

"Abby, that's twice you've mentioned money. Were Elliot and his wife not insured?"

"He was a minister, Ben. The church provided minimal benefits, and including a small life policy. Blair's grandmother left her this house and a small trust fund, which as near as I can tell they tapped to pay the yearly property taxes. Since taxes have gone up, the fund's now defunct. Blair should probably have rolled it into mutual funds. Maybe then it would've grown enough to meet the rising cost of inflation. On Elliot's salary, I think they did well to feed and clothe themselves and five kids.''

"Considering that Elliot had to struggle to make ends meet after your parents' accident, I'd have thought he wouldn't make the same mistake.''

"Unless you're talking about one of the big evangelists, money is always short for people in the ministry. It's not a field anyone goes into to get rich. It's a calling, Ben.''

"So are medicine and teaching and science. I don't know if baby lawyers and stockbrokers sit around and talk about where they can make the most money before they choose a profession. But most students gravitate toward a particular career because it speaks to them. They also expect it to make them a decent living.''

"I never heard Elliot or Blair complain. Their house was filled with laughter and love. I hope I can do as well by the boys.''

"I'm sure you will, Abby. Give it time.''

They both realized what he'd said at the same moment. "There I go mentioning that darn word again.'' Ben laughed self-consciously. "And speaking of time, the clock is ticking and my mountain of laundry isn't getting any smaller.''

"Okay, I should go, anyway. I hear Sam fussing. Before I hang up, though—about Friday. Just bring a bottle of wine. I'm planning pot roast with all the trimmings. I'll feed the boys early and keep ours in the oven. If you can get here by eight-thirty, I ought to have the boys in bed and the food should still be good.''

"Pot roast is one of my favorite meals. You're on. And

Abby, I can't tell you how much I'm looking forward to spending a quiet evening alone with you.''

FRIDAY, at approximately eight-twenty, Ben whistled cheerfully as he bounded up the steps to Abby's house. The front door stood ajar, but the screen was latched. Inside, Ben expected virtual silence. In reality the place sounded noisier than it had at his last visit.

The bird squawked raucously above the excited shrill of children's voices. Someone yelled, there goes Poky. Grab him! A hollow but higher pitched tone, shrieked, "pretty bird." Ben deduced that was the cockatiel. More distant, but equally annoying, the dog barked loudly enough to wake the dead.

Shifting the bottle of chilled wine from his right to left hand, Ben pounded as hard as he could on the door casing. Otherwise, he had no hope of being heard.

One of the younger twins galloped into the hall, skidded across the tile and dashed out again. "Aunt Abby," he bellowed at the top of his lungs. "That doctor guy you said was coming is here."

A worried-looking Abby, red-faced from exertion, popped her head around the wall. "Ah, Ben. Is it that time already?" She hurried over and unlatched the screen. But she barely gave him room to squeeze past. "Be careful where you step," she warned. "Speedy and Poky got out. Ruffian chased them under Reed's bed. I crawled under and I thought I had them captured. Brad went to find a cage. I didn't realize he and Reed had taken both of them into Noah and Mike's room. Well, the minute he opened their door, those little suckers smelled freedom. They streaked past me. Brad saw them race downstairs. So here we are an hour later, still hunting for them."

"I see." Ben didn't, of course. "Who are Speedy and Poky, might I ask?"

"Our hamsters," stated two anxious, round-eyed boys. The two instantly began blaming each other for the animals' great escape. The verbal blaming ended up in a fistfight of sorts.

Abby grabbed each boy by an arm and sat one down hard on the couch and the other in a wing-backed rocker. "We'll have none of that. Brad, Reed, you'll each stay put for five minutes. And be quiet. I told all of you this tearing around is scaring the hamsters half to death."

"What's that you got?" Mike Drummond sidled up to Ben and inspected the bottle of burgundy Ben gripped so tight his knuckles had turned white.

Noah joined his twin. "It's wine, stupid. For Eucharist." Then he added, "We only do that the first Sunday of the month."

"And Daddy uses grape juice 'stead of wine," piped up one twin from the couch.

Abby, now on her hands and knees behind the curtains covering the bay window, backed out. Raking red curls out of her eyes, she blinked at Ben. "Oh, Ben. I didn't get the kids fed. Do you mind putting the wine in the kitchen?"

Ben assumed from the way she rolled her eyes, she meant they'd share the wine later, after she put the kids to bed. *If* she put them to bed, he found himself thinking.

A sudden, mournful wail rolled down the hall.

"Holy cow, Aunt Abby," Mike declared. "You left Sam sittin' on the toilet."

Abby leaped to her feet. "Blast, so I did." She checked her watch and her face got redder. "The poor child's been there half an hour. Why didn't somebody remind me?"

Ben held up a hand. "This seems like déjà vu. Remember, I said bathroom duty is right up a pediatrician's alley.

Mike, if you'll put this bottle carefully on the counter, I'll help your brother.''

Noah and Mike started a minor scuffle over who should be allowed the honor of carrying the wine. Ben opened his mouth, but he really wasn't surprised when the bottle slipped out of their hands and crashed on the entry tile, spreading glass and bloodred wine from one wall to the other.

''Don't move!'' Abby screamed. ''None of you.'' She glared at the other two as if daring them to leave their seats.

Since Ben was closer to Mike and Noah, he gingerly hooked an arm around each skinny waist and hoisted both to the safety of the living room. Of course, the boys legs and bare feet were stained red.

''I'll clean up the wine,'' Abby said, in spite of a sigh she couldn't restrain. ''Ben, would you rescue Sam as planned? Noah and Mike, finish hunting for your pets. No one, I repeat, no one, extends his search to the kitchen until I have this latest mess mopped up.''

Oddly enough, Ben watched the boys responsible for the crisis, obey quietly. He tapped on the bathroom door and announced himself to Sam before entering. ''Hey, buddy, remember me? I'm the other Dr. Galloway.''

''Yep, the nice one. Dr. Ben.'' Sam smiled mischievously, hunched his sturdy shoulders and pressed a finger to his lips. ''I'll tell you a secret.''

Ben eyed the child a moment, then slowly nodded.

Reaching into the deep pockets of his bathrobe, Sam Drummond withdrew his chubby hands. In each, he clutched a nose-twitching hamster.

''Sam!'' Ben exclaimed. ''Abby and your brothers are tearing the house apart looking for those guys.''

''I know. Poky and Speedy ran in here and I bent down

and scooped 'em up. I coulda falled on my head, but I didn't.''

"Why didn't you let someone know you'd found the hamsters?''

"'Cause.''

"Because why?'' Ben asked, thinking he probably shouldn't play Sam's game.

"'Cause Brad and Reed won't let me play with their hamsters. And Mike and Noah say the same about Harry.'' The child's eyes filled. "The day I got hurt, Daddy said he'd buy me a rabbit for my very own. Only...only...now I'll never get one.''

Ben swiftly took care of Sam's needs, righted his clothes and hoisted the boy high against his chest. "What about Ruffian?'' he inquired. "Whose dog is he?''

"He belongs to the fambly. I want my own pet.''

"I saw fish out there, and a bird. I'll bet your Aunt Abby will put you in charge of them if you tell her how you feel.''

The boy shook his head, and doggedly stuffed the hamsters back in his pockets. "Daddy gave Mommy the bird, and the fishes were his. I did tell Aunt Abby. She said all she needed underfoot was a smelly old rabbit. I don't think rabbits smell, do they, Dr. Ben?''

Ben felt he'd landed in a situation over which he had no control. While he could certainly sympathize with Sam, he owed his allegiance to Abby. "You know, son, I don't have any experience with rabbits. I'll bet no one in your family does. But that isn't a good reason to punish your brothers by hiding their hamsters. Brad and Reed are really worried that something bad happened to their pets. I think they'd be plenty appreciative if you told them you'd captured the little guys.''

Sam mulled that over as Ben carried him down the hall.

"They still won't let me play with them, I bet. And even if I tell 'em, I won't get my rabbit."

"Until your casts come off, you won't be able to take care of a rabbit, anyway. It'd just mean more work for your aunt Abby. Rabbits need food and water and clean grass in their cage. That I do know."

Sam nodded slowly, his face a solemn study of freckles. "'Kay. I'll say I've got Poky and Speedy. But Dr. Ben, could you maybe ask Aunt Abby to think about gettin' me a rabbit after I can walk again?"

"I can do that, Sam. I can't promise I'll be able to convince her. Meanwhile, how about if the next time I visit, I bring you a book on raising rabbits? That way, if Abby relents, you'll be ready to own and care for a rabbit."

"What's re…relent?"

"Uh, it means change her mind. Remember, though, I'm not making any promises on her behalf."

"When are you coming back?"

"I don't know. First, I have to get through this visit without further mishap."

"Why is Aunt Abby scrubbing the floor?" Sam asked in a stage whisper as Ben skirted her and carried the boy into the living room.

"A spill," Ben said, carefully placing Sam on the blankets in his recliner. "I'll go see if I can help. I believe you have some news to share with your brothers," Ben said more loudly; shooting the boy a meaningful glance as he walked away.

Dropping to one knee, Ben stared at the wicked stain still showing on the light tile. "Will that come off? I'd hate for you to have to explain that wine stain if a group of well-wishers happen to drop by from Elliot's church."

"I might tell them it's where I murdered the last well-wishers.'' She laughed. ''Awful, isn't it, that I have so little excitement in my life I need to make up tales.''

''Jeez, I was just thinking I don't know how you stand all the excitement you have around this place. One good bit of news. Listen…'' He nodded to where Sam was handing over the runaway hamsters.

''Thank heaven.'' She stood. ''I'll worry about getting all the red out later. ''Boys,'' she announced. ''Put those animals back in their cages, feed Ruffian and wash your hands. I want everyone seated at the dining room table by the time the little hand reaches nine and the big hand's on the ten.''

''Need help setting the table?'' Ben asked, assisting Abby to her feet.

''You mean you want to stay for dinner after everything I've put you through so far?''

''Hey, I went to all the work of booking a sitter. I can hardly go home before she earns the amount I promised to pay her. Besides, if this is the appetizer, I want to stick around for the main course—to see what you do for an encore. A striptease on the dining table, maybe?'' He wagged first one eyebrow, then the other.

Abby punched his arm hard. ''Ben, shh. You have to be careful what you say around here. I guarantee, explaining the wine spill to Elliot's board would be far easier than trying to get out of *that* comment with inquisitive boys. Hey, you and Sam seem to have hit it off. Would you do me another favor and carry him to the table?''

''I guarantee you won't be pleased about the shine Sam's taken to me, Abby. I promised to bring him a book on the care and feeding of rabbits.''

''You didn't!'' Disbelief leached all color from her face. ''You did? Ben Galloway, I swear! Men are nothing but overgrown kids. If we get one more animal in this house, I'll have to apply for a zoo license.''

''Sorry, but it's only a book. And it might take his mind off other pursuits.''

''You're right again, Ben. It might take his mind off the fact he's tied to his chair. I owe you once more. Thanks.'' Abby rose on tiptoes and brushed a kiss across Ben's lips.

Surprised, he slid his arms around her waist and pulled her close for a better kiss. It wasn't until they broke apart a satisfying moment later that Ben discovered he wasn't the only one who'd been surprised. Four boys wearing identical shocked expressions stood around them.

CHAPTER SIX

THE KISS galvanized the children. Ben had never heard the house so quiet. The only sound was an under-the-breath collective gasp uttered by the gaping boys.

Ben hadn't reckoned on being so affected by a simple kiss. They shouldn't have started something they had no hope in hell of finishing. "Abby, I...we—"

"I, ah—we'll talk about this later," Abby mumbled in Ben's ear, although she was clearly rattled. "Boys, I gave you each a dinner assignment. Time to get at them, please. If our pot roast isn't shoe leather by now, we can eat in five minutes."

"And Ben, would you carry Sam to his chair at the table? It'd help me if you'd get him settled."

Suddenly glad of the offered distraction, Ben hastily escaped the ring of suspicious faces. "Phew!" he muttered.

It was a much subdued group who finally took seats around a large mahogany table. They sat at opposite ends, with the twins between them on either side. Sam was closest to him. In the kitchen, Ruffian slurped his bowl clean, then galloped to the dining room, looking for a handout. A stern word from Abby sent him to his bed beside the fireplace. Ben noticed the animal slink back in on his belly, to lie quietly under Noah's chair.

Abby's pot roast in no way resembled shoe leather to Ben. And the vegetables she generously dished into steaming bowls smelled heavenly. More than ready to dig in,

Ben lifted his plate in anticipation of Abby's filling it. An extended silence occurred before Ben tumbled to the fact they were patiently waiting for him to join hands.

Fervently hoping Abby wouldn't ask him to say a blessing, he felt his heartbeat resume gratefully when she said, "Tonight it's Michael's turn to say grace."

It humbled Ben to feel the tremors in Sam and Brad's small hands as Michael added a prayer for their folks, and one for Ben's sister at the end of the blessing. "Amen," Ben murmured in a deep voice, several seconds behind the boys.

"Since you're near Sam, Ben, do you mind cutting his meat into bite-size pieces?" Used to being obeyed, Abby forked slices of roast onto the other boys' plates. Each accepted a spoonful of vegetables without grumbling, which amazed Ben. Hardly a day went by that at least one parent didn't ask him how to get kids to eat veggies. He'd have to cajole Abby to tell him her secret method.

"You're sitting in my daddy's chair," Brad declared, glaring at Ben.

Four other forks stilled, and four heads shot up lightning fast. Only Sam seemed content to have Ben seated in that position.

It was Reed who ventured tentatively, "Are you coming here to live, Dr. Ben? Is that why you kissed Aunt Abby? 'Cause you two are gettin' married?"

Ben dropped his knife. It clattered against Sam's plate, splashing gravy on the white tablecloth.

Abby choked on water, spewing it all over with a gurgle that Ben deciphered as an emphatic *no way José*.

"Kissing doesn't always lead to marriage," he said carefully. He decided it was in keeping with his professional duty to enlighten the boys. "Adults kiss for any number of reasons."

Four pairs of eyes looked skeptical.

"Really, it's okay, guys," Ben assured them. "Your aunt and I are friends. Friends often kiss one another."

Sam abruptly started to cry. "Why won't you come here to live, Dr. Ben? Don't you like us? Is it 'cause we're all naughty?"

Flustered, Ben resorted to stammering. "It's, ah, nothing like that, Sam. I like you a lot," he said, tossing Abby a pleading glance.

Noah stretched to poke Sam in the ribs. "Quit bawling. If he moves in, he's gotta bring that loser, Erin, too."

"And Mollie? Mollie's okay for a girl," Reed said around a mouthful of potato. He kicked the table leg in time to his chewing.

Abby clasped his knee. "Boys, eat. Erin and Mollie are sweet little girls. It bothers me to hear name calling. It's hurtful. How would you feel if someone called you boys losers?"

Sullen-lipped, Noah shoved his nearly full plate away. "I'm not hungry, and Ruffian wants to go outside. Please, may I be excused?"

Abby glanced at the dog, who seemed to stare woefully back as if to suggest they leave him out of the discussion. "If you've eaten all you want, Noah, you may shower and get ready for bed. Reed and Brad have early soccer practice tomorrow. You and Mike have karate. This time, I'm holding each of you responsible for packing your duffles. We'll be pressed for time, and since some streets are still cordoned off, there'll be no returning to the house for anything you might have forgotten."

"What's cordoned off?" Brad asked.

"Your aunt means some roads were damaged in the quake. Police have blocked them to car traffic." Ben answered because Abby was responding to Mike's request for more potatoes.

"Brad asked Aunt Abby, not you," Noah said, clearly belligerent.

Abby set the potatoes down hard. "Noah, you are excused from finishing your food. You are not excused for taking that tone with an adult. Apologize immediately to Dr. Galloway and sound as if you mean it."

Flinging back his chair so hard it toppled over and frightened the dog, Noah evaded Abby's outstretched hand as he ran from the room.

She righted the chair, stood, then sat again and calmly stacked Noah's plate on top of hers.

Ben massaged a tight cord running up the side of his neck. "Surely you're not letting him get away with such rude behavior?"

"I'll deal with Noah later. If you've finished, Ben, I'll take our plates to the kitchen."

"I am. It was a tasty meal, Abby." From the corner of his eyes, Ben saw the other boys, who hadn't cleaned their plates, meekly mumble excuses to leave.

"Maybe I should go have a little talk with Noah."

"I said I'd deal with him, Ben. And I will," Abby said sharply, stacking plates in a lopsided manner. More than she could carry.

Before she could march off and drop half her load, he said coolly, "Discipline is only effective if it's delivered in a timely manner. Steve and I compiled a discipline pamphlet called *Dealing with Johnnie's Bad Behavior*. Remind me to bring you a copy next time I come over." Having donned his pediatrician's hat, Ben ignored the fact that he had his own problems at home.

"Don't trouble yourself." Abby wheeled to face him, her hazel eyes snapping. "To get a degree in elementary education, I had to take quite a few psychology classes. Perhaps as many as you took to be a doctor. Instead of waltzing in here telling me how to handle my boys, *Dr.* Galloway, fix your own household. At least relax some of your stringent rules. Erin acts positively repressed. She's nothing like the carefree kid I had in class last year." Executing a military-like turn, Abby stalked off, leaving Ben gnashing his teeth.

Mike must've been lurking near the door, because he scooted out from the hall and grabbed his aunt Abby's arm. "My karate uniform's dirty. You have to wash it tonight."

"If you'd put it in the hamper after class, Michael, it would get washed on wash day. But...okay this once. Leave it by your door. I'll do a load tonight."

Only Ben and Sam remained at the table. Probably because Sam's casts prevented him from departing without assistance.

"Dr. Ben, you got on Aunt Abby's nerves," the boy said in a hushed tone.

Like *his* nerves weren't stretched thin? Ben realized how thin when he noticed that he'd wadded his napkin into a ball. Regardless, Sam's comment made him smile. Putting down the napkin, Ben ruffled the boy's mop of red curls. "You got that right, sport. I'd better go home and let your aunt cool off. Can I deposit you someplace first?"

Sam nodded. "Would you take me upstairs to my room? And...will you read me a story before you go?"

Seeing the guarded expression in the child's eyes, which all but said Sam expected to be turned down, Ben capitulated. "One story, buddy. But I get to choose."

"*Really?* You'll read to me? All riiight," Sam crowed. "Let's go now."

"Sure. Just let me make sure it's okay with Abby." Poking his head into the kitchen, Ben spelled out his intent.

At the wary sound of his voice, Abby turned from filling the sink. A dishwasher was one appliance her town house had that Elliot's lacked. And one she sorely missed. It'd be her first purchase once she returned to teaching. "You *want* to read to Sam?" Abby used her forearm to push hair out of her eyes. Softening visibly, she said, "He'll love it. I know the other boys often forget he's incapacitated but no one leaves him on purpose. It's more that everyone's used to Sam dawdling."

"I wasn't criticizing the way you care for the kids," Ben said. "Remember, I walk in your shoes. And I'm not so old that I can't recall what a terror I was at Noah's age. I do know there's been a change in Erin. Just because I wrote a pamphlet on discipline, doesn't mean I think I have all the answers, Abby. The other day Erin walked out in the middle of one of my lectures. She glared at me in a way I remember glaring at Kirk. I backed off and gave Erin her space. So I *am* capable of learning, Abby."

"Oh, Ben, I know you're the city's top pediatrician. I shouldn't have lashed out at you." Abby lowered her lashes in embarrassment as she gripped the edge of the sink.

"My mom was one of the foremost cardiologists in the country before she turned her back on her kids and ran off to marry an Italian count. And Dad…well, you've seen his credentials. Degrees after people's names don't qualify them as good parents. Listen, Sam's squirming to get down. I'll go read him a book, and when I'm done I'd still like it if we could talk."

"I'll put on a pot of coffee. I'm sorry I can't offer you a beer or some wine."

"Wine. Well, that was a fiasco I'll add to my résumé of life experiences." Ben chuckled warmly.

Abby smiled. "Every first-year teacher learns not to give a kid anything breakable."

"Point taken. Clearly a doctor's education is sadly lacking in certain areas."

"Maybe. Or since you're so gifted with steady hands, you assume everyone's born that way."

"Hmm. If the kids were in bed, I'd demonstrate how gifted I am with my hands."

Abby blushed to the roots of her red hair, and Ben withdrew wearing a cocky grin.

Sam raised his arms expectantly. "You're smiling, Dr. Ben. Did you make up with Aunt Abby?"

"I hope so, sport. I like your aunt a whole bunch. I'd hate to think I'd done anything to make her unhappy."

"Is unhappy like being sad?"

Ben had to take a second look at the boy. *Sad* in his line of work was often synonymous with depression. *Unhappy* more often meant that a parent had thwarted his or her child. Ben answered Sam's question with one of his own. "How do people act when they're sad?"

The little chest rose and fell. Finally Sam hooked an arm around Ben's neck and murmured near his ear, "Like Noah, I think."

"Shh." The little boy clapped a pudgy hand over Ben's mouth. "Noah doesn't want us to know he cries about Mama and Daddy going to heaven. But sometimes he forgets I'm in the room."

Ben faltered on the last step. He paused outside the door to the bedroom Sam had identified as his. Had the kid inadvertently hit on something that needed further investigation? Ben entered the room and set Sam in the middle of his bed. "Okay, point me toward your books."

Sam pointed to a case brimming with mostly Bible stories. Checking through them, Ben dismissed some as being too involved for a quick read. He settled on a book with large, well-drawn pictures. A story about hiding baby

Moses in the bullrushes. Ben started out seated on the edge of the bed, but because Sam almost toppled over trying to see the pictures, he turned and rested his back against the headboard.

Downstairs, savoring the uncommon silence, Abby started a pot of coffee and left the roasting pan to soak. She began to worry that it had grown too quiet upstairs. Definitely time to see if twins one and two had complied with her earlier edict. If they'd gone to bed without an argument, it would be a major first, she mused, detouring to scoop wet towels off the bathroom floor. All the boys tended to have selective hearing when it came to doing chores or getting ready for bed. They seemed to invent a million excuses. She always told them that as a teacher, she'd already heard every excuse in the book.

Each set of twins shared a bedroom that connected to a central bath. The one that had flooded at Ben's last visit. Abby's mind wandered as she dumped the towels into an overflowing laundry basket inside the guest bedroom she'd moved into. Were she and Ben destined to have their relationship crumble as they stood helplessly on the sidelines and watched? Twice he'd made an effort to spend time with her, but the chaos of her household had ruined their dates—which weren't really dates.

She pushed open the door to Brad and Reed's room and found it empty. That meant all four boys were in Mike and Noah's room, along with Ruffian, the gerbil, and both hamsters. Uh, oh. They were being far too quiet.

Tiptoeing to the door, Abby jerked it open without warning. That started a chain reaction of boys leaping up, and set Ruffian barking. Mike looped skinny arms around the TV in an attempt to hide the picture. Noah dived for the control, fumbling to shut it off. Brad and Reed headed for the bathroom door, obviously figuring they'd escape before

Abby prevented their exit. But knowing they were up to something, she'd already locked that route from the other side.

Snatching the remote control, she swept Mike out from in front of the tube. "HBO? Boys!" The X-rated movie on the screen made her face flame. "I know for a fact that your mom had this channel blocked. How did this happen? When? *Why?*" Closing her eyes, Abby silently counted to five.

"Noah did it." His brothers gave him up willingly and fast. As a result, he pummeled his nearest brother, who happened to be Mike.

Abby waded into the melee. "Brad and Reed! Take Speedy and Poky to your room, then go brush your teeth. I'll expect you both to be in bed with the lights out by the time I get in there to check." She pointed dramatically toward the door.

"Mike, you take Ruffian downstairs. Put him in the backyard. Then I want you back doing the same thing as your brothers."

Noah shook loose from her grip. He slumped against the lower bunk bed, his face an angry mask.

Once the room was cleared, Abby sat beside him. She chewed on her lip and fiddled with the remote control. "Okay, let's start with you telling me how you got the HBO access code."

At first Noah said nothing. There was no sound except the rhythmic squeak of Harry's frantically rolling wheel. He finally muttered, "Jason Bingham said for ten bucks his big brother would phone the cable place and say our power went off. Jason said it's a no-brainer. When the power goes off, it knocks out the programmed codes. The company'll give it to an adult over the phone. So, me, Mike, Brad and

Reed all chipped in our lunch money, and Jason's brother got our code."

Abby knew Jason Bingham. The kid was the bane of her school's existence. If he applied half the amount of ingenious thought to his schoolwork, Jason would be an A student. As it stood, he was a hoodlum-in-waiting.

"Let's say, for the sake of this discussion, that I understand why you and Mike are curious about TV shows another student in your class has access to—and you don't. But, any way you cut it, Brad and Reed are practically babies. You and Mike exposed them to stuff they shouldn't have a clue about at their age."

"We told them to get out. They said if we didn't let 'em stay, they'd tell on us."

"Well, gee, Noah. That didn't make it plain enough you were doing something wrong? What would your parents say about this kind of behavior?"

His blue eyes narrowed and he bolted upright. "They're not here to say anything. Who cares what we do?"

"I care. Enough to put my job on hold so I can cook and clean and wash your clothes. Doesn't it prove that I care when I get Sam to the doctor, and Brad and Reed to their soccer games? Don't I show you I care by transporting you and Mike to karate?"

"I hate karate. I'm quitting." He walked over and kicked the end of the bed so hard the upper bunk shivered.

Abby heard Mike shut off the water in the bathroom, which meant he'd be reappearing at any moment. She'd seen it before, Noah clammed up if any of the other boys came around. And all the kids followed his lead.

She got to her feet and went to unplug the portable TV. "I'm not going to force you to attend costly lessons I know your dad struggled to provide, young man. As of now, your TV privileges are revoked until I feel you've been appropriately punished. Smarten up, Noah, or this is only the first privilege that will disappear.''

When Mike slipped in, looking worried, she reiterated the punishment for the HBO debacle. ''Lights out in ten minutes, or you boys will be grounded.''

Abby didn't even have the door all the way shut when she heard Mike hiss, ''I told you Aunt Abby was gonna be PO'd.''

If Elliot and Blair were still here, Mike would've been in big trouble for using even an abbreviation of *pissed off.* She probably ought to go back and add to their punishment. But frankly, she didn't have another confrontation in her. Not tonight.

Across the hall, Abby shoved the TV onto the top of her closet. The bed beckoned. Instead, she rubbed her temples and made her way down the hall to see how Sam and Ben were faring.

She saw that Sam had burrowed beneath the crook of Ben's arm as Ben read a story Sam could probably recite from memory. Abby watched the child's eyelids slowly drift closed, and she saw him scrub his face to stay awake. Her heart went out to the fatherless child. And to Ben who, however fleetingly, was fulfilling an injured boy's need.

Sam couldn't see Abby. Ben did, because her shadow fell across his page. He glanced up, noted how tired her eyes were and started to close the book.

She shook her head, pointed to Sam and mimed with hands against her cheek to indicate how near he was to falling asleep. She silently withdrew.

Ben felt the soft wiffle of Sam's snore a page before the story ended. Afraid of waking him if he moved too soon, Ben finished the book. Setting it on the nightstand, he carefully slid off the bed.

Ben held his breath, afraid that Sam's eyes would pop

open again. He needn't have worried. The boy was out, his limbs as floppy as the Raggedy Andy that Ben retrieved and tucked next to him. As he flipped off the light and left the room, Ben's thoughts returned to the woman he'd come here to see.

He found her in the kitchen, nearly asleep over a cup of coffee. "I guess that's decaf," he said, sliding into the chair across from her.

She jolted awake. "Ben!" Abby stifled a huge yawn. "I take it Sam finally conked out? Thank you for removing his robe and covering him with his blanket." She stood up. "Let me pour you some coffee. Then I need to make a last check of the other boys before I let Ruffian in. Oh, and I'd better cover the birdcage."

"I'll do that."

"Thanks. The stars are bright tonight. If all's well upstairs, we can take our coffee out on the porch and talk awhile."

"Are you sure you're not too tired?" Ben accepted the steaming mug.

She shoved cream and sugar closer to his hand. "I don't know what's wrong with me lately. I used to go from dawn till dark and then some. You'd think I'd have a lot more energy since I'm not expending it on work."

"Surely you don't buy the myth that parenting isn't work?"

Her shoulders slumped. "If I'd ever believed that, I don't after today." She paused, staring down at the table. "I could really use your advice on how to handle a stunt Noah pulled tonight. Not his behavior at the table," she hastened to say. "Something worse."

"If I can help, you know I will, Abby. Earlier, though, I had the distinct impression you'd rather I kept my advice to myself."

She rubbed her chin with her index finger and looked abashed. "I'll admit I'm touchy. I'm a good teacher, Ben. I always assumed I'd be an equally good parent. All of this…" She blinked fast and waved one hand. "Blair handled the house, the kids, Elliot's parishioners, plus this menagerie. And she did it without a problem. Since I took over, it's been one crisis after another."

Ben took her trembling hand. "Go check on the boys. I'll cover the bird, then see if I can corral that mangy dog. He won't take a chunk out of me, will he? I mean, if I show up suddenly in his dark yard?"

"Put a handful of kibble in his dish and rattle it at the kitchen door, and he'll follow you anywhere. If that fails, the second light switch turns on the back floodlights. Even if he's at the fence sniffing out shrews, which is his favorite pastime, the light brings him running."

Abby left and Ben took care of his chores. The dog bowl did the trick. Ruffian immediately chowed down the small amount of kibble and drained his water dish. Ben was just refilling it when Abby returned.

"Everything okay upstairs?" Ben asked.

"Fine. I detoured past the laundry room to throw in a load. Mike has karate tomorrow, and his uniform missed getting washed." She dumped her cold coffee and refilled her cup. She topped off Ben's cup, then led the way to the back porch.

The view over the water, even though it was some distance away, was every bit as fantastic as Ben had imagined the first time he laid eyes on the house. "I'm afraid if this were my place, I'd never get any work done. The view is terrific. Was this your family home? Is that how Elliot came to own it?"

"Are you kidding? My folks were missionaries, remember. When Dad came here and took a church, it was the first time Elliot or I had spent more than a brief furlough on U.S. soil.'' She sipped from her cup and curled into one corner of the porch swing, giving Ben room to spread out a bit. ''This house belonged to Blair's grandparents on her mom's side. Her granddad was a salmon fisherman. He made a fortune around 1910 and built this house. Over time, his fortune eroded, but his wife managed to hang on to the house. She left it to Blair.''

''Eroding fortunes would explain the tired look of the place. All the same, it's great. The property is probably worth a fortune today.''

''That's what Elliot said. He said they'd sell it to ensure the boys could all attend college. His salary didn't run to making major renovations or upgrades, though. And frankly, my brother wasn't good with a hammer and nails.''

''Ministers, doctors, teachers. We shore up minds, bodies and souls instead, I guess.''

''So you're not a handyman, either?''

''I never had to be. My folks were in orthopedic and cardiovascular surgery. Both are top-money fields. We had people who watered our indoor plants and changed our lightbulbs.'' He grimaced.

''Do I detect discontent in a life most people would consider paradise?'' Abby asked lightly.

The muscle in Ben's jaw flexed. After a long pause, he sipped his coffee. ''Weren't we going to discuss a question you had concerning Noah?''

Abby studied Ben's profile in the flickering moonlight. For the time being, she tucked away the subject of Ben's feelings about growing up in obvious wealth. ''Noah.'' A sigh escaped Abby's pursed lips. ''You didn't know the boys before they lost their parents, so you can't see how they've changed. But Noah's always flouted authority to some degree. He's much worse now.''

As rapidly as she could, Abby recounted her nephew's latest transgression. "I know what Elliot would've done tonight. He would've given the TV to Goodwill. I removed it until they apologize."

"No second chances with a man of God?"

"Not many." Abby told him about an outfit she'd wanted during her sophomore year. "Elliot and I had already gone five rounds over it. He said the skirt was disgracefully short, and the peasant blouse was cut too low. I saved up, went behind his back and bought the outfit anyway. In what I thought was a brilliant plan, I stored the clothes at a friend's house."

Ben saw what was coming, but he let Abby tell it.

"It was my bad luck to be wearing it one day when I forgot Elliot planned to pick me up early for a dental appointment."

"Man, I can imagine sparks flew."

"No. He didn't say a word. He simply took me home to change into slacks and a blouse he yanked out of my closet. The outfit disappeared, never to be seen again."

"I'm curious. Did that end your rebellious ways?"

"It did," she admitted. "I hated having let him down. I told you how much Elliot gave up to provide me with a home. Seeing his disappointment kept me on the straight and narrow. But when I told Noah I thought his parents would be disappointed in him, he kicked the bed, flew into a rage and announced he was quitting karate. He's always loved it. I don't know what's going on with him, but I felt his distress. I punished him because I couldn't let the TV episode go. It hurt me, all the same."

"Sam said something interesting after the blowup at the dinner table. He said Noah cries over losing his folks, but only when he doesn't think anyone will see."

She shook her head. "Noah's the only one who didn't cry his eyes out at the service. He's been the stoic one."

"But if it's all an act..." Ben shrugged.

"Then what?"

"I'm only suggesting his sadness or fears may be manifesting themselves in temper tantrums."

"Is that your professional opinion?"

Ben set the swing rocking with his foot. "I'm just tossing it out as a possibility. I've seen a similar regression in Erin. Lord, Abby, in one visit you noticed that Erin's acting differently. I'm afraid I've overlooked a problem because Erin's naturally quiet."

"She is. And I'm sorry I jumped all over you, Ben."

"But that's what I'm getting at. While Erin's always been quieter than Mollie, she used to be quick with hugs and smiles. She's gotten downright bossy lately."

Seeing the brooding shadows creep into Ben's eyes, Abby set her cup aside and moved closer to touch his forearm. "If Noah and Erin are having real problems coping with all this upheaval, their teachers have probably picked up on it, too. Would you like me to swing by the school on Monday and make a few inquiries for both of us? Ordinarily, the staff won't discuss a student's behavior with anyone other than a parent or guardian, but Erin's in Jill French's class, and I think Jill would confide in me. She knew you and I were loosely dating."

"What's this *loosely* stuff? And *were?* Don't you mean *are dating?*" Placing his cup on the porch floor, Ben slipped his arms around Abby. He shifted her until she curved against his chest, much like Sam had earlier.

She laid her head on his wide shoulder. "I say *loosely* because look at the situation we're both in. And tonight can't count as a date. Ben, I can't manage dating on top of everything else. I just can't."

Bending his head, Ben skimmed a kiss over her lips. Starting slow and languid, he increased the pressure until he felt her sigh. His heart started to beat a great deal faster.

Forced, finally, to let them both breathe, Ben smiled, and Abby could feel it on her lips. "If circumstances hadn't changed—or if we could turn back the clock—would you still agree to go to Whistler with me?"

Abby snuggled her cheek against his solid chest. In the agony that came in the aftermath of the quake, she'd reacted as each crisis appeared—all the while studiously ignoring what this new reality meant to her future. She'd blocked that out, taking life day by day.

Tonight, in Ben's arms, she admitted how terribly she'd missed seeing him. Missed touching him. Missed talking about even mundane things with him.

"My answer wouldn't change, Ben. Although I have to confess I felt guilty. I never told you, but I put off telling Elliot and Blair until the last minute. Not only did I always give them a break from the kids, I knew Elliot would be unhappy at what he'd consider me jumping the gun on my wedding vows. I told him that Friday morning, and I didn't give him an opportunity to object. I've felt guilty ever since."

"Guilt's a funny emotion. It sneaks up at the worst possible time."

"Yes. I've lived with it, I suppose. And I'm sorry we didn't get our week, Ben. But just imagine how long it would have taken us to get back if we'd already left the city. What if I hadn't been here for the boys, or you for Marlo's girls? Well...your father's here, but my nephews have no one but me."

The muscles along Ben's arm grew rigid. "Believe me, Erin and Mollie are alone except for me. I've only ever asked Dad for help twice in my life. Both times he failed me miserably.''

''Really? He operated on Sam when you asked. For that I'll be eternally grateful.''

''Save your gratitude. I'm sure Kirk weighed the request carefully and decided it was an opportunity to show his hospital board how vital his expertise is to them.''

''His expertise was vital to Sam. Two nurses and the chief orthopedic resident said that if Sam walks again, we'll owe it to Dr. Galloway—uh, your father.''

Ben pulled his gaze back from the moonlit waves. ''I didn't realize there was a question about whether Sam would walk.''

Abby's fingers dug into Ben's shirtfront. ''Your dad expressed grave concerns about the condition of Sam's hip and thigh. He put in pins and wires, but even with that, he's afraid too many ligaments and tendons may have permanent damage. Sam's mobility will probably always be restricted. Dr. Kirk recommended physical therapy. Long-term. The hospital is in the process of contacting therapists in West Seattle, so getting him to and from therapy won't pose such a hardship to me and the twins. His therapy is the main reason I took leave from teaching. Otherwise, I ought to be working to earn the money for Sam's therapy.''

Ben frowned. ''I know you said Elliot's health insurance left a lot to be desired.''

''I'm looking into whether or not it's possible to add the kids to my policy with the district. I paid my premiums in advance for my leave. It worries me that they've got no medical coverage after the end of this month.''

Gathering her hands, Ben turned her so he could massage the tense muscles in her arms. ''I'm sure you're aware that almost any insurance company will refuse to cover Sam's preexisting condition.''

"So I learned last week. But if I can provide better health coverage for other problems that might arise with the twins, I won't feel as bad exhausting Elliot's policy on Sam."

"Abby, I'll take care of the boys without charge. You only had to ask."

She started to answer, but a yawn overtook her words. Sitting up, she clapped one hand over her mouth, then touched two fingers to Ben's lips. "Your big heart is just one of the things I find so appealing about you, Ben," she finally murmured after a second yawn. "But I really hope you don't see me as someone who'd ever take advantage of our friendship by asking such a huge favor."

Ben kissed her fingers. "Don't we have more than friendship between us? Besides, didn't you offer to talk to Erin's teacher for me on Monday?"

"That's not costing me. Plus, it's a one-time occurrence. If our relationship goes nowhere, I've lost maybe twenty minutes, as opposed to you investing hours of care when you could see paying patients."

Ben picked up his coffee cup and got to his feet. "Steve and I frequently comp services. This issue goes deeper than whether you and I are friends or lovers, Abby. I thought you knew me. I'd never turn away a child in need because his family lacked money for treatment."

"One child, sure. But you're volunteering to take on all medical care for five boys for God knows how many years." Rising on tiptoe, Abby looped her arms around Ben's neck and kissed him soundly. "Please, can we agree to disagree about this? It's late. We're both tired, and we each have more urgent problems to deal with first."

"All right. I wish I could stay and talk this out, though." He raised his arm to catch a shaft of moonlight on his watch. "But I have a sitter waiting. And I heard your washer shut off, which means you need to throw Mike's karate uniform in the dryer.''

Arms linked, they walked through the house to the front door. Ben stepped outside but leaned in to kiss Abby tenderly. ''Honey, there's nothing we can't work out if we communicate openly.''

Watching Ben take the front steps two at a time to reach his car, Abby pinned her hopes on that one thin possibility. Even if Ben hadn't, she'd added up their separate long-term commitments. Both lists were staggering.

CHAPTER SEVEN

BEFORE ABBY'S porch light had disappeared from Ben's rearview mirror, he punched his father's number into his hands-free cellular. A woman with a soft southern drawl answered. Lily or Millie. Well, she'd lasted longer in Kirk's bed than Ben would've expected. "Is Kirk available?"

"Benny? Is that you?"

Ben clenched his teeth. Not even as a kid had he gone by Benny. He didn't know if it was the woman's Southern background, or if calling him Benny made her feel older— old enough to be Kirk's girlfriend. "Yes, it's Ben. I have a question for Kirk."

"Your father's gone upstairs to bed. Let me take him the phone. He'll be pleased to hear from you, I know."

Ben doubted it. "Is he sick?"

"Not that I know of. Why?"

"It's Friday, and the night is young. Isn't that usually all the reason you two need to party at the old homestead?"

"Why so bitter, Benny? I've tried to tell you Kirk and I like nothing better than spending quiet evenings by the fire, reading or doing crossword puzzles."

Ben snorted. He heard a door open and Lily—yes, he was sure her name was Lily, not Millie—announced his call.

"Ben? What a surprise." His dad's cultured baritone sounded chipper enough. "How are you? Everything okay with Marlo's girls?"

"I'm calling about Sam Drummond. Is there really a possibility he won't walk?"

"I believe I sent you an official thank-you note for the referral. I didn't include a progress report because it's my understanding that Jase Belltower is the boy's primary care physician."

"He could be. But…I may be taking over the children's care," Ben replied stiffly. He wasn't about to mention his evolving relationship with Sam's guardian. That wasn't his father's business.

"I'm sure Belltower's office will forward Sam's records to you."

"Is his condition a big secret, for God's sake? Or don't you want to talk about his case because the great Galloway didn't pull off a miracle this time? What's the matter— your skills slipping?"

"I don't answer to you on this case." His father seemed annoyed. "Especially not when you assume that tone. Just once before I die, I wish we could hold a civil conversation, Benjamin."

"Which of those possibilities is more imminent, do you suppose?" There was a loud slam in Ben's ear.

Punching the button to lower his car window, Ben welcomed a blast of cool night air. Damn, the old man could shoot Ben's temperature from zero to ninety in ten seconds flat. Always had. That was Kirk's way of dealing with his children; he dangled material things and his approval— which they'd craved above all else—in front of them. Tonight Kirk could easily have given Ben the information he wanted, as one professional to another. Hell if he would, though. Ben hadn't risen to the level of Kirk Galloway's expectations and therefore didn't qualify as an equal.

Ben revved the BMW's engine while waiting for the light at the intersection to change. Why was Kirk in bed at this hour? He was only—what? Sixty? Sixty-one? Counting backward, Ben concluded his father was sixty-three. Far from old. Still, age and blood deserved some respect. Any way you sliced it, Ben should apologize.

Expelling a deep breath, he hit redial. It was galling how fast the phone was snatched up. This time Kirk got right down to business. "Sam Drummond had compound, comminuted fractures of a femur, tibia, fibula and patella. Add to that a crushed ilium and punctured lung. We're talking chips and fragments in his right hipbone," the older man said gruffly. "It took ten hours to piece him together with steel pins and platinum netting. Why else do you think I came out midway through surgery to change my sweaty scrubs? It was damned tedious work."

Ben sucked in a harsh breath, but his father continued, "When the casts come off, will the kid have full range of leg motion? Half? None? Will bone continue to work out through the netting I wove piece by piece over every fragment? Damned if I know. Only time will tell. But if there's any miracle in this case, son, it's that Sam Drummond is still alive. Period."

"There is that. The bridge collapse was awful for so many families, us included." Ben swallowed rapidly to keep his voice from breaking. "Uh...thanks for the update. I shouldn't have started off so rude, Kirk. If I could ask one more thing—who, in your opinion, is best equipped to handle Sam's PT? Which physical therapist in West Seattle, that is?"

Kirk rattled off two names and Ben committed them to memory. In the background, he heard his dad clearing his throat. "Do, uh, the little girls need anything? Clothes, shoes? Anything? My accountant said you returned the check I sent to help out."

"How about a visit from their grandfather? They get home from school at three."

"I can't, Ben." His voice caught. "Marlo wouldn't approve. I'm surprised she didn't tell you about our big fight. In January, I asked Lily to deliver Mollie's birthday gift. I was in Europe. The women had words meant for me. Marlo threw Lily out and said neither one of us was ever to darken her door again. That's why I refused your request to have Lily watch the girls until you found a housekeeper."

"I didn't know. Marlo never said a word about this to me. But I doubt Erin and Mollie are aware of it."

Kirk's response was testy. "According to Lily, the girls heard every word. After I got home from my trip, I tried to straighten things out. Marlo...wouldn't even talk to me. And now...now—what's done is done. It's probably for the best, considering how you feel about me."

"Well, you can only ignore relationships for so long, Kirk, and then they unravel."

"What the hell is that supposed to mean?"

"You don't know, and never did. That's been your problem from the day you and Mom had children, when you were trying to outdo each other by being the best in your fields. Sorry, I just pulled up outside the house. I have a sitter to pay and dictation to do. Goodbye." Ben hit the disconnect button. The years of his father's emotional neglect had hit Marlo hardest. Neither she nor he liked the constant parade of women passing through Kirk's house after their mother left to marry an Italian count. What did Kirk expect? That Ben could suddenly snap his fingers and make all those years disappear? Not even the great Dr. Galloway could command *that* miracle.

Ben called out to give his sitter advance warning, so she wouldn't think someone was breaking in. "I'm home, Miriam." He stuck his head into the living room and saw the young woman rocking Mollie and reading a book. The kids' fat cat, Blackberry, was stretched out on the couch, paws draped over a pillow. "Hey, pickle," Ben said, stopping in front of Mollie. It was a nickname he'd given her at birth because she'd been the reddest, most wrinkled baby he'd ever seen. Now they both considered it an endearment. "It's way past your bedtime."

"Unca Ben, where'd you go? My tummy hurts. Bad."

"Again, Mollie?" Ben swung her up into his arms and shot an apologetic glance at the sitter. "I should've mentioned this, Miriam," he murmured. "It's a nightly event."

"That's okay, Dr. Galloway. She didn't have a fever, and after Mollie told me she'd had a lot of stomach aches lately, I phoned my mom. She said it's probably psychosomatic." The teenager shrugged.

Mollie buried her head in Ben's neck. He kissed her ear as he endeavored to work his money clip out of his pants pocket. Ben peeled off the agreed amount, then added five for good measure. "Thanks for driving out here this evening. Tell your mother I may be phoning her for an appointment. I'd hoped the symptoms would abate in time." The sitter's mother, Jane, had a private child psychology practice across the street from Ben's clinic. He massaged Mollie's back. She didn't feel the least bit warm through her nightie.

"I'll tell Mom to expect a call," the girl said as she started for the door. "The kids were really good, Dr. Galloway. I don't know if I told you, but I'm trying to earn money to tour Europe this summer with an ensemble I'm in. I'll sit for you anytime."

"So you're a musician? Piano, by chance? I can't get Erin to practice."

Miriam shook her head. "It's an all-brass ensemble. Maybe Erin needs to change instruments, or needs different songs. At dinner she said her mom promised she could take violin lessons this summer. I'm only bringing it up because she wasn't sure you'd let her switch from piano.''

Ben stood at the door feeling in over his head. He'd had no inkling his sister had made such a promise to Erin. He wondered what other important details he'd missed. ''Uh, thanks for the tip, Miriam. I'll talk to her about it tomorrow.''

The mewling cat wrapped herself around Ben's legs. Miriam scooted out with a wave. ''That's an awesome cat you've got, doctor. I've never seen a house cat so big.''

''She's not so awesome at 5:00 a.m. when she sinks her claws in my head.'' Ben felt Mollie droop in his arms, her breathing leveled in sleep. Poor kid, she'd worried about his going out. That was why he'd hesitated about leaving them at night. Tonight, though, he'd really wanted time alone with Abby. Was that so selfish?

Ben watched Miriam climb into her car. He shut the screen so Blackberry couldn't sneak out, but waited to close the door until he saw the girl drive off.

He had to shove a pile of stuffed animals aside in order to tuck Mollie back in her bed. Ben left the door ajar so he could hear if she became restless again. He paused to peek at Erin, who slept in an adjacent room. Her night-light glistened on a trail of tears streaking her narrow, elfin face. ''Erin, hon. Are you still awake, too?,'' Ben whispered.

She didn't stir, not even as he stepped into the room. Deciding the tears must be old ones, Ben backed out. He'd definitely have to carve out time to sit down and really have a heart-to-heart with Erin. She reminded him so much of Marlo at the same age. Marlo was ten when their mom took off. Weeks had gone by before Kirk bothered to tell his kids their mother had left for good. Marlo got very proficient at silently crying herself to sleep. Their dad should have paid attention to her tears.

At thirteen, she stole painkillers out of Kirk's medical bag and tried to end her life. It took years of therapy to determine what Ben suspected all along—Marlo felt forsaken and abandoned by everyone who was supposed to love her. He vowed on the spot that his nieces would not suffer the same fate.

ABBY PARKED outside the school at two-thirty on Monday. A wave of nostalgia and envy swept over her as she watched teachers walking their students out to the busses lined up in the turnaround. Until now, she hadn't let herself dwell on the job she loved but had been forced to leave in the hands of a substitute.

Deciding she wouldn't even go to her classroom, Abby unbuckled Sam from the battered booster seat that had somehow survived the crash. What she needed was a bigger car. Buying a van sat at the pinnacle of her to-do list. Elliot's had been insured, and once the company paid the claim, she'd sell her compact and buy a used van. As it stood, she couldn't take all five kids anywhere at the same time and renting a larger vehicle got expensive.

Thrusting that depressing thought aside, Abby hugged Sam a little tighter. "Sammy, how would you like to look at books in the library until I finish talking to my friends?"

"You won't be gone long, will you?" It was a question Abby noticed all the boys were preoccupied with since the quake, particularly whenever she had to ask a neighbor to watch them. They all wanted to know precisely where she was going and how long she intended to be. And if she was the slightest bit late returning, their anxiety registered on their faces.

"I'll be quick like a bunny." She kissed his nose as she

deposited him in the reading circle and spoke to the librarian.

Mrs. Burkholder trailed Abby to the door. "It's good to see you. How are you getting along?"

"Okay, I guess. It takes time to settle into any new routine."

"Well, we sure miss your smiling face around here."

Abby felt a wave of yearning. "Only three more weeks," she murmured. "Then I'll be back. Unless I have to request an extension. Thanks for letting me park Sam here while I visit with the twins' teachers. I also told Ben Galloway I'd catch a word with Jill French. He's worried about his niece, Erin McBride."

"Another tragedy. Our school suffered so many. Mr. Conrad said twelve of our students lost one parent. Three besides your twins lost both mom and dad."

"And our staff didn't fare well, either. One lost a teenage child. Two, their spouses. What do we have, four subs?"

"Yes. It's hard, breaking in subs so late in the year. Some will go permanent in September. Have you met Stacy Thorpe, who has your class?"

"No. I requested Celia Myers. They said she'd already agreed to take the music slot. I know that's her first love. And it may turn into a permanent job." There was something in the librarian's voice when she mentioned Stacy Thorpe that prompted Abby to ask, "Isn't my sub working out?"

"I'm probably not the best person to ask. Maybe Raina Miller could tell you more. I only see Ms. Thorpe two periods a week."

"Hmm. I'll make time to telephone Raina. I'd better go now or I'll be late for my appointments." To make it easier on the twins' teachers, she'd suggested a group meeting.

Both women were already in the conference room. Abby

hugged them before she sat down. "I doubt you ever thought you'd see me on this side of the table," she joked.

The older twins' teacher agreed. The younger twins' teacher, Karen Wheeler, shook her head.

"I believe we should get right to it," Abby said, clasping her hands. "You both know the boys' home situation. I'm looking for areas in which you think I can help them. Obviously, I'm more familiar with Brad and Reed's curriculum. It's Noah and Michael I'm worried about. Particularly Noah."

Susan Sutton, the fourth-grade teacher opened a folder. "I've tried to ease my students back into lessons after spring break. The kids who were at school at the time of the quake have taken longer to assimilate. But Noah hasn't completed one assignment. As a result, his grades have slipped. Michael's fallen behind, but his attitude is better."

As Abby studied some of their work, the second teacher spoke. "My experience is that Brad's picked right up. Reed was struggling before and is falling further back. I don't know what to suggest, Abby. Like you said, you know the second-grade curriculum as well as I do. Maybe if you spent extra time with Reed and Noah in the evening…"

Abby groaned. "Time," she muttered. "I don't know where it goes. We're at the end of the bus route, so it's almost five before they get home. I let them play while I prepare dinner. Then…well, I doubt you want to hear my woes. I'm certainly gaining a new appreciation for a parent's role. I was never particularly sympathetic when moms whined about fighting with their kids over homework. Now I'm whining with the best of them. It's a constant battle of wills, especially with Noah. And next week I'll be adding physical therapy sessions for the twins' younger brother. I assumed the therapists handled all the exercises at the clinic. Wrong! I have to repeat them at home."

The older boys' teacher reached across the table and stilled Abby's restless fingers. "These aren't learning disabilities, Abby. They're behavioral setbacks caused by trauma. I'd like to say they're temporary. But with Noah, I'm afraid if we don't nip his attitude in the bud, it may well become habitual. Probably the last thing you need is for me to suggest counseling. Honestly, though, that's my recommendation for Noah. Which will be even touchier if Michael doesn't have to go. That's one reason I don't like putting twins in the same classroom. Their mom insisted. She said that splitting two sets of twins presented too much of a hardship at open houses and parent-teacher conferences. Blair went to Mr. Conrad and he caved in."

Abby nodded.

"I heard the school added extra counselors. I didn't see a list. Is there one you'd recommend over another?"

The teachers conferred for a moment, then Susan said, "Dave Keeler. He's younger than Paul Caputo. Noah will benefit more from talking with a man, I think."

"Keeler is probably too macho for Reed," Karen murmured. "He's the sensitive sort. Bonnie Reavis would be my choice."

Abby jotted down the names. "Thank you both for being candid." She checked her watch. "I'd better dash. I'm seeing Jill French next. Erin McBride's uncle asked if I'd talk with her teacher."

"That's right, you're dating the uncle. Lucky duck," Susan, the unmarried teacher, said as she closed her folder and rose. "I heard he's raising the McBride girls. Hey, Abby, his kids need a mother, and your boys need a dad. Ever thought you two might want to join forces?"

Abby skidded to a stop at the door.

"You seem shocked," Karen said. "If you ask me, it's a brilliant suggestion. You and the good doctor were already a hot item. Or is the bachelor not inclined to give up the singles scene?''

The teacher who first introduced the suggestion tossed out a parting shot. ''His bachelor days are curtailed, anyhow, now that he's become an instant dad.''

Abby still didn't respond. What could she say? Just how active had Ben's bachelor days been? The day he'd invited her to go to Whistler, he said he considered them to be dating exclusively. These women didn't sound as if that could be true. Since she and Ben hadn't spent all their free time together, Abby had no idea what he did those other evenings.

''If coming to school is difficult to manage, Abby,'' Susan said, ''we can communicate by phone or notes. Let's give counseling two weeks, then talk again.''

''Sure. But I hope to be back teaching a week after that. Perhaps if I'm here, I can keep better tabs on the boys and their progress.''

''To say nothing of reestablishing control in your class.'' This comment was tossed out casually by Karen.

''Isn't Stacy Thorpe handling my class well?''

''I don't like talking out of turn, but she has zero discipline. Of course, she's young. She's fresh out of college, which may account for part of the problem. Although being young doesn't stop her from voicing her opinions. She had a lot to say in our meeting last week. Belinda thinks Stacy has her eye on replacing you for good. I don't bring that up to add to your stress, Abby. But if possible, I'd advise not adding to your current leave request.''

Abby pursed her lips. ''Thanks. For everything, guys. Gosh, I'd better hurry before Jill gives up on me. And Mrs. Burkholder's keeping an eye on Sam. She'll be wanting to lock up the library.''

Abby found Jill French at her desk. She glanced up when

Abby walked in. "Hi! You know, when the front office gave me the note about you wanting an appointment, I couldn't imagine why on earth you would. I thought it was a mistake. But at lunch, Ben Galloway left a message with the office saying he'd asked you to speak with me."

"It's hard for Ben to get away from the clinic or to phone at a set time. He said his patient load has doubled since the quake. He knows I taught Erin last year. In fact, that's when I met Ben. He came to a conference in his sister's stead."

"Erin is such a sweet child."

"Then you haven't seen any change in her since she lost her mom?"

"I didn't say that. The quake affected so many of the kids. I have Erin and another girl who lost her dad. I've tried to imagine myself in their shoes. It's difficult. The other child has reverted to some infantile behavior, like wetting her pants and throwing tantrums over nothing."

"Erin's not doing any of those things, is she?"

"No. And she's always been a shy, studious girl. Now, she alternates between drifting off into her own world and acting too bossy for words."

"I've just spoken with my nephew's teachers. They think two of the boys need counseling. Should Ben explore that avenue for Erin, do you think?"

Jill tapped her pencil on her lips. "I'm not big on sending kids to shrinks. Especially as most school counselors are overworked. Still, I know we've added some to our staff since the quake." She paused, frowning.

"Let me mull it over for a couple of days. I'll make a point of observing Erin in the meantime. Or maybe Dr. Galloway would rather make Erin an appointment with a private counselor. There are some good ones around."

"You're saying the ones hired by the district aren't?"

"No. Just that I don't really know much about them.

Someone in private practice can probably devote more time to an individual child and maybe get faster results. That's all I meant. Plus it's expensive. But you'd know Ben Galloway's financial situation better than I do.''

"Why? Because we sometimes dated? That's all we did, Jill. I'm not privy to his finances.''

"You mean to tell me you didn't run a check on his portfolio to see if you'd want to marry him?'' Jill exclaimed.

"That would *never* have occurred to me! Not even if we were serious about each other. Jill, you're kidding, right? Women don't really investigate the men they're thinking of marrying—do they?''

"Sure do. Most of my friends run background checks on a guy after three or four dates. A lot of them work at jobs where they make as much or more than the guys. Hey, if a woman doesn't look out for herself and demand a prenuptial contract, she could lose everything she's worked for.''

Abby shook her head. She didn't know Jill French all that well. But she'd heard rumors to the effect that Jill's family had money. "I think that's sad. If I didn't trust someone, I wouldn't marry him.''

"You'd be surprised how many creeps are running around looking for a wealthy wife. But getting back to Erin. What do you want me to do?''

"That's up to her uncle, not me. I'll pass on your comments. Meanwhile, go ahead and observe her for a couple of days. Ben can call you toward the end of the week and you two can hammer out some course of action.''

"Good idea. Hey, If you're not serious about Galloway, Abby, I wouldn't mind giving him a try. Tell him to phone me for an appointment. Or perhaps I'll call him and suggest we meet for drinks. Oh—to discuss Erin, of course.'' She gave a coquettish grin that grated on Abby's nerves. It was a side of Jill French she'd never seen. It shocked Abby enough that she failed to comment one way or the other.

She disliked thinking it was jealousy she felt as she left Jill's room. After all, Ben was a free agent. He probably *would* meet Jill for a drink. He'd had no difficulty arranging for a sitter so he could go out.

Hurrying back to the library, Abby collected Sam and thanked Mrs. Burkholder for watching him. She stopped at the counseling office and set up times to phone the counselors recommended for Noah and Reed.

"Can we stop and get ice-cream cones on the way home, Aunt Abby? Me and Mama used to do that."

Abby glanced at her watch. "Sam, I'm running late. I'm afraid the boys will get home and they'll worry if we're not there."

Sam slumped in his seat. His eyebrows met over the bridge of his nose as he pouted. "I don't like you, Aunt Abby. I wish Mama and Daddy didn't go to heaven." He started to cry.

It was probably wrong to give in to emotional blackmail, but Abby had too much on her mind and already felt fragile in her new role. "Sam, sweetie, we don't have time to stop for cones, but I'll run into our corner market and buy a half gallon of ice cream. That way your brothers can share in the treat."

"'Kay. But I get chocolate." Sam rubbed at his tears with the heels of his hands.

Abby realized she didn't know if any of the boys disliked chocolate. Or worse, were allergic to it. "Sam, I want the truth now. Do any of the twins have a problem with chocolate?"

"Michael only likes 'nilla."

"Vanilla?" At his nod, which Abby managed to see via

the rearview mirror, she tried desperately to recall if she had enough cash to buy two cartons. She hadn't been to the bank since last week. It was scary how fast two burials had depleted her meager savings. Except for a document naming Abby guardian of his estate, after Blair, her brother had been ill-prepared to leave his family. Fortunately, Blair's grandmother's trust kept the house from being lost in probate. Abby would've hated being forced to sell it and further uprooting kids who'd had trauma enough.

She dug through her purse, and by emptying every conceivable pocket, she came up with enough to buy both kinds of ice cream, plus a nickel to spare.

Sam clutched the sack, as she lugged him to the car. "Sammy, boy," she panted. "Before the casts, you were no lightweight. Now, we're going to have to find an ingenious way to move you from point A to point B, if your casts don't come off soon."

"We've got a wagon, but it broke," he explained as she drove the short distance home.

"A wagon might work. Maybe I can fix it."

"Girls can't fix wagons," Sam scoffed. "You'd better call Dr. Ben. I'll bet he could make it go."

"What do you mean? I swear, Sam Drummond, you're too young to have such outdated ideas."

"Guys fix toys and stuff," the boy said stubbornly. "Girls cook and wash clothes an' clean house."

Abby sputtered. "Who fixed our broken toilet? Not Dr. Ben."

"I'll ask him. There he is." Sam pointed.

"Who?" Abby, still flustered by Sam's blatant chauvinism, frowned.

Sam continued to grin and stab an excited finger toward the house. "Dr. Ben's on the porch, but he brought those girls. The ones Noah don't like."

She followed Sam's finger and sure enough, Ben Galloway sat on her porch steps between his nieces, who didn't look happy. Ben hadn't mentioned stopping by today. Yet when Abby climbed out, and he got to his feet, a warm feeling spread through her. It was silly, she knew, and tried convincing herself she was glad only because his being there would save her playing phone tag with him that evening.

Noticing Abby struggling to lift Sam out of the back seat, Ben started toward her. Part of the problem seemed to be a bulky grocery sack Sam must have refused to part with. "Erin, you and Mollie wait here. I'm going to help Abby." Ben wondered why Abby didn't have a wheelchair for the boy.

"Ben, this is a surprise! I just spoke with Jill French." She lowered her voice to make sure Erin couldn't hear. "I thought you were going to call me later for a report."

Ben hoisted Sam easily into his muscular arms, bulky sack and all. "Our housekeeper fell down her front steps and broke her hip this morning. Her son phoned me at the clinic. He came from Everett to take her home with him until she recovers. The long and short of it is, I had no one to meet the girls after school. So I picked them up. I saw your car in the lot." Now Ben lowered his voice. "I didn't think it'd be a good idea to hunt you up just then, in case you were with Erin's teacher. Besides, I promised this guy I'd find him a book on rabbits."

Accepting the sack, Abby dug out her house key. "Hey, girls, you must've been happy to see your uncle show up to give you a ride home."

"I figured it meant something else bad happened," Erin said, her narrow face pinched with concern. "Now Mollie and I don't have anywhere to go after school."

Ben tugged her braid. A better one than his fledgling

attempt, but still far from perfect. "That's my worry, button eyes. I promised I'd take care of you and Mollie. Have I ever let you down?"

Whatever might have been Erin's answer was interrupted by the arrival of the twins' bus. The boys disembarked in a rowdy pack. Brimming over with energy after their confinement on the bus, they kicked and punched at one another as they raced to reach the house first.

Noah, who always won because he was the tallest, drew to a halt the moment he spied the McBride sisters. "What are *they* doing here again?" he demanded sullenly of Abby. "We had to ride the stinking bus. Why didn't *they* have to?"

Leaning across Ben's broad shoulder, Sam piped up, "Noah, me'n Aunt Abby bought ice cream for a treat. I bet you don't get none for saying that."

The other boys whooped over the prospect of ice cream. Both girls shrank from their roughhousing. Abby felt a major headache coming on. It grew stronger after Ruffian bounded out the door, happily licking anyone within licking distance. Unfortunately Erin was his first conquest. She screamed bloody murder and nearly knocked Ben off his feet in her attempt to crawl up his leg.

Noah made things more difficult by laughing loudly at Erin's plight.

"Ruffian!" Abby grabbed his collar. She also grabbed Noah by the shirt. "The rest of you go in and make yourselves at home. Noah and I are going to put Ruffian in the backyard. Ben, will you dish up the ice cream? Bowls are over the sink. Scoop's in the drawer to the right of the stove. One scoop each, and the rest goes in the freezer."

"I didn't do nothing," Noah sulked. "It's not fair they get ice cream and I don't."

"Did I say you weren't getting any?" Abby asked

calmly. "You're jumping to conclusions again. I had errands, which meant Ruffian was cooped up half a day. You and I are going to turn him loose in the backyard. Then I want you to fill his water dish."

Unable to hear what Abby said after she and Noah disappeared around the corner, Ben shooed the remaining kids inside.

Boys and girls were scrunched into the breakfast nook savoring their treat, while Ben patiently waited for a pot of coffee to brew, when Abby and Noah entered the kitchen.

"Noah, would you like chocolate or vanilla?" Ben asked, picking up the last bowl.

"I want a scoop of each."

"I didn't hear a please with that," Abby said sternly. "And everyone else got one scoop. Tell Ben which flavor you'd prefer, Noah."

"I don't want any of his stinking old ice cream." Noah slammed open the French doors and bounded up the stairs. The other children fell instantly quiet.

Michael gave a final lick of his spoon and slid out of the nook. "I'll take Noah his ice cream. He likes chocolate."

It was no less than Abby expected, because it was one of the phenomena of twins. One minute they battled each other tooth and nail; the next they'd make sure their twin didn't get short-changed. "Let's give Noah some space, Mike. His ice cream isn't going anywhere. He knows what he has to do in order to get some. If you're finished, put your bowls and spoons in the sink, please. You may play a game or watch TV in the living room. Sam, you need your face washed. Afterward, would you like me to carry you to the recliner?"

"Dr. Ben do it," he mumbled through the washcloth Abby scrubbed him with.

She glanced helplessly at Ben, who merely lifted Sam

and carried him to the living room. On his return, Ben poured and passed Abby her coffee. "You need a shot of rum in this, but I know you don't have any squirreled away in the cupboard. Were you able to talk to Noah's teacher? That kid is totally out of control."

Abby sighed. "I'm consulting with a psychologist tomorrow. Also about Reed. He's falling miserably behind in school." She sank onto the stool next to Ben.

"Is that what Erin's teacher recommends I do, too?"

"Actually, she thinks you're hot and says you should meet her for drinks one evening. To talk about Erin," Abby said, rolling her eyes.

Ben slopped coffee over the edge of his cup. He grabbed a napkin and wiped up his spill. "What?"

"I'm sorry, Ben. That was totally unprofessional of me. You'll need to call Jill and set up a time when you'll be available."

"Available for what?" He scowled.

"To, uh, talk—about Erin. I'm botching this, Ben. For all I know, she was joking about drinks. Have you met Jill? Her dad designed half the buildings in Seattle. She's single and very attractive. Erin will verify that if you ask her."

"What does her appearance have to do with how Erin's doing? I don't have time to meet with her. I have to find somebody to take care of the girls before and after class. I phoned an agency," he said. "They have no qualified nanny-housekeepers needing work. My secretary called a dozen day cares, and they're all full."

"You're kidding! I hoped to find one that runs a bus to the elementary school after I go back to work. I have to find a place soon. Ben, you're welcome to drop the girls off here until you make other arrangements. It may be out of your way, but for now the girls could ride the twins' bus."

"I can't ask you to overload yourself, Abby."

"You didn't. I volunteered. Really, Ben. What's two more kids? In class, I'm used to twenty-five. And at least the girls know me. Erin will warm up to Ruffian in no time, and I'll make sure Noah behaves."

"Abby, jeez, I could kiss you."

"There's a plan. At the moment, however, I'd rather you helped me make dinner. Show me how to light the gas grill. Just don't tell Sam I need help. He's under the impression girls aren't capable of doing stuff like fixing wagons or lighting barbecues."

Ben laughed. He kissed her, too. Then he sat back with a sigh. "I've been thinking about kissing you since I saw you pull in. Before my thoughts go too far in that direction, you'd better point me toward your big, bad barbecue."

Doubling her fist, Abby socked him on the shoulder. Ben did nothing but continue to grin at her wolfishly.

CHAPTER EIGHT

THE SMOKE from the barbecue enticed Noah out of his bedroom. "Hi, guy, feeling better?" As he loped past her, Abby ruffled his reddish-gold cowlick. "I was about to come dig you out. We're taking burgers to the beach. We'll let Ruffian chase waves and you kids can run off your excess energy. How does that sound? We shouldn't let our good weather go to waste."

"Who'll carry Sam?"

"Me," Ben said from behind Noah. He held a heaping plate of piping hot hamburger patties and brandished a spatula.

"Great," Abby exclaimed. "I placed buns on the counter. Each one has a name written on a lunch sack underneath. I've also bagged chips and an oatmeal cookie for everyone. You and Noah are the only ones who haven't said if you want ketchup, mayo or mustard, lettuce, onion and relish on your bun."

"You've been busy." Ben gazed at Abby with a teasing glint in his eyes. "How about if I fix mine and Noah's while you load the others into plastic bags?"

Abby had a cooler on wheels and a big tote bag sitting next to the counter. She'd bought both as gifts for Elliot and Blair, and found herself crying earlier when she hauled them out of their catch-all closet. It seemed that small things popped up without warning, driving home the fact that she'd never see them again. She wondered if things in

Marlo's house affected Ben the same way. Or maybe he hadn't spent as much time at his sister's as she had in her brother's home.

Twenty minutes later at the beach, Abby had an opportunity to discuss personal matters with Ben. She'd spread two quilts on the sand for the kids. She and Ben carried their lunch sacks to an old driftwood log, which placed them between the kids and the water.

He stared out at the waves, sparkling in the sun, and heaved a deep sigh. "This is so relaxing. I could get used to living in a place like this."

"Elliot and Blair rarely had time to enjoy the beach. I guess people who have beach property or a mountain view accept it as commonplace."

Sliding off the log onto the sand, Ben leaned back against Abby's legs, sending pleasure rippling through her.

"Steve and I want to reach a point in our practice where we can each take off one full afternoon a week, just to kick back."

"You probably should've figured that into your initial schedules. Now, I imagine patients are used to having you both on duty full-time."

He munched a chip and watched the dog scrabbling in the sand. "Marlo couldn't believe I went into medicine. We hated that our parents never had one iota of free time, for us or each other. Marlo assumed I'd end up working some nine-to-five job, like she did. I thought so, too."

"What changed your mind?"

Ben set his chips down and inspected an oatmeal raisin cookie. Idly he picked it apart and tossed sections out to the hovering seagulls. When it was gone, he reached over his shoulder and took Abby's hand. "Something you don't know about me is that I was a hell raiser as a teen."

"Ah. That's why I'm drawn to you, Dr. Galloway. Women love a rebel."

"I was a bit more than that. I had some scrapes with the law. Several."

Abby tightened her grip on his hand. "Drinking and stuff?"

"That, and I broke into the country club on a dare. I swam naked at midnight in their pool. I was booked on a B-and-E. Kirk had no more than bought me out of that mess than I stole his girlfriend's Porsche and drove it to Mount Rainier. Tore the undercarriage all to hell on a side road, trying to outrun the cops. Kirk got her to say I had permission to take the car. He had to promise to replace the Porsche with a brand-new model. It pissed him off royally, which did my heart good."

Abby's shock showed. "And you were judgmental when I didn't discipline Noah the other night over a little rude behavior?"

"That's how it starts, Abby. First mouthiness, followed by bouts of delinquency. All fed by an I-don't-give-a-damn attitude, which—if it isn't channeled properly—ends in self-destruction."

"You did okay."

"Two reasons. My old man pointed out I was leading Marlo down the same damaging path, and in the next breath, he said I'd never amount to anything. Said I was stupid, and he doubted I was really his kid. It was a lie and we both knew it. I looked exactly like my paternal granddad at the same age. I asked for Kirk's help in straightening out. He told me to go to hell, stomped off and left me to deal with the cops while he took care of his latest girlfriend's car."

Abby wondered how the gifted surgeon, who'd knit Sam's bones so skillfully together, justified treating his own children so badly. Slipping down to sit beside Ben, she said nothing, but simply laid her head on his shoulder in a gesture of support. Secretly she was thinking Ben and his father probably needed a gentle push to start them communicating again. Both were such talented men.

Absently Ben stroked Abby's hair. "One of the cops said something that clicked with me. He said, 'you ought to show that fool he's wrong about you. Make him eat his words.'"

"That was it? That's all it took?"

"That, and a lot of determination on my part. A friend posted my bail on the careless driving charge. The night I got out, I made a pact with Marlo. If she'd forego liquor, drugs and chasing around with a bad crowd, I'd straighten up and apply myself at school. She said we should both study to be social workers. She wanted to save throwaway kids, I guess."

"A worthy endeavor. Marlo wasn't as determined as you? She told me once she didn't finish college, and mentioned how difficult it was raising two kids on an insurance clerk's salary."

"As a sophomore, she got pregnant with Erin. She wanted a baby, but didn't plan to get married. Neither of us had seen much to recommend it. By then, I'd decided I was more suited to medicine than social work.. or marriage. In fact, I'd just completed my internship. I wasn't in any position to help her financially. Kirk and I had another major falling out—he ordered me to do my residency in orthopedics. When I refused, he cut off what support he was providing. My mom came through and bought Marlo a house."

"But…Marlo did get married? I thought Erin and Mollie had the same father."

"Yeah. Kevin McBride hung around until he wore Marlo

down. They tied the knot a month after Erin's birth. I lost count of the times he moved in and out after that. They had a stormy marriage. Right after Marlo learned she was pregnant with Mollie, Kevin announced they were moving to Florida. He had no job. Had never held a steady one. Marlo was afraid to abandon her only means of support—her job at the insurance company. She assumed he'd eventually agree. One day, she arrived home from work to find an empty house. Kevin had cleaned out every stick of furniture except for Erin's bed. He didn't even leave a note. Nice guy, huh?''

"Ben, how awful! And she never heard from him again?''

"No such luck. A mutual friend told her where Kevin had gone. Marlo filed for divorce. He didn't contest it. About the only good thing was that I made enough in my residency by then to help her refurnish. For a while, I even moved in to help her out with some rent money.''

"That was wonderful of you.'' She thought briefly of Elliot. "I don't know why I always assumed Marlo's husband had died. So what was his reaction to her death?''

"I didn't notify him. As far as I'm concerned, it's good riddance to bad rubbish.''

Abby started to tell him that as a teacher, she'd seen some nasty custody fights. But before she could, Erin dragged Mollie over, complaining about the wind blowing off the bay. "Mollie and me wanna go home, Uncle Ben. It's cold and the boys are kicking sand all over us.'' She shook her long braids and sand did fly.

Mollie glanced back to where the boys were playing tag. Her expression didn't suggest that she agreed with her sister about leaving.

"Want to sit with me for a while, Erin? Mollie can play for another little bit.''

"No. We're ready now, aren't we, Mollie?" Erin squeezed the younger girl's arm. "I have reading to do. And nobody's home to feed Blackberry."

"Abby and I are enjoying our conversation. Are you sure you can't give us half an hour, button?"

Erin had perfected an aggrieved pout, but she seemed genuinely distressed. Taking pity on her, Abby rose and collected their lunch sacks. "This has been a nice interlude in a hectic day, Ben. But the boys probably have homework, too. It takes time for them to settle down after an outing."

Ben climbed to his feet. "I suppose all good things must end. Girls, I do have exciting news. Until I can find someone to replace Mrs. Clark, Abby has offered to watch you before and after school."

Mollie let out a whoop and threw her arms around Abby. Erin scowled defiantly. That disturbed Abby, since she and Erin had always gotten along famously. "Erin, I know it's not ideal," Abby said, after hugging Mollie back. "But I think we can have some fun..do some girl things in this predominantly male household."

"Hey, that reminds me," Ben said. "Abby, do you play the violin, or know anyone who does? A little bird told me Erin hoped to take violin lessons over the summer. I couldn't find a reference in Marlo's daily planner to indicate she'd contacted a teacher."

"That's 'cause renting a violin was too expensive," Erin said, still pouting. "But that's okay. I'll stick with piano. Next year I'll be old enough to take band at school. Clarinets and flutes are cheaper to rent."

"Honey, I can afford a violin if that's what you have your heart set on. I haven't got a musical bone in my body. I applaud and encourage anyone who does."

Abby glanced from girl to man and back again. "Phone

the office of the Seattle Youth Orchestra, Ben. I'll bet they keep a list of instructors. Or maybe our school music director can recommend someone. Erin, have you asked Mr. Gilcrest?''

''No. I said just forget it. But…if I have to come here after school, Uncle Ben, how will I practice? They don't have a piano.''

''I saw an electronic keyboard in Blair's closet. She played for church weddings and sometimes for the youth service. I'll dig it out after I get the boys to bed. Ben, could I prevail on you to carry Sam up to the house? With those casts, he weighs almost more than I can manage. Depending on how long he has to wear them, I might need to fix the boys' broken wagon.''

''I saw it in the garage. Shall I take a look at it? Oh, by the way, I spoke with Kirk about which therapists he thought would most help Sam. I'll give you the names before the girls and I take off.''

''Thanks, and thanks again. I should have phoned his office for that information a week ago. To be honest, my time's been spent bugging the insurance company to finalize the claim on Elliot's van. I have to replace my car with something bigger. I can't keep asking neighbors to watch the boys while I run one or another to practice, or take Sam to therapy. The neighbors have been wonderful, but I hate to wear out our welcome.''

''I know what you mean. Girls, go tell the boys we're cleaning up. You two shake out the blankets, fold them and put them in Abby's tote.''

Neither girl moved very fast. But when it became clear that Ben wasn't budging until they obeyed, they dragged themselves back to where they'd left the twins and Sam.

''I didn't want to say this in front of them,'' Ben said after the girls were out of earshot. ''I've felt guilty over the number of times I've phoned Marlo's neighbors to beg favors. Mrs. Clark was very adamant about leaving on the dot of five. Even on good days, that's an almost impossible goal for me."

"I'm sure," Abby murmured. "I hadn't thought of after-hour staff meetings. Once I return to teaching, I'll have to deal with conferences, professional development days and breakfast duty."

"Even if I cut appointments at four, emergencies have a way of cropping up. I frequently run by the house, grab a minute with the girls and leave them with a teenage sitter. On-call nights are the worst. I can't know for sure whether or not I'll need them. And it might be at six o'clock, or ten, or midnight. Two nights last week, I had to wake the girls at 2:00 and 3:00 a.m. I took them to the hospital with me because I had no other choice."

"Ben, that's terrible. For you and for them. I don't know how you pop in and out of sleep, either, but I suppose you're used to it. If that happens too frequently, I think you'll begin to see ill effects in the girls' school performance."

"Tell me something I don't know. I'm doing the best I can, Abby."

"I'm not making accusations. We both need live-in help. I'd like to consider that option myself, but it's prohibitive on a teacher's salary."

"Pediatricians are at the bottom of the doctors' pay scale. We don't do specialty work like surgery. I have to manage, whatever the cost. It's just…finding a motherly sort willing to take the job is next to impossible, according to the agencies I've phoned."

"What you need is a wife," Abby teased, elbowing him playfully. She sobered quickly when she remembered the teachers' comments.

Early on in their relationship, he'd said marriage was way down on his list. If he had free time, he wanted to enjoy sports and other recreational pursuits. He'd said forty might be an age at which he'd consider marrying. Abby knew he was barely thirty-two.

She hadn't teased him because back then, his announcement pretty much matched her timetable. Teaching came with stress. Abby loved not answering to a single soul when she arrived home. Several nights a week, she'd turn on whatever music struck her fancy, and indulge in two-hour bubble baths. Marriage and babies tended to make that pretty well impossible. In fact, she couldn't name a working mom who didn't rush home from her job only to don the hats of cook, housekeeper, chauffeur and occasionally hostess to her husband's clients. Showers were a luxury grabbed on the run, and then only if the woman was lucky. Abby hadn't so much as thought of taking a bubble bath since she'd assumed care of the boys.

A wrestling match broke out between Michael and Brad farther down the beach. Abby went to break it up, not waiting to hear Ben's response to her joking remark.

Getting seven kids and one rambunctious dog back to the house consumed Ben and Abby's attention, and they forgot their previous conversation.

Ben's pager beeped seconds after they'd herded their charges inside. He hardly had time to put Sam in his recliner before pointing the girls toward the front door.

"Are you on call?" Abby asked. If so, she supposed they were lucky Ben had managed any free time at all.

Indicating no with a brief shake of his head, he called back his answering service on his cell.

From the one-sided snatches of conversation, Abby gathered that Ben had a patient in trouble. "Would you like to leave the girls here while you go to the hospital?'' she asked after he signed off.

Erin flung her arms around Ben. ''I wanna go home. Blackberry will be *starved.*''

Ben patted her head. ''Erin, hon, either way it's going to be a while before your cat gets fed. She always has food left in her bowl, anyway. Fat as that cat is, it's not like she's in danger of wasting away.''

''You could buy a timed cat-feeder, Ben. It would keep the girls from worrying if this ever happens again.''

''I've never heard of such a thing.'' Ben pulled out his car keys and tossed them to Erin. ''Tell the boys goodbye, get your sister, then go unlock the car and buckle in. Abby,'' he turned to grip her hands. ''I won't take you up on your offer tonight.. but thanks. But I'll bring them here tomorrow if that's okay.'' At her nod, he added, ''Can I take out the trash we brought from the beach. I go right past your bin.''

''The boys earn their allowance by taking out the trash, mowing the lawn and feeding Ruffian. We'll be fine. I hope you're able to stabilize that sick child.''

''I want Dr. Ben to read me a story before he goes.'' Sam's lower lip protruded, and his eyes glossed with tears.

''Another night, sport.'' Ben bent and smoothed back Sam's wind-blown hair. ''Here, color a picture and save it for me.'' Ben gave the boy his coloring book and a half full box of crayons.

''Okay. *Then* will you read me a story?''

''Tomorrow?'' Ben straightened. ''Sure, provided Abby says I can come again.'' Hearing his car horn honk, Ben stepped to the door.

Abby walked outside with him.

He fit one broad hand around her waist and nudged her behind one of the wide porch pillars. ''Kids sure wreak havoc on a person's love life, don't they? The hell of it is, I don't foresee it changing for us anytime soon. Do you?''

It was one thing that he'd asked her such a provocative question and quite another that his very thorough kiss prevented her from answering. Ben's fingers inched up under Abby's T-shirt, eliciting shivers of desire. She automatically pressed the lower portion of her body against Ben's. They both reveled for a moment in the result. Ben shifted away first, but not before uttering an apologetic groan.

''I should be shot for instigating something that's going nowhere fast. Forgive me, Abby?'' In the background, the twins clamored for their aunt. And in the foreground, the girls yelled for their uncle.

Tipping her head to one side, Abby swayed in his arms. ''Frustrating as this is, Ben, we're the lucky ones. We're alive, and our homes are virtually undamaged. I remind myself of that whenever things get too hectic. You'd better go. Right now, your patient has first call on your time.''

He slowly withdrew his hands from under Abby's shirt, enjoying her softness to the last tingle of his fingertips. Ben knew she spoke the truth. Yet, when he thought about the larger picture—being responsible for the total well-being of Erin and Mollie 24/7, 365 days a year for the next twelve to fourteen years—it scared the hell out of him.

Perhaps that was why he yanked Abby close again and gave her one last feverish kiss. Releasing her just as quickly, he charged headlong down the front steps.

''Hey,'' she called. ''The school bus picks kids up at the corner around eight every morning. Unless you call to say you've made other arrangements, I'll expect the girls before then.''

''We'll be here,'' he shouted from the street. His car door opened and he disappeared inside.

Abby's fingers flew to her lips, and she sagged against

the pillar, letting her eyes follow the BMW until it made the turn. Something about Ben's last kiss was different, suggesting more than the desperation dictated by haste. She stood for a minute, feeling jumpy and disconnected, but still couldn't place a finger on what made it different.

Once the street was empty and she'd gone into the house, facing the normal uproar, whatever fleeting thought she'd had about Ben's last kiss faded to a pleasant memory.

MORNING WASN'T Ben's best time of day. Especially now that he had to pry two kids out of bed, prepare a nutritious breakfast for them, braid hair and feed a cat. Even on the days Mrs. Clark breezed through the door at eight on the dot, he'd indulged in his old habit of hopping from bed at the last minute, flying out to grab a Starbucks latte and muffin on his way to the clinic. Getting the girls up earlier and changing routines in order to drive them an extra two miles to catch a bus made them grouchy, and it didn't do much for him, either.

"We don't know any of the kids on that stupid bus," Erin whined in a tone that grated on Ben's already frayed nerves. He bumped into Mollie as he sought a suitable reprimand for her sister. "Mollie, good grief! Why are you underfoot no matter which way I turn today?"

Mollie burst into tears, and Erin rushed to comfort her sister. Glaring at Ben, she said in her snottiest eight-year-old fashion, "Mommy never made Mollie cry. She's tired. Me, too. We didn't get home till midnight. We're both just kids, you know."

Feeling guilty, Ben pulled out the nearest kitchen chair and sat. He held both girls in a single hug, and understood Erin's stubborn resistance. "Hey, girls. Times are tough all over. I'm doing my best. We all are, aren't we, button?"

Mollie crawled into his lap. "I love you, Unca Ben, but

I miss Mommy so bad. I always see Mommy's face before I go to sleep. Last night I lost her and I'm scared.''

"Oh, pickle.'' Ben swallowed the lump in his throat. He wrapped the girls tighter and practically felt Erin's iron will slipping. Her quivering body might well be his undoing. Ben had managed to hold up at Marlo's funeral and afterward for their sake. Dammit, he ought to be able to handle his grief—and theirs. In medical school, doctors were taught to deal with death. There were ways a physician could hide his or her personal feelings while speaking with the family of a loved one who'd died. There'd been no lessons on how to deal with it if the loved one was the doctor's own.

Ben kissed Erin's forehead and brushed another on Mollie's fair hair. "Girls, remember all the boxes we put in the attic the day I moved here?'' Both heads bobbed. "Well, in one box I have pictures of your mom when she was your age and even younger. I also have her high school graduation pictures and a few taken shortly after you were born. This weekend, how about we find the box and then we'll get each of you a set? We'll buy photo albums, and that way, you'll be able to see your mom's face any time you're feeling sad.''

"It's not the same as having her here,'' Erin muttered.

"I know. I know,'' Ben murmured, dragging his shirttail out of his pants to dry the girls' eyes. "Her…leaving left a huge hole in my heart, too.''

"Are you ever mad at her for going away?'' Erin asked in a small, teary voice. "I am sometimes, and I don't think I should be.''

Ben's throat closed. "She didn't have a choice, sweetheart.'' He lightly touched the ribbon he'd tied cockeyed at the end of Erin's badly done French braid. He didn't think he'd ever master French braiding.

Erin frowned, studying him warily. "But Mommy said our daddy chose to go away and leave us."

The mantel clock chimed the half hour. Ben knew he'd never get their book bags loaded and lunches fixed, plus get them to Abby's before the bus arrived. But he didn't plan to have a discussion with the girls involving Kevin McBride. Not right now, anyway. Marlo had tended to make Kevin out as a bad guy. Ben wouldn't lie to them about either parent, but he preferred not to even mention the jerk if he could avoid it. Although something in Abby's eyes yesterday had nagged at him to notify the jerk.

"This subject is deeper than we have time for today, kids. I need you to finish eating and then go brush your teeth. I'll phone Abby and tell her I'm driving you both to school. That way I can stop in at the office and arrange for you to ride the bus home with the Drummond boys. It'll give you all day to ask around your classes and find out if any of your friends ride that bus. I'll bet some of them do."

"Yes, please, Uncle Ben." Erin's frown disappeared. The first smile Ben had seen in days brought dimples to her thin cheeks. Mollie still clung to Ben like a monkey. He carried her to the table, thinking she did look sleepy. But then why not? He'd had to keep them at the hospital until eleven-thirty. Sure, Mollie had fallen asleep on the couch in the doctors' lounge, but he'd roused her when it was time to leave, and again once they got home. So many disruptions in one night couldn't be good.

No two ways about it, Ben thought as he added milk to their cereal, something had to give. He had to locate a housekeeper. Soon.

Returning the milk carton to the fridge, he closed the door and reached for the wall phone. "Abby, it's Ben," he said on hearing her cheery hello. "I'm a ways from getting the girls moving. I thought I'd drop them at school and arrange for them to catch the bus to your place afterward. Will that work for you?''

''Fine. I tried calling you last night to let Erin know I found the keyboard. Have her bring her music, will you? Gosh, you must've been tied up at the hospital until late. I think the last time I tried phoning you was nine-forty-five.''

''I didn't check my messages. Did you call my cell?''

''No. It wasn't that important.''

''I had a baby with breathing problems. A touch-and-go situation for a while. I suspected asthma, since the mom is an allergic mess. Turned out the baby had pneumonia. Took time to stabilize her and for the oxygen and antibiotics to kick in.''

''Are your evenings always so frantic?''

''Some are worse than others. I never thought about it before…I…uh…'' He glanced over his shoulder at the girls. ''Until my life underwent major adjustments,'' he finished lamely.

''I know exactly what you mean. In fact, there's a scuffle taking place in my kitchen as we speak. I'm sure it's because one little piggy got the last of the Cocoa Puffs and another got none. Want me to let you know when the girls get here?''

''Thanks, that would ease my mind. They're nervous over this switch in routine. Not that anything can be called routine these days.''

''You sound stressed, Ben. Is there more going on with the girls? Problems I should be aware of?''

''No. I don't know. Probably.'' Ben shut his eyes and wished he'd phoned from another room.

''Ah. Nothing you can mention with the kids in the same room, huh?''

"Right. Teachers must be intuitive. Or else it comes from being female."

"Lord, I only wish that was true. But I'm as in the dark about what goes on in kids' minds as you are. I think sometimes it helps to talk over stuff with another adult who's in the same boat. I hate to sound needy, but is there any chance you can stay for dinner? Sam's counting on you to read him a story, so if you can't, I need to start preparing him now."

"I'm on call tonight. I've arranged for the student who baby-sat the other night to come over at a moment's notice. But if my phone's quiet, I might stay for dinner. Oh, and Abby, don't let me forget the picture Sam promised to color for me. As far as dinner goes, you fed us last night, so let me buy tonight's meal."

"Don't be silly. The girls eat like birds. And cooking for this crew, two or three extra makes no difference. Besides, the twins begged me to fix corn bread and macaroni with cheese for dinner. I'll include a veggie of some kind. I hope the girls like mac and cheese."

"Girls?" he said, turning to them. "Abby's asking if you like macaroni and cheese. If so, we'll eat with them before we leave for home."

"Again?" Erin rolled her eyes. "Why do we always have to eat with those stinky boys?"

Ben caught himself to keep from snapping back. Mollie, bless her heart, clapped. "Macaroni and cheese is my favorite food," she sang out.

"Plan on us," Ben said into the receiver. "And Abby, if I haven't said so before, you're the bright spot in my life which is otherwise going to hel—" He broke off suddenly, saying goodbye as he hung up.

RUFFIAN STARTED BARKING and jumping at the door, and the bird suddenly squawked. Abby glanced up from the project that claimed her attention. Reed dropped the cars he'd been playing with, charged down the hall and pressed his nose to the screen door. "It's that doctor guy," he said, galloping back, all out of breath, to confront his aunt.

"Ben? Already?" Abby dragged her watch out from under her sleeve. "Wow, it's later than I thought. Don't stand there, Reed, let the poor man in. And hold Ruffian."

Ben walked in on a much cosier scene than usually greeted him in the Drummond house. The girls and Abby sat on the floor around the coffee table. They were stringing beads for bracelets or maybe a necklace. The girls wore contented expressions. Abby, too. Her bright-red curls refused to be contained by a string ribbon she'd used to tie them back.

Ben could see Noah and Michael in the kitchen. They appeared to be diligently writing. The younger twins, including the one who'd let him in, flopped on the carpet around a city built of blocks. From the number of police cars, fire trucks and other emergency vehicles scattered among the buildings, Ben figured the boys must be recreating the city's recent disaster.

Mollie left her spot to run and hug Ben. She held up her prize. "Abby's helping me and Erin make bracelets to give our teachers at the end of school. That way, they won't forget us over the summer."

"Students give teachers presents at the end of the year? I wouldn't have known that," Ben said after approving Mollie's enterprise.

"All the kids were talking about it in my class today. The girls," Erin said as she added two colorful beads. "I didn't know if you'd have time to help us make anything, Uncle Ben. I hope you don't mind that I asked Abby instead."

"Are you kidding? When it comes to stuff like that, button eyes, your uncle is totally inept. I can barely manage to do my Christmas shopping."

"You always bring us presents on time," Mollie said in his defense. "Not Grampa Drummond, though."

Ben recalled his father mentioning an altercation surrounding Mollie's last birthday gift. The girls rarely mentioned their grandfather. And that suited Ben fine.

"I have a book picked out for you to read me, Dr. Ben," Sam said, holding his arms.

Jumping at the chance to ignore Mollie's reference to her grandfather, Ben lifted the boy.

Abby smiled. "If you read fast, you might finish the book he's picked out before I get dinner on the table, but I'm warning you, don't try skipping any words. Sam has most of his books memorized."

"Okay, short stuff. I'll read every word of...*Cloudy With a Chance of Meatballs*? That's a funny title. Hey, is this the picture you colored for me? Great! It's going on the cork board in my office." Ben tickled Sam, and he giggled so hard the boys came from the kitchen to see what was going on. Noah appeared to be more carefree than Ben had ever seen him.

Dinner was harmonious—far different from previous tensions that had radiated from the boys.

"Ben, do you know anything about the inner workings of a car?" Abby asked when talk died away.

"Some. I know more about the inner workings of kids," he said, winking at Mollie who sat to his right. Sam, whose eyes had already begun to droop, had leaned against Ben's left arm ever since they'd sat down. "Why?" Ben asked after Mollie stopped laughing.

"Tomorrow the insurance agent is bringing me a check for the replacement value of the old van. I'm hoping to pick up a used one with whatever I can get for my car plus the insurance check. I need whatever I buy to be in good working order.''

''Will all the kids fit into our two vehicles? If so, I'll go with you to browse car lots after I come to collect the girls tomorrow. There may be some good deals among cars slightly damaged by the quake.''

''Really? Noah and Michael are big enough to sit in front. Sam's booster takes up half my back seat, though. If you can fit four and I take the rest, we've got it made.''

''Okay,'' Ben clapped his hands. ''I'll help Abby clear the dishes, if you continue to get along for a while.''

''Abby rented us a movie. None of us have seen it. So take your time helping with the dishes, Uncle Ben,'' Erin said.

''Yeah,'' chorused the boys. ''Aunt Abby, Mike and I finished our homework.''

''Good going. Noah, you may start the VCR. And remember, I said this is a special treat. It doesn't cancel out the TV down time you still owe me.''

Sam raised his arms again. ''Please carry me, Dr. Ben.''

Abby nearly had the table cleared by the time Ben returned. ''You can either watch the movie with the kids or have a second cup of coffee in the kitchen with me,'' she said.

''No contest.'' Ben pinned her against the dining room wall and pressed a kiss on the gentle curve of her neck. ''Hmm, you even smell tasty.''

''Hmm. Let's take our coffee out to the back porch.''

''And neck on the porch swing? It suits me, but can we hear the kids?''

''Of course. But if we're lucky, they'll be glued to the screen.''

Like conspirators, Abby and Ben tiptoed out the back

door, taking care to leave it ajar. A golden moon, a peaceful night sky and the prospect of a lovely woman in his arms set rockets off inside Ben's head and in his bloodstream. Setting their cups aside, he tasted Abby's lips. Growing bolder by the minute, he slid his hands up under her blouse and lazily thumbed the tips of her breasts.

Weak-kneed, her heart pounding against Ben's palms, Abby slipped sideways, allowing him to reach her breasts with his lips. So great a heat sizzled around them that neither felt chilled by the wind blowing off the sound. Ben felt the strain behind the placket of his slacks long before he unsnapped Abby's jeans and sneaked in two fingers....

A firecracker ready to explode, she moaned and moved against his seeking hand. She attempted to give him some relief at the same time.

Loving the soft glitter in her eyes, knowing he was the cause, Ben felt a deep yearning in the pit of his stomach..and felt as though her light touch might make him explode. Suddenly, something Abby had said the previous evening popped into his head. *He needed a wife.* She'd meant he needed someone to help with the girls. Tonight, an all too different reason thrummed through his veins. If he and Abby joined forces, they wouldn't have to steal moments on the back porch to cop a feel or do a half-assed job of assuaging basic human needs.

As Ben felt Abby convulse around his fingers, he cried her name in a raspy whisper, and fought to hang on to his own control. "Abby, let's get married," he blurted out.

"Wha-a-at?" Her bones were twice as wobbly as a bowl of jelly.

"Married. You and me." He sat up. "Think about it— if ever two people had good reason to get married, it's us. Neither of us feels comfortable sneaking around. And that's what we're doing right now."

She gaped at him for several seconds, then shot upright, hurriedly buttoning her jeans. Her face flamed and her breath came in short spurts. "But...marriage! Ben, that's such a...huge leap. The kids—" She waved a hand feebly toward the house.

"—need a mom and a dad," he finished. "Abby, we both admitted we need help with them."

"Yes, but..." Her tongue stumbled over her racing thoughts. Surely there were other cautions she should bring up. But her brain felt numb. And Ben's cell phone rang, ripping apart her concentration.

He frowned as he took the call. Abruptly he clicked off. "Four teens are coming in at County, the result of a two-car crack-up on the freeway. The two youngest are my patients. Their dad requested me. Abby, could I leave Erin and Molly with you until I evaluate the situation?"

"Of course you can leave them." She managed to get to her feet semigracefully, even though her head still spun from his marriage proposal. She wondered if she'd heard him correctly.

Ben went on instant doctor-auto pilot. He hurried inside, spent two seconds explaining his hasty exit to the girls—then like that, poof, he was gone. Like a rabbit disappearing into a magician's hat.

Desperate for something ordinary to focus on, Abby ran water to wash the dishes. As the tempest inside her slowly subsided, she began to weigh the merits of Ben's proposition. A business merger was all it had been. He'd made no mention of love. The absence of such a tiny word shouldn't bother Abby. But it did....

CHAPTER NINE

BEN LEFT County Hospital shortly after midnight. A night breeze and brightly shining stars should have rejuvenated his spirits, but didn't. Not when the boys' blood still spotted the lab coat he stripped off as he hunted up his car. And no matter how hard he and the E-room team fought to save him, the older boy's life had slipped away from them.

Crazy kids. Their story was similar to many Ben had heard throughout the years, and no less sad. Four hotheaded teens, two newly purchased cars. Each driver taunting the other to prove which car could go fastest. Two friends now lay dead because of it. Two clung to life. Their families would never recover.

Ben slid under the BMW's wheel. He scrubbed his hands over his face, barely feeling the rough prickle of his beard. He ought to phone Abby to check on the girls.

What he needed, though, was a stiff shot of bourbon. He'd like to fall into a sleep deep enough to block out the gut-wrenching sobs of the mothers he'd left in the hospital waiting room.

By and large, pediatrics was a happy profession. But when cases went bad, doctoring was a bitch. Tonight was the first time in Ben's career that he couldn't just give his tires a damned hard kick, and then go home and wallow in solitude.

After warming up the engine, he flipped on his lights and drove back to Abby's house.

It surprised him to see her living room still lit. His heart tripped faster. Was Mollie having another nightmare? Or had Erin refused to go to sleep?

Abby's front door was jerked open before Ben rang the bell. A rumpled Abby stood framed in softly glowing lamp light. "I thought if you rang, it might wake the kids, so I waited up. Ben, you look awful. I guess I don't need to ask how things went."

"No." He stood there, waiting in the doorway. "I saw your lights and worried that maybe you'd had difficulty with the girls."

"They're asleep in my bed. Erin fretted all evening about her cat. Ben, you're really going to have to buy an automatic feeder."

He gazed at her blankly, and Abby knew his mind wasn't on Erin's cat. "Would you like to crash on my couch? I'm not sure you ought to drive in your condition."

Two steps, and Ben had Abby wrapped so tight in his arms, she found it difficult to breathe. Still, without hesitation, her arms circled his waist. She rubbed his lower back. Abby had never seen Ben anything but clean-shaven. The prickliness of his unshaven cheek against her face told her how badly he needed to hug someone.

"I can't stay the night," he said, his voice a low rumble in the ear she'd pressed to his chest. "The girls need fresh clothes for school. And the cat. Erin would have conniptions if Blackberry had to go without food for a night. Poor thing depends on us."

"Sam and Reed gave Mollie stuffed animals to sleep with, but Erin refused to take one," Abby said. "Erin made a valiant effort to stay awake until you got back. At ten, I finally took her book away and turned off the light. I'd say she held out maybe ten seconds after that, bless her heart."

Ben sighed wearily. "I don't know what to do anymore,

Abby. None of this is their fault. But I am what I am—a doctor. Patients sometimes come first.''

Abby had spent the whole evening mulling over Ben's forthright if not so flattering marriage proposal. She had to admit she saw benefits in it for her and for him. ''Watching how hard you struggle to work with two kids makes me doubt I'll ever manage it with five.''

''Especially when you add Sam's therapy.''

''Ben, I, uh, I've been thinking about what you said before you left. About us...merging our responsibilities. Merging our lives.''

Turning Abby so her face was fully illuminated in the light from the living room, Ben fiddled with her hair. ''So? What did you conclude?''

''It'll mean more change for all the kids. Your nieces and my nephews would be affected. One set uprooted.''

''Wouldn't it be easier on them now, while they're still in transition from the first turmoil, as opposed to later? We're young, Abby. We have certain...needs, too.''

''I suppose. But Ben, mine is the larger house. The girls...''

Ben recalled Mollie's anxiety at breakfast. She already felt worried that she was somehow forgetting Marlo's image. ''The girls both like you, Abby,'' he said hesitantly. ''I believe having you in their lives will outweigh any problems attached to a move.''

Abby toyed with the buttons on his shirt. ''I have to admit, this isn't exactly the proposal I imagined I'd get from the man of my dreams.''

''Just so I am the man of your dreams,'' he muttered gruffly. ''I realize this lacks the romantic trappings. But can starting off with seven kids possibly be romantic?''

As if to counter his statement, Ben dipped his head and gave Abby a knock-your-socks-off kiss.

She came out of it weak and with her heart fluttering. "Okay, so I see definite potential for improving that part." She took a deep breath. "If you're sure it can work, Ben, why delay?"

In spite of the late hour and the circumstances bringing him to Abby tonight, Ben crushed her tight. He spun her into the living room. "Tomorrow night we're slated to find you a van. Wednesday's the first afternoon I can get away to pick up a license. We could set an early-Saturday appointment with a J.P.

With any luck, I can find a mover who'll meet me after the ceremony. Thankfully our house is pretty small. I'll leave the furniture I've stored there, which will turn it into a viable rental. That way, I can hang on to the house for the girls rather than sell it."

A hard knot formed in Abby's stomach. It expanded with each new plan Ben laid out. She'd just agreed to marry the man. Who'd suspect she'd be so anxious to have him leave? But frankly, she needed him to go.

Indeed, a weight seemed to lift off Abby after Ben carried the last sleepy girl to his car. Of course, the clock chimed 2:00 a.m. then, and her day had begun at six. She was totally beat. Perhaps that was the only thing wrong with her.

For most of the following day, Abby thrust all thought of marriage out of her mind. In the morning, she met with the insurance agent and collected a check. When Sam went down for a rare nap, she phoned used-car dealers to find out who had large used vans. In the middle of one such call, a florist arrived, delivering a dozen peach-colored roses. From Ben.

He'd enclosed a handwritten note that said, "No rose can compete with the fire in your hair. But when I saw these in a shop today, I pictured you on our wedding night wearing something silk in this color.'' He'd signed it simply, ''Ben.''

The note, written in broad-tipped felt pen, brought a blush to her cheeks. Yet, her mind focused on the absence of the word, *love*. Why didn't he sign it ''Love, Ben''?

She intended to ask him point-blank when she called the clinic to thank him.

His receptionist, Pat, answered Ben's private line. The woman said he was with a patient. ''I'll take a message. I can't say when he might get to his call-backs.''

Abby didn't care to have the clinic receptionist relay her thanks. ''I'll call again later,'' she mumbled. ''It's not urgent.''

The floral arrangement looked too formal for her kitchen. Abby was afraid the kids might knock it over and break the crystal vase she'd unearthed in Blair's dining room hutch. So she stopped phoning car lots long enough to take the vase upstairs to her bedroom. It was time she checked on Sam anyway.

He was dead to the world, allowing Abby to make more calls. But now her concentration was disrupted by the presence of the roses. Her senior prom was the only other occasion on which she'd received flowers from an admirer. Well, Elliot and Blair had given her a pair of white roses at her college graduation, but that didn't count. Abby finally decided it was the thought that mattered. The fact that Ben had bought and sent her roses meant more than how he'd signed a silly card.

She had five possible dealers listed by the time the bus dropped off the kids that afternoon. By then, Ben's lack of the *L* word had faded from importance in her mind.

Abby fed all the children a snack of apples and peanut butter crackers. While they ate, she dragged two sacks out of the closet. ''Come here, girls. I cleaned the attic this morning, and I found a trunk with some of Blair's mom's old evening clothes. There are hats, high heels, sequined tops and silk and satin skirts. Perfect for dress-up. There are even a few lace scarves and a satin cape.''

''Can we take them home?'' Erin asked, getting up from the table to examine the booty.

Abby groped for a nice way to refuse. She and Ben hadn't discussed when they'd tell the children about their impending wedding. He obviously hadn't told the girls they'd be moving here on Saturday. ''The room at the head of the stairs has a full-length mirror,'' she finally said brightly. ''That'll be your special play area. Just for girls.''

''Oh.'' Erin closed the sacks. ''Today we'll wait on the couch for our uncle to get here, won't we, Mollie? He said he'd be early today.''

''Because he's helping me select a van we'll all fit in.''

''Why?'' Erin's pointy chin shot up, and her eyes were suspicious.

''Why what, hon?'' Abby glanced up from where she was cleaning up crumbs from under Sam's chair.

''You sounded like you're looking for a van big enough to hold all of you, *and* Mollie, me, and Uncle Ben.''

''I am.'' Abby was growing flustered. ''Ah…in case one of you gets hurt and I have to drive to the clinic. I can't very well leave some of you home alone. And it'd be nice sometimes to pick all of you up from school.'' *Phew! Had she managed to pull her foot out of her mouth with that explanation?*

''Oh.'' Erin carried her plate to the sink, then went to sit primly on the couch.

Abby wondered where the girl who'd cuddled with her yesterday had gone. ''Kids, I'll be upstairs in my bedroom folding laundry if anyone needs me. Yell when Ben gets here. We'll have to take off the minute he arrives if I'm going to close a deal today.''

Ben himself came to find Abby about thirty minutes later. "Hi," he murmured, bending her backward for a sensual hello kiss. "I see you got the flowers. Do you like them?''

"I love them. I tried to call and thank you, but Pat said you were booked really tight all day.''

"I was. Today was a zoo. So, did you tell the kids?''

"Tell them what?'' Abby frowned at him.

Ben eased her upright. "I thought since you had all seven of them here this afternoon, you'd let them know we're getting married.''

"I'm not getting married alone, Ben. Why should I break the news by myself? Erin and Mollie are your nieces.''

His expression blanked momentarily. "They're crazy about you. They'll be delighted. Noah, now, he's the problem. He'd as soon see me take a flying leap off Mount Rainier without a parachute.''

"I'm sure Noah's anger isn't directed solely at you. But if it is, that's all the more reason we should make our announcement together.''

"Okay. Let's do it. There's no time like the present.''

Suddenly suffering cold feet, Abby rushed to say, "Ah…shouldn't we test-drive vans first? If there are objections, I'd rather not deal with the fallout while we're dragging the kids from dealership to dealership.''

"Good point.''

"Here, Ben. I jotted down a list of car lots that have used vans in stock within the right price range. There are five. I tried to keep within a manageable radius.''

"This looks good,'' Ben said after perusing the list. "So what's the plan?''

"The older kids can take books to read. I thought coloring books for the younger ones. If a van shows promise, I'll sit with the kids and you can test-drive it.''

"Sounds workable. I'm familiar with this lot. It's near a pizza place and has an arcade my nieces love. Let's promise that as a treat, provided they're good.''

"Perfect. They can play games while we order. Once we have everyone at the table chowing down, we'll spring our news about the wedding. I think if we ask them all to take part in the ceremony, even though it's small, they'll feel involved and therefore happier.''

"If that's what you want, Abby." Ben took her hands and kissed each knuckle. "I know you said this isn't how you imagined your wedding. But we'll do whatever you want at the ceremony..it's just for you. Sometimes kids have to accept things just because the adults know it's in their best interests.''

"The ceremony is just for me, Ben? Not for you?''

"Well, uh...sure. The thing about men is—we focus on what *follows* the ceremony. Show me a guy who gives a damn about tuxedos, boutonnieres, engraved napkins and the like. Men go along because it's the way to get to the together-naked-in-the-bedroom part of marriage.''

"Ben!" Blushing, Abby cast a glance toward the open door. "You've certainly blown away any visions a woman might have about her wedding being the most romantic day of her life.''

"That's hype fostered by wedding planners and chapels wanting to make a buck. None of that stuff ensures a marriage will last. Besides, weddings aren't romantic. I've been best man in five. The bigger the affair, the greater the couple's stress. Two of my friends weren't even speaking to each other by the time they walked down the aisle. Believe me, sweetheart, showing up at the courthouse with one friend each to make it legal is by far the smartest way to do the deed.''

"Shh. You're raising your voice. Honestly, Ben, you don't need to worry that I'll try to trick you into a big wedding at the last minute. Once we get our license, I intend to ask Raina Miller to be my one attendant.''

"And I'll ask Steve. In fact, I penciled it on his calendar. I expect a huge reaction when he flips the page over to Saturday. Tomorrow, I'll pick up our paperwork.''

"Great. Since that's settled, shall we round up the kids and go find me a van?'' Abby took one last soulful look at the beautiful roses sitting on her dresser before she tossed the final pair of Mike's socks on the stack and exited the room ahead of Ben. The pretty blossoms stirred a bleak feeling in her stomach. Or perhaps that was a result of the pragmatic exchange she'd had with the man who'd soon become her husband.

Abby descended the stairs, thinking she'd better reprioritize the need for romance in her life. The roses and his poetic note seemed at odds with Ben's views on marriage. Once again, she noticed he'd avoided using the *L* word.

"Can I ride with Dr. Ben?'' Sam begged at the outset.

"Sweetie, no,'' Abby said. "Your booster seat's already in my car. I'm not switching it to Ben's only to change it again when I buy a van.''

"Why not?'' Sammy's lower lip stuck out an inch.

"Because it takes an engineering feat to move booster seats from car to car. That's why. But maybe Ben will carry you out, Sam.''

"Sure. Mollie, Erin, Brad and Reed, you four ride with me,'' Ben announced. "Erin, sit in front.''

"I don't see why we have to help Abby find a van.'' Erin herded her sister down the walkway. "Mollie doesn't want to be squished in the back seat with dumb ol' boys.''

''She'd better get used to it. You, too, Erin. Boys aren't dumb. I was one once, you know. Watch what you say.'' Ben tweaked Erin's braid. He was getting better at the braiding chore, even if he was the only one who thought so.

Noah shoved Ruffian's nose back inside before slamming the house door. ''Aunt Abby, if Erin gets to sit in front, I want to do the same in our car.''

''Okay. But only until we buy a van. Then you'll ride in the back with the other kids.''

''I ain't gonna sit next to no puky girls.''

Unlocking the car, Abby sent him a stern scowl.

''I told Mr. Keeler I hate havin' Erin and Mollie hangin' around our house,'' he said.

''You've seen Dave Keeler? When?''

''Twice,'' Noah muttered. ''He's okay. He coaches fifth-grade boys' soccer, you know.''

Abby started her car and swung in behind Ben, who'd stopped at the corner light. ''Out of curiosity, Noah, what did Mr. Keeler say when you complained about the girls?''

''He said I gotta ignore 'em, and act like they're not there. Even if Mollie bugs me to play with my trucks and stuff. Mr. Keeler said guys need their privacy.''

Groaning, Abby began to doubt that counseling was the way to go for Noah. Certainly, she'd have to phone Dave and tell him the girls were becoming permanent fixtures in Noah's life. Abby hoped that if Bonnie Reavis had seen Brad, she'd been more in favor of peace and harmony. *Love,* was hoping for too much. Especially since one adult in the equation, it seemed, had trouble with the concept.

''I'm hungry,'' Michael shouted too close to Abby's ear.

''You ate an entire apple by yourself, mister. Plus, you gobbled down Brad's leftover peanut butter crackers.''

"I can't help it if my stomach likes food. When's dinner? And what are you fixing? I didn't smell anything cookin'."

"That's because after we find a van, we're all going out for pizza. Ben's treat." Abby named the place, knowing the boys loved the arcades there, but had rarely been allowed to play them. Elliot thought arcades were not only a waste of money, but might lead to a propensity for gambling. Abby knew her students all enjoyed pitting their skill against machines. She found the games at the pizza parlors harmless, and occasionally indulged her nephews in spite of Elliot. "I expect good behavior from everyone while we're deciding on a car. If you don't all behave, there'll be no pizza and games for anyone."

"Gol…ly," Michael griped. "That's not fair. What if the kids in Ben's car act up?"

"They're being offered the same deal."

"How many vans we gotta look at?" Noah asked.

"Five, maximum. Unless we fall in love with the first one we see." Abby turned into the lot and parked next to Ben.

He spotted the oversize van in the back row. "Abby, if that's the one this place told you they had, don't bother unloading the kids. I can tell by looking that vehicle's been through hard times."

"I'll wait here if you want to run in and ask if that's their only one."

He returned shortly. "That's it. Salesman looked up the stats. It has a hundred and forty thousand miles on it. A guy from Alaska traded it in."

"Well, that explains the wear and tear. I hope this isn't a bad omen. You lead out to the next lot."

The next used car lot showed more promise. They actually had two vans. Abby and the kids looked them over inside and out. Ben carried Sam inside for her, then left with the salesman to test-drive the vehicles.

"Can me and Michael go, too?" Noah asked Ben, surprising him as Noah had been so standoffish. "It's gonna be our car, not yours."

"Well..." Ben clamped down on what he was about to say. "I, uh, guess you can go if it's okay with Abby. You guys can test the rear seats."

Abby didn't object. She wanted the boys to warm up to Ben. Thankfully they all seemed to come back in good moods. "So what's the verdict?" she asked.

"The boys and I agree the green van is better. The catch is, it's more than you want to pay. If you like it, I'll cover the difference."

"No. No, Ben. You have your car and this will be mine for all intents and purposes."

She was so adamant, Ben shrugged. "Then we should go to the next dealership. I'll give this salesman my cell number. I think he'll phone and offer us a lower price."

"Might he sell it to someone else in the meantime? I can qualify for a small loan."

"Abby, how large do you think the used market is for nine-passenger vans? He's had this van on his lot for five months. A few hours won't matter, and it may save you money. If he doesn't, my offer to pay the difference stands."

"I thought we settled that, Ben."

"Suit yourself." He waited, letting the final decision be hers.

"The kids are already restless. I guess I shouldn't be hasty. Even though it's a chore loading and unloading seven kids." Abby herded them out to the cars.

The next stop produced a van just short of being as big

a loser as the first one they'd seen. Ben said it drove like a tank.

"The salesman with the green van hasn't called back."

"Relax, Abby. We still have two stops left. He may know the condition of what his competitors have for sale. Car buying is a game. Let's play out our hand."

"All right. But the kids are antsy and now they're all whining about being starved."

"I wish you'd just let me cough up the difference. Aren't we going to merge our bank accounts soon?"

Given what Jill French had said about her friends all getting prenuptial agreements, Abby hadn't imagined Ben would want to join their incomes or their bills. His announcement gave her pause. "I want my own car, Ben. Come on, kids."

"It *would* be yours. Jeez, you're stubborn. Come on, kids. Load up again." At the next stop, Ben got his call from the salesman with the green van. "Hmm," he said noncommittally to the man on the phone, "my fiancée and I are moments from signing a deal on a white van at Herb's Auto Mall. I think she might reconsider if you come down another thousand dollars on yours. Seven-fifty? Just a minute." Ben covered the mouthpiece. "I was hoping he'd knock off another five bills. Seven-fifty's even better. Reload the kids, and let's go buy you a van." Ben told the man he had a deal, kissed Abby's nose and grinned.

She felt unabashed about Ben kissing her in front of the kids.

"What's a fiancée?" Reed asked as he skipped toward the cars. "Why didn't Ben just call you Abby like he always does?"

Erin, wise beyond her years, stuck out her tongue. "Fiancée is someone who is going to get married, birdbrain. You just didn't hear Uncle Ben right."

Noah thrust out his square jaw. "Watch who you're calling a birdbrain. That's what he said. But my dad used to marry people. Fiancées wear big diamond rings. And Aunt Abby ain't wearing no diamond."

Ben realized too late what he'd revealed on the phone. He also saw that the kids were heading for a knock-down-drag-out. Gathering them into a circle before loading the cars, Ben lifted both Mollie and Sam. "Kids. We… Uh, Abby and I planned to tell you over pizza. But since I let the cat out of the bag, I'll give it to you straight. Abby and I *are* getting married. I, uh, haven't had time to shop for a ring yet. Noah, she'll have one by Saturday. That's when the wedding is. We'd like all you kids to attend."

Noah shoved Erin down and dashed toward the street. Both adults were stunned by his reaction. Abby recovered first. She raced between cars, leaving Ben to deal with the remaining six.

Thirty minutes later, except for Sam who was beaming from ear to ear, the others refused to listen to either Ben or Abby's further attempts to explain.

Ben's phone rang again. It was the salesman with the green van wondering where they were. "We're on our way," Ben promised. "Okay, listen up, all of you," he said, pocketing his phone. "I've had enough of your bad behavior. Everyone's getting into the cars and we're going to buy the green van. Then we're going for pizza. I expect attitudes to have improved immensely by then. Abby and I thought you were old enough to see that we're doing you a favor. But sometimes kids have to understand that the adults know best. There's not going to be a debate. Get used to the idea. There'll be no further argument."

The two loudest objectors threw themselves into opposite cars. Abby assisted Mollie and Reed in last. Clearly Reed thought he was to blame for the blowup because he'd asked about *fiancée*. Abby did her best to reassure him.

Wonder of wonders they were able to complete the paperwork on the van in near silence.

However, a full-scale war broke out again two blocks from the pizza parlor. "Stop, or this van goes straight home," Abby warned. "I guarantee that if I have to pull over, the perpetrators will not be happy campers." Her scowl in the rearview mirror stopped a scuffle between Noah and Erin that was headed for bloodshed. Abby had to marvel at how neatly Ben had engineered her taking all the kids. He'd blithely remarked that this presented a great opportunity to make sure all the seat belts worked and that seven kids could indeed ride comfortably in the van. But in all fairness to Ben, he couldn't just leave his car and ride with them.

Nevertheless, when they met at the restaurant, Abby didn't hesitate to point out that he'd fooled her. "I hope you enjoyed your moments of peace and quiet."

His endearing, if not guilty grin, accepted full blame.

"I thought teachers knew all the tricks," she muttered after he'd readily dispensed tokens for the arcade. "That was a sneak attack from the rear I didn't see coming. You won't find me so gullible in the future."

"Let's face it. I blew my cool and needed a time-out. The kids are going to have to learn to get along. What better way than to toss them together buckled in separate seats?"

"Some have longer arms than others," Abby complained.

"I'm really sorry. Why don't I drive the van back to your house and give you some time alone?"

"I'm afraid that when we finally leave here, the kids will have had a bellyful of togetherness. It'd be better if I took my brood home, and you took your girls. That way we can each answer whatever questions they still have. Tomorrow, I'll drive the lot of them to school. I can also ask Raina if she'll stand up for me on Saturday.'' Abby also wanted a word with the boys' counselors, but she didn't mention that to Ben.

''Sounds like a plan. I'll corner Steve tomorrow, too.'' Ben curved a warm palm around Abby's neck. ''It'll work out, you'll see. By the way, how do you like driving the van?''

''It's a dream. Thanks, Ben. I'd never have been able to work the deal you pulled off. You even talked them into paying my license fee.''

He sneaked in a fast kiss just before the waiter called out their order number. ''Men do serve some purpose in this world,'' he teased. ''Don't try to deny it, Abby.''

She laughed and punched him lightly. Together they went to collect pizza and sodas for nine. Abby paused, wondering whether she and Ben were really doing the right thing. Talk at their table was stilted. The girls snuggled up on either side of Ben; the boys sat sullenly across the table. Abby had to warn the twins several times to stop kicking the girls. She and Sam were crowded together at one end, since his casts made it impossible to slide him between the table and the attached bench.

Less was said on the drive home. The boys were full of pizza and yawning loudly. Abby broached the subject anyhow. ''I'm sorry for springing the news on you that way, guys. Ben and I thought it'd be easier to wait until we were all together. This is your chance to ask me any questions.''

''Ben said it won't do no good,'' Michael stated.

''Yeah,'' Noah said sullenly, ''nobody listens to kids.''

''I'm listening, but I can tell you right off the bat, Noah, that your current dislike of the girls is not a valid reason for Ben and me to call off our wedding.''

No one made a sound after that. The boys went straight to bed, and Abby soon followed.

Next morning, the children remained subdued. Because Ben had a consultation at the hospital, he dropped the girls off early and sped away.

Raina provided the single bright spot in a day that should have been one of Abby's happiest. "Hey, that's fantastic news! I'm honored you asked me to be your witness or whatever it's called when you're married by a J.P. I so hoped you and Ben would get married. I must admit, with him being such an important doctor, I did figure you'd have a splashy church wedding. But married is married. So, how soon after do you expect to be back teaching?"

"I just spoke to Mr. Conrad about a two-week extension on my leave. I'm not expecting major problems joining our households, but on the other hand we're throwing a lot of changes at kids who've undergone a lot already. I've gotta tell you, Raina, I'm anxious to get back in the classroom."

"I'm anxious for you to be back. Stacy Thorpe has completely loused up your schedule. And I think she's pressuring parents into asking the district to keep her on in your slot."

"That's silly, Raina. I'm tenured."

"Yes, but you know how the district caves in to parent demands. They might decide to let Stacy stay here, and move you to another school in the fall."

Abby bit her lip as she watched Sam showing his casts to some of Raina's students. The women had left him in Raina's room while they stepped into the hall. "I've taught here throughout my whole career," Abby said. "I'll work out any problems. Two measly weeks is all I've requested. I don't anticipate any flak."

"Good. Now I'd better do my roll call. Didn't you say you're on your way to Sam's doctor's appointment?"

"His first physical therapy session. I'm hoping they'll tell me when he can go from the hard casts to air casts. They're light enough to improve his life and mine."

The friends parted at the door. "See you Saturday at eight. Marrying Ben is the best thing for you and the kids, Abby." Raina sounded so earnest, Abby was convinced.

SATURDAY, Abby arrived twenty minutes late at her own wedding. The boys had not cooperated in dressing up. Nor had she taken Sam's casts into account with regard to his suit. He cried over wearing baggy shorts when his brothers got to dress in church clothes. For the first time, the twins decided to ask why Abby wasn't being married in their father's church. "Dad said people who don't get married by a minister aren't really married," Michael tossed in.

"Ministers, justices and sea captains all have the power to perform weddings." Abby had found time, while Sam was at therapy, to buy an ivory suit. Now, looking at herself in the mirror, she decided it made her freckles stand out like…like warts on a hog.

"If Sam can wear shorts, I don't see why we hafta dress up," Brad wailed.

"We're running late as it is, guys. I'm not going to argue. Sam has to wear a white shirt and tie with his shorts. Other than pjs, he doesn't have any other pants that'll slide on over his cast."

A worried Ben Galloway met Abby some twenty minutes later at the J.P.'s office. "Where have you been?" He tapped his watch. "The J.P. is sure you stood me up. Steve, too. By the way, Abby, have you met my partner?"

Reaching across Ben, she shook hands with Steve—and didn't realize until afterward, how sweaty hers was.

Erin, the picture of a little princess except for the ferocious scowl she wore, blurted out, "Mrs. Clark is back in town. She called last night and said she's ready to come to work. So you and Uncle Ben don't hafta get married.''

Abby shot Ben a stunned glance.

''Erin, you said Mrs. Clark makes yucky cookies. You and Mollie both agreed Abby's were far superior. And have you forgotten that Mrs. Clark didn't like you to practice your piano, and Abby found you a keyboard? Oh, what am I saying? Mrs. Clark did a crappy job, which is beside the point. I'm not marrying Abby because she's a better cook or because she indulges you, Erin. Come on, we're overdue in the J.P.'s office. It's next to Courtroom Five, where I left Raina and Mollie.''

Ben lifted Sam out of Abby's arms. He remarked how comfortably Sam was dressed. Yet he said nothing about Abby's new suit. Not that he'd know it was new. Nevertheless, she'd hoped he would at least say she looked nice.

As the group lined up in front of the J.P., Ben produced a wide gold band set with a row of sparkling diamonds. It was only when he doled out the rings to each attendant in a matter-of-fact-manner that Abby found herself wondering why Ben Galloway was marrying her.

CHAPTER TEN

THE KIDS FIDGETED throughout the simple ceremony. Abby couldn't blame them. It was stuffy in the small room. The vows were the usual ones, read from a small, tattered manual. Tightly clutching Elliot's worn Bible, she held her breath when the J.P. asked Ben, "Do you promise to love, honor and cherish this woman?"

Ben answered, "Yes," without hesitation or equivocation. Only then did Abby release the breath she'd been holding. Ben certainly shone when it came to the part where the J.P. said he could kiss his bride.

But Abby already knew Ben was a good kisser. The best in her limited experience. This time, however, having a bunch of kids giggling in the background, forced him to shorten a kiss he'd otherwise have made more memorable.

Mere seconds after Steve had signed their certificate, he raised a sleeve on his white shirt and checked his watch. "Well, buddy, I hate to sign you over to this woman and run, but I have office hours starting at nine."

The J.P.'s assistant went to his desk to get a folder for the certificate.

Ben squinted at his own watch. "Holy smoke, I'm due to meet the movers at nine-fifteen. Abby, can you take all seven kids back to your place? I'll have to hang around for a while after the movers load and leave, because a cleaning crew is set to show up at two o'clock. The sooner we rent the second house, the better for us financially."

Raina gaped at the lot of them. "Hello, folks! This is your *wedding*. I thought you'd at least indulge in a celebration breakfast someplace."

"Yeah, Aunt Abby," Michael chimed in. "We ain't had our breakfast yet. Me and the guys are starving."

"Ain't? Mike, you know better than to use that word around a teacher."

"We're hungry, too," Mollie interjected. "Unca Ben wouldn't let us eat cereal this morning. He was afraid we'd spill milk on our pretty new dresses."

"That settles it," Raina announced, grabbing Abby's arm. "Breakfast at the Pancake Cottage. My wedding treat for anyone who can attend." She sent dirty looks at Ben and his partner.

"Gosh, Abby, I'm sorry. I hope you'll give me a rain check," Steve mumbled.

"You and the kids go and enjoy," Ben urged his wife of ten minutes. "Steve has patients booked and…and I'm scheduled to move today. I don't know what I was thinking. Hell, I must not have been thinking." He raked a hand through his brown hair. "Forgive me?"

"Aunt Abby," the youngest twins gasped in unison, "Ben said a bad word. Daddy said only preachers can say hell, and then it has to be in church."

"Boys, enough. Ben's not a member of our church. Sometimes people…well, not everyone follows your daddy's rules." Abby noticed the gleam passing between the boys, and quickly said, "It's never appropriate for boys to say bad words. Got that, guys?"

Straightening their faces, all the boys nodded solemnly. Except Noah, who asked, "Does that mean it's okay for Erin and Mollie to cuss?"

"Not them, either," Ben stated firmly. "Hereafter I'll try to watch what I say." He glanced sheepishly at Abby's face as he made the promise. In the next breath, he said, "Will you take charge of our wedding certificate, Abby? The J.P. gave this to me, but it'll end up in a box if I take it. You know movers, they box everything that doesn't wiggle, and a few things that do."

Erin started to cry. "We left Blackberry at home. I don't want those old movers putting her in a box. How will she breathe?"

Ben knelt and wiped away a flood of tears. "Hey, I'd never let that happen, button. I got out the kitty carrier last night. Blackberry will ride to Abby's with me."

She didn't look convinced. "What if Blackberry doesn't like it at Abby's? She's never lived anywhere but at our house."

"Mc, neither." Mollie's small face crumpled. "Mommy decorated our room."

Steve pounded Ben on the shoulder, then touched three fingers to his forehead in a mock salute. "You've got your work cut out for you, Daddy Ben. Better you than me, pal. See all of you later. Abby…good luck. Have a good life."

The boys had started to wrestle, placing the J.P.'s podium in jeopardy. Abby put two fingers to her lips and whistled sharply, capturing everyone's attention.

"Where's your playground whistle?" Raina asked around a broad grin. "They make some really snazzy ones to coordinate with just about any outfit. With your motley crew, I foresee a whistle as a required accessory."

"Raina—?"

"Do the math, kid. How many women go from zero to seven kids before they even have their honeymoon? Speaking of which—"

"Don't even say it," Abby cautioned as her eyes followed her spanking-new husband. Ben had reached the front door, still peeling clingy little girls off his slacks as he made his way out behind Steve. "With all the adjustments the kids have already gone through, and given Sam's ongoing condition, it didn't make sense for us to spend a night at a hotel."

"Hmm. Did Mr. and Mrs. Brady have a honeymoon on that show *The Brady Bunch?* I can't remember."

"Mrs. Brady had Alice, a live-in cook-housekeeper. Ben and I are it, Raina. Are you sure you want to take this bunch to breakfast?" Abby sounded tired and it was only a little after nine.

"Snap out of it, Abby. Two teachers juggle a lot more than seven kids on a field trip. Shall we meet there? The restaurant on California Avenue may be less busy, even though it's smaller. Anyway, the area around their bigger restaurant is messed up from the earthquake."

"Whatever," Abby answered, feeling strangely depressed. "It takes me a while to get everyone buckled in."

"Do you need me to take a few kids in my car?"

"No. Ben helped me find a used nine-passenger van. I have to tell you I feel so much more in control of the situation now."

"Then why don't you look more like it?" Raina said, hugging her friend.

Abby sighed. "I don't know. Still getting used to things, I guess." What else could she say? She was lugging Sam, who was only four but astute.

Raina caught the shift of Abby's eyes to the child, and quickly changed the subject. "How do you propose to shuffle these new responsibilities so you can teach again, Abs?"

For a minute Abby looked puzzled. "Uh," she said half under her breath, nodding at Sam. "Day care for what remains of this year. If I can find one that doesn't eat up my whole salary," she added in a more normal tone. "Next year, Sam will only need half days."

"With Ben being a doctor, I shouldn't think money will be an issue."

"Oh? Well, we haven't discussed how we'll sort out the bill paying, Raina."

"Sort out? Won't you both throw your earnings into one kitty? He didn't ask you to sign a prenuptial agreement, did he?"

"Nothing like that. It's just, well, I'm bringing more mouths to feed than he is."

Raina shot Abby an odd glance. She might have said more, but they'd reached the parking lot and the boys all begged Abby to let them unlock the van.

"Who did it this morning? Michael, wasn't it?" At his glum nod, Abby did a short version of *eeney meeney miney mo*. She was pleased *mo* turned out to be Mollie.

"Will it ever be my turn?" Sam wore the longest face.

Abby tickled his tummy until he giggled. "Yes, tiger, it'll be your turn one of these days. Maybe next week after physical therapy. I'm hoping they'll switch your casts to some that are lighter weight."

"Then can I walk like I did before?"

"Not then, but soon," Abby said as if there was no doubt. "Sam, you broke a lot of bones. They take a while to heal. I'm going to say this right now to everyone." Her stern gaze traveled the faces of the kids climbing into the van. "Everyone has to be extra careful of Sammy for a long time after his casts come off. The first person I see playing roughly with him, will be grounded for life." On witnessing their horrified expressions, she held up a hand. "Okay, that's extreme. But you'll definitely have privileges taken away for longer than any of you would want."

At the restaurant later, the kids were angels. Abby allowed the three oldest to sit at a table by themselves. Raina and Abby took a big horseshoe booth with the others.

"You kids order anything you'd like," Raina said.

Abby smiled at the chorus of unprompted, "Thank you, Mrs. Miller."

"This was a good idea you had, Raina. Treating the kids never entered my mind. You know, occasionally taking them someplace nice is something I'll need to program into Ben's and my schedules. I tend to look at transporting this mob anywhere, and I panic. Look, they're all getting along fine. Up to now, Noah and Erin haven't said a civil word to each other."

"The first year I taught, I had two kids from a blended family in my class. Their mom didn't work outside the home. I remember she said that for months she wondered if settling disputes was to be her permanent lot in life. The marriage was two years old by the time we met. She said her house was closer to normal by then."

"Two years?" Abby groaned. "I don't have the luxury of two years. I have more like four weeks to establish a routine."

"Good luck." Raina opened her mouth as if intending to add to her previous statement, but the waitress came with their meals. Between cutting up sausage for Sam and pancakes for Mollie, there wasn't time for more adult chitchat.

They'd eaten, Raina had paid, and everyone was loaded into the van before she again mentioned Abby's lack of a honeymoon. "If we didn't have plans with friends from Bob's squad, Abby, I'd spend tonight at your house. I know you said Ben's dad lives in town. Why didn't Ben ask him to keep the kids for one night? For that matter, why wasn't he at the wedding?"

Casting a concerned eye toward the girls, Abby stepped around the front of the van. "Shh, not so loud, Raina. I gather Ben's at odds with his father, which I hope to change. I mentioned inviting him to our wedding, and Ben came unglued.''

''That's too bad.''

''Yeah, but I'll bet if they'd just communicate, they'd see how much they have in common. Two adult men should be able to rise above the past for the girls' sake. Erin and Mollie have lost too much of their family. Having one set of grandparents would be beneficial. I feel as if I have to try to smooth over Ben's differences with his dad. He doesn't know, but I invited Kirk Galloway and his wife to Sunday dinner.''

''Well, I hope it turns out well. But getting back to your wedding night. Can you think of anyone else who'd stay with the kids? I know you and Ben aren't exactly virgins. Neither were Jerry and I. But the first night after you're actually legal is—I don't want to say more inventive, but in a way it's true. Having kids in the house curtails adult playtime, if you get my drift.''

Abby did. Up to now, she'd tried not to dwell on the sexual aspects of being married to Ben Galloway. Raina evoked a vivid picture. And Abby was very glad tonight wasn't going to be their first time. Even though it had been evident the few times they'd slept together that Ben was the more experienced of the two, Abby didn't think she'd be uncomfortable in the role of his wife.

But inventiveness! What exactly did that entail? Getting naked with him in the same room, down the hall from seven kids and a host of pets, seemed risky enough. Abby wished Raina hadn't said anything. Just how good was the sound-proofing in her bedroom, anyway?

Although Elliot and Blair's room was larger and more secluded, Abby still didn't feel right about moving into it. Ben had agreed it'd be the most likely room for the girls.

He said they had doll beds, buggies and an entire toy kitchen, in addition to twin beds, dressers and toy chests.

"Raina, I appreciate your concern. However, Ben and I aren't starry-eyed young lovers. Sex isn't our number-one priority."

Her friend tsked and shook a finger under Abby's nose. "I'll bet any counselor would tell you both what an important part of marriage sex is. Especially when a couple starts out with his and her kids. You and Ben need to establish a strong bond early in the marriage. It'll be what gets you through later frustrations and difficulties."

"Be that as it may," Abby murmured, "we've already weathered about the hardest times anyone can imagine. Getting married is supposed to solve our frustrations and difficulties."

"Okay, have it your way. But do yourselves a favor and find a few hours tonight to enjoy each other." That was Raina's final word on the subject before she climbed into her own vehicle and drove off.

Abby stared after her for so long, the kids began to fret.

Once she'd buckled in, Abby noticed Erin and Mollie huddled in the back looking exceedingly miserable. "Girls, I'm going to swing by to see how Ben's doing with the movers. I thought we'd take him a hamburger and a soft drink, and grab a box of your toys. I doubt we'll have time to do much more than set up your beds tonight."

"Can we take Blackberry to your house, instead of toys?" Erin asked.

"Honey, you can stop referring to it as *my* house. It's your home now, too." Abby wasn't prepared for two rows of piercing eyes.

"Boys, married people live together forever. You know that."

''Not forever! Me and Mollie are going home in a couple of weeks, aren't we?''

''Girls, Ben's moving all your stuff and his in with me and the boys. Because our home is larger than yours. What were you thinking this move meant?''

Erin frowned. ''We thought our house had to be fixed or something. Uncle Ben said the basement got cracked in the earthquake. Last year we stayed at Uncle Ben's apartment when Mommy's stove caught fire. After it got fixed, we went home.''

''I can't believe Ben didn't make it clear that this move is permanent. Erin, you, Mollie and Ben will be living with me and the boys from now on. We're going to be a family.''

Neither girl made a sound. Their eyes filled with tears that spilled over and dripped down their cheeks. Noah, Brad and Reed set up a racket that forced Abby to pull over and stop before they reached the fast-food drive-through. For a moment she was too mad at Ben to utter a word.

At last, she controlled her anger enough to set the emergency brake. That allowed her to climb into the back. Midway between the seats, she sank to her knees. ''I am so sorry Ben and I didn't make our intentions clear. We need to drive on to your home, girls. Even though Ben will be busy, I think the nine of us need to sit down and discuss what's involved in this marriage.''

She stumbled back to the driver's seat, managing to complete the absolutely silent drive on guts alone.

A moving van was backed up to the McBride garage. Ben's BMW sat across the street. Following his lead, Abby made a U-turn and parked behind him.

Ben looked startled when the kids trooped inside where he and the moving crew were taping and labeling boxes.

He spared a questioning glance for Abby, who carried

Sam on her hip, and held out a burger sack. Especially as they were still dressed in their wedding finery. By contrast, Ben's hair flopped into his eyes. He wore scruffy jeans and a T-shirt streaked with dirt and sweat.

"Is there a quiet spot we can talk?" Abby included the kids with a sweeping gesture of one hand.

He brushed her lips with a quick kiss. "Thanks for the food," he said, pausing to look around.

"Pretty much everywhere's a mess at the moment. Fred," Ben called to a man muscling a child's dresser down the hall. "I need a minute alone with my family. How about if we hole up in the dining room? I think that room's staying as is."

The man nodded. Ben stepped aside once the coast was clear. He let Erin and Mollie lead the way as he unwrapped his burger and began to chow down.

"What's this about?" Ben cocked an eyebrow as he pulled the sliders shut.

He knew something was amiss even before Erin threw herself, bawling, against his legs.

"Uncle Ben, you never said we had to live with Abby *forever*. That's what she just said."

He cupped the child's head, throwing Abby a baffled look.

She'd set Sam on a chair next to one on which Brad and Reed had crowded together. Crossing her arms, she leaned against the wall. "Apparently *we* failed to inform the children that our marriage is going to last more than a few weeks."

Ben scanned the circle of accusing eyes. "I distinctly recall settling that issue the night you bought the van." He loosened Erin's grip, then squinted at each child before striking his forehead with the heel of one hand. "I bungled it, huh?"

There were nods all around.

"Look, kids." Ben cleared his throat. "Everything that's happened has been no easier on Abby and me than on you. We lost people we loved. Neither of us had kids—until the earthquake. Suddenly, it's up to us to keep the seven of you safe, fed, in good health and decent clothes. We thought...*hope* we can do a better job together. Because no matter what you think, Abby and I love each and every one of you. That's something you can all count on."

Abby's throat tightened. She blinked rapidly to ward off threatening tears. The man speaking to the children from his heart was the Ben Galloway she hadn't hesitated to marry. Whether or not he eased their fears today, he gave her reason to believe their marriage could succeed.

Mollie flung herself into his arms. "At night, when Mommy looks down from heaven, Unca Ben, what if she can't find us at Abby's house?"

He seemed stricken for a moment, then said in a strained voice, "Remember how far you could see from the top of the Space Needle? Well, heaven is so much higher, your mama will find you no matter where you are, pickle." He hugged the girl and her sister. "Okay, kids, I need to talk privately with Abby." They weren't given time, however. The mover, Fred, slid open the pocket door, and announced he needed Ben, who quickly swallowed the last bite of his lunch.

"Kids, we'd better let Ben get back to work. We actually came to get toys for the girls. Oh, and play clothes."

Erin still scrubbed at tearstained cheeks. "Abby said maybe we can take Blackberry with us now, Uncle Ben."

"That'd be great." Ben sighed with relief. "I can't tell you how afraid I've been that she'd accidentally get out. Give me a sec to see what Fred needs, then I'll gather up some breakables you can take, too."

The coal-colored cat yowled from the instant Ben shoved her fat body into a too small carrier. The boys clapped their hands over their ears. "That's the biggest domestic cat I've ever seen," Abby murmured. "Are you sure she's not part panther?"

Ben sent the girls after food and litter. He pulled Abby aside. "Fred'll be at your place to unload in an hour. I have to wait here for the housecleaning crew, so it's up to you to corral the kids and pets at your end."

"I'll do my best," Abby promised in such a small voice, it prompted Ben to give her a bolstering hug.

"Would you like to leave Mike and Noah with me? I'll put them to work carting out trash bags or something."

"I would, Ben, but they're still wearing their suits. I'll manage. Although you may owe me big-time before this day is over."

"Tonight. I'll make it all up to you tonight after the kids go to sleep." Ben waggled his eyebrows. "Maybe you think I've forgotten this is our wedding day. I haven't, Abby."

"It's okay, Ben. I agreed to this marriage, which is one of mutual convenience. I went into it with my eyes open."

Ben studied her a moment and frowned faintly. Fred bellowed for him from the other room. "I've gotta go see what he wants," Ben said, backing out the door. "Abby, I'll wind up here as quickly as possible. I'll try to be home before dark."

"I'll fix the kids' supper. Shall I hold back two plates and wait to eat with you?"

"That'd be great." He plucked at his T-shirt. "Leave me time to shower." Hearing his name echoing down the hall from the far end of the house, Ben gave a last shrug and jogged off to see Fred.

Abby rounded up her brood. She carried Sam out first

and buckled him into his booster, then returned for the monster cat, who howled during the entire trip home.

BEN DIDN'T MEET his arrival goal, nor did he call. The movers had come and gone. Abby assembled the girls' beds, which was no easy feat. She made them up with flowered sheets she found in a box marked Kids' Room.

The really fabulous lasagna she'd whipped up from scratch was wasted on the kids, who picked at their meals. The leftovers began to shrivel.

The kids had been in bed for over an hour and most were fast asleep by the time Ben pulled in and parked behind her van. Not wanting him to see her peering out the window as she'd been doing off and on for two hours, she rushed back to the kitchen and began brewing coffee. She'd set the kitchen table for two with china from her hope chest. Unlit tapers stood in crystal candle holders she'd also bought for herself. In the last hour, she'd put out champagne flutes, then put them away again, thinking it was a foolish gesture as there hadn't been time in her busy schedule to buy champagne. Anyway, Ben might think she was being silly. After all, they hadn't planned a champagne kind of union. That notion had sprung from old dreams. Old yearnings.

Suddenly embarrassed by her attempt at romance, Abby raced to the table and snatched off the candles. She stuffed them in a drawer, then hid the holders in the cupboard. Tomorrow she'd pack them away again.

Ben, who'd made a point the day before of having his own set of keys made, walked in on the remnants of her efforts to provide a wedding supper. Grimy as he looked, and in spite of the weariness in his eyes, he had stopped on the way home to buy a vase of carnations and a bottle of cold champagne. He plunked both down on the kitchen counter. "I'm so sorry, Abby. The cleaning crew showed up late. On top of that, they were slow as molasses in January. If I hadn't tackled the attic myself, I swear we'd still be there. I would've phoned, but I'd had the house phone disconnected yesterday. And I discovered that in all the rush, I'd forgotten to recharge my cell battery."

Drawn by the sweet aroma of the peach-tinted carnations, Abby buried her nose in the blooms and said, "Teachers give a lot of credit for effort, Ben. Go see if the girls are still awake. They wanted you to kiss them good-night. I left clean towels for you in the bath closest to, uh, our bedroom. I had the movers set the boxes labeled as your personal stuff in there, too."

"But…I smell supper. Unless it's already ruined."

Abby set the vase in the center of the table and put the champagne in the fridge. "If it's edible now, it'll still be edible half an hour from now."

He turned her toward him and bracketed her face with his hands. Nibbling softly on her lips, he licked his tongue along her jaw, feather-soft, stopping to circle her ear. "Teachers aren't the only people who give gold stars for effort," he growled. "So do doctors. At least, pediatricians," he added, nipping her earlobe sharply.

Abby shivered. The timber of Ben's voice held the same sensual promise she recalled hearing the day he'd invited her to spend a week with him in Whistler. So much had happened in their lives since then. She'd nearly forgotten the languid heaviness a mere inflection of his tone could stir in her body.

The feeling evoked a memory of the lacy, sexy nightwear she'd packed for their ill-fated trip. In the aftermath of straightening up from the quake, she'd never unpacked, but had tossed the suitcase in a closet. Ben's lazy kisses made

Abby think about dragging out that suitcase now. She gave a needy sigh as Ben pulled back.

His smile, the crooked smile Abby loved, stoked fires deep within her. And she seemed to have lit a spark in him that drove the tiredness from Ben's eyes.

"Fifteen minutes," he muttered. "That's all I need to shower and look in on the girls. Make this dinner snappy. I want to get on to what comes afterward."

Abby registered his tread on the stairs, but it was some moments before she commissioned her legs to move.

Out came the crystal holders again, and the tall white tapers. When the shower went on, Abby zipped into the hall, found the suitcase, and after some rummaging, pulled out a yellow silk nightie. Racing upstairs, she thrust it beneath her pillow. At the time she'd made her purchase, she hadn't known about Ben's preference for peach. Oddly enough, she'd bought matching undies in the color he liked. Even as she tucked them in her drawer, the shower shut off. Judging by how fast Ben had showered, Abby figured there was no time to trade them for the plain white set she had on. She tiptoed from the room, then she rushed down the hall to briefly check on all the kids.

Out of breath when she reached the kitchen, Abby couldn't say why she didn't want Ben to catch her plotting. The prospect of spending the night in bed with a man she'd married less than ten hours ago—in more of a business arrangement rather than a love match—left her with a case of nervous jitters.

Ben smelled traces of Abby's tangy orange-blossom perfume the moment he entered the bedroom to hunt for his shaver. He'd half expected, or maybe *hoped,* to see her waiting for him in bed.

Of course she was downstairs slaving over a ruined dinner. Which made him feel thoroughly guilty. He hadn't planned to be so impatient about rushing her into the consummation part of their marriage. The eagerness he experienced had dogged him since Abby's odd remark about their getting married for convenience.

Coupling of convenience was how Ben tended to label Kirk's frequent alliances. His father no sooner discarded one bombshell than he'd seek out another, younger version who set his hormones alight. And because the great Dr. Galloway wouldn't risk creating even a breath of gossip in the medical community, he'd made numerous trips to the altar—until Lily. By then Kirk must've tired of forking out alimony.

Ben wanted more from his marriage than a willing sex partner. Not that he was averse to sex—he wasn't. In fact, the permanent state of his body since their morning kiss attested to his true feelings.

Hurriedly plugging in his shaver, he finished making himself presentable for his bride. Studying his face in the mirror, Ben renewed his determination to make this a memorable night for Abby. Thanks to the many conversations he'd had with his sister, Ben knew that trappings were more important to women than to men. After checking on the girls and adjusting the covers they'd kicked off, he went downstairs prepared to eat a meal for Abby's sake. In fact, the tantalizing odor of food did draw him to the kitchen. There he saw her dishing up squares of lasagna to go with a crisp green salad and toasted French bread already assembled on china plates. Ben tried to remember how long it had been since he'd been greeted by such a thoughtful domestic scene. Abby had cooked for him in the past, but no one had ever set such an enticing table just to please him. His heart tumbled end over end, and he all but felt it plop at Abby's feet.

Yet being a man, Ben was easily distracted. As Abby

straightened from the table, the curve of her bare neck, soft and pale below where she'd clipped back her fiery curls, demanded his attention. Nuzzling her, he made a feral sound deep in his throat.

"Shh." She laughed and ducked away from his lips. "Blackberry may hear you and think this is the mating call of the wild."

"And if it is?" He yanked her into his arms.

"Ben, will you please light the candles on the table? Oh, did you take a peek at how we set up the girls' room?"

He gave up and released her. "I noticed it looks amazingly like their room at home, complete with Blackberry draped over Erin's feet. I expected to find them in sleeping bags. I didn't know the movers put beds together," he said, lighting the candles with the battery-powered barbecue lighter Abby shoved in his hand.

"The kids and I assembled the beds. I hope they don't fall down tonight. When it was time to climb into them, Erin and Mollie both cried. I hope they adjust."

"Kids are remarkably resilient. Hey, this is our wedding night. We ought to be eating this great meal and toasting each other with champagne. There'll be plenty of nights for us to discuss the kids."

Abby got the champagne from the fridge. "You'll have to open the bottle, Ben. I've never so much as tasted champagne, let alone opened any."

"Really?" He smiled and let the cork fly up to hit the ceiling. He laughed at the way Abby jumped. Ben poured her flute full of bubbly, and stole a kiss as he placed the icy glass in her hand. "To many years of enjoying quiet dinners." The crystal clinked musically as Ben touched the rim of his glass to Abby's.

She tasted the champagne and licked her lips. "You've eaten here, Ben. Meals are pretty much always chaotic."

"Not tonight. Tonight we'll pretend we're at a five-star restaurant."

Abby tested the lasagna with her fork. Noodles that should pierce easily resisted her efforts. "If this were really a restaurant of any kind, you'd send this food back to the chef. I'm sorry, Ben. Three hours ago it would've been good."

"Don't worry. Bread and salad will fill our stomachs. Do newlyweds ever eat much on their wedding nights, anyway? Or do they feed a different kind of hunger?"

Startled by his comment, even though she'd made her own preparations not long ago, Abby dropped her fork.

"If you're nervous about sleeping with me, Abby, finish your champagne."

"I'm not…exactly nervous," she said. Yet she drained her glass and promptly refilled it.

Ben ate his salad. He removed the crisp top of the lasagna, exposing the softer center.

Abby found the way Ben separated the layers of sauce and cottage cheese too erotic for words. She finished off her second glass of champagne.

It pleased Ben to watch her hazel eyes grow luminous in the flickering candlelight. In spite of what was happening in his lower body, Ben slowly fed her bites of his lasagna. They spoke little. Neither seemed to need words.

Pushing his chair closer to Abby's, he sucked on her full lower lip. Abby was content to stroke Ben's broad hand, and occasionally she played with a lock of damp hair that insisted on drooping across his brow.

Of one accord, both appeared to know when their meal was at an end, and they were ready to move their wedding night upstairs.

"Let me blow out the candles and make sure my good

china's out of the kids' reach before I go up, Ben,'' Abby murmured.

Not wanting to wait, Ben tugged her into his arms. He delivered a kiss that turned her mind to mush. ''I'll clean up here while you go slip into something more comfortable,'' he said. ''And I'll bring up what's left of the champagne.''

Her knees knocking, Abby climbed the curved stairs. Perhaps two glasses of champagne had dulled her natural inhibitions. Whatever the case, Ben couldn't join her fast enough to suit Abby.

Hearing the creak of the bedroom flooring overhead, Ben counted the minutes, as he put their dishes in the sink and wondered if he'd given Abby long enough to change. Reaching his limit, he felt his heart pounding fast as he ran up the stairs and down the hall to their bedroom door.

Abby stood at the mirror, holding a small decanter of perfume. The angle gave Ben an unrestricted view of the woman he'd married. Flame-red hair. Milk-white limbs gleaming in the lamplight. Lemon-yellow silk molded to her narrow waist, barely skimming her thighs and breasts. He almost dropped the champagne and the two flutes he carried. He barely managed to place them on the table nearest the bed.

Kicking off his loafers, he began stripping off his shirt and slacks. He did take a moment to rip open a box of condoms.

Abby watched in the mirror. Clearly Ben had no false modesty. Her hand shook when she returned the perfume bottle to its spot on her dresser. She'd doubted that she'd be able to make love in a loveless marriage. However, she'd discovered she had enough love in her heart for both of them. Hearing the bed creak slightly under her husband's weight provided the last stimulus Abby needed. She locked the door and flicked off the lights.

Within minutes, Ben was caressing her, and soon—very soon..there was nothing between them but the blackness of the night and the trickle of moonlight dancing across Abby's big feather bed.

CHAPTER ELEVEN

SHOUTING KIDS, a barking dog and a caterwauling cat mixed with the shriek of the cockatiel. Abby was jolted straight out of a sound sleep. She'd expected to wake up slowly to Ben's expert kisses and more of the loving they'd enjoyed throughout the night.

Totally groggy, Abby leaped for the door. Her hand slipped on the knob because the door was locked—for which she was thankful. Especially after Ben's sleep-roughened, slightly amused tone cautioned, "Abby, I don't think you want to go out in the hall looking like that!"

She glanced over a bare shoulder and saw him propped up in her bed on an elbow. *Bare shoulder.* "Oh, my God," she yelped. "Where's my robe? I don't have a stitch on." She found it on the floor where it had fallen last night after she'd worn it downstairs to cut them each a piece of the chocolate cake she'd baked. She and Ben ate cake, drank flat champagne and giggled over the frosting that fell on her breasts, which Ben happily licked off.

"You'd better put something on, too," she suggested, right before she yanked open the door and sped into the hall. Except now the commotion appeared to have shifted to the stairs and below in the living room.

Her head hurt as she leaned over the bannister and was suddenly assailed from all sides by whining kids. Boys and girls demanding she fix their problem. At the top of their lungs, each kid blamed the other. Abby figured they were moments from a major fistfight. "Stop! Hold everything right where you are! Noah, get a grip on Ruffian. Erin and Mollie, you're responsible for that cat. Brad, cover the bird."

Hearing Sam bellowing from his room, Abby straightened and appealed to Ben, who leaned nonchalantly against their bedroom door frame. "Will you please see to Sam? He needs help getting out of bed."

Hurrying downstairs, Abby ordered the children to line up and hush. "All right," she said, completely winded, "one at a time, tell me what happened."

They outshouted each other. She put two fingers in her mouth and gave a sharp whistle. "Erin first." The girl had tears streaking her face. She clutched the monster cat so tight, the animal's ears lay flat against her wide head. There was a constant low growl in Blackberry's throat.

"Noah sicced that horrid dog on our poor cat."

"Poor cat?" Brad shouted. "Aunt Abby, that moose of a cat sneaked into my room and tried to eat Harry. I *saw* her."

Reed sobbed openly. "Yeth, and Harry ran away and he's gooonnne!" The boy ended in a shriek loud enough to take the top off Abby's champagne-addled head. "Gone? What do you mean, gone? Has anyone opened either outside door?"

Ruffian refused to stand still. He quivered all over and slobbered on Noah, who had the boxer in a neck lock. The dog dragged the boy in circles. His barking got louder when Ben appeared on the stairs carrying a sleepy-eyed Sam. At that point, the cat tried to claw its way up poor Erin's skinny torso.

"What's all the ruckus at this hour on a Sunday morning?" Ben demanded, gazing loftily down from the landing. "Sundays are for sleeping in."

Erin ran up to him, the cat's tail dragging on the steps. The explanations Abby had just heard were repeated all over again.

She waded into the center of the fray, grabbing the arms of the two nearest children. "I am not interested in who or what started the altercation. At the moment we need to find Harry and get him back in his cage. Boys, you know the routine. We each take a room and search in and under everything until Harry shows up. Noah, put Ruffian in the pantry with a bowl of water. Erin, take Blackberry into your room and shut the door. Make sure Harry's not in there first," she called belatedly. Erin had already gone crying down the hall.

"Aunt Abby, when's breakfast?" Sam asked from his perch in Ben's arms.

"My sentiment exactly." Ben descended the remaining steps. "Somehow, this isn't my ideal Sunday. Come on, cowboy," he muttered to Sam. "If that was the newspaper I heard hitting the porch, let's you and me go find the sports section. Then I'll read you the funnies."

"Don't open the front door!" Abby shrieked. She hadn't taken in his statement until he had a hand on the knob. "Honestly, Ben, haven't you heard a thing I've said?"

"Yeah, Ben." Sam shook his head vigorously. "Mike and Noah's gerbil might get out and we'd never find him. A car could run over him."

"Aren't gerbils supposed to be caged?" This from Ben.

Abby, who'd dropped to her hands and knees to search under the credenza in the hall, glanced up at him. She blew curls out of her eyes. "Yes, now that there's a cat residing in the house, gerbils and hamsters should be kept caged. I'm sure the boys didn't give Blackberry a thought. Harry, Poky and Speedy have always had free run of the house. Ruffian used to chase them, but now he doesn't bother."

She sighed. "I can't understand how the cat got out. I know I shut the girls' bedroom door last night."

Ben blinked. "I left it ajar when I checked on them while you went to get cake. Abby, you put her litter box in the bathroom. You can't deny a cat access to the litter."

"I found Harry," shouted Reed. "He's under the bookcase by the fireplace. Somebody with a longer arm than me has gotta dig him out."

"Don't scare him." Abby scrambled across the hall and into the living room, nearly falling on her nose when her brushed cotton robe refused to slide on the carpet. "Drat!" She hitched her belt tighter, suddenly aware that she was stark-naked under a robe held together with nothing but a narrow tie. Using the couch to aid her in standing, she gathered the drooping collar beneath her chin. "Ben, uh…maybe you should get Harry. I'll take Sam upstairs and dress him. You can have him again after Harry's safely caged. Then I'll, uh, go throw on something more suitable than what I'm wearing."

Ben grinned broadly as they made the transfer. "Need any help?"

Deliberately misunderstanding, she drawled, "No, thanks. I've managed to dress and undress Sam by myself for weeks now."

Ben's chuckle followed Abby up the stairs. She noticed she ached in unusual places, which called to mind how she'd spent the night. The claim that sex relieved tension must be true. The tired lines had disappeared from around Ben's eyes, and as for her, in spite of the hectic start to her day, she felt exhilarated. She wondered if she'd finally learned why Blair had never seemed harried or ruffled by the antics of five rowdy boys.

Order had been restored below, Abby saw, after she'd showered, dressed and made her way downstairs again. Ben sat on the sofa reading the paper. His gold-rimmed glasses, teamed with sun-bleached hair, gave him a decidedly distinguished look. Abby realized she'd never seen him wear glasses before. What else did she not know about her husband?

Mollie and Sam sat on the floor near Ben's feet. They colored in the same book. The four older boys were grouped around a lively board game. Battleship. Abby knew that Elliot and the boys had loved that game. Erin sat alone in the window seat staring listlessly outside. Abby's heart ached for the sad, lonely girl.

"Erin, would you like to help me fix breakfast for this hungry mob?"

"Pour cereal, you mean? No, that's okay, Abby, you can do it."

"On weekends, when no one has to go to work or school, I generally make things like pancakes, French Toast or waffles."

"Waffles, waffles," chorused the boys.

Erin's face was pinched. "Me and Mollie don't know what waffles are."

"We obviously like them," Abby said. "But boys, maybe we should save waffles for another day. Let the girls choose, since this is their first day in our family."

Ben peered at her over the top of the paper. "You're starting a bad precedent by catering to the kids' whims, Abby."

"Catering?" She shifted her gaze to see if he wore a joking smile. He looked serious. "I think it's a democratic solution to what could be a royal battle. Between Saturday and Sunday, this household accommodates two different choices of breakfast. Eventually we get to everyone's preference. I write down on the kitchen calendar who picked what. Not only does it save the cook from always having to decide the meal, but at least one day a month, everybody gets to eat something he or she likes.''

The paper rattled. ''Suit yourself, Abby. Meals fall into your domain.''

Abby had held out her hand to wiggle her fingers at Erin. She and the girl were at the kitchen door when Ben's remark penetrated. She stopped and turned back. ''What does that mean, exactly? *My domain?''*

He carefully folded the section of newspaper he'd been reading and let it fall to the floor. ''What else but the usual divvying up of male and female chores?''

Her frown became more marked. ''Those aren't things you and I really ever discussed, Ben. I guess I thought we'd split household tasks fifty-fifty. Maybe not during these next few weeks while you three are settling in and I'm still at home. But once I start back to work, I'll be coming home tired, too. I don't intend to be the only one responsible for making family meals.''

''Why would you go back to work now?'' Ben sat straighter, ripped off his glasses and stuck the end piece between his teeth.

''Why? I *am* going back, Ben. In a matter of weeks.''

The children reacted to the sudden tension between the adults. All of them grew very still, and worry darkened seven pairs of eyes.

The teacher in Abby noticed their behavior faster than Ben did. Cutting off their argument, she said, ''Erin and I have a lot to do in the kitchen. Obviously Ben, you and I have a few logistics to work out. All couples make adjustments early in their marriages,'' she assured the children. ''Oh, wait—we didn't settle on what to fix this morning. Girls, pick something, quick.''

''Smiley-face pancakes,'' Mollie chirped.

''She always wants those.'' Erin rolled her eyes. They're

regular pancakes, Abby. Mama put faces on them with chocolate chips. She made eyebrows from whipped cream.''

"Yum, chocolate chips.'' The boys, chocolate lovers one and all, threw their weight behind Mollie's request.

"Chocolate for breakfast?'' Ben muttered.

Abby shrugged. "Can it be worse than syrup or jam? Luckily we have Erin's expertise when it comes to making pancake faces.''

Ben swallowed his protest the minute he saw the first spark in his oldest niece's eyes. "If you say so, Abby. I'll give them a try.''

Abby, who generally made dollar-size or slightly larger pancakes, wasn't sure at first that she'd be able to flip the plate-size ones Erin poured. "Hey, this is easier than I thought,'' she said, getting the hang of flipping them up and letting them fall back into the pan. "I'll put this one in the warming oven. Once we've made enough and everyone's at the table, we'll do the faces. You know, I'll bet blueberries would work as well as chocolate chips.''

"Yuck!'' Erin made a gagging sound.

"Blueberries might fit better with your uncle's notion of a balanced meal, kiddo.''

"Yeah, but there's orange juice. Won't that balance us?''

Abby smiled halfheartedly. "Uh, Erin. In case you think it's your job to help me cook, I want you to know I believe in equal opportunity. The boys' mom insisted they pull kitchen duty as well as yard and trash. I see no reason to alter that.''

The girl wrinkled her nose. "You'd better tell Uncle Ben. He visited us lots for dinner. Mama used to get mad 'cause he'd leave without helping wash or dry the dishes.''

Raising her head, Abby stared out the archway to the living room, where Ben sat like a bump on a log with the paper. "Yes, well, honey, I'll handle him. Don't you worry."

Abby tucked the idea of a showdown with Ben aside for now—to save an evening when the two of them were cozy in bed. She recalled a lunch conversation between some young, newly married teachers who said it was far easier to get agreements out of their mates in the aftermath of lovemaking. At the time, Abby remembered thinking that was sneaky and manipulative. Now, she could see merit to their method.

She was prepared to be flexible in how she and Ben split chores, but she couldn't imagine what had given him the notion she'd walk away from her job. Not after all the years she'd trained and had taught. Abby was sure they'd discussed her eventual return to work the night they'd talked about how joining forces would improve their lives.

The family was seated around the table tucking into breakfast when Abby launched a topic that upset Ben more than the prospect of her return to teaching.

"I hope breakfast tides everyone over until this afternoon," Abby said. "I'm planning a late lunch, or call it an early dinner. We're having company."

"Who?" the kids asked in one loud voice.

"I could say just wait and see because it's a surprise. Except I'd like everyone to be on his or her best behavior. Plus, I want you all to look nice."

"We've gotta wear church clothes again?" Mike and Noah exclaimed in disgust.

"Not dress up like you did for the wedding. But I expect clean hands, faces and hair combed by two o'clock. Tied sneakers, too. I've invited the girls' grandfather and grandmother to have dinner with us. I told them we'd eat at three. Roast chicken, mashed potatoes and gravy, with baby peas and carrots. Oh, and apple pie for dessert. Anyone who'd like to help me make pies gets to eat the leftover crust, rolled, baked and sprinkled with sugar and cinnamon.'' It wasn't until the last word rolled off her tongue that Abby chanced to glance down the table and see Ben's murderous expression. The girls, too, appeared slightly stunned.

''Ben? Give their visit a chance before you get into a snit. Consider how many relatives the kids have lost. Lily was very gracious when I explained about the move. She said she understood why we had just us at the wedding, and she said they'd be delighted to come to dinner today.''

Ben clenched and unclenched his hands. He clamped his teeth over his lower lip, trying not to blow up at Abby. ''My family!'' he said with deadly softness. ''I should think it would've occurred to you to consult me before you issued an invitation.''

Abby swung her eyes away from his dark fury. ''I figured you'd probably say no.''

''I'd definitely have said no.''

It was easy to see Ben's tight jaw as he spoke. Abby felt her anger stir, too. ''Haven't both our families suffered enough trauma as a result of the quake? Shouldn't those of us left attempt to coexist harmoniously? Your father pieced Sam back together, for crying out loud.''

''Kirk's skill as a surgeon has nothing to do with his failure as a parent.''

''Was he also a failure as a grandparent? Lily said he adores the girls. When I mentioned you'd taken on the job of fathering five boys' as well, she said Kirk would be tickled pink to serve as an adopted grandfather.''

''Dammit!'' Ben sprang to his feet. Vaguely registering the puzzled expressions on the kids' faces, Ben stalked from the room. The back door slammed, and a minute later the gate screeched. Abby heard Ruffian, then his barking grew fainter indicating Ben had taken the dog for a run on the beach.

She picked up her fork with a far from steady hand. Yet she felt it imperative to put on an act for the sake of the children.

"Is Uncle Ben gone forever?" Mollie inquired, her chin quivering more than Abby's hand.

"Certainly not," she told the child, sounding more assured than she felt in her aching heart. "Ben's not upset with you kids. He's just unhappy with me right now."

"Why?" Sam asked, his small face a mask of concern.

Abby tugged nervously on her lip. "I, ah, invited people into our home without talking it over with him first. I'm used to making decisions on my own. But Ben and I are partners now, so dinner invitations ought to be a joint decision. I shouldn't have tried to surprise him."

Erin poked her fork aimlessly at what remained of her smiley pancake. Its whipped cream eyebrows were sadly askew. "Mommy had an awful fight with Mimi Lily on Mollie's birthday. Mimi is what Grandpa's wife wants Mollie and me to call her 'cause she's not old enough to be a grandma. Anyway—after Mommy threw Mimi Lily out, we never saw her or Grandpa Kirk again. I miss them," she said in an afterthought.

A tic started below Abby's eyes, followed by a throbbing in her skull. Whatever had possessed her to meddle in a relationship that she suspected, deep down, needed more than surface TLC? If Marlo McBride had such a huge disagreement with Kirk Galloway's wife, maybe she *was* an ogre, although Abby found that difficult to believe. On the phone, the woman couldn't have been sweeter.

"Eat up, kids, before your pancakes get stone-cold," Abby urged brightly, although she couldn't swallow another bite. "Noah? Mike? Seconds, anyone? I have more batter. It'll only take a minute to reheat the grill."

They all shoved their plates back and asked to be excused.

"Thank you for your good manners. Leave your plates. I'll stack them all when I'm done. Don't forget to brush your teeth and wash any stray chocolate off your hands and faces. You can play until it's time to dress for our guests."

Mollie and Sam continued stuffing their faces with pancakes. Erin pushed her plate away and followed the boys out. A moment later she returned to whisper to Abby. "Do you think Uncle Ben will call Grandpa Kirk and Mimi Lily on his cell phone and tell them not to come?"

"Oh, I don't think he will." But Abby wasn't at all sure of that.

Erin fidgeted. "I'm a bad girl, Abby, 'cause every night I pray they'll come see us again."

Abby gazed deep into Erin's troubled blue eyes. She smoothed a hand over the fine hair kinked from daily braiding. "Oh, honey. Prayers are private conversations between you and God. They're never bad."

"Not even if I started praying 'cause Mimi Lily left Mollie a birthday present, and then didn't bring me one on my birthday?"

"Not even then." Abby hugged the girl. "Run upstairs and find your comb and those cute butterfly clips. I'll fix your hair in twists for your grandpa's visit."

"Really? Uncle Ben tried to learn twists. They always fall out before I get to school." She scampered off, seemingly relieved of her concerns.

Abby pictured Ben attempting the new hairstyles. It said a lot about him—that he'd try to fix a little girl's hair in the current fashion. How could a man possessed of those fine qualities be so unwilling to accept..and forgive..his father's faults?

Erin returned to have her hair done before Abby had the table cleared. She ended up carrying Sam in to play with his brothers. Resisting the urge to look for Ben, she went upstairs, saying she'd fix both girls' hair. "I'm letting the cat out of Erin's room," she called. "That means keep the gerbil and hamster cages closed, boys."

Abby was finished washing the dishes when Ben returned. His shirt was soaked with sweat from his run, and his hair was a windblown mass of curls. He saw her as soon as he walked in, but he went to the fridge and pulled out a bottle of water without saying a word.

"We need to have this out before the kids discover you're back, Ben. Tension between us only adds to their unrest. God knows they've experienced enough turmoil."

"You should've thought of that before you phoned that woman."

"*That woman* being your father's wife?"

"They're not married. And she's lady love number five. Or is it six? Sorry, I've lost count."

"If she loves your father and he loves her, isn't that what counts?"

"Love, hell! With Kirk it's showing the world he's virile enough to attract a woman half his age. For a woman like his current Marilyn Monroe look-alike, it's plain greed." Ben tipped back his head, drained the bottle, then recapped the empty. He threw it into the recycle bin sitting in one corner of the kitchen. "Oh, yeah, they're great role models for seven impressionable kids."

Abby tried to read between the lines of Ben's angry diatribe against his father. Since he himself had married not for love but for convenience, what was it about Kirk Galloway's situation that his son found so reprehensible? The difference in their ages as opposed to hers and Ben's? Lily's blatant sex appeal, as opposed to her own lack thereof? Or the fact Ben had felt honor-bound to tie the knot when his father didn't?

The headache that had hovered all morning kicked in with full fury. "They're not staying a week, Ben. We're sharing one simple meal. I admit I shouldn't have tried to surprise you. But what would you have me do at this late hour? Phone and uninvite them? Well, I won't," she said. "If you want to disappoint them and your nieces, who by the way don't bear any animosity toward Kirk and Lily, then you handle it. And you tell the girls. I already bought the food, so I'll prepare it anyway." Turning her back on Ben, Abby wrenched on the hot water faucet. She could tell when he left the room, taking the tension with him. The fine hair on the back of her neck had been prickling. Now only the breeze from the overhead fan cooled the sweat brought on by the heated exchange with her husband.

Her *husband*. What precisely did that word mean to Ben? It was a question that rose again and again in Abby's mind as she prepared the chicken, popped it into the oven and peeled potatoes for later boiling. In a frenzy, she set the table with her good dishes, then swept the kitchen and dining room floors. She made a last-minute check on the kids and various pets before heading upstairs to change her own clothes.

Ben, unshaven and still in the pants and shirt he'd worn to go running, sat at the desk in their bedroom. Stacks of envelopes covered the surface. His chin rested on one palm. With the other, he rubbed the back of his neck.

"What are you doing?" Abby asked as she opened the closet and pulled out a dress.

"I unpacked a few boxes and ran across my unpaid bills.

I decided to combine them with yours before setting up our long-range budget.''

''Did you phone your father?''

''No. How would that look, Abby? Like my marriage was already as screwed up as the one he and my mother had..thanks to their endless game of career one-upmanship?''

His tone gouged Abby's tender feelings. Giving up, she lashed back at his earlier statement regarding their joint budget. ''We never discussed whether or not to merge our bank accounts. I think we should each pay into a fund for property taxes and any repairs on either house. Splitting food fifty-fifty is easier than keeping track of who eats what. With clothes, though, and pet expenses, it's probably more fair to do it individually.''

Ben's jaw went slack. ''Whoa! Hold it just a damned minute. Are you insinuating I can't afford to support this family?''

Abby, who'd bent to untie her sneakers, plopped down on the end of the bed and threw Ben a look of confusion. ''Why is it every time I open my mouth, you jump down my throat? Pardon me, but I thought I presented a rational solution to sharing expenses. I brought the greater number of kids into this union, so I'm willing to pay the greater share of their overall expenses.''

''I wouldn't have proposed if I hadn't thought I was capable of caring for you and the boys,'' he said harshly. ''I've designated the top right-hand drawer as a place to put bills as they come in. Writing checks will be my job.''

''All right. Good grief!'' Abby left the bed, hung the dress back in the closet, then rummaged until she found a matched blouse and slacks set. She wanted to look nice for Ben's family, but not so dressy as to make Ben and the kids appear shabby.

As she stripped, a host of unanswered questions played through her mind. For instance, Ben hadn't said they'd put all their earnings into one joint account. Neither had he spelled out whether he'd write checks from both their checkbooks, or did he mean he'd pay for everything, including gifts? What about Christmas and birthdays, some of which were imminent? Would he expect an accounting of every dime she spent?

Feeling his eyes on her, she turned from the closet and glanced over her shoulder. Ben's face reflected a broad range of lust-filled thoughts. Abby smiled. In the area of sex, they were definitely compatible. "You'd better put what you're thinking on hold for another six or so hours. The only time it's safe to indulge in adult games around here, is after the kids are sound asleep."

"Isn't that why there's a solid lock on the door?"

"Kids have a sixth sense about locks. Either they pound until you let them in, or they figure it's an opportunity to do all manner of nifty experiments—like shaving the dog or each other. Or finding the matches."

"I should know that. I've listened to enough parents complain." Ben shook his head. "I always planned on having perfectly angelic kids."

Abby laughed as she buttoned her blouse and tucked it into the waistband of her slacks. "In another universe. Not on this planet. Oh, they all have their angelic moments. And not only when they're sleeping. But by and large, all kids test their limits."

"Add up all the experience we have between us, Abby, and you'd think we could make this household operate like clockwork in say…another month?"

"That's a joke, right?"

Ben leaned back in his chair and propped a sneaker-clad

foot on the desk. "I notice you're still lax about discipline. Exactly what are your views?"

Abby stopped at the door. "Lax? Not really. Ask any teacher at my school. They'll tell you I run a very orderly class."

"I'm talking about here. There's the scene I walked in on the first day I came to visit. And this morning was pure bedlam."

Arching an eyebrow, Abby studied the man who acted as if he didn't have a care in the world. "What was your contribution to a peaceful settlement today?"

"That's the point. *You* settled it, Abby. Not the kids. Child psych books recommend giving kids two rules. Solve the problem, and do it quietly."

"What fool wrote that book? I'll bet if you dig deep enough, you'll find they never actually worked with kids. Maybe lab mice or something. Speaking of quiet, I haven't heard a peep out of the little darlings since I came upstairs. Now, in my teacher's mind, I suspect they're up to no good. But, you know what? I have a meal for eleven to prepare. So I'm placing our kids in your capable hands, Dr. Galloway. You and your favorite child psychologist go see what's up, why don't you?"

"Oh, ye of little faith." Ben rose, and followed Abby out. He let his hand rest warmly on her butt as they descended the stairs. She hoped that meant he'd forgiven her for inviting the elder Galloways over.

In the living room they saw that Mollie and Sam had closed their coloring books. Both were engrossed in painting a mural of stick people on the living room wall. Reed and Brad giggled in hushed tones while pulling the stuffing out of sofa pillows. They rained it over each other's heads like snow.

When she saw Ben's face, Abby wished she had a camera. One with audio that would catch his enraged bellow.

She doubted he realized three of the seven kids were missing from this charming scene. Ducking away from his wild gestures, she went in search of Mike, Erin and Noah. And found them in the kitchen mixing watercolor paint with glitter. Someone had carved stamps out of her peeled potatoes. As Erin and Noah each wielded a paring knife, Abby was afraid to shout the way Ben was doing. These kids had at least stamped their carvings on large sheets of art paper she kept in the cupboard for that very purpose. Of course, someone had to climb to the top shelf to reach her stash of paint and glitter.

The thing that truly amazed Abby was how quickly they'd all gotten into mischief. She hadn't been upstairs fifteen minutes. Well...more like twenty-five. Ben's folks were due to arrive within the hour.

"Hi, guys." Abby announced her entry, walking gingerly around drying paintings set about the tile floor.

Mike and Noah stopped carving. "Ain't this cool, Aunt Abby? Erin's teacher showed her how to do potato art for open house. Me, Mike'n her are makin' pictures for Dr. Kirk's office wall."

"I see. Noah, please use *isn't* instead of *ain't*. While potato art *is* cool, you're using potatoes meant for Dr. Kirk's dinner."

All three faces fell. They laid down their knives and brushed paint-covered hands on their formerly clean shirts and pants.

Abby sighed. "You've stamped enough pictures for twenty walls. It's time to start cleaning up the mess. I'm not helping, either. I have to peel more potatoes."

Ben poked his head into the kitchen. "Abby, what takes crayon off flat paint?" Directly behind him, a weeping

Mollie and red-faced Brad burst past him, rushing to throw their arms around Abby's legs.

"Sam and me drawed Grandpa Kirk a picture of our new fambly," Mollie cried. "Unca Ben's gonna wash it off."

Brad's voice rose. "The little kids asked Reed and me to glue fluffy clouds in their sky. *He* says we gotta vacuum all our cloud stuff up right now." Brad pointed a finger at Ben.

"Ben, the kids didn't mean any harm. They want to make your father and Lily feel welcome." She wanted to side with her husband, but the kids' tear-streaked faces weakened her resolve. "You children should have asked us first." Lifting her eyes, she sent Ben a pleading glance.

"Okay, we'll leave the mural for now. But clouds are out. Jeez, Abby, did you see the living room floor? It looks like a train wreck."

"The kids will put the cloud stuffing back in the cushions. Then they'll vacuum. Won't you, guys?"

Two heads bobbed solemnly. Sam and Reed could still be heard sobbing in the living room.

Ben caved in totally after Abby walked over and kissed away his lingering protest. Automatically, his arms circled her waist. He let their foreheads touch, and his breath fanned red curls already escaping from the clasp Abby had employed in hopes of taming her untamable hair. Ben loved her hair. And he supposed the wildness of it represented something that said his life would never be dull.

"You win," he muttered. "I'll go help Reed and Sam restuff the darned cushions. Mollie, you and Brad come put away the paints."

Order was restored in the nick of time. Ben had barely shaved and donned a clean shirt and slacks and run a cursory check on how the kids looked when the front doorbell chimed, and he panicked.

"They're here," Abby called from the kitchen. "I'm whipping the potatoes now. Ben, will you get the door?"

"Erin, why don't you and Mollie go greet your grandfather? I need to bring Sam downstairs. Go on. Don't keep them waiting."

It was all the encouragement the girls needed. Both raced for the door. Surprisingly, the boys started after them, but hung back when the door swung wide. Ben had never known the Drummond boys to be shy. Today, they presented a new side.

Ben's first glimpse of his father brought old resentments flooding back. Kirk wore a three-piece suit and shoes shined to a high gloss. It was Sunday afternoon, dammit. Kirk knew he was visiting a house filled with kids.

Oddly enough, Lily had dressed more appropriately. Granted, her jeans and blouse bore Ralph Lauren labels, but her makeup had been toned down a lot from what Ben had expected. And she'd changed her hair from white-blond to wheat. The new look had aged her. Surprisingly, Ben saw lines around her lips and eyes. Had her formerly youthful appearance been a product of cleverly applied cosmetics?

Ben set Sam on the ottoman, then stood back near the birdcage, watching Lily dole out gifts to all the children. She oohed and ahhed over the mural, pointing out to Kirk that the kids had included her in their stick family. Ben thought nastily that poor Lily had probably unwittingly revamped herself right out of Kirk's life. She should take a really good look at her lover. If there lived a more vain man than Kirk Galloway, Ben had yet to meet him.

The surgeon himself had stopped to examine Sam's casts. "Haven't those bonehead therapists switched his plaster for air casts yet? Son, what's wrong with you?" Kirk wheeled to confront Ben. "You've got to know that leg's gonna atrophy if it doesn't get air soon. Or are you boycotting the moon boot he'll wear because it's my invention?''

Ben's lip curled. If Abby hadn't entered the room then, he knew there would've been an ugly scene.

"Dr. Kirk and Lily. Welcome. Sorry I didn't greet you. I was just putting the finishing touches on dinner. If everyone will go straight to the dining room, we can catch up over the meal. I hope you like roast chicken and mashed potatoes.''

It took five minutes to get the lot of them seated. The older kids had to present Kirk and Lily with the stack of potato art pictures. Lily hugged each and every child. Abby noticed Kirk was more reticent.

She'd arranged seating to maximize the space between Ben and his father. She and Lily both kept up a pleasant smattering of chatter. Sparks continued to fly from Kirk to Ben and back again during the meal.

"I hear there's a big pediatric convention in Vienna this summer. Are you presenting a paper?'' Kirk asked Ben, declining Abby's apple pie with a shake of his head.

"I'm not going.''

"Why not? That's how your work gets noticed and you climb the ladder of success. I've heard via the grapevine that you're doing some innovative studies in infant leukemia.''

Abby cocked an interested ear. This was the first she'd heard of Ben's interest in kids with leukemia.

"I have other obligations, Kirk. Eight others to be exact,'' Ben said, letting his gaze sweep the table.

Kirk waved a dismissive hand. "There's your mistake. Tying yourself down when you're young. As I learned the hard way… That's when you can make your mark in the medical world.''

Lily quickly squeezed his arm, but not before it was clear his thoughtless words had hurt Abby.

"Nothing personal against you, Abigail. Some careers don't lend themselves to domestic bliss. It's well known that medicine is one."

As if to make Kirk's point for him, Ben's pager sounded. He hurried into the kitchen and called his answering service on his cell phone. Returning, he looked directly at Abby. "I've got a patient who took a header over his skateboard and plowed into a brick wall. I'm sorry, Abby, but I've got to run."

"I thought Steve was on call this weekend?" She frowned unhappily at Ben.

"He is, but he's tied up at another hospital."

Kirk Galloway studied his son, then his son's new wife. "Better get used to the disruptions," he advised Abby. "You married a doc, and if you want to continue feeding all these kids, this'll be your life. Of course, if Ben had gone into a speciality where he could make more money—" Ben cut his dad off in midsentence. "I'm in the field I like. Abby, I'll phone when I know how long I'll be."

His car keys rattled and he jerked the door open, creating a wind through the room. Then, just like that, Abby was left to entertain her in-laws alone—a prospect she suddenly found less than thrilling.

CHAPTER TWELVE

NEVER HAD Abby been so glad to say goodbye to anyone as the elder Galloways. When they'd finally filed out, she leaned against the door, her jaws aching from gritting her teeth to keep from saying something she'd regret.

Kirk Galloway had an irritating habit of paying compliments in one breath and arrogantly wiping them out in the next. He praised the house, remarking on how valuable the property was. Then he gave a mile-long rundown of everything that needed upgrading if she and Ben hoped to sell the "eyesore" for a decent profit.

"We're not planning on selling," Abby had repeatedly said. "Ben and I agree this house and the antique furnishings passed down through the boys' mother's family will eventually be equally split between them. Ben's hanging on to Marlo's home for the girls."

Abby would later wonder why she thought Kirk would be impressed by that fact. He wasn't.

"Where is that boy's head?" he'd exclaimed in exasperation. "In today's market this property is worth an easy half mil. Ben could buy you a nice house in a new development and invest the remaining funds with a top broker. That would allow him freedom to write and present a paper to his peers on his work in leukemia."

"Ben's a man, not a boy," Abby said stingingly. "And this isn't our home to sell. My brother and his wife wouldn't want that. They intended this to be their boys' legacy.''

"This old house isn't worth squat, you know." Kirk started ticking off reasons. "But land's hot at the moment," he finished. "Who knows, in the future, prices may fall."

"I think the house has a warm, homey feel," Lily ventured.

"That's why you leave the thinking to me, Lily. Which reminds me, who did your hair yesterday? It looks like a haystack. I have a good mind to call the salon owner and give him a piece of my mind.''

Lily's cheeks paled, but Kirk didn't seem to notice he'd embarrassed her. Which must have hurt. To her credit, the woman rose gracefully and went into the other room to play a game with the children.

Luckily the kids were all playing in the living room with the toys the couple had brought. Abby wouldn't want them witnessing Kirk's behavior.

After Lily left, Kirk regaled Abby with approximately ten years of his own accomplishments in the field of orthopedic surgery. The visit couldn't draw to a close fast enough for Abby. Now it was clear why Ben had opposed her extending an invitation. She couldn't wait for his call. She wanted to tell him how wrong she'd been.

Once the visitors had departed, Abby cleaned up their dishes. She played a couple of board games with the kids, supervised showers, then laid out clothes for school the next day. As she pulled the drapes against a growing darkness, she worried that something might have happened to Ben.

Erin came looking for Abby when the girls were ready for bed. "Has Uncle Ben phoned? Mollie says she won't go to sleep unless she gets to tell him good-night."

"You probably know his hospital routine better than I

do. I'm afraid the skateboard accident required more than slapping on a few Band-Aids.''

''He still oughta call us. Uncle Ben knows Mollie's a worrier.''

As was Erin, Abby noted without comment. ''I'll tuck you both in. And if Ben finds an opportunity to phone, I promise I'll come see if you're still awake. That way you and Mollie can tell him good-night.''

''Okay. Abby, what should I do about Blackberry? Brad and Reed are going to let Speedy and Poky out of their cages. They said if my cat eats their hamsters tonight, they'll vote…and…and we'll have to go someplace else to live.'' Her small chin quivered.

''What?'' Abby rubbed at the nagging pain between her eyes. ''Erin, the boys are pushing your buttons, as adults say. They're teasing, but this time they've gone too far. I'll have a word with them. As Ben pointed out earlier, Blackberry's litter is in the bathroom. Here's the deal. At night, the cat has free run of the house, but takes her chances with Ruffian. Once the boys get home from school, they can go in their rooms, shut their doors and let their gerbil and hamsters out to chase around.''

The girl looked even more distressed. ''Noah said if I tattled on Brad and Reed, even worse things are gonna happen to me and Mollie.''

''Not true. Or, they'd better not. Come on, sweetie. This is your home now, same as it is theirs. We operate as one family. I intend to make that perfectly clear right after I tuck you in.''

''But…but…I don't want to cause trouble.''

Abby worried about the slump of Erin's shoulders. Where was Ben when she needed his help? ''Erin, hon, we owe ourselves time. It's a big adjustment for you girls, the boys, your uncle and me. I have faith we will adapt. Someday, I bet we'll all look back on these early weeks and laugh.'' Abby squeezed the girl's small, trusting hand.

Erin offered a shy smile that almost broke Abby's heart.

Once she'd kissed the girls and turned out their light, Abby paid a visit to each of the boys. She loved those little rascals, but that didn't stop her from laying down the law. ''No more tricks on the girls, understand? Noah and Mike, you're older. Big brothers have the honor and responsibility of being role models. It's an important job. I know you guys are up to it.''

AT THE HOSPITAL, once things had calmed down and nerves were less on edge, Ben glanced at the clock in the doctors' lounge. He was stunned to see how late it had become. Eleven-thirty. It'd taken a team of doctors and nurses eight hours to stabilize his young patient. Ben scrubbed the tired ache from his face, and recalled his promise to phone Abby. Would she understand how dicey the situation had been? None of the team had time to breathe, let alone break for a call home.

''Good work, Galloway.'' The ER senior night staff man clapped Ben's shoulder. ''The rest of us were so worried about the kid's head injury, we overlooked the bleeding spleen you picked up on. As I said a few weeks ago, I need a good pediatrician on ER rotation here. Someone adept at diagnostics. Have you given my offer any thought?''

What Ben had thought about was the stack of bills he'd sorted this morning. His stack and Abby's made a mountain. He also remembered Kirk's dig about his specialty being so low-paying. Ben couldn't deny that pediatrics paid less than other fields. It had never bothered him until he'd assumed responsibility for a big family.

Looking at long-range costs for seven kids—well, he must have been delusional to think he could afford to do right by all of them. To say nothing of the fact that he'd hoped, sometime in the future, he and Abby might have a child together. Of course, there hadn't been time for them to discuss the possibility yet.

"I notice you didn't say no, but neither did you say yes. Did I hear whispers among the nursing staff that you recently got married?"

"Yesterday," Ben admitted with a giant yawn.

The ER doctor laughed. "I could joke about why you're falling asleep on your feet, but I'll be nice. Tell you what, Ben, I'll hold the position open for a couple of weeks. If I don't hear from you, I'll go to the next victim—" he grinned "—er…pediatrician on my list."

"No. Listen, I've decided. I'll take the job. My wife and I are raising my sister's and her brother's kids. Their folks died in the recent earthquake. To make a long story short, I can put extra cash to good use." Ben had already made up his mind to beef up his private practice by stretching his clinic hours. If he added just four patients a day, plus put in a few nights a week here in the ER, that ought to let Abby stay home full-time with the kids. Ben was positive she'd see that was best all the way around.

"Good, Ben." The senior staff man shook Ben's hand. "I'll courier a contract over to your clinic tomorrow. Can you give me four nights a week starting this Wednesday at, say, 7:00 p.m.?"

"That'll be great. My wife's a teacher, presently on leave. She'd planned to go back to her old job, but one of our boys needs extensive physical therapy due to injuries he received in the quake. My putting in extra hours will allow Abby to tend to him without feeling guilty about quitting her job."

"You're undoubtedly right. My wife's a nurse. She was working when we got married. She continued to work, but finally admitted she'd held on because she thought I expected her to add to the coffers even after we had kids. One day I found her in tears. She was due on shift, but our son had awakened with chicken pox. Day care refused to take him. I can't tell you how happy I made Luanne by merely saying, honey, call in and quit. Robby's more important than a few extra bucks.''

"Thanks for sharing your experience, Don. I've been having second thoughts over whether I should've run the extra job by Abby first. But as you say, who wouldn't prefer staying home over slogging to work every day, rain or shine?''

Feeling his tension lift, Ben decided to just go home rather than call.

The house was dark when he pulled in, except for a night-light in the hall. Ruffian barked a few times, but loped up and sniffed Ben's shoes as he removed his key from the lock. "Hi, guy. You the only one awake?'' Dropping to his heels, Ben gave the dog's belly a good rub, then Ruffian padded back to his bed. Dog tags clanked as he laid his head on his paws. Ben leaned down to pick up one of the Rock 'Em Sock 'Em Robots Kirk and Lily had given the middle set of twins.

Always keyed up after an emergency, he prowled the lower floors looking for something to occupy his excess energy. He fed the fish and checked to be sure the cockatiel had water and food. Turning, he remembered the mural. Ben was surprised when he snapped on a lamp and found it gone. Abby's doing, he'd bet.

Ah, Abby! He glanced over at the neat pile of new toys. It struck him how hard she worked trying to please everyone. Him. The girls. Her nephews. Abby so wanted a warm, loving, extended family for the kids' sake. Enough to try and mold Kirk and Lily into replicas of normal grandparents. Ben recognized that those unselfish traits were what had drawn him to Abigail Drummond in the first place. She was an inherently good woman. And a warm, generous lover.

He turned off the lights on the lower floor and carried the toys upstairs. One by one, he looked in on the kids and distributed their toys. In Sam's room, he rearranged the menagerie of stuffed animals. He pulled up the blankets Brad and Reed had kicked off. In the older twins' room, he switched off a tape player that would otherwise run all night.

Tiptoeing into the girls' room, he dropped a light kiss on Mollie's forehead, then pried a book out of Erin's hands. She stirred and opened her eyes. "Hi, Uncle Ben. Am I dreaming, or are you home?"

"I'm home, button eyes," he murmured. "It's late. You go on back to sleep."

"Mollie cried 'cause you didn't call. Abby rocked her for a long time."

Guilt washed over Ben. Especially when he thought about all the future nights he'd promised to put in at the ER.

"Uncle Ben, do we hafta move again?"

"That's a funny question. No, Erin. I hope we're staying put for a long time."

"I heard Grandpa Kirk tell Abby if you sell this house you'd get lots of money."

Typical Kirk. Nevertheless, Ben experienced a burn in his chest. "What was Abby's reply?"

"She said it's the boys house. 'Cept Abby didn't like that Noah and Mike told me if Blackberry hurts the gerbil or hamsters, they'll send me and my cat away. Abby said we're all family." Her voice broke.

Ben smoothed a hand over her soft, dark hair. He remembered a time when her mother lay awake at night, fighting the same night demons that apparently plagued Erin. "Button, the boys don't really own the house. Not until they're grown. It's complicated, but the house is in what's called a trust. I've done the same with your mom's place. We'll rent it out until you and Mollie are old enough to decide if you want to sell it or live there yourselves."

Erin snuggled back into her pillow. "That's what Abby said. 'Kay, Uncle Ben. G'night!" She sighed, shut her eyes and turned on her side.

Blackberry stretched and batted Ben's hand. Ben scratched the big cat's ears, then he left the room. He recalled seeing the caged gerbil and hamsters when he'd looked in on the boys.

Figuring he could probably sleep now, Ben made his way into his and Abby's darkened bedroom. He made every effort to sneak in quietly, but apparently he hadn't been quiet enough. She shifted, sat partially up in bed, and raked a hand through her tangled hair. "Ben, is that you?"

"Were you expecting someone else?" he asked, laughing softly.

"What time is it?" She yawned. "It seems I only just got Mollie to sleep. I thought maybe she woke up again, and that you were Erin coming to get me. I told her to do that if Mollie started crying."

"It's straight up midnight. I checked. All the kids are snug in their beds."

"Oh. So late? Are you all right, Ben? I mean—is your patient… Did he—?"

"He's stable." Ben tugged off his tie and began unbuttoning his shirt. "The boy's blood pressure kept dropping. We ran a million tests and took as many films. I finally ordered an MRI. Sure enough, Tommy had a ruptured spleen. Once the surgeon removed the bleeding organ, his

BP started to climb. He's got some swelling in his brain so he's still comatose. I'll check him tomorrow before I go to the clinic. I think he'll be fine.''

''Oh, good. I heard about his accident on the ten o'clock news. I had it on while I scrubbed crayon off the wall.''

''I noticed you'd done that.'' Ben put his wallet and keys on the nightstand before taking off his slacks. ''How late did Kirk and Lily stay?'' The bed gave under his weight as he turned back the covers and slid in beside Abby.

''Too long,'' she said hesitantly.

''Oh?'' Ben found her face mere inches away from his.

''I owe you an apology, Ben. Your father is mean-spirited.''

Ben knew what it must cost her to admit as much to him, especially when he stopped to consider how briskly she'd defended her decision to invite his family. There were several things he might say. But suddenly, Abby's warm body awoke other needs. He could smell faint traces of perfume she'd splashed on earlier.

Slipping his arms around her, Ben pulled Abby flush against him. His erection was instantaneous. They both felt it.

Abby reached for Ben at the same time he slid his hands under the silky top of the pajamas she'd put on in case Erin did come to fetch her.

''Big improvement over the cold sheets I used to come home to from night hospital runs,'' Ben crooned, filling his hands with Abby's breasts. They peaked under his rasping thumbs.

''So you're not going to make me grovel over being wrong about inviting your dad and Lily to dinner?''

''Hmm, I'll have to think about how I might punish you.'' Ben kissed her breast just to make his point. Her hand found his solid erection.

"Abby...that feels...ah...good. But much more, and we'll see who's punishing whom."

She laughed and stopped attending to him long enough to peel away the lower half of her silk pjs. Feeling him pause to strip off his shorts, Abby asked a question that popped into her head, "Did you remember to lock our door?"

"I forgot." He groaned and struggled to sit.

"I'm nearer. Don't move and I'll be right back." Ben watched her streak naked through the tiny shaft of moonlight that filtered in the window. At that moment, he didn't think he could move a muscle if his life depended on it.

Ben found the strength, however, to lift her onto him when she returned. It suited him fine tonight to let Abby take charge of their lovemaking. And she didn't disappoint him. She drove him to the edge of insanity with her hands, lips and the blunt tips of her hair, which brushed his chest, then his belly as she kissed her way down his body.

He discovered that a man could only take so much. Panting, he hoisted her up and flipped her onto her back. He took the time to see that she was ready before he entered her. Midway through a wild ride, Ben was flat on his back again. This time, when Abby cried out in ecstasy, he clamped his mouth over hers and swallowed the sound.

Ben's body vibrated pleasantly as they fell limply back against the pillows and curled together in the center of the bed. Ben loved it when Abby's satisfied smile brushed his shoulder in a series of love bites.

"You make me want to move mountains for you." His words were lost in her hair.

"I don't need you to move mountains, Ben," she said, lazily scraping her fingertips through his sweat-damp chest hair. "But I do need more from our marriage than good sex."

"Sweetheart. If it's within my power, I'll get it for you."

"I want you to spend more time with the kids. They're all at such crucial ages. They need a mom and a dad, especially now."

Ben said nothing. Abby assumed he'd fallen asleep. She sighed. So much for what her teacher friends had said about a husband being more cooperative after good sex. Obviously their mates didn't come home dog-tired or as late as hers did. Fitting her head to Ben's shoulder, she succumbed again to the need for sleep.

Ben remained awake. He'd heard every nuance of Abby's request. He knew exactly what she wanted—what she'd begged for, and begged so sweetly. He honestly didn't see how he could grant her wish, yet pay all the bills he'd added up this morning.

It worried him so much that the moment he felt her sink into slumber, he threw off the sheet and got out of bed. Sliding stealthily into his pants, Ben collected the bills from the desk as well as the budget sheets he'd put together. He unlocked the door and made his way down the dark stairs. He soon had everything spread out across the kitchen table. By 3:00 a.m., Ben had confirmed his worst fears. His income simply wouldn't stretch far enough. They needed what the shift in the ER would pay. Even with that, Ben figured he'd still need to increase his clinic patient load in order to pay for Erin's violin lessons, summer camp and sports for the boys. It would help if he could rent Marlo's house right away. But the Realtor had said that since the quake, rentals had bottomed out. He understood new people not wanting to move here. But as he and Abby had discussed at Marlo's funeral, their own roots were deep in Seattle.

Ben paid and stamped the bills he had funds to cover. He stuck them in his jacket pocket to mail on the way to work, and carefully rubber-banded the rest. If his clinic staff kept his office hours on track, he ought to make it home most nights for supper. Some evenings he might manage an occasional half hour to read to Sam or help kids with homework. It wasn't ideal, but it'd have to do. He'd show Kirk he could provide for a family *and* succeed at his profession.

Sneaking upstairs again, Ben returned the accounts to the drawer. If he didn't get some sleep, he'd be useless tomorrow. And yet he couldn't resist spending ten minutes gazing lovingly down on Abby. She made no sound when she slept, not even an occasional soft wifflc. But the rapid jump of her eyelids told Ben her sleep wasn't relaxed. As he lay down and curved his body around hers, he wondered if she was worrying about the children. Sam would start PT the next day. If that concerned Abby, she'd kept it to herself. Ben's last coherent thought before sleep was that this woman he'd married never seemed outwardly fazed by much of anything—one of the traits he admired so much in her. Abby was the calm in the eye of a storm.

WAKING UP, Abby heard kids tramping down the hall. Glancing at the clock, she saw that it was a full fifteen minutes before her alarm was set to ring. She reached for her robe, and once again realized she'd slept naked. Smiling down on her sleeping mate, she decided all thc money she'd spent buying sexy nighties at Victoria's Secret had been a waste.

Deciding to let Ben sleep for an extra half hour, she hung her robe in the closet and quickly, but quietly dressed.

The minute she stepped into the hall, gleeful giggles wafted up the stairs from the proximity of the kitchen. She spared only a moment to see if the kids were up. All except Sam were missing from their rooms. If she was truly going to let Ben rest, she ought to take Sam to the bathroom. Otherwise he'd holler down the roof until someone came to help him.

Anyway, Mike and Noah were old enough to prepare cold cereal for themselves and the younger twins. Erin could take care of herself and Mollie.

Sam, bless his heart, always woke up in a jolly mood. Abby spoke to him about letting Ben sleep late, and Sam nodded. As she helped the boy dress, she went over what he might expect today during his therapy.

"Will it hurt?" Sam asked.

"Honey, I'm sure no one will hurt you on purpose. But you do know your legs might not work right away, even after these casts come off?"

"Uh-huh. Ben said my leg could look like a prune. That's funny, isn't it?"

Abby didn't think it was, but she smiled and ruffled his fiery curls all the same. "Okay, tiger. Let's go see what your brothers and the girls are up to. I hear an awful lot of frivolity from kids who should be eating."

"Aunt Abby, if Noah, Mike, Brad and Reed are my brothers, are Erin and Mollie my sisters?"

"Sort of, but not really." Abby stuttered, not knowing how to explain the concept of merged families. "You can certainly think of them as your sisters," she said, stepping over the threshold, into the kitchen. Anything else Abby might have added flew right out of her mind at the utter chaos facing her.

No wonder the kids were having such a high old time! Yesterday, one of Kirk's gifts had been a game called Jumpin' Monkeys. Abby had taught them all how to play it last night. It was simple enough, consisting of a plastic tree needing some assembly. Each child had a springboard playing piece and several plastic monkeys. Turn by turn, the players were supposed to try catapulting their monkeys into the tree. Those with the most monkeys in the tree at the end won. Only…this morning the monkeys and trees remained in the box. Her darling, ingenious sextet had substituted Cheerios for the playing pieces. Half the kitchen stood ankle deep in crunchy cereal.

Crunchy because Abby walked on them as she entered the room.

A ring of guilt-stricken faces spun toward her at Abby's muffled, ''Oh, my God!''

Noah, the guiltiest-looking and therefore probably the ringleader, leaped up and crunched across to meet her. ''Au-Aunt Ab-Ab-Abby. I've been watchin' the clock on the stove. We were gonna clean this all up before your alarm went off. Honest.''

Torn between wanting to laugh or sit and cry, Abby expended a herculean effort in maintaining her cool. She might have pulled it off if a half-asleep and barefoot Ben Galloway hadn't shown up to step on the cereal, too. His yelp as he hopped around swearing woke Ruffian.

In defense of his territory, the big dog sank his teeth in the flapping cuff of Ben's jeans, prompting a loud, ''Dammit!'' from Ben.

Abby wished she could go back upstairs and restart her day. ''Ben, stop leaping around like a demented fool. Kids, somebody put Ruffian outside. The rest of you, find brooms and a dustpan or two.''

Shoving Sam, who was sobbing hysterically, into Ben's arms, Abby knelt down and swept away enough cereal to allow some of the kids access to the pantry where the brooms hung on the wall.

''I'm not even going to ask the obvious—like what in God's name happened in here,'' Ben hollered at Abby's stiff back.

"I guess if you wanted to reach far enough, you could add this to a list of your father's sins." Abby duckwalked through the space she'd cleared with her hands. "But that would really be reaching. He and Lily gave the kids that monkey game. These darlings, however, have taken it upon themselves to completely remake the rules."

"I guess it'd be too much to expect a cup of coffee to magically appear."

"That's an excellent idea. Take Sam and run to Starbucks. There's one three blocks down the street, toward the school. Sam likes their hot chocolate with a double shot of milk. Bring me something strong and black—please."

"Should I bring donuts, too?" Ben asked, backing from the room.

"Are you kidding?" Abby glared. "Do any of these little monsters look like they need to start their day with a sugar high?"

Ben withdrew with as much composure as he could muster. He made a side trip upstairs to get his shoes.

Abby waited until the front door shut behind them before she launched into a string of lectures. Soon after, the floor tiles gleamed again and bags of dirty cereal had made their way into the trash.

Twenty minutes later, Ben returned, holding a take-out carton with two cups of coffee, and Sam, whose mouth was ringed by the hot chocolate he'd consumed.

Six kids sat silently scarfing up toast and scrambled eggs, even though Ben knew for a fact that Mollie detested scrambled eggs.

Abby accepted a steaming coffee from him. She set the other at Ben's usual spot. "Sit, and I'll dish you up some eggs and toast. These guys are almost done. That's good, as they have a school bus to catch."

Ben didn't like eggs in any form. He grabbed his cup,

dropped a kiss on top of Abby's hair and transferred Sam to her arms. "Thanks, but I've gotta scoot. I have exactly thirty minutes to get to the clinic. Kids, have a good day. Sam, remember what I said about trying everything the PT asks you to do."

"Hey!" Abby clutched Ben's sleeve. "Doesn't your clinic open at ten?"

"We're starting summer hours. Did I forget to mention it?"

"Does that mean you'll be home early?" Abby brightened at the possibility.

"No guarantee I'll get out any faster. I rarely do. Our receptionist uses summer hours as an excuse to book more patients." Noting how fast Abby's eagerness fled, Ben felt bad for blaming Pat, his receptionist, for his longer office hours. "Look, I'll do my best to get out on time. And when I'm home, I'll do some fun stuff with the kids."

They all shouted, "Hooray!" There ensued a series of suggestions. One brave—or foolish—kid proposed teaching Ben how to play Jumpin' Monkeys.

"No way." Abby rejected that idea. "This game's going into the hall closet until you convince me by your behavior that I can trust you to play it right."

They all sobered. One after another, they scooted back their chairs, carried their empty plates to the sink and filed out of the kitchen, mumbling, "Excuse us."

Ben wagged an eyebrow. "Wow! Apparently I didn't need to bring you a copy of my discipline brochure."

"I told you I can get tough when it's warranted."

"I wish we knew why, all of a sudden, they're provoking us at every turn. Or is this normal for boys?"

"No. Wait. You assume the boys led your nieces down the garden path?"

"I used to baby-sit the girls. Except for Mollie being stubborn as hell, they're usually sweet as cotton candy."

"You could be right." She sighed heavily. "I've requested counseling at school for—" Cutting her gaze to Sam, who was far too alert, she finished lamely, "For two of them. Today I'll drop by the school to see if they have results on the preliminary psych workups."

"Good plan. Like I said, I've gotta dash. Sam, see you later." Ben did some complicated handshake he and the boy had obviously worked out. Sam puffed up like a peacock. Any fool could see he'd taken a shine to Ben.

Abby waved Ben off, and handed lunch money to the older kids as they came down to collect their backpacks. She finished her coffee, then gave Sam a sponge bath, taking care not to get his cast wet. "Okay, kid, now it's our turn to fly out of the house. With luck, we'll squeak into the PT clinic just in time for your appointment."

"We don't got wings." Sam laughed, his dimples reminding Abby so poignantly of a youthful Elliot. Whenever things like that happened, it struck her like a body blow, reminding her of their loss.

Halfway through Sam's appointment, Abby's cell phone rang. The elementary school, she saw from the readout. Her heart dropped to her toes. The wall clock indicated it was recess-time for second- and third-graders, and she immediately feared one of the kids had gotten hurt on the playground.

"Hello," she said, gripping the phone tightly. "Abby Drummond, er—Galloway, I mean."

Mr. Conrad, the principal, stammered. "So it's true you got married, Abigail?"

"Yes. Is that the reason for your call, Mr. Conrad? Do you need to change school records?"

"I'm calling because I have your nephew, Noah, in detention. Well, he's getting patched up by the nurse. Later he'll be in detention for getting into a fistfight with Jason Bingham.''

"Did Noah start the brawl?'' Jason was the boy Abby considered a hoodlum-in-waiting.

"I'm punishing them both because neither will talk. As usual I can't reach anyone at the Binghams'. Oops, I forgot you're on leave. I shouldn't say things about one parent to another. But please, Abby, could you drop in and see what you can pry out of Noah?''

"Sure. I'm at the physical therapist's with Sam. I can be there by noon, unless they decide to exchange Sam's cast for braces today. I'll phone back if it looks like I'll run late.''

The therapist did cut off Sam's cast. Abby phoned Mr. Conrad back, and then she called Ben. "Do you have a minute? You do? Good. I asked because we never discussed your policy about wives bothering you at work.''

"Wife, singular. Bother me anytime,'' he said with a smile in his voice. "Is everything okay? You sound—I don't know—harried?''

"I am. They're cutting off Sam's cast and he's crying his head off for you. On top of it, the school phoned. Noah's in trouble for fighting on the playground.''

"Can I talk to Sam? There's no way I can leave. I have a full waiting room. As for Noah, I'm probably the last person who should intervene in that situation.''

Abby kicked her toe against the PT's metal desk. "I disagree, Ben. I'm expected to deal with the girls. One of these days, you'll have to take a hand in correcting the boys. Wait, can you hear Sam? They're bringing him back from X ray. We'll discuss the older boys another time. Please just see what you can do to calm Sam.''

Whatever Ben said worked like magic. Sam's tears dried

instantly as he listened raptly to his new best friend. Abby couldn't help feeling somewhat put out. But maybe, as Ben said, she was just extra harried today.

When Sam handed the phone back, Abby's irritation flared again at his remark. "If I stop fussing, Ben's gonna take me to get an ice cream cone when he gets home." *Bribery?* That was Ben's answer to a tantrum?

She let her anger slide once she learned that Sam still had to be carried everywhere for two more weeks. At least his moon boot and brace harness were half the weight his full casts had been.

"Can we stop for a cheeseburger?" Sam asked from his booster.

"No, honey. I have to go to the school. Mr. Conrad needs to see me a minute."

"But I'm hun-gry," Sam wailed.

"So am I. Hey, it's nearly time for Mollie's class to eat. Would you like to have lunch with her in the cafeteria while I talk with the principal?" As it turned out, it was a great solution to what Abby had feared might turn into a problem. Namely what to do with Sam while she grilled Noah.

She hurried into the detention room. Noah sat slumped on one side of the room; Jason did the same on the other. A student monitor from the high school occupied a desk in the middle. He waved to Abby. "Hi, Ms. Drummond."

"Hi, yourself, Vic. But it's Ms. Galloway now. I got married since we last spoke. May I have a private word with my nephew?"

"Sure. Jason's been bugging me about going to the bathroom." The monitor left with the other boy in tow. Abby squeezed into the desk beside Noah.

"I know you boys think silence is macho. That doesn't work with me, Noah. I have the power to ground you until you're twenty-one."

Noah shot her a sullen look. "So what! Jason yanked off Erin's glasses and threw them on the ground. They didn't break, but they could have. He's a big bully. When she started crying, he just laughed. I told him to stop picking on my sister. He called me a liar."

"Oh." The air fled from Abby's lungs. "Uh…how did Erin react? Did she tell the playground teacher what happened?"

"She tried. Wouldn't nobody listen."

"I'll set them straight today. And Noah, even though you were wrong to solve your differences with your fists, I'm proud of you for standing up for Erin."

"It's no big deal." Noah shrugged.

Abby thought it was a very big deal. She spent half an hour with Mr. Conrad. When she'd collected Sam from the cafeteria, she tried twice to call Ben from the van. Abby thought Noah's good deed deserved a reward—like going out for ice cream. Ben had already promised Sam an ice-cream cone; this way, Ben wouldn't appear to be favoring Sam.

But it wasn't to be. Not only did they not connect, but Ben rang the house ten minutes past the time he was due home. "Abby, count me out for the evening. I just got a call from an obstetrician who sends Steve and me the majority of his new babies. He's got a diabetic mom in premature labor. Unless we're damned lucky, her baby's in for a rough start."

"Oh, Ben, I'm sorry for her. But can't Steve take this one? I mean, you were at the hospital half the night. And I have some remarkable news for you about Noah's trouble at school." She lowered her voice, in case one of the children was in a position to overhear.

"Abby, I have to run. Premature babies don't wait. Whatever it is with Noah, you deal with it. That's why it's a good thing you're at home. Oh, and don't wait up. I have no idea how late I'll be.'' The phone went dead in Abby's ear. She held it against her breast until it started to bleat loudly. Anger cruised through her, setting her heart thumping. She slammed the phone back in its cradle, all the while muttering unkind things about Dr. Benjamin Galloway.

CHAPTER THIRTEEN

ABBY LOADED the kids in the van. She'd waited until she could talk calmly about Ben's emergency. "He promised to take Sam for ice cream to celebrate getting his cast off. I say we *all* deserve double-dip cones."

It was in the ice-cream parlor that Abby first noticed how disreputable the boys' sneakers were. Not the girls; theirs were pristine by comparison. The boys' shoes had holes, caked dirt and broken laces. The tongue on one of Reed's was gone. Never one to use shopping as a balm, Abby found that tonight the diversion held more appeal than spending a long, empty evening arguing over baths and homework.

Taking seven children to a shoe store at one time, she soon discovered, was not the brightest decision she'd ever made. First, the store had a buy-one-pair-get-a-second-for-a-dollar sale in progress. Then Sam and the girls began to cry the minute Abby said they *weren't* getting new shoes.

Mike tugged at Abby's sleeve. "Sam's the one Mommy was taking to get shoes the day of the earthquake."

Abby recalled her last conversation with Elliot. How could she refuse Sam's request after that eloquent appeal by his brother? And the therapist had indicated he'd want Sam to start bearing weight soon. But if she reversed her decision for Sam, how could she tell the girls no? They coveted sneakers with heel lights, plus black patent dress shoes.

"We could add the black ones for only a dollar apiece," Erin pointed out.

The seven dollars for add-ons didn't bother Abby. Math happened to be one of her strengths. She didn't need to see the register tape to know the final bill was staggering.

Amid the kids' happy chatter on the drive home, it struck Abby that perhaps she should've run a purchase this large past Ben. *You didn't spend a dime on yourself,* a niggling voice said. *And you wouldn't have shopped for shoes if Ben had followed through on his promise to Sam.*

Clearly the kids needed shoes. But what about *her* needs? Abby had entered this marriage with an image of her and Ben sitting on the porch over coffee, jointly setting guidelines for raising their brood. So far it was a pipe dream. She shrugged, somewhat disconsolate. Oh, well, when it came to spending money on the children, once she returned to work, she'd feel freer to do that.

Typical of kids, they ran into the house and dropped their shoe bags on the living room floor. Each took the pair he or she wanted to wear to school, tore off the tags and left stuffing paper strewn across the carpet. The mess greeted Abby, who'd had to close the garage and carry Sam and his shoe boxes inside.

"Kids, clean up this mess," she ordered. "Noah and Mike, feed Ruffian, please. Erin and Mollie, Blackberry's water dish is dry."

"It's late. We have homework," the three older children announced.

Of course they did. In two weeks, the Iowa tests would be administered district-wide. Teachers took stock of low grades and poor performance about now. Panicked, they made last ditch efforts to cram learning into their students' vacant little heads.

"Okay. I'll feed the animals tonight, but don't forget

who bought your shoes. You can clean this room when you're finished with homework.''

"Thank you, Aunt Abby!" Their voices chimed together so sweetly, she couldn't help smiling as she set Sam in the living room and went to care for the pets.

"Did anyone feed the fish today?" She stopped to read the schedule Elliot had taped to the wall. "Yikes," she muttered. "It was time to put in fresh water and the solution designed to keep the tanks clean." She mentally added that to her list of must-dos before bedtime.

Because the kids were excited over their shoes, their energy levels rose. For every notch theirs went up, Abby's dropped. By eleven she was dragging. When the last muffled giggle died, there was still no message from Ben. As Abby toured the house, shutting off lights and checking door locks, she saw that the living room still looked as if a cyclone had hit. Those little connivers hadn't picked up one tag or sack. They'd counted on her to do it. "Too bad!" Getting her body up those steps one last time tonight was all she could manage. Tomorrow the little angels would learn she wasn't their maid.

BEN STUMPED UP the front steps. He was almost too exhausted to choose the right key and shove it in the lock. If the night had been a bit warmer, he might have sacked out on the glider. April was still cool. Tonight, he couldn't work up any enthusiasm for the salty smell of the wind blowing off Puget Sound—or even Abby's warm and willing body waiting upstairs. All he wanted was sleep.

In spite of modern medical miracles, he'd left a struggling baby in the hands of infant ICU nurses. Prematurity had been the least of their worries. A fragile, three-pound diabetic baby couldn't tolerate normal glucose feedings. But the red, wrinkled prune of a kid was a fighter. That, plus prayers, might get her through the night. He should have stayed. But once he'd done all he could, the staff, knowing he was a newlywed, had literally kicked him out. Any minute, though, he could get called back.

A dark, silent house suited him. Having taken on a ready-made family, Ben understood, for the first time, why his colleagues wanted calm and order in their own lives. After long, draining nights of yanking kids back from the brink of death, all they wanted to do was make sure their own kids were safe and sound.

The multicolored glow from the wall of fish tanks seemed brighter tonight. Ben stepped into the living room to see why and tripped over boxes and lids scattered everywhere. *Shoe boxes?* "What the hell?"

Scrabbling for the lamp, he finally found a switch and blinked at the stuff strewn clear across the floor. He heard a rattle and a crunch coming from the biggest pile. Blackberry wiggled out of a large bag, sprang into the air and pounced on the heap as if she were a kitten again. Ben laughed in spite of himself. Then sobered suddenly.

Even if the kids had been playing hide-and-seek with their pets before bedtime, Abby ought to have made them clean up this room afterward.

It wasn't until Ben began gathering up sacks that he discovered not all the boxes were empty. Some were filled. *With new shoes. A lot of new shoes. Girls' dress shoes.* A receipt fell out of one bag as Ben tried to stuff the box back. Casually, he glanced at the slip, then did a double-take. He took the slip over to the lamp.

"Holy shit!" His eyes bugged at an amount totaling more than he'd earned in a ten-hour shift today. Add that to Friday's grocery tab, which he'd stuffed in the drawer upstairs, and he was a man fast headed into debt.

Forgetting how tired he was, Ben smacked off the light. The receipt clenched in one hand, he bounded up the stairs.

Abby emerged from sleep, blinking at a sudden infusion of light. She could do little but gape at the wild-eyed man pacing back and forth by her bed, spouting words her sleep-fogged mind couldn't comprehend. Ben still wore a wrinkled lab coat, and his tie hung loose, flapping as he paced.

She covered her eyes. "Stop, Ben! I can't make sense of anything you're saying."

He leaned close to her. "I want an explanation as to why seven kids need fourteen pair of new shoes in one fell swoop."

"Oh, the shoes! I can explain."

"Good."

Abby licked her lips, but said nothing.

"You can begin anytime."

Where to start? At the beginning? "We went for ice cream."

Ben waved the foot-long receipt under her nose.

"I have to tell this my way, Ben. You'd promised Sam ice cream, if you recall. And Noah did a good thing today. Well, good and bad." She shrugged, and her strap fell off her shoulder. She stopped talking to tug it up.

"It's almost one o'clock, Abby. Can you get to the point?"

"I am," she said, raising her voice. "Noah got in trouble on the playground. Because he stuck up for Erin. And Ben—you won't believe this. In explaining what happened, Noah referred to Erin as *his sister*."

She smiled so prettily, Ben was left opening and closing his mouth like a guppy.

"Isn't that progress?"

"Hey, that's great!" Ben nodded—but then he frowned. "Back to the shoes, Abby. Or should I say back to how ice cream led you to buy fourteen pairs of shoes.'' Again he shook the receipt, and Abby sighed.

''The ice cream didn't. Well, not exactly. As the kids ate their cones, I noticed the boys' sneakers were falling apart. I planned to replace the worst. But once we piled into the store, I realized that Mike and Brad's shoes were too small. Sammy cried, because I said he didn't need shoes yet. Mike reminded me that Blair was taking him to get shoes the day of the quake. It's why she rode downtown with Elliot. So I capitulated. But how could I leave out the girls? If you'd seen their faces, Ben…''

''All right. All right.'' He opened the desk drawer and threw the credit card receipt on the stack. ''That accounts for seven pairs. What about the others?''

''Erin brought my attention to a store sale. If we bought full-priced sneakers, the dress shoes cost only a dollar a pair. I need to get them back into Sunday school, and at that price, it just made good sense.''

''I see. After being hit with the national debt, you mean seven bucks wouldn't sink the fleet? Except it might,'' Ben muttered, dragging a hand through his hair.

''Oh, dear, did I bring us into financial ruin?''

''No. I can take care of my family, Abby.'' He practically snarled as Kirk's taunt flashed through his mind. Dropping into a chair, Ben slipped off his loafers. Wadding up his stained lab coat, he jammed it into an overflowing laundry basket. ''I'm down to my last clean lab jacket. What day do you do laundry?''

''Ben, I do laundry almost every day. Do you have any idea how many loads it takes to keep this family in T-shirts, socks and underwear?''

He shook his head. ''A bunch, I'm sure.'' He looked guilty for adding his shirt to the growing heap. His sigh actually shook the bed when he pulled off his pants and fell back on the pillow, flinging one arm over his face. "God, I'm tired."

"How'd it go with the baby?" Abby asked as she switched off the lamp.

"So-so. Don't be surprised if I get a page before morning."

Abby glanced at the glowing clock. "Technically it *is* morning." She rustled the covers as she turned toward him and grazed her fingers lightly over his bare chest.

Ben had thought he was too tired to perform tonight. Kissing Abby's fingers, he knew he was dead wrong.

"Did you stop in Sam's room to check out his brace and air casts? He gets to remove the brace and harness at night. Or were you too furious at me over the shoes to look in on the kids?"

"I intended to, until I tripped over the damned boxes. I'm sorry if I sound petty, Abby, but dammit, I don't expect to kill myself walking into my house at night."

"That's my fault. I told the kids to clean up. Later, when I saw they'd ignored me I was too tired, and I decided they could just clean it up tomorrow."

Ben slid his hands up and down the slick satin of her nightgown. "How tired *are* you?" he asked, inching up the fabric with one hand while groping for a mylar packet with the other.

"Not that tired," she whispered against his lips.

Their lovemaking that night was slow, sensual and delicious. They fell into a rhythm that left them both satisfied.

Sleep claimed Ben first. Abby snuggled against him, spoon fashion, feeling boneless and exquisitely tired. Just now, she really believed there was no problem they couldn't solve as long as they continued to communicate so well in bed. She understood why Ben worried about the growing number of bills. Which only underscored that the sooner she got back to work, the better. A yawn interrupted her musing. She let her eyes drift shut. At breakfast, she'd talk to Ben about a realistic timetable.

SHE WOKE UP to sunlight streaming through the window and a note on the pillow. "Hey, Sleeping Beauty. I've gone to meet Steve at the gym. I'll grab coffee on the way to the clinic. Tell Sam I said his new cast looks really space-age. I saw his list of exercises. I should have fifteen minutes or so to work with him before I head back to my new job in ER, provided you have supper on at six." He'd signed it, *Ben.*

Frowning, Abby tucked the note into the pocket of her robe. What did he mean *new job?* Didn't he see patients in the ER whenever he was on call? Granted, during their dating phase, days had passed without their even speaking.

Downstairs, she found the living room devoid of last night's clutter. The kids were grouped around the breakfast table, except for Sam, who tended to sleep late. She knew he'd feel bad about missing Ben.

"Hi, troops. This is a much improved scene over yesterday morning. I'm glad to see you're all so self-sufficient, but why didn't you get me up?"

"Unca Ben said to let you sleep," Mollie said. "Are you sick or somethin', Abby?"

"I'm fine, honey. Why?"

Erin paused with her spoon halfway to her lips. "Uncle Ben was really grouchy. He said we need to help you more, 'cause you're too tired to pick up after us. Abby, are you gonna have a baby?"

Abby, who was putting on water to heat for tea, spun around. "A baby? Where on earth did *that* notion come from?"

"Noah said his mama got real tired before she had Sam."

"Well, ah, that's not the only reason a woman gets tired." The second the explanation left her lips, Abby formed a clear and vivid picture of her and Ben's nightly ritual, which definitely contributed to her tiredness. A ritual that could lead to pregnancy if one of those condoms ever broke. *Perish the thought.* "Like we have space for a baby," she muttered darkly.

They continued to eye her as if expecting her to conjure up an expanding belly. "Look, I'm not pregnant, okay? Do you have any idea of the work involved in caring for this family, let alone a baby? Let me learn how to juggle seven of you, before you wish an eighth on me."

"Don't you like babies?" Mollie asked, sounding as if that were unthinkable.

"I do. I love them. I'm just not having one. Yet," she added firmly. "Now finish your cereal."

Later, the kids' comments nagged at Abby as she folded and put away the fourth load of laundry—between entertaining Sam, making out a grocery list and readying the evening meal. The bus delivered the kids from school, and shortly thereafter, Ben walked in. Abby realized she hadn't yet showered or put on so much as a coat of lipstick.

"I must look a fright," she murmured to Ben, who was drop-dead gorgeous as always. She made a lame attempt to control several escaping curls.

She didn't know whether his grunt meant Ben agreed, or that he felt it best to remain noncommittal. Either way, after a kiss that almost couldn't be called a kiss, he charged up the stairs. "Where's the list of Sam's exercises?" he called down over the railing. "This morning it was on his dresser."

"Don't ask me. I spent the day washing and folding

clothes. You now have four clean lab coats. Can you run your slacks to the cleaners on your way to the Emergency Room? Oh—how often will you be working there?''

"Four nights a week." Or at least that was what Abby thought she heard him say. Ben must have his head in the closet or under the bed, looking for the paper with Sam's exercises. *Four nights a week!* Her heart fell to the floor.

"Abby, I found the list folded in a towel under our bathroom sink. I've wasted ten minutes searching when I could've been working on Sam's routine.''

She wanted to ask how long Ben expected to cope with such a hectic schedule. But he disappeared into Sam's bedroom. And the doorbell rang. Abby sprinted down the hall and jerked the door open, expecting to find one of the boys' friends or a door-to-door salesman. Instead, Raina Miller smiled at her through the screen.

"Wow, this is a nice surprise.'' Abby unlocked the screen and stood aside to let her friend in. From the backyard, Ruffian went crazy barking; she heard the kids yell at him to be quiet.

"Did I catch you at a bad time, Abby? You seem frazzled.''

Ruefully, Abby smoothed a hand down her stained shirt. While she was fixing spaghetti sauce to pop into the microwave for supper, she'd splashed some on her clothes. "I'm afraid all this parenting is getting me down, Raina. I can't seem to get organized. Do you have time for coffee? I just made a fresh pot.''

"One cup, then I have to dash back to school for a parent conference.''

"I guess it's conference time, isn't it?'' Abby murmured wistfully as she filled two mugs. "I took the notices out of the kids' backpacks today. I haven't had a chance to ask

Ben when he'll be free to go. We have so many conferences, we may have to split up, even if that's not ideal.''

"When I think about your situation, Abby, I can't see
how you can possibly come back to finish out the year.''

Abby's jaw tensed. "I'll get more organized. I *am* coming back, week after next.''

Raina sipped from her cup. "I'm glad to hear it. I think
you ought to know I overheard Stacy undermining your
work to a couple of parents the other day. She's subtle but
as deadly as a black widow. I'm not the only teacher who
heard her casually tell a mom she might want to speak to
Mr. Conrad if she's happier with Stacy than with you.''

"That little bit—uh, witch," Abby stuttered. "She
wasn't my first choice as a sub, you know? Not even my
second. The others had been spoken for by the time I
phoned the district. The quake created chaos with several
schools. Most teachers will eventually reclaim their jobs.
Doesn't the little idiot understand tenure?''

Raina drained her cup and stood to hug her friend. "You
know Conrad's retiring at the end of this year. Well, last
week we all got to meet his replacement. A young stud
from one of the rural districts. I missed this, but Jill said
that at his reception our Stacy flirted outrageously. Which
he ate up. Jill thinks they may have even made a date for
drinks later that evening.''

"So, what are you saying? That this new principal has
the hots for my sub, and he might shuffle me off?''

"Exactly." Raina moved toward the door. "Conrad
won't, not if you come back as planned. But the new broom
is going to get involved next month. If Conrad steps aside
early, and if you need to start taking time off for Sam…''
She let her comments hang. "Speaking of Sam, how's he
doing?''

"He's in a moon cast and a new brace. But he has therapy three times a week. By next week they hope he'll take a few steps. Holding on to my job is important to the family. And it's vital to my sanity, Raina. Ben obviously has to figure out a way to adjust his schedule so he can take Sam to therapy.''

''Where *is* the hunk?''

''Upstairs working on Sam's at-home exercise program.''

''Will Ben be able to get away from his clinic, do you think?''

''He'll have to.'' Abby started to mention the tussle they'd had over the shoes, but thought better of it. Raina complained frequently about the low pay her husband received as a cop. She was among those who thought the word *doctor* was synonymous with *rich*.

''Well, see ya, Abby. If I don't run I'll be late.''

Abby had closed the door behind her friend, but lingered in the hall with her hand on the doorknob.

''What are you doing, Abby?'' Ben tripped lightly down the stairs. ''Are you calling the kids in for supper?''

She glanced at her watch. ''I haven't put the spaghetti noodles on yet. And I still have to make garlic bread. Want to come give me a hand? We haven't had time for any real conversation lately.''

''Didn't I say in my note that if I'm going to eat dinner with you and the kids, it has to be ready at six?''

She stared at him blankly. ''Yes, but we never eat until seven. Especially now with the weather warming up. The kids want to play outside with their friends.''

''Oh. No problem, then. I can grab something at the hospital cafeteria. I left Sam in the living room watching TV. Are the girls out with the boys? I probably have twenty minutes or so to shoot hoops. I think Sam said that's what they're doing.''

Abby watched him stride out the back door. She wrestled with the question of managing supper by six. She got off work at four, but depending on how far away Sam's new day care was, she'd arrive home anytime between four-thirty and five-thirty. Unless Ben picked him up. Abby figured there were enough after-school activities to keep the older kids at the elementary until four o'clock. Okay, with a lot of carefully planned meals, she ought to make it work. No doubt about it, she *would* make it work.

She hummed while preparing the garlic bread. Ben breezed in again. He paused behind her to nuzzle a kiss on her neck. Abby began to turn around, only to find him dashing away, out of the kitchen.

"Hey," she hollered. "That was a miserly kiss, Dr. Galloway."

He poked his head back into the room. "Sorry. That's all I've got time for. Pity me. That sniff of your perfume is enough to drive me nuts all evening. I honest to God have no idea when you can expect me home."

Abby bit her lip. "You mean, you're not just on call tonight?"

"Yes and no." He pulled his medical bag out of the hall closet. "This is my first night on this particular job. Oh, and I don't know if I said I'll be at West, not Children's Health Hospital."

"Why?" Abby was really confused now.

"They've been after me for months. It's in a big, new residential area. I guess they get a lot of bike, skateboard and football accidents involving kids. The ER chief needed a pediatrician on evenings and nights."

"Kids skateboard after dark?"

Ben shrugged. "We'll have to talk about this later. I don't want to be late my first night."

Unhappily, Abby wondered when Ben thought they'd

make time to talk about anything when he was continually on his way in or out of their revolving front door.

"Jeez, if I don't get out of here now, I'll end up staying. That spaghetti smells great. Save me some and I'll warm it up for breakfast."

"Spaghetti for breakfast?" she scoffed.

"Sure. We single guys eat all kinds of leftovers for breakfast."

"You're not single," Abby snapped. Too late, because Ben's booming goodbye to Sam overrode her words. Next thing she heard was the slam of the front door, followed by the distinctive growl of Ben's BMW.

With seven boisterous children to fill her evening, Abby wasn't exactly sure why she felt lonely. But the feeling persisted long after she'd tucked the last kid into bed. She missed Ben, and longed for him to call. She could phone him, she supposed. But her memory of the busy emergency room at Mercy General held her back. How happy would she be if Ben had to brush her off, anyway?

Abby cleaned the bird's cage and put fresh wood chips in the gerbil and hamster cages. There was nothing on TV fit to watch. She picked up a book of Elliot's she'd been meaning to read. Finding it difficult to concentrate, she eventually put it aside. Hating to just pace, she dug through her long-discarded schoolbag, pulled out a ruled tablet and sat down at the table with a cup of Earl Gray tea. Within the hour, she'd drawn up a typical week's schedule for their household.

Although, what was typical for them? At this point, she had no real idea. She sipped her tea and pondered that until the phone rang. Sure it was Ben, she snatched it up. The caller turned out to be Lily, although at first her voice was almost unrecognizable.

"Abby, I shouldn't phone you so late. But I wanted you

to know I've left Kirk. Something in your expression on Sunday, when Kirk acted like such an ass, gave me the courage to tell him a lot of things someone's needed to say to that man for a long time.''

"Oh, Lily! I'm sorry. It wasn't my place to object to his treatment of you.''

"It woke me up. Oh, I love the jackass. He's brilliant, you know. But I told him that doesn't give him the right to think he's God's gift to the world. Today I found a job. But...if you and Ben don't object, I'd still like to play adopted grandmother to your kids.''

Abby's eyes misted over. "It would be good for them, Lily. I can't speak for Ben, but you're certainly welcome here anytime I'm around.''

"Thank you. Well, I'll let you go. I'll phone again after I get my life in order.''

Rinsing her cup, Abby wandered upstairs, and tried to imagine Ben's reaction.

BEN DROVE SLOWLY up the street toward a house which should, by now, feel as if he belonged there. He didn't know why, but he still felt like a stranger coming to visit Abby. It was nothing she'd said or done that he could identify. So it probably had more to do with his own upbringing. Kirk, and his mom when she lived with them, considered an address more important for its ability to impress colleagues than for any type of family life. Ben didn't want that to be the case with him. Yet tonight, when the ER chief introduced him around, Ben caught the murmurs in response to where he lived in the high-rent beach district. Later, he realized he hadn't corrected the staffs' assumption. Could it be that, like his dad, he derived satisfaction from his colleagues' envy?

He answered that with a resounding *no*. He ought to have

set them straight about the condition—and the fact of the house—and the fact that it actually belonged to the boys. Now it troubled Ben to think he hadn't admitted that straight away.

Maybe that was the crux of his unrest. Taking into account the hours he spent away from home and family, what *was* his role in this house? Was he uncle, friend or simply Abby's always absent husband? Did a man have the right to claim the title of stepfather by virtue of being the main breadwinner?

Gazing at the black windows, it struck Ben that he spent more time on the outside looking in on a slumbering household than he did looking out.

He unlocked the door. He probably just needed to get used to working day and night again. He'd managed okay during his internship and residency. Ben knew he could handle a tough schedule. So what if the hiatus of the past few years had seemed a happier existence?

Or was that a fair description of his bachelor days? From the first night he met Abby, he'd pictured her in his future. He thought the feeling was mutual.

Ben greeted Ruffian before making his nightly circuit of the fish tanks and birdcage. The blue, green and violet hues cast by the tank lights relaxed him. All was quiet downstairs.

As he made rounds of the children's rooms, not even the rodent pets, as he'd labeled Harry, Speedy and Poky, were up running in their wheels. Everyone but him had apparently settled down for the night. Did that mean they'd also settled into a family routine?

Ben noticed that Mollie slept with her arms above her head the way she'd done as a contented infant. And Erin's face, bathed in moonlight, didn't twitch. Nor was her brow creased in a frown, which had become habitual after Marlo's death.

Shuffling out, Ben pulled off his tie and unbuttoned the cuffs of his blue shirt. This afternoon, in the short time he'd spent with the kids, Erin had clued him in about Noah's playground fight. Ben realized belatedly that it was the incident Abby had tried to tell him about when he dashed off to see the diabetic baby. He hadn't found time to fill Abby in on that case, either. Maybe tomorrow they could grab coffee together and catch up. Could they sit on the back porch and watch the sun rise?

An attractive prospect—although not as attractive as feeling her curl against him in her sleep before he nudged her awake to make love as they'd done every night.

Ben supposed he shouldn't be disappointed to find Abby dead to the world. But he was. She didn't move even slightly when he locked the door. Nor did she wiggle as he crawled in beside her. And he didn't expend all that much effort on trying to be quiet. He reached across her to reset the clock, which would allow them that half hour on the porch.

Still not so much as a tic of her eyelids.

Ben lay there for a moment, debating whether to wake her. In the end, he decided against it, and rolled over, placing his back toward her. The kids had probably worn her out. Surely this didn't mean the bloom had worn off their marriage. There were a lot of reasons newlyweds didn't make love nightly. Except that he knew from comments made by his newly married pals, this wasn't the norm. Nightly bouts of lovemaking was a feat those guys bragged about ad nauseam for months.

But then, few aspects of their marriage could be described as normal. Flopping flat on his back, Ben shut his eyes. The soft mattress and Abby's warm skin eventually had a drugging effect that soon overpowered his physical need. And he slept.

ABBY'S EYES FLEW OPEN. Bolting upright, she reached for her robe. Someone was trying to kick down her bedroom door. Goodness, had she inadvertently locked Ben out?

But no, he vaulted up beside her. "The sun—what time is it?"

She grabbed the alarm clock. "Holy cow! This says eight-thirty. Is that a.m. or p.m.?"

"A.M." Ben leaped off the bed, yanked slacks and shirt out of the closet and slammed into the adjoining bath. "I thought I set the clock last night to give us time to have coffee together. I must've screwed up."

"Obviously." Dragging on her robe, Abby opened the bedroom door. Six of the seven kids huddled outside, eyes big as saucers.

"Noah said we missed the bus," Brad announced.

"Ohhh," Abby moaned. "Have you eaten? I'll have to drive you to school. Is Sam awake? If not, Mike and Noah, get him up and help him dress. He's due in physical therapy in forty-five minutes." She shut the door in their faces and threw on yesterday's clothes.

"I'm taking the kids to school," she called to Ben, who'd jumped in the shower. "Write your schedule on the kitchen blackboard. From school, I'm taking Sam to PT. Darn," she grumbled. "I'm dying to tell you about Lily's phone call. She left your father."

Ben had his head under the water and didn't hear a word.

Abby expected some kind of response, but shrugged when she got none. "Huh!"

Boy, she hated days that started off behind the eight ball. Abby didn't draw another full breath until Sam's therapist escorted him into the exercise room. She opened a magazine, but couldn't concentrate. Sam's loud cries had her flinging the magazine aside and forging her way into the room.

"It's okay, Mrs. Galloway. We put Sam on the stationary bike. It hurts because his muscles haven't had to work in weeks. By the end of this visit, he'll be taking a few steps with a walker."

Tears flooded Abby's eyes. "Oh, Sammy. I know it hurts, hon, but you want to walk and run again so you can play with the other kids."

"I want Ben," he sobbed. "Call Daddy Ben."

The term sent Abby into a tailspin. "Ah...wouldn't it be better to do what the therapist says? When Ben gets home, you can show him everything you've learned."

The child nodded and clenched his teeth against the pain. When the session was ended, Sam and Abby were both sweating. But he took two steps with a walker.

"Do you want him walking only here at the clinic?" Abby inquired. "Or is there someplace we can rent a walker for home use? His fath—er, my husband is a doctor. He helps Sam with the patterning exercises. It would mean so much if Sam could meet Ben at the door."

"Not yet. We don't want him to overdo it. No more than three steps at a time, two or three times a day for a week. On Monday, we'll repeat X rays. Depending on how well the bone has knit with Kirk Galloway's mesh and pins, we may increase Sam's time with the walker."

"I've been meaning to ask. By next week, I have to return to work. I'm a teacher. I'll need to find a suitable day care for Sam. Can he safely go to day care?"

"Not to a regular facility. Down on California Avenue there's a great spot set up for handicapped kids, and they're equipped to keep up Sam's therapy. If you'd like, I can phone them and ask if they have any openings. It'd be perfect for Sam. The only thing is, it's a bit more costly than regular day care.''

''How much more? Like I said, I teach. Everyone knows what we earn.''

The PT laughed. ''I doubt you'll find it more than ten bucks a day beyond the regular fees. Here, I'll dial the number and let you speak with Pam Lenz. She owns the center. She's an occupational therapist who started the school when her own son fell skiing and needed both knee-caps replaced.''

Abby found Pam to be sympathetic and understanding of her budget constraints. The center did have an opening, and Mrs. Lenz said Abby could probably get partial assistance through Elliot's medical policy, which was in effect to the end of the year.

Feeling that things were finally falling in place, Abby returned home in a better frame of mind after stopping at the home health store to rent Sam a walker.

Ben hadn't left her a note on the community blackboard. Nor any message on her machine. She tried calling him to say she was going grocery shopping but that she'd definitely have dinner ready by six.

''I'm sorry, Mrs. Galloway. Ben had to rearrange his appointments so he could see a very sick baby at the hospital. Thyroid cancer, he believes. Rare but hopeful, if they've caught it in time. He's running all the tests himself.''

''So, are you saying he won't be home by five?''

The woman laughed. ''Definitely not. I've just spent an hour rescheduling his afternoon. He wants to see the last patient and be out of here by seven-fifteen, which just gives him time to grab a bite and get to his duty at West. He asked me to phone you and explain his predicament. I tried three times, but never caught you at home. You ladies of leisure are hard to pin down.'' The receptionist chuckled, setting Abby's blood pressure soaring.

She barely managed a civil thanks. And burned under the collar the entire time she took Sam grocery shopping and back. Hauling him and a ton of groceries up from the car was no fun, either. Especially as the sack filled with oranges ripped, sending a million of them—or so it seemed, rolling into the street.

Her bad mood only grew worse as the day wore on. Abby spoke crossly to Sam, who asked every five minutes when Ben was coming home to watch him walk.

At dinner, the older kids wouldn't stop horsing around. Someone, Abby couldn't determine who, knocked a gallon of milk onto the floor. Most of it drained out, to the delight of Ruffian and Blackberry.

''That's it! I've had enough of your hijinks for one day. After dinner you'll all do your homework, then go straight to bed. I want the lot of you asleep by eight-thirty.''

''That's not fair, Aunt Abby.'' Looking unhappy, they whispered among themselves. ''What are hijinks?'' she heard someone ask.

But she closed her ears. And not wanting to hear any excuses from Ben, Abby unplugged the phone, turned off her cell and sank neck-deep into a rosemary-and-lavender bubble bath. There wasn't a sound from the kids' rooms, and she steeped until her skin wrinkled. All the while, she wondered why her marriage wasn't turning out the way she'd always dreamed. Remembering Lily's call, it entered Abby's mind that Ben Galloway might be more of a chip off the old block than he'd care to admit.

CHAPTER FOURTEEN

IN THE MORNING, Abby saw that Ben had come home sometime after she went to sleep, but he hadn't disturbed her. Not that she would've welcomed him with open arms. The fact that he didn't wake her and suggest they make love proved which direction their marriage was headed, didn't it? Straight down the drain.

She went through her morning ritual, attempting to be quiet. Her eyes kept straying to her sleeping husband. The state of his side of the bed indicated he'd suffered a restless night. Abby worried that something bad had happened to the baby Ben's receptionist, Pat, had told her about yesterday. Thyroid cancer in one so small sounded heartbreaking.

Was it her imagination, or did Ben's face look more drawn than when they were dating? Leaning closer to the mirror, Abby peered at her own face. She saw the same corkscrew red curls. The same freckles that so irritated her. Maybe she had more fine lines fanning out from her eyes, which were otherwise the same shade of hazel. She didn't have time to worry about a few lines.

A scruffy face suddenly appeared in the mirror cheek to cheek with her. A gritty voice rumbled near her ear, causing her to shriek.

Ben laughed, spun her around and smothered her shriek with a mind-numbing kiss. A hard, demanding kiss, which made perfectly clear that while he may not have awakened her to make love last night, it was uppermost in his mind now.

The minute Abby caught her breath, she wedged a space between them. "Ben, the children," she said shakily.

"Can, um, fend for themselves while I say good morning to my wife." As if he couldn't hear pounding feet or loud voices in the hall, he lifted Abby and carried her into the bathroom. Deliberately locking the door, he spun the shower dials. As he was already naked, he proceeded to divest Abby of the clothes she'd just donned.

"Ben, I took a bath last night." Because she was ticklish, Abby wiggled and squirmed and laughed against her will. And when Ben pulled her under the warm spray, closed the shower door and backed her against the cool tile with his hot, pulsing body, her protests grew feeble and then trailed off. This was new territory for Abby. She'd always found Ben's hands fascinating and manly. And that was before she'd experienced the delight of watching those same hands smooth soapy lather over every inch of her body. At first she didn't participate, but as the steam built in the tiny enclosure and along the exposed skin Ben stroked with his clever hands, Abby's desire exploded.

She returned his ministrations, loving the friction as she soaped the hair-roughened portions of Ben's muscular body.

Then he cupped his hands beneath her thighs and instructed her in a husky order to, "Circle my hips with your legs, Abby." She shivered uncontrollably and felt as if she were drowning in the stinging pinpoints of cooling water. Sensations and textures came alive. Heat built inside her until all at once Abby was rocked by a series of small convulsions. Again and again and again. Clinging to Ben, she was positive she had nothing left. Then he wrung from her one final orgasm. A volcanic eruption sending her sky-rocketing like nothing had before.

Ben's arms, braced against the back wall of the shower, shook. His broad chest heaved.

Slowly opening her eyes, Abby expected to see herself flying in electrically charged bits around the stall, mixed with water and steam. What she saw were Ben's brown eyes, dark and bottomless with tender passion.

"Good morning." He smiled devilishly, yet his kiss was soft.

"Good morning yourself." Abby needed the shower wall for support. She discovered that all trace of her earlier anger had miraculously disappeared.

Ben positioned them so the water sluiced away what was left of the soap. As if it were something he did every day, he squeezed shampoo into his hands and washed her hair.

Abby's tension continued to seep away. "Did anyone ever tell you that maybe you'd missed your calling, Dr. Galloway?"

"Hmm. For sure the hours at a salon would probably be better." He moved her directly beneath the now cooler spray. But even as he combed the shampoo out with his fingers, his kisses warmed her.

"On second thought," she murmured when he shut off the spray and handed her a towel for her hair and one to wrap up in, "the local vice squad would shut down any beauty salon that offered your method of shampoos."

From the moment they exited the bath, it was obvious there was a ruckus in the hall. "Hey, hold it down out there," Ben hollered. "Give us time to dress and we'll come out to settle the fuss."

"What's on your agenda today?" he asked, again turning to Abby.

"This is my day on the road. Two of the boys have Little

League sign-ups after school at their coach's house. I'm dropping them off and taking Erin to her first violin lesson. After I leave her, I promised Mollie we'd have a look-see at the dance studio next door. Apparently they had a talent show at school last week, and Mollie came away entranced with tap and jazz. Her music teacher lent her a video she watched last night. She's more sure than ever that she wants to dance.''

Ben took the comb out of Abby's hand and ran it through some tangles she'd missed in back. "How much do dance lessons cost?"

"I won't know until we pick up the information today." He pulled her hair accidentally. She yelped, ducked and grabbed the comb from his hand. She was at the door when Ben said, "Did you know one of the kids unplugged the phone yesterday? I found it when I came in last night."

"I unplugged it—because you hadn't bothered to call and let us know you weren't coming home as usual. I had to find out from Pat, and I was too angry to want to speak with anyone." She wrenched open the door. The kids had all gone downstairs.

"It was an emergency, Abby." Buckling his belt, Ben stalked after her.

"You disappointed Sam. He counted on you being here. At the very least you could've called him."

"It couldn't be helped," Ben said, rallying. "Didn't Pat explain about the baby with thyroid cancer?"

Abby paused at the head of the stairs. "You trained her well, Ben. She's convinced your patients are more important than your family."

"Sick patients *do* have first call on my time, Abby."

She wheeled and faced Ben. "I wish you'd told me that before we decided to jointly raise seven children."

"Come on, Abby. Medicine is my job. What did Sam need that was so important you couldn't handle it?"

"Be-en." Sam's trembling little voice drifted from his room. It halted the argument beginning to heat up between the adults.

He whirled around, expecting to go fetch Sam from his bed. To his shock and dismay, Sam stood in his doorway. He took two shaky steps toward Ben, sliding a metal walker forward one inch at a time.

Abby clapped a hand over her quivering lips. "That's the unimportant thing you wanted me to handle, Ben," she said hoarsely. "Sam took his first step yesterday. And he wanted to show you what he could do. He's only supposed to take a step or two at a time. I know it's farther than that from his bed to the door. And as doctoring is your job, *you* deal with any problems." Her breathing uneven, Abby ran headlong down the stairs.

She was still moderately annoyed with Ben when she reached the kitchen.

"Why were you and Uncle Ben yelling?" Erin asked, her eyes round behind her gold wire-rims.

Abby hadn't realized their voices would carry so far. But from the anxious expressions regarding her all around the table, it was obvious all the children had heard. "Ben and I had a disagreement. Nothing that should worry you guys."

They still acted nervous as Abby ground beans and prepared coffee. Clearly, they hadn't bought her explanation.

"I see the school lunch menu today is stew. None of you wants stew, correct?"

No one did. Abby cleaned the counter and laid out slices of bread for sandwiches.

Ben carried Sam into the kitchen just as she asked Mike to feed the fish and uncover the bird. "If that's your special chore," he said, "you ought to take care of it daily without Abby having to remind you, son."

"It's not my chore, and I'm not your son. Daddy took care of the fish and the bird. Me and Noah feed Harry and Ruffian. Brad and Reed gotta do the same for Poky and Speedy. Like Erin and Mollie are in charge of the cat."

"Hey, that ain't fair," Noah said. "Two of them for one cat. And Sam don't gotta feed nobody. Aunt Abby, shouldn't Sammy hafta feed the fish?"

"*Ain't*, and *don't gotta* are words that do not register with me, young man. You may as well learn right now that life is rarely fair. What's with you kids all of a sudden? If I had a dollar for every time one of you claimed something isn't fair, I'd be well on my way to being rich."

Noah, nothing if not stubborn, pressed his point. "Us kids asked for the dog and the gerbil and hamsters. Mama said that's what made feeding them our responsibility. We didn't ask for no fish or bird."

"Abby and I didn't ask for them, either," Ben pointed out, pausing as he dumped cereal into Sam's bowl. "Since no one in this room requested fish or birds, what's the solution?" He stared at each kid in turn. "Shall we take them back to the pet store?"

"No, Unca Ben." Mollie leaped out of her chair and threw herself in Ben's arms.

"I like to get the bird to talk. I'll feed him if you show me how."

"That leaves the fish to Sam," Mike declared, plopping back into his chair.

Abby reached over and stood him up again. "Not so fast. Your brother can't reach the dispenser. He's not old enough to read, and comprehend the difference between feeding and overfeeding. Even if he could I don't want him standing on a chair. I'll type up a new chore schedule for the fridge. From today until further notice, you'll each feed the fish on a rotating basis, except Sammy.''

"Gol-ly," Mike groused. "It's not fa—"

"Don't say it," Abby warned. "Since we're all gathered in one room, this is as good a time as any to let you know that beginning a week from Monday, I'll be expecting more out of each of you."

"Why?" the kids asked before Ben could. He eyed his wife speculatively.

"Because that's when I start back to work. I've arranged for Sam's day care, where they'll continue his therapy. The advantage to you kids is that you get to ride to and from school with me instead of taking the bus. The downside is you'll have to get up earlier and may have to eat breakfast in the school cafeteria."

No one said a word, except for Ruffian, who lifted his head and howled.

"My sentiments exactly," Ben muttered when he found his voice. "This is awfully sudden, isn't it?"

Abby raised her eyebrows. "Sudden? I'm on temporary leave, Ben, which I already extended once. If I don't go back next week, I'll lose my job at Sky Heights."

"So, lose it. Isn't caring for a house, seven kids and a hodgepodge of animals enough for you?"

"Is it enough for you?"

"Don't be silly. I went to school for ten years to become a doctor. Medicine is my career."

The kids' heads whipped back and forth. Abby spread peanut butter on the same slice of bread twice. Jamming the knife deep into the jar, she propped her fists on her hips. "Teaching is *my* career. I have a master's degree. So I stopped short of getting my doctorate, but I— This argument is purely asinine, Ben."

"Really? As a teacher your salary's a drop in the bucket compared to what I make as a physician."

"My working isn't just about money, although you're the one always griping about what I spend." Abby couldn't believe he'd thrown the disparity in their wages at her.

"You're saying I can't support this family by myself?" Ben pointed at his chest. "Well, I can. Furthermore, I can bring you study after study that shows how much better kids do in school if one parent stays home."

"Hogwash! It's not the quantity of time a parent spends with kids, it's the quality. I'll match your studies with ones that show kids excel when moms and dads are happy and fulfilled in jobs they love. You're never home, Ben. The kids have seen you for maybe one hour in three days. Count them. Three!" She held up her fingers.

Ben quickly stood up and let his gaze sweep the pinched faces of the children. "I recommend you take a good look at the children this morning, Abby. Do they look happy and fulfilled? Ask yourself if this is the life you're prepared to condemn them to." Shoving his chair under the table, he turned and stalked from the room.

"Where are you going?" she shouted after him.

"To work, where every father goes in the morning. I have fifteen minutes to get to the clinic if I don't want my first patient to beat me there."

Smoldering, Abby pulled the knife out of the jar and slapped way too much peanut butter on the next slice of bread. She gritted her teeth as the front door slammed. "I'm surprised he didn't stop at the door and give his king-of-the-jungle bellow," Abby mumbled between clenched teeth.

Brad and Erin meekly finished their cereal and carried their bowls to the sink. No one said a word, except for Mike who paused briefly to watch his aunt slice through the sandwiches like an angry Samurai. "I'll feed the fish and Cayenne," he said, referring to the cockatiel by the name Blair had given her bird, which Abby had forgotten until now.

"Thanks. And don't let the girls see you flush any dead fish."

"Nah, I won't. Yesterday, Erin saw Noah do it, and I thought she was going to go into orbit."

One by one the other kids stacked their bowls in the sink and slunk away.

Memories of how her day had begun filtered into Abby's thoughts. Her anger slowly receded, leaving her drained. As she opened sacks and filled them with sandwiches, fruit and chips, she felt her youngest nephew's eyes follow her every move.

"Sam, are you finished? Are you ready to get down? I think *Sesame Street* might be on TV." He didn't answer, so Abby glanced his way. The boy's scrawny arms were crossed on his chest in a display of anger. Blue eyes shot barbs in her direction. He looked so much like Elliot when he got mad. Abby flinched at the sad reminder.

She felt guilty about heaping her quarrel with Ben on a child who had experienced more than his share of unhappiness. Anyway, she was sure Sam would side with Ben.

"Adults argue, sweetie. It doesn't mean I don't love Ben." Sighing, Abby folded down lunch sacks. *She did love Ben just like Lily had claimed she loved Ben's dad.* "Sammy, honey, people can disagree and still love each other." Of course, she had no verification that her feelings for Ben were reciprocated. Not even in their most passionate lovemaking today had the words *I love you* passed Ben's lips.

Abby transferred the sacks to a spot where the kids would pick them up. She sat down facing Sam and took a sip of her cold coffee. "Thing is, Sammy, I also love teaching. I love what I do at school."

He stared at her so seriously, Abby felt another dart hit its mark.

"You kids take top priority in my heart. Do you see any reason I can't enjoy you kids, Ben, *and* the job I love?"

Sam put his head down on the table.

So he was having a sulk like the big kids often did. Abby released the air trapped in her lungs. "Okay, tiger, time to go see what your brothers and sisters are up to. What shirt do you want to wear to therapy today?"

Abby might as well have been carrying on a conversation with herself. "You do want to go to therapy? So your bones get strong and you can play like the other kids?"

Still no response. Abby made a mental note to check a child psych book regarding hero worship in four-year-olds. For instance, how long could she expect it to last? And how long could a boy sulk?

Doggedly figuring she had right on her side, Abby went about her day by working through the checklist she'd written out the night before. She phoned the district office and Mr. Conrad, informing one and all of her intent to resume her classes one week from Monday. Step two. After Sam's PT appointment, she stopped by the recommended day-care center to pay and sign the appropriate papers.

"Ah, his father is a pediatrician." Pam Lenz, the school's owner, pounced on that fact and beamed widely. "I'm in the market for a medical advisor on my board. It would be a double coup to get one with a child in our program."

"Ben isn't Sam's father. I'm Sam's legal guardian. I'm not sure about all the legalities when it comes to Ben's nieces and my nephews. He and I were only recently married. Frankly, we haven't discussed adoption yet." She paused. "You see, I lost my brother and his wife in the earthquake. Ben lost a sister. We…thought it made sense to—oh, it's complicated."

"Sounds like it. But yours isn't the only case we've seen since the earthquake," the woman said, gazing through the office glass at her students, which included Sam. Abby appreciated Pam's suggesting that Sam join the class to see how he liked the activities while the two women spoke candidly.

"However," Pam went on, "I honestly can't point my finger at another family who's assumed the huge responsibility you have. I hope you'll at least convey my request to your husband, Mrs. Galloway. The commitment to our board only takes a little time. We meet twice a month for an hour. Plus, we encourage board members to attend holiday parties and fund-raisers."

"I'll pass your request on to Ben. But if I may be frank, finding time to be together as a family is perhaps our biggest obstacle at the moment. Did I mention that between us, we have seven children?"

"Yes. Or Sam's PT did." Mrs. Lenz buried her nose again in Abby's paperwork. "I see this is in order, but I must admit, the fact that Sam's not verbal concerns me."

"What do you mean? Oh, I understand. Sam talks. He's punishing me today for a tiff I had with Ben this morning. His silence is temporary, I assure you. You'll probably end up wishing he was less verbal." Abby grinned.

"Before I accept your deposit and the first month's fee, I'd like to ask Sam's opinion on whether or not he wants to spend his days with us. If you'll wait, I'll do that now."

Abby extracted her checkbook from her fanny pack. "I'm sure he'll get over being angry with me. Of all the kids, he's our model child. Your facility is ideal—it's close to work and home. And you provide the therapy Sam needs to walk again.''

"Yes, well, there is that. All right. From what I've observed, he's coloring and drawing age appropriately. I'll be happy to part you from some of your hard-earned money, Mrs. Galloway.''

"Please, call me Abby. This account is still in my maiden name of Drummond. The bank is my next stop after we leave here. Sam was wearing heavy casts until recently, so I delayed tending to the smaller issues, especially if I had to carry him very far. He's a load.''

Pam nodded. "I had three children when I remarried. My husband is a dentist, and I own the school. We still maintain accounts that are his, mine, and ours.''

Abby weighed that as an option as she drove to the bank. Ben seemed bent on paying their bills. Judging by the fit he threw this morning, he probably wouldn't want her pitiful earnings tainting his funds. So, for now, maybe she'd change to her married name and otherwise keep her own account. Why hadn't she said in the beginning that after being independent for so long, it embarrassed her to have to confer with him over every little purchase? Like shoes. Granted, fourteen pairs did seem excessive at first—but not in hindsight.

At the bank, that was what Abby did—switched her account to the name Abigail Galloway. It took so long to do the paperwork, she barely made it to the elementary by the time school was dismissed. Sam still stared through her without talking.

"Hurry, hurry,'' Abby called to the others. "Sam and I had a busy afternoon and it's about to get busier. Next up, Little Leaguers get dropped off at Coach's house.''

Sam unbuckled his harness as the boys disembarked. Abby knew Sam loved to watch the twins play ball. "Hon, they're only signing up today. Coach's wife is having a small party for team members only.'' She buckled him in again, and kissed his nose. He reared back and pushed her face away.

''Would you like to go hear Erin play her violin? I'm taking Mollie right next door to check on the cost of dance lessons.''

Sam made a wry face and cupped his hands over his ears.

Afraid Erin would be insulted by his behavior, Abby winced and telegraphed an apologetic glance at the girl.

''Don't worry, Abby, I just started playing. I don't want anybody to hear me yet.''

Reed grimaced. ''Like Erin thinks we can't hear if she goes in her room to practice. Noah says she sounds like a dying swan in a snowstorm.''

Abby took her eyes momentarily off the road. ''And how would Noah know what dying swans sound like in or out of a snowstorm?''

''He probably heard one on Animal Planet,'' Reed said in his brother's defense.

''Honestly, guys. Be nice. You've been getting along so well. Don't spoil your record by picking on each other now.''

Brad piped up from the rear seat, ''So how come it's okay for you and Ben to yell and shout, and not us?''

Shocked, Abby didn't know how to respond. She fell back on the usual lame excuse. ''We're grown-ups, and we know when to quit. Kids tend to keep it up and keep it up until feelings are irreparably hurt.''

Except, a distant voice in Abby's head reminded her, Ben had hurt her feelings in placing the importance of her career so far below his. Even so, they shouldn't argue in front of the children. She, of all people, knew how kids tended to blurt a family's deep, dark secrets at inopportune times. Abby would die if one of them went to school and told their teacher anything about her and Ben's petty squabbles.

For the remainder of that week and the next, Abby kept a tight rein on her feelings. Sam persevered in ignoring her. She found it unsettling.

"Ben," she said one evening, catching him on the fly. "Would you check Sammy's throat? Even the kids have noticed that he's simply quit talking."

Ben found a tongue depressor in his bag and checked then and there. "Sam, is your throat sore?"

He slumped and gagged, but didn't answer Ben, who tried numerous times to get a response. "I can't see anything amiss, Abby. If it persists, we'll run some tests. You're right about him clamming up. It's probably a phase. Some kids can be stubborn." With that, he tossed the tongue depressor in the trash and tore out of the house, headed for the ER.

Disgruntled, Abby mulled over making Sam an appointment with Jase Belltower, his old pediatrician, before she returned to classes. Getting Sam to a doctor thereafter would be difficult. But as Ben had pronounced Sam okay, perhaps she shouldn't worry.

Abby said something about it to Lily when the woman phoned that afternoon to see how everyone was doing.

"Honey, isn't Benny considered the city's leading children's doctor?"

"He is, Lily." Agreeing left Abby feeling somewhat better. And talking to the older woman was comforting.

Yet, as the week waned, Abby waited for Ben to mention her working. Or did he think his last word on the subject was law? He came and went from the house in keeping with his busy agenda. The scant time he had at home in the afternoons, he spent playing with the kids or helping Sam strengthen his legs.

Abby went out of her way to have meals ready by six. Dinners were actually pleasant, except for Sam's notable silence. The older kids began using the opportunity to talk to Abby and Ben about their lessons, their sports and their friends.

"Ben, have you had a chance to look at the brochure I gave you from the tap and jazz school? Mollie would like to begin classes next week. They have an opening at the same hour Erin takes violin. It's right next door, so I can drop them both off after school, then swing around and collect Sam."

Ben, who'd come in from playing ball with the boys to get a drink of water, drained the glass before he answered. "Is Mollie old enough to stick with this? What if in a month she decides she'd rather take ice-skating or gymnastics or horseback riding?"

"That's the beauty of this school. You're only committed for a month at a time. Some places ask that you pay six months in advance to insure against dropouts."

"Is that why it's so expensive? It's twice what we pay for Erin's violin lessons."

"The price includes both tap and jazz. Seems reasonable to me."

"Pat, our receptionist, has two girls. She thinks it's out of line compared to what she had to pay."

"Oh. So are Pat's girls taking lessons somewhere less costly?"

"Her girls are in high school and college now, Abby. Which you'd know if you ever found time to bring the kids by to meet my staff. They're starting to think you're unfriendly."

"They might not have that impression if you'd tell them

how busy I am. Pat's of the opinion that I'm a pampered lady of leisure. Now she'll add that I'm a gold digger trying to spend all your money on expensive dance lessons. Why would you discuss our private business with a member of your staff?''

"We're like family at the clinic, Abby."

"Great. What are we at home? Strangers?''

He frowned. "Sometimes it seems as if we are.''

"Whose fault is that? Oh, for pity's sake, Ben. We'll come tomorrow. Sam and I will load up the kids after school and we'll descend on your workplace en masse.''

"Good. While you're there, I'll culture Sam's throat.''

True to her word, Abby waltzed into Ben's clinic during one of their busiest hours. And as she might have predicted, his staff had no time to spend getting to know her or the kids. Steve and two nurses made brief forays past Ben's office. Steve did the honors of introducing his partner's family, as Ben was tied up with a vomiter. "Very likely a kid,'' Steve informed Abby, "who has a hot appendix.''

Pat, the receptionist, remained glued to the phone. She acknowledged them with a nod. She stopped talking only long enough to tell Reed to leave the stapler alone. And she had the nerve to glare at Abby, as if to say Abby ought to have better sense than to inflict seven kids on an already overloaded work space.

"Tell Ben we'll see him later,'' Abby murmured to Anita, Ben's nurse. They'd commiserated briefly over the antics of boys.

When Anita tried to culture Sam's throat, he threw a fit the likes of which Abby had never seen. He flung his arms around Ben's chair and went limp when Abby tried to lift him. Embarrassed, she wondered what the families in the waiting room must think about the doctor's unruly child. Sam had a temper to match his red hair. He pounded on the floor in lieu of the usual kicking and knocked things off the desk in his rage.

Abby had a redhead's temper, too. And she was bigger. Their tussle ended with her hauling the equivalent of sixty, maybe sixty-five, pounds of deadweight, including his air casts and braces, from the clinic to the van.

That was Thursday. Ben didn't make it home for dinner that evening. He dragged in from the hospital after midnight, again without phoning. This time, Abby waited up. She'd fine-tuned a schedule she labeled Abby and Ben's Domestic Chore Calendar.

As he entered the hallway, Abby shoved a rum and cola, Ben's favorite drink, into his hand. "What's this for?" he asked suspiciously. "Okay, might as well tell me. What now?" he muttered wearily. "There hasn't been so much as a bottle of beer in this house in the two months we've been married. Is this because of the fit Sam threw at the clinic? I heard all about it, but I'm sure it's nothing my staff hasn't seen. And so far, his culture looks clear."

"This isn't about Sam. Although I'm worried sick over his silence. Buying rum and handing you a drink has more to do with giving you a chance to relax before I show you this." Abby produced her masterpiece.

Ben read it between sips of his drink as he followed her upstairs. "Nice work with the computer calendar program. I'm virtually computer-illiterate. What does it all mean?" Ben flashed Abby one of his boyish grins.

"Exactly what the heading says, Ben. I've drawn up an equal split of the duties required to keep this house running. There's three copies for each of us. That way we'll have one at home, one at work and one in each car. You'll notice you have more at-home tasks because I drive the van and carpool the kids to all their activities."

"I see what you've done. But what's this for? Are you taking a class or something?"

Abby sank down on their bed. "I can't believe you've blocked out the fact that on Monday I go back to teaching."

Ben gaped at her. "I thought we'd settled that issue the last time it came up."

"Settled it how? Well, in a way we did. I told you I intended to take back my job."

He gulped down his drink. "Abby, this is insane! Surely you can see from the hours I keep that there's no prayer of this…this…schedule working. I can't do laundry for instance, in the forty minutes I'm home between jobs. Furthermore, it's not necessary for you to work."

Her eyes blazed green fire. One thing Ben knew: when Abby got her dander up, the brown and blue flecks in her hazel eyes always lost out to the green.

"I suggest you take tomorrow to make adjustments in your work schedule to accommodate us. This calendar goes to the end of the school year. I've already turned down a request to teach summer school. But I'm going back in September."

"No. No, you're not. I can and will provide for this family's financial needs. But one of us has to be at home and available. What's wrong with the routine we've had for the last couple of weeks? I thought things had calmed down and were going well."

"Really? Because you come and go as you damn well please?" Abby ticked things off on her fingers. "I take Sam to therapy. Cook. Clean. Do laundry. I make a grocery list and shop for food. I chauffeur the kids hither and yon. If you find time to work us in for an hour a day, we're blessed with your presence. If not, too bad."

"Abby, I'm doing my level best here."

"Really? When I'm not being a housekeeper, I'm expected to be available for your sexual pleasure."

"Give me a break, Abby. I haven't heard you complain about our sex life."

She went to the closet and pulled the bottle of rum off the top shelf and pushed it against his midsection. "Fill a water glass, big fella. Drown your sorrows. Starting tonight, mama's gonna sleep alone. Paint me on strike until I get some respect around here. Or until you decide to share my highly overrated job of domestic engineer."

"For God's sake!" Ben stumbled as Abby pushed him to their bedroom door. Opening it, she shoved him out, then drew back and turned the lock.

He knocked softly, calling, "Abby, get real."

"I am. You get real, Ben Galloway." Five seconds later, she banged the door open, tossed a pillow, a sheet and a quilt at his feet. "I finally understand why Lily walked out on your father. You claim not to like him, Ben, but in some ways you're exactly like him."

His jaw dropped. "I am nothing like Kirk Galloway. And why would you listen to a...a bimbo like Lily?"

"Stop with that talk! You don't really know her. She's smart enough to leave your father and get herself a job." Again the door closed with a slam, and Ben heard the double locks he'd installed click and click again.

That grated on his nerves as nothing else in their ludicrous conversation had. He stomped downstairs and put the rum in the cupboard over the sink. Marching upstairs, he pounded on their bedroom door again.

Abby didn't budge.

Ben pounded harder. "Dammit, Abby, let me in. This is stupid. It's midnight."

Still nothing.

He rattled the knob. That got a response. She yelled, "Go away, Ben."

Suddenly, Ben felt as if he was being watched. Glancing first over his right shoulder and then his left, Ben saw a circle of white faces and big eyes staring out from each of the children's rooms, including Sam's.

"Uncle Ben, what's the matter?" Erin called anxiously.

He cleared his throat. "Nothing, button. Uh, Abby and I are having a little…" Ben didn't want to say *fight.* If he said that, the kids would worry all night. But if he said they were having a problem, it wouldn't be any better.

"A little what?" Noah demanded in a froggy voice.

"All of you, back in bed." Ben made shooing motions with his hands. "This is between Abby and me."

Seeing the light wink out under Abby's door, Ben figured he'd lost round one of their battle tonight. With as much dignity as he could muster, he dropped the bedding over the bannister, to the hallway below.

"Come on. I'll tuck each of you in again. Then I'm going to get some shut-eye. Tomorrow we'll all be bright eyed and bushy tailed."

That brought the desired giggle from everyone but Erin and Sam. She wasn't easily mollified, and Sam remained mute. His round eyes followed Ben with suspicion.

"Abby sounded really mad at you, Uncle Ben," Erin muttered.

"At me, not at you, button."

Once Ben settled all the boys, Mollie climbed slowly into the bed adjacent to her sister. "But, if Abby frowed your stuff out of her room, she wants you to go away. Are you going away, Unca Ben?"

Ben knew it probably looked like that from a child's perspective. Hell, it didn't look good from *his* perspective. "You know what, pickle? You hit the nail on the head.

Abby is determined to go back to teaching regardless of what I think. I thought we got married so we could take better care of you kids. Apparently Abby and I don't agree.''

He thumbed his lower lip. "Girls, get dressed. Pack a few things. I'll find Blackberry's carrier. We're returning to our other home. I'll phone Mrs. Clark in the morning and offer her back her old job. If Abby wants her career more than she wants us, she can have it.''

"But…Mollie and I like it here," Erin sobbed into Ben's shirtfront. "Blackberry's happy, too. I like school and violin. And Abby's a good teacher. Ask anyone in my last year's class. She's really, really good, Uncle Ben.''

"If you love us, Unca Ben, you'll tell Abby you're sorry," Mollie added, her voice breaking.

"That's ridiculous. Of course I love you girls.''

"Don't you love Abby?" Erin demanded.

It struck Ben that he'd deliberately shied away from using the word *love* in his relationship with Abby. Who knew better than he that love broke your heart and left it bleeding on the floor? His and Marlo's love for their parents hadn't held their family together.

But yeah, he did love Abby with her freckled face and riotous curls. Why couldn't she understand his other commitments? Abby was being unrealistic.

"I do love her," he said. "I don't think she loves me. Not in the same way, at any rate." Scrambling up, he pulled their suitcases out of the closet. "It's better to cut our ties now. The longer we wait, the harder it'll be to go back to our old life.''

"It's hard now," Erin cried. "What about Sam, Uncle Ben? Sam needs you. I think he's sad inside. That's why he quit talking, I'll bet.''

Ben hesitated. His heart gave a painful lurch. Tears bubbled along the lower rim of his eyes. Turning away from the girls, he dashed them away. "Have I ever lied to you girls? You have to believe me now. Leaving tonight is best for everyone, maybe even Sam.''

"'Kay,'' they both murmured, tears continuing to drip down their small faces.

Downstairs, Ben folded the bedding. He set the pile on the kitchen table and wrote Abby a hasty note. It was brief because he didn't possess the words to explain everything that was in his heart.

Pinning the note to the pillow, he went to the broom closet and got the cat carrier, and set it and a sack of cat food beside the front door. By then the girls had dragged their suitcases downstairs. Ben led the way to his car, refusing to look squarely into their long, accusing faces.

It was over. His marriage was over. Ben should have known. After all, juggling careers was the very thing that had torpedoed his parents' union. Yes, he should've known, he thought bitterly.

CHAPTER FIFTEEN

SUFFERING MORE than a little guilt over their fight, Abby fully expected to find Ben asleep on the couch when she hurried downstairs early the next morning to make a pot of coffee. Instead, she was met with the shock of her life.

She reread the note she clutched in her shaking hand. Not believing what she'd read, she ran upstairs to look in the girls' room. It was true. They were gone. Like a thief in the night, he'd taken them away.

Tears streamed down Abby's face. It was over. Her marriage was over. But what did she expect? Ben had never loved her. And it was now plain that he had no interest in finding solutions to their problems. Her parents had gone through some pretty rough times. Abby remembered her father saying, the tougher times were, the more he and her mom had learned to pull together.

What hurt Abby even more than Ben's terse note was that he'd left her to face telling the boys alone. *Sam!* Poor little guy. He'd been locked in silence for weeks. The only times he perked up and seemed his old self—except for not talking—were those afternoons Ben was available to play with or read to him. She'd have to make him an appointment with his old doctor.

Abby scrubbed at her already puffy eyes. The twins knew at once that something was wrong. ''Where are Erin and Mollie?'' Mike asked. He set out cereal bowls for all the kids, including the girls.

Abby returned two bowls to the cupboard. Hard as it was, she forced herself to look at them as she said, "Ben and the girls have moved out. They've gone home. It's just us again, guys."

Noah's chin shot up. "Aw, jeez. The other day I should'na said he was a lousy pitcher. Call him up. Tell him I'm sorry, Aunt Abby." The boy rummaged frantically in her purse and yanked out her cell phone.

"Noah, Noah, Noah." Abby threw her arms around the surprising child. "Ben didn't leave us over anything you kids said or did. He and I—" Her voice broke. "Honey, we…just couldn't make our marriage work."

"Then work harder," Mike cried out. "Ben's cool. Aunt Abby, there are things a guy can't say to…well, to his aunt."

"Yeah," Brad blustered. "Like Dr. Ben understood all the stuff me'n Mr. Keeler talk about. And Mr. Keeler said he knows it's been better for me 'cause we've got Ben here for us. Only…only…now we don't."

Frankly, Abby hadn't been prepared for the hard time the boys were giving her. Stiffening her back, she got out their cereal. "I didn't marry Ben just to give you boys a dad," she attempted to explain. Fumbling, she nearly spilled the Cocoa Puffs. Guiltily she acknowledged that had been precisely why she and Ben had decided to marry. To give the boys a father and the girls a mom. She'd been foolish enough to fall madly in love with Ben Galloway somewhere along the line. *Dumb, dumb, dumb!* Abby whacked her forehead with the heel of her hand.

"Look, we managed before Ben came here to live. We'll manage again. Eat, please. I'll drive you to school. I need you guys to act adult about this breakup. I'm worried about Sammy, okay? I'm going up to tell him now. You know it'll be hardest on him. Can you be strong for me?"

They all nodded unenthusiastically. Abby felt their eyes boring into her back as she left the room.

Sam was awake. She tried to be stoic in telling him about his idol's departure. Abby didn't know quite what reaction she expected. Certainly not the wide-eyed, tearless stare she got while she helped Sam dress.

The older boys remarked on his odd response, too. "What're we supposed to say to Erin and Mollie?" Noah asked grumpily when Abby pulled into the circle to let them off at school.

"Act normal. It's no more their fault than yours. Truthfully, I've got no idea what Ben might have said to Erin and Mollie. It'd be better if you let them set the tone of any conversation you might have."

Abby noticed the boys' shoulders were bowed. She bit her lip hard watching them trudge into the building. And Sam. She glanced at him in the rearview mirror. He remained eerily quiet. She carried him into his school and left him at his play station while she had a word with the school's director.

"I don't know if you'll see aberrant behavior from Sam in the next few days, Pam," Abby said, shaking her head.

"I know you said your husband, er, former husband, examined Sam's throat and found nothing wrong. His muteness concerns me and his teacher. Sam pinched his hand in a drawer the other day and didn't so much as peep. Perhaps when you get back to the elementary school, you could arrange to have him evaluated by a speech and hearing pathologist."

"That's a good idea. I've considered taking Sam back to his old pediatrician. But…Ben is…well, tops. A hearing evaluation is the next logical step. After that, I'll consult a psychologist. Thanks for the tip. I've been at my wits' end."

She thought that sometime over the course of the day, she'd hear from Ben. But she didn't.

Saturday afternoon, Abby arrived home from the twins' Little League game, to discover Ben had come in and cleaned out his closet and the girls. He'd left a note indicating he'd find someone to move the girls' beds, and that he'd let her know when.

That act made the split so final. She'd actually held out some hope that he might call her after the boys said Erin and Mollie spent every recess complaining about Mrs. Clark. Erin referred to the woman as an old witch. She apparently didn't want Erin to practice her violin.

Abby had to smile at that. Erin did screech abominably.

"Guys, tomorrow I'm rolling everyone out of bed early. It's time we started going to Sunday school and church again."

The boys groaned. "Don't you need the day to get ready to go back to teaching, Aunt Abby?" Reed asked diplomatically.

"I'm ready. Have been for a week. It'll be good to settle into my old routine again."

"Mollie said Ms. Thorpe's PO'd about you taking over her class."

"It's my class, Michael. I taught them the first half of the year. And don't say PO'd. It's like swearing."

"Who's gonna take us to ball practice Tuesday afternoon, Aunt Abby?" Brad inquired.

"Oh, I nearly forgot. I've arranged for you to get a ride with Bobby Peterson's dad. I'll pick you up, though. It may take a week or so to work out the transportation quirks, but we'll manage, guys. Trust me."

"Yeah, sure," Noah muttered, slamming out of the house.

The weekend before Abby was due back at school flew by in a pleasant haze.

Sunday night, she tossed and turned. It was the first night she'd allowed herself to miss cuddling up next to Ben, and once the memories started pouring in, she couldn't stop them. Drat! Giving in to the pain that was always in her heart, Abby indulged the tears she'd never let the boys see. She put the pillow over her head and cried and cried and cried.

Monday lent new meaning to the word *frenzied*. Bleary-eyed, Abby stood in front of the bathroom mirror when one of the boys let out a yelp. Noah pounded on the bathroom door. ''Aunt Abby, Ruffian's sick. He's throwing up all over the kitchen.''

Dressed only in panties and bra, Abby snatched up a robe, and raced downstairs.

Sure enough, the dog was still heaving. ''Mike, get me our vet's emergency number.'' She got the on-call vet, who said to bring him in. ''Boys, I'm trusting you to stay by yourselves until I return. The clinic is only five blocks away. Eat breakfast and get dressed. I'll be back before you're finished.''

''Ick,'' Reed exclaimed. ''How can we eat with throw-up all around.''

Sighing, Abby wet a handful of paper towels, knelt and mopped up every spot.

''Aunt Abby, are you goin' to the vet's in your robe?'' Brad exclaimed.

Abby, who'd been halfway to the front door, squealed. ''Noah, come hold Ruffian's collar. Don't let him get near the living room carpet. I'll run quick and jump into my clothes.'' She had a suit waiting. Changing her mind, Abby threw on a pair of slacks. She left the younger twins crying.

Reed was lisping badly again. "Ruffian's gonna die, I know he ith."

"He is not," she insisted. "The vet will give him medicine and fix him up." Abby prayed that was true during her entire drive with a barfing dog.

"He probably ate something out in the yard, Mrs. Galloway," the vet said. "That last rain brought out some poisonous toads. I've flushed his system. But it'd be best if you left him here this morning. Call first, but I'm betting by noon he'll be good as new."

Calculating what the visit would cost, Abby said okay. Buying a spray from the clinic to use on the van after she hosed it out, she went home. In the meanwhile, Sam had climbed from his bed, and unnoticed by his brothers, was attempting to scoot down the stairs.

"Sam, what on earth?" Abby left her keys dangling in the door and dashed up to grab Sam before he fell head over heels. Her heart pounded a mile a minute. "What if you'd fallen? Noah! Mike! Where are you?" She found all four boys in the older twins' room, playing Nintendo.

All was not paradise or even close to it when Abby bundled Sam off to his school and returned to the elementary with the boys. She felt decidedly frazzled.

It was bad enough that the twins were sure Ruffian was going to die. They carried on in the car until Abby raised her voice. "Stop being so dramatic, Reed. The vet said Ruffian's going to be fine. Be thankful you're not the one who's sick. Ruffian got a shot with a needle that would make you guys faint."

They glared at her in typical male fashion.

Parking in the teachers' lot, Abby shooed them from the van. "*Wiki wiki*. That means *hurry* in Hawaiian," she said, brushing a hand through Noah's uncombed hair. As it was, with the morning's delay, her timetable was thrown off.

She locked the van and gave instructions for meeting after school. "I'll call the vet during my lunch. If Ruffian's okay, I'll run to the clinic and take him home."

Abby felt haggard and out of breath when at last she unlocked her classroom door.

Raina had been right, she soon discovered. The entire landscape had changed. Her desk sat at the back of the room, and the children all faced the opposite blackboard.

Those changes Abby could have dealt with. But the kids were different, too. Instead of welcoming her back excitedly as she'd anticipated, children she'd known and taught for six long months filed in and stared at her as if she were some space alien landing in their midst.

She thought she'd get back into the swing by reading a few chapters of a book last year's class had loved. She'd barely read the first paragraph when a hand shot up at the back of the room.

"Tiffany, what is it?"

"Ms. Thorpe said that's a sissy book. She's reading us *Harry Potter*."

"*Wind in the Willows* is considered a children's classic," Abby sputtered. But all the students agreed with their spokesperson. Abby put the book away.

"Well, then. We'll forgo a story and start on social studies."

Another hand waved. "We do social studies only on Tuesdays and Thursdays."

"No," Abby said firmly. "My schedule calls for it every day at this period."

By day's end, Abby's head had split in two. She also felt faint, as she'd used her lunch hour to retrieve Ruffian and take him home. Abby didn't think she could take one more, "Ms. Thorpe didn't make us do that," or "Ms. Thorpe did it this way."

She thought she'd scream. And felt like crying when two parents came back to the room with their students and one said, "Stacy rearranged the schedule so the children had their easy classes before lunch. Stacy said they were more awake after lunch. Do you think you can stick to her schedule, Ms. Drummond—er—Mrs. Galloway. You know, that confuses the children, too—having to learn a different name for you so close to the end of the year."

"They can call me Ms. Drummond," Abby said sweetly.

"You mean you aren't married to Mr. Galloway?" The second mother sounded shocked.

"It's Dr. Galloway, and we are…married." God, but Abby didn't want to explain their separation. "You brought up the name change. I agreed—why confuse kids?" She dredged up a smile. "Believe me, I know about confused kids. I'm raising my nephews. Five boys," she confided.

The two women looked even more sour. One of them said, "That's a shame. Stacy had energy to burn. She wasn't too tired or stressed from handling her own kids. We asked Mr. Conrad to let her stay on, you know."

Abby kept silent, afraid that anything she said would bring the school board down on her neck. She maintained her composure until the women left. Then she dug in her purse for a headache remedy.

Raina Miller popped in as Abby shook out four pills.

"I saw Stacy's cheerleading committee leave." She screwed up her face. "Were they four-pills bad?"

Abby swallowed. "Is it me, Raina? I feel as if I've been away for years instead of two months." She picked up her purse and her briefcase. "Actually, I fumbled around today like a rookie. Can you believe Stacy left me a spiral book filled with notes? Me, a veteran teacher. And kids who started out the year as angels have developed discipline problems. The ones I said couldn't read, she's moved into higher reading groups.''

''Part of it's because of the earthquake. But who knows about that better than you?''

''Yeah. Oh, Raina—on top of everything, Ben and I have split up. My nephews are back on a roller coaster.''

Obviously trying not to appear shocked, Raina said, ''My friend, you've got a full plate and then some. Returning to teaching takes an adjustment for anybody who's been on leave. You've undergone a triple whammy. Give it two weeks.''

Abby hugged her friend. ''Thanks, I needed that. But school's out in five. It better not take me two of those to adjust. Ah, there's my brood. Speaking of which, we had a tizzy at the house this morning over a sick dog. He ate something that made him barf everywhere.''

''We can only hope he ate that squawking bird. That parrot or whatever it is wouldn't last a minute in my house. He'd be fricasseed Sunday dinner.''

Abby laughed, her good humor restored.

She was very thankful when Ruffian met them at the door that afternoon, his greeting bark normal and vigorous. The mob of kids and dog ran off to play. No one asked Abby how her first day back at school went. *Just as well.*

During dinner, she dished up rice and carrots to go with the chicken strips she'd microwaved. ''Sammy, next week, while the boys are at their game, I'm taking you to the elementary school for some tests. Fun ones,'' she said quickly.

''Why does he have to be tested?'' Noah wanted to know.

''Uh, the usual stuff before going to kindergarten. Speech, hearing, those kinds of things,'' Abby said as if all kindergartners had testing.

Noah, tuning in to a problem, patted Sam's hand. "Tests are cool," he said. Sam looked up from his plate, not so much as flickering an eye.

An hour after dinner, as Abby made lunches for the next day, Mike strolled into the kitchen to swipe an apple. "Is something wrong with Sammy? Erin said Dr. Ben asked if he was talking yet. That school he's going to—will it help him be normal again?"

"He's there for physical and occupational therapy, Mike. I'll be honest, honey. I have no idea why Sam suddenly quit talking. Does he ever speak to you kids?"

"Not since Ben and the girls left. He misses them, though. 'Specially Ben."

"How do you know?" How sad, she thought, that she and Ben had been reduced to communicating through the kids.

"Easy. Sam's always drawing pictures of our house. He always draws in Ben and Erin and Mollie. And Ben's dad and mom. For a squirt, he draws good."

Abby made a mental note to check his drawings before she went to bed.

She did gather up a stack of pictures, but got distracted by Reed who couldn't find his school assignment. Once calm descended, she found herself too exhausted to remember where she'd put Sam's drawings. So she showered and climbed into bed.

Brad's counselor had cornered Abby on the playground that day. Bonnie Reavis still had concerns. Ha, so did Abby. Yesterday afternoon she'd caught Brad in the garage kicking the spokes out of his bike. He'd raged at God for taking his mom and dad. Abby hadn't known what to do. Almost three months since Blair and Elliot's death, and suddenly, this delayed reaction. It frightened her.

"Brad's grown recalcitrant and noncommunicative during our sessions,'' Bonnie had said. Abby knew the change coincided with Ben's departure, and promised Bonnie she'd look into the problem.

That night, when sleep wouldn't come, Abby toyed with the idea of phoning Ben to see if he'd be amenable to carving out a few minutes to visit the boys. At the very least, they needed to hear from Ben himself that his leaving wasn't their fault.

Abby picked up the phone and dialed the ER room. With her breath constricted in her throat, she quickly slammed the receiver down, not waiting for a clerk to answer. What if he thought she was phoning because she missed him? Well, darn it! She *did* miss him. So much, she ached to feel his touch again.

In the morning Abby battled gritty eyes. Still, she broached a subject she'd mulled over during the night. ''Boys, the lilac bush out back is blooming. I think we should cut bouquets and put them on your mom and dad's graves.''

Everyone but Sam stopped eating. Reed kicked a table leg. ''I don't wanna go see that sad ol' place. I don't understand why God took 'em when we need them more.''

''I can't answer that, Reed. Death is one of life's great mysteries. I know your mother planted that lilac tree when you and Brad were born. The snowball she planted for Noah and Mike. The climbing rose by the front door, is for Sam. It's just starting to bud. They were planted with love. Leaving flowers at their headstones is a sign that your parents are loved and not forgotten.''

''Will Mama and Daddy know we're giving them flowers?''

''I'd like to think so, Brad.''

''Okay, then. I'm real sorry about my bike, Aunt Abby. Dad wouldn't like what I did. Neither would Ben, I bet.''

"Oh, Brad." Abby hugged him. "Come—help me cut the blooms." She cut half a dozen branches. At first Brad just stood there. The minute Abby said she thought they had plenty, he grabbed her hand. "What about flowers for Erin and Mollie's mom? Erin said she's in the cemetery, too."

Tears collected in Abby's eyes. "Remembering Marlo would be a nice gesture, honey. You take these flowers to the kitchen and put them in water. I'll cut more."

It was a sobering trip. The children were terribly quiet on the ride to school.

At recess, Erin approached Abby on the playground. She acted shy. "Erin, how are you? How's Mollie? And Blackberry?" Abby tried to inject a light note.

"Awful," Erin blurted. "We don't like Mrs. Clark. She's crabby. Mollie and me want to move back in with you. Uncle Ben won't listen. He goes into his office and shuts the door. I, uh, came to thank you for taking flowers to my mom. Brad told me. I forgot and left Mommy's picture at your house next to my bed. Uncle Ben said he's gonna rent a truck and get all our stuff." Erin threw her arms around Abby's waist and burst into tears. Such copious tears she had to take Erin into the nursing office. As she did so, Abby was forced to admit the shambles her life had become. And she had to admit that it now affected seven children. She had no idea what to do.

Over the weekend, she picked up the phone to call Ben, then set it down again. She hoped he'd phone. She was sure the school nurse would've contacted him about Erin's outburst.

Saturday, Sunday and Monday came and went without a word from him.

On Tuesday, two of Abby's students had a free-for-all

on the playground. One set of parents reamed her out in the hall outside her classroom.

"You should've kept a better eye on those kids! I've heard you have seven of your own. You probably come to work exhausted. It's no wonder you're asleep at the switch during playground duty."

"I was wide-awake, Mrs. Lyons. The fight blew up fast. After it happened, another student said your son and Mark Taylor had words on the bus. If someone had told me, I might have warded off further problems by separating the boys."

A sixth-grader ran down the hall, stopped and handed Abby a message. "Excuse me, Mrs. Lyons." Abby read the note thinking it might concern the recent fight.

But no. James Peterson, the father who was supposed to collect Brad and Reed from their ball game, had to cancel at the last minute. The boys had been dismissed early and were already at the field. Abby rubbed at the furrows creasing her brow.

"Problem, Mrs. Galloway?" Mrs. Lyons hadn't gone away.

"It's nothing." Abby shrugged, rather than indicate the call was personal. She ignored the rest of the woman's petty bitching and tried to figure how she could juggle picking up Sam from the center and reaching a field at the opposite side of West Seattle to collect the twins and their stranded friend.

The three o'clock bell rang. She walked her students to their busses in a daze. Just as Abby thought she had a plan, Mr. Conrad tore out of his office calling her name.

"Noah, find Mike," she urged. Wait for me by the van. I need to see what Mr. Conrad wants."

"Abby, I'm so glad I caught you before you left. Some-

place called the Lenz Center phoned the office. The owner
told Caroline that Sam Drummond ran away.''

"Sam? Ran—? That's preposterous! Sam can barely
walk." Abby started to ask if the secretary had misunderstood the center's administrator. But of course she hadn't.
Caroline had worked for Mr. Conrad for fifteen years. She
was a jewel. Besides, it was illogical to think she'd pull
Sam's name out of a hat.

Once Abby cut through her initial disbelief, fear gripped
her heart and turned her stomach inside out. "Thank you,
Mr. Conrad. I have my cell phone. I'll call Mrs. Lenz from
the road. Brad and Reed are stranded at Park of the Lakes.
Mr. Barber checked them out of school early for their game
and Mr. Peterson's unable to pick them up as planned.''
Oh, what was she saying? Sam was the immediate priority.
She needed to phone Pam Lenz ASAP and find out how in
the world they'd misplaced one handicapped four-year-old
boy.

She punched in the number as she ran across the parking
lot. "Pam, this is Abby Galloway. What? Slow down. How
is it possible that Sam took his walker and simply left the
building?''

Abby made herself breathe slowly in and out. Even at
that, she realized how much she must sound like the hysterical Mrs. Lyons of half an hour ago.

"Mike, here are my keys. Unlock the van. And be quiet
for a minute. Sam seems to have disappeared from the center.''

"You mean he got kidnapped?'' Noah gasped.

Those words were like a dagger through Abby's heart.
"No! Of course not. According to his teacher, Sam left the
grounds without permission.

"Pam, I appreciate that you've phoned the police. I'm
leaving the school now. Hopefully they'll locate him before

I arrive. I'm sure he can't walk far." Logic told her that and brought a measure of calm. "They'll probably find him sitting on a curb less than a block from the center." *Please, Lord, let him be sitting on a curb.*

Abby's hand shook so hard, she had difficulty fitting the key in the ignition.

Five minutes later, she made an impulsive decision to phone Ben. For some reason, she had an overwhelming need to hear his solid, reassuring voice. She barely managed to punch in the number for his clinic.

"This is Abby Drummond, Pat. Er…it's Mrs. Galloway. No, not Mrs. Kirk Galloway," Abby stressed and almost shouted. "Pat? Is this Pat? It's Abby Galloway. I need to speak to Ben. Tell him it's an emergency."

"I'm sorry," the receptionist said, cutting Abby off. "Dr. Ben has an emergency of his own. He's sewing up a child who was bitten by a very nasty dog. I'm afraid he'll be tied up for half an hour, at least."

"Tell him… Tell him—Brad and Reed have no way home from Park of the Lakes. And Sam. Sammy's run away from the center." Abby's voice hit a high note, rising and falling raggedly as tears threatened to impair her driving skill. "Please, Pat, please relay my message to Ben. Oh…never mind. Just never mind." She clicked off and threw the phone into the front passenger seat. Grabbing it up again, she hit speed dial for Lily. Abby almost cried with relief when the older woman said she'd go after Brad, Reed and Bobby Peterson.

"If you have to find Sam," Noah said, "and if Ben can't leave his office, Aunt Abby…who's going to see that Brad and Reed get home?" He strained against his seat belt. His face had turned ashen.

"Erin and Mollie's grandma Lily." Abby didn't know how to explain her any more clearly than that. Dashing away her tears, she concentrated on driving to the center as fast as the van would take her. Forcing a semblance of calm, she smiled at Noah and Mike in the rearview mirror.

Moments later, she wheeled into the center's parking lot, praying her worry would be for nothing. But a frantic Pam Lenz paced in front of the building. She met Abby, apologizing profusely. "I swear to you, this has never *ever* happened at our school before. I've never lost a child."

"Neither have I. Did you ask his teacher if Sam seemed unduly upset today?"

"No. That's just it. He's always such a good, quiet child."

Abby heard crying, glanced over to discover Mike and Noah hugging one another. Bless their hearts. For fourth-graders, they'd been through so much already. They were the reason Abby had to hang on to what remained of her sanity.

"Mrs. Lenz, I need to borrow your phone book. My youngest set of twins got stranded at one of the parks. They had a ball game, and the person responsible for picking them up canceled at the last minute. My husband's—" she'd started to call Lily Ben's mother. "A friend of the senior Dr. Galloway has gone to collect them. I need to let Callie Peterson know Lily will drop off her son."

Ushering her into the office, Pam handed Abby the local phone book. Two phone calls later, she reached Callie Peterson, who insisted a man had dropped Bobby off and driven away with Brad and Reed.

"A man, Callie? But, who?" Abby's heart tightened in her chest. "Who said it's the twins father? Callie, you—everyone knows Elliot is…" Abby shuddered before she whispered, "…is deceased."

"Abby, what's wrong?" Pam guided Abby to a chair at her desk.

"My Lord, Pam. I can't think what to do. Bobby's mother said a man has Brad and Reed." Burying her face in her hands, Abby began to shake uncontrollably.

Noah threw open the door to Pam's office. "Aunt Abby, Aunt Abby. Come quick!"

She jerked upright. Was Noah heralding good news or bad? Surely, nothing else could happen today.

"Dr. Ben's here."

"Noah, that's not funny. I don't have time for games today."

"He is so here! And he's got Brad and Reed. He asked where you are, and where's Sam. And Erin and Mollie's grandma Lily drove right in behind him."

No sooner were the words out of Noah's mouth than Ben and Lily burst onto the scene. Ben wore a blood-spattered lab coat. His stethoscope hung half out of a ripped pocket. Tufts of his hair stood on end, and deep worry lines fanned around his lips.

Abby was shocked to see him gazing at her with pain in his eyes. Their time apart melted away. She forgot their differences, and the strife he'd put her through. "You came," she exclaimed brokenly. "For Sam. For me. You left your patients for us. Ben, I'll never be able to thank you."

"Nonsense." He hugged Abby a moment, burying his face in her wild array of red curls. Swaying to and fro, Ben ran his hands up and down her slender back. "Why would you doubt that I'd come, Abby? Pat's message scared the hell out of me. What happened with Sam? More important, what's being done to find him?"

Pam Lenz stepped forward, all but wringing her hands. She introduced herself. "I hate meeting you under these circumstances, Dr. Galloway. I've filed a report with the police. They and my staff are out combing the streets.

We've only got one student's word as to which direction Sam took.''

"I don't understand.'' Ben still cradled Abby. "Exactly how could a boy who can barely hobble about get past so many adults? And where would he go? Where's the child who saw him? Did Sam say anything before leaving? Did he give any clue at all? And what's *she* doing here?'' He pointed at Lily.

Abby hung her head and massaged her temples. "Ben, since the boys told me you'd asked Erin, I assumed you knew. Sam hasn't spoken since…ah…since the day of our first big blowup. Remember? You examined his throat and said physically he was fine. And just be nice to Lily. She dropped everything to go after Brad and Reed when your receptionist said you were unavailable.''

Lily gathered Noah and Michael's hands. "Kirk is coming, too. I took the liberty of phoning him about Sam. Now wipe that scowl off your face, Ben. In his way, Kirk loves you and Sam and all the kids. We've been, uh, dating. I think you'll see some positive changes in your father.''

The lines crisscrossing Ben's brow cut deeper. "I think the girls may have tried to tell me there was still a problem with Sam,'' he said, continuing to ignore Lily. "They've tried so many tactics to get me to call you, Abby. I'm sorry for suspecting his silence was another ploy. If he doesn't talk, what does he do at school all day?''

Mrs. Lenz walked around her desk. "He listens. And he draws. In fact, the student who saw him leave gave me this picture Sam left on his desk.'' The woman retrieved an eight-by-ten sheet and passed it to the couple.

Ben and Abby's heads touched as they studied the drawing. "He's drawn himself. There's his walker. Oh, look, Ben. In the picture he's not using the walker. It's by the door. But a door leading to what? There's a desk, and a man. Sam's reaching his arms out to the man, who seems to be reaching back. Could that be his old therapist's office? The background seems sort of familiar. Is it your father's office?"

"The kid's remarkably talented for his age." Ben tilted the picture so he could see it better. "Abby, I think he's drawn my office. See the framed certificates on the wall behind the desk? Those could belong to his therapist, or Kirk, of course. But notice the items on the desk. A photograph and a statue of a doctor surrounded by kids. Steve's mom bought each of us one when we opened the clinic."

Abby followed Ben's finger as he traced things he'd mentioned. "I believe you're right. Oh, but Ben—" She clapped a hand over her mouth. "Your clinic's five miles from here. Sam can't have the faintest idea how to reach it."

"Thing is, if we agree that's where he's headed, we can alert the police."

Brad and Reed, who'd come in and now hovered between Pam's office, Lily and the outside door, started hopping up and down, shouting, "Aunt Abby, Dr. Ben, there's two cop cars just drove up. And there's Erin and Mollie's Grandpa Kirk." The awed boys pressed their noses to the window, mostly excited about the cool black-and-whites with the flashing lights.

The adults, followed by Lily and the boys, all raced out of the building to converge on the nearest car. Tears streamed from Abby's eyes the moment she saw a dear, bright red head bobbing next to a female officer in the back seat of the vehicle. Sam's walker occupied the front passenger side.

Abby beat everyone—Ben, Lily, the boys, Pam and Kirk—to the door. "Sammy," she cried when the policewoman opened it. "What on earth possessed you to just walk away from school?"

"'Cause I wanted to visit Daddy Ben." The child's dirt-smudged, freckled face became beautifully animated the instant Sam spotted him. "Daddy Ben! Daddy Ben! I went to tell you we all love you. Please come home." Sam stretched out his grubby arms to Ben, whose step faltered and whose eyes began to fill.

Abby dashed away her tears. Tears of sadness mingled with tears of joy at having Sam safe and sound. "Sam... Ben... He's found his voice again! Oh, thank God. I've been worried sick."

"We picked the boy up jaywalking, ma'am," the male officer said. "Five blocks due south of here. My patrol was on the lookout after the chief called out a child alert."

"Five blocks south of this school?" Abby turned to Pam. "He walked so far and on rough concrete. Dr. Kirk, might Sam have reinjured his hip and leg? I mean—this could impede his progress, couldn't it? Set back his recovery?"

"Bring him inside. I'll check him out," Kirk said, blinking his own watery eyes. "Don't worry, Abby...Benjamin. Look at him. He doesn't seem any the worse for wear."

Abby did look, and her heart swelled. Sam had both arms wrapped around Ben's neck. His face was wreathed in smiles, and he seemed to be pouring out all the words he'd kept locked inside for weeks. The simple beauty of it hurt. Once again, she felt tears of sorrow brimming in her eyes. What would happen to Sam after this brief reunion with Ben? Tomorrow, life in the Drummond house would go back to the way it was.

"Pam, I can't tell you how troubled I am over Sam's escapade. He has the Drummond stubborn streak. If he sets his mind on a course, nothing short of full-scale disaster will deter him."

She turned to the officer in the car who'd delivered Sam to them. "Do you need anything from me? I teach at a local elementary school. My husband, er, the gentleman holding Sam, is a pediatrician on Thirty-Fifth Street. The other man is a surgeon. We're all so grateful for your quick response, and your help in finding Sammy."

"We're happy to be of service. Happier still there's a quick and easy solution."

Abby's knees felt spongy.

"The female officer extracted Sam's walker from the front seat. "The little guy told me he has two sets of twin brothers, and two sisters. I have to say, I expected you'd be much older, Mrs. Galloway." Both cops chuckled.

Abby couldn't even appreciate the compliment. She felt as if her world hadn't yet caved in around her.

Pam led Ben and Kirk inside, together with Sam. The police waved goodbye.

The two concerned physicians had almost finished examining Sam's reflexes and muscle tone when Abby's phone rang. Brad and Reed's ball coach was on the other end.

"Mrs. Galloway? What's this about the boys leaving the game with a stranger? I saw Dr. Galloway drive in. I was sure the twins got into his BMW."

"They did. We temporarily misplaced the boy's younger brother, Coach. It's a long story, and it got very confusing."

"Oh, but everything's all right now?"

Abby, afraid nothing would ever be right again since she'd botched things so badly, first with Ben and the girls, then with Lily and Kirk, and now with Sam, nevertheless assured the coach all was well.

She hung up, suddenly feeling the weight of the day sapping her last ounce of energy.

Lily hugged her.

Pam Lenz murmured, "You poor dear, what a day this has been for your family. Paul, that's my PT, just said Sam might have leg cramps tonight. If so, ice packs will help. But why am I telling you this when you have a pediatrician in the family?"

"And an orthopedic surgeon," Lily reminded them.

"Pam, Dr. Kirk Galloway is Ben's father, but neither man is actually related to Sam," Abby murmured.

Ben walked up behind her. "I...think we need to let these good people close up so they can get home to their families. And as we seem to be on the subject...of families, Abby, I think you and I need to go someplace and talk." He lowered his voice. "So we can clarify once and for all Kirk's and my relationship to, uh, Sam."

Bravely, Abby pasted a smile on her face, even though she died a little inside at the prospect of severing all connections with Ben Galloway.

She put the boys in the van and attempted to pry Sam away from Ben.

"No, Aunt Abby. Daddy Ben said I could ride home with him."

"Sammy, it's getting late. Ben's due at the ER in less than an hour. He wants a word with me before he goes home to check on Erin and Mollie." Suddenly cold to the bone, Abby felt her teeth begin to chatter.

"Doctors are allowed to take sick leave sometimes. Tonight I honestly don't feel so well," Ben said. "Abby, you're in no shape to drive. I'll leave my car here and take you and the boys home. Actually, I'd like to swing by my house to pick up the girls."

"Ben, there's no need to draw this out. To make another parting worse."

"Shh." He touched two fingers to Abby's lips. "Since

the night I walked out on you, I've slowly been working everything out in my head. I have to tell you, when I arrived here and saw the pain and worry on your face, it hit me like a ten-pound sledge hammer. I knew I'd become my father—just like you said. I'd let my work become my life. I'd let my career assume more importance than the woman I love. Well, I'm not going to allow that to happen, Abigail. Please tell me it's not too late to erase these past few weeks and start all over.''

Abby sagged against the side of the van. ''Say that again.''

''Since the night I walked out on you—''

''No,'' she interrupted, surging forward to grab the lapels of his lab coat. ''Just repeat the part where you said you loved me. Or I think that's what you said.''

Awkwardly, because Ben had a four-year-old wrapped around his neck, he lifted Abby's hand and kissed the ring he'd placed on her finger without ever saying he loved her. ''I've never made a secret of the fact that Marlo and I never had anyone at home to show us how to love. I used two yardsticks. Kirk's, which measured love in dollars and cents and an ability to provide material things for his family. And yours, Abby. Where love was a matter of compromise and sharing. You, Abby, and seven kids showed me what love really is.''

Lily took Kirk's hand and tugged him toward their cars. ''Time for us to skedaddle. Kirk, tell them before you go that you can teach an old dog new tricks.''

He cleared his throat several times, and actually managed to look contrite as he grasped Ben's free hand. ''I'm sorry…for—I'm just sorry, son. Lily's made me see, well…a lot of things. You go and make it right with your family. You and I will talk later.'' The older couple walked away hand in hand.

Abby skimmed her fingers over Ben's lips. "Even though I wasn't sure you loved me, Ben, I never doubted how you felt about the children. And not just Marlo's girls. I was hurt and angry when I accused you of being like your father—the old Kirk. If you really love me, I know I can handle anything else life throws at us."

"Even when love hurts? Like when Pat stuck her head in my exam room today and said you'd called, saying Sam had run away I felt like a meteorite had dropped on my head."

"Even then." Feeling had seeped back into Abby's weak limbs. "Love manifests itself in many different ways."

"Well, I thought I was showing you how much I cared every night."

"Without the words, I came away…uh…believing you'd filed our lovemaking under the meaningless category of good sex," she murmured almost too softly for Sam to hear.

"Grreat sex, you mean." Ben smiled one of his most charming, slightly off-kilter smiles.

"I'd rather know it's love. Love makes the difference, Ben. Love is the glue that binds couples together through thick and thin."

"You'd think I'd be smart enough to figure that out for myself. I know now."

"As a teacher, I have a soft spot in my heart for slow learners."

He kissed her, fully, passionately. And she kissed him back until they heard giggles and gagging sounds at the van's open door.

"Uh-huh! Time to go get the girls and take these little monsters out to dinner," Ben said, winking at Abby.

"I'd offer to fix you a home-cooked meal, Ben, but I'm afraid everything I have needs thawing out."

Ben buckled Sam into his booster seat and then helped Abby into the passenger side. "That's okay, we'll grab burgers someplace that has a play area. Wear the kids out, and then we can wear each other out, if you catch my drift."

Abby blushed. "I'm afraid Pam's PT thinks Sam will be up tonight with leg cramps."

"Hmm. I believe we can find something to keep us occupied during his catnaps." Ben started the van and drove out of the lot. He switched on the radio to a rock and roll station, then turned the sound to the back speakers. "Now we can talk without eavesdroppers."

"I'm trying to be serious, Ben. What Sam did this afternoon—running away—was our fault. Yours and mine."

"I wasn't running away!" Sam shouted. Clearly the music hadn't kept him from listening in on their conversation. "Daddy Ben never came home no more, so I decided to go to his office and then he'd hafta bring me home. You guys said we were gonna be a fambly. We can't be a fambly if no mom and dad are ever home."

Abby and Ben shared a surreptitious, guilty look.

"The kid's right," Ben acknowledged quietly.

"Yes. But, Ben, I have to finish this year of work. I…found out teaching isn't so much fun anymore. Add to that the trauma my working has caused our family, and well, it crossed my mind that we'd be ahead if I tutor instead of teach."

"Really? When did all that cross your mind?"

"At recess when Erin told me how much she and Mollie dislike having Mrs. Clark as their sitter. I had to go back to the classroom to appreciate the advantages I had in staying home."

"You know what? I came to the same conclusion about working in the emergency room. That's not what I want to do. I want to do more in pediatric oncology. Study cancer in children,'' Ben explained. ''Months before the earthquake, I applied for a grant to do research on cancers affecting children under the age of eight. Not leukemia. Other types of carcinogenic tumors. Yesterday I learned I got the grant. It pays more than I earn in the ER. And for me, the work is more rewarding.''

''Ben, that's great! I'm not saying that just because you'll be home more—although that is important. I love you, Ben. With or without a fancy specialty that makes oodles of money. I'm thrilled that you'll have an opportunity to get involved in meaningful work you'll love.''

''Abby, I want you to know I'll support whatever you decide to do. If you want to teach, we'll find a way to accommodate you. Watching Kirk examine Sam in there— well, my father seemed genuinely worried about…us. If he's not too old to change his stripes, there's sure hope for me.''

''When do we get to eat?'' Brad yelled. ''I'm starved.''

''Hmm. Me, too.'' Ben let his eyes drift slowly over Abby. ''Here we are at my house. My *old* house,'' Ben made a point of saying. ''Noah, will you run in and get the girls? Instead of burgers out, I suggest we all go home…to your place—ours,'' he corrected. ''We'll order something in.''

''Too bad Elliot never got around to adding that Jacuzzi. After the day I've had, I could go for that over food,'' Abby said, leaning back in her seat.

The boys began bartering over pizza toppings as Noah opened the side door of the van and ran toward the McBride house. Under cover of the kids' din, Ben pulled a long white envelope from his pocket and tapped Abby's freckled nose. ''This is the first installment on my grant. I thought we could use it for a belated honeymoon. But if you'd rather put in a Jacuzzi, I'm A-okay with that.''

"A belated honeymoon sounds heavenly." Abby snatched the envelope and peeked inside. "Ben—I've got an idea. I uncovered something in my stacked-up mail at school. A brochure offering a two-week, summer family getaway, complete with a Magic Kingdom card.''

"A California amusement park?" Ben grimaced.

"A cruise ship. With loads of activities designed to entertain kids. Leaving their parents free to entertain each other.''

Glancing at her, Ben saw that the sparkle he loved, had returned to Abby's ever changing eyes.

"Sold. Tomorrow when I go in to work, I'll block out the time.''

"Let's go home so we can eat," came the chorus at the door. Erin and Mollie stood with their arms looped around Noah. They all grinned from ear to ear. The boy hauled a spitting, meowing cat in a too small carrier.

Laughing, Abby and Ben leaned across the console to share another stolen kiss. Ben pulled back, saying, "Load 'em up. This van's heading home. *Home,*" he said again, underscoring the word with every last bit of love he'd been storing up for so many years.

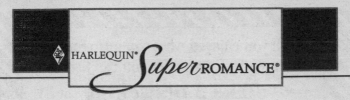

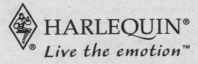

Is your man too good to be true?

Hot, gorgeous AND romantic?
If so, he could be a Harlequin® Blaze™ series cover model!

Our grand-prize winners will receive a trip for two to New York City to
shoot the cover of a Blaze novel, and will stay at the luxurious Plaza Hotel.
Plus, they'll receive $500 U.S. spending money!
The runner-up winners will receive $200 U.S.
to spend on a romantic dinner for two.

It's easy to enter!

In 100 words or less, tell us what makes your boyfriend or spouse a true romantic
and the perfect candidate for the cover of a Blaze novel, and include in your submission
two photos of this potential cover model.

All entries must include the written submission of the contest entrant, two photographs of the model
candidate and the Official Entry Form and Publicity Release forms completed in full and signed by
both the model candidate and the contest entrant. Harlequin, along with the experts at
Elite Model Management, will select a winner.

For photo and complete Contest details, please refer to the Official Rules on the next page. All entries
will become the property of Harlequin Enterprises Ltd. and are not returnable.

Please visit www.blazecovermodel.com to download a copy of the Official Entry Form and
Publicity Release Form or send a request to one of the addresses below.

Please mail your entry to: **Harlequin Blaze Cover Model Search**

In U.S.A.
P.O. Box 9069
Buffalo, NY
14269-9069

In Canada
P.O. Box 637
Fort Erie, ON
L2A 5X3

No purchase necessary. Contest open to Canadian and U.S. residents who are 18 and over.
Void where prohibited. Contest closes September 30, 2003.

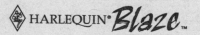

HARLEQUIN BLAZE COVER MODEL SEARCH CONTEST 3569 OFFICIAL RULES
NO PURCHASE NECESSARY TO ENTER

1. To enter, submit two (2) 4" x 6" photographs of a boyfriend or spouse (who must be 18 years of age or older) taken no later than three (3) months from the time of entry: a close-up, waist up, shirtless photograph; and a fully clothed, full-length photograph, then, tell us, in 100 words or fewer, why he should be a Harlequin Blaze cover model and how he is romantic. Your complete "entry" must include: (i) your essay, (ii) the Official Entry Form and Publicity Release Form printed below completed and signed by you (as "Entrant"), (iii) the photographs (with your hand-written name, address and phone number, and your model's name, address and phone number on the back of each photograph), and (iv) the Publicity Release Form and Photograph Representation Form printed below completed and signed by your model (as "Model"), and should be sent via first-class mail to either: Harlequin Blaze Cover Model Search Contest 3569, P.O. Box 9069, Buffalo, NY, 14269-9069, or Harlequin Blaze Cover Model Search Contest 3569, P.O. Box 637, Fort Erie, Ontario L2A 5X3. All submissions must be in English and be received no later than September 30, 2003. Limit: one entry per person, household or organization. **Purchase or acceptance of a product offer does not improve your chances of winning.** All entry requirements must be strictly adhered to for eligibility and to ensure fairness among entries.

2. Ten (10) Finalist submissions (photographs and essays) will be selected by a panel of judges consisting of members of the Harlequin editorial, marketing and public relations staff, as well as a representative from Elite Model Management (Toronto) Inc., based on the following criteria:

Aptness/Appropriateness of submitted photographs for a Harlequin Blaze cover—70%
Originality of Essay—20%
Sincerity of Essay—10%

In the event of a tie, duplicate finalists will be selected. The photographs submitted by finalists will be posted on the Harlequin website no later than November 15, 2003 (at www.blazecovermodel.com), and viewers may vote, in rank order, on their favorite(s) to assist in the panel of judges' final determination of the Grand Prize and Runner-up winning entries based on the above judging criteria. All decisions of the judges are final.

3. All entries become the property of Harlequin Enterprises Ltd. and none will be returned. Any entry may be used for future promotional purposes. Elite Model Management (Toronto) Inc. and/or its partners, subsidiaries and affiliates operating as "Elite Model Management" will have access to all entries including all personal information, and may contact any Entrant and/or Model in its sole discretion for their own business purposes. Harlequin and Elite Model Management (Toronto) Inc. are separate entities with no legal association or partnership whatsoever having no power to bind or obligate the other or create any expressed or implied obligation or responsibility on behalf of the other, such that Harlequin shall not be responsible in any way for any acts or omissions of Elite Model Management (Toronto) Inc. or its partners, subsidiaries and affiliates in connection with the Contest or otherwise and Elite Model Management shall not be responsible in any way for any acts or omissions of Harlequin or its partners, subsidiaries and affiliates in connection with the contest or otherwise.

4. All Entrants and Models must be residents of the U.S. or Canada, be 18 years of age or older, and have no prior criminal convictions. The contest is not open to any Model that is a professional model and/or actor in any capacity at the time of the entry. Contest void wherever prohibited by law; all applicable laws and regulations apply. Any litigation within the Province of Quebec regarding the conduct or organization of a publicity contest may be submitted to the Régie des alcools, des courses et des jeux for a ruling, and any litigation regarding the awarding of a prize may be submitted to the Régie only for the purpose of helping the parties reach a settlement. Employees and immediate family members of Harlequin Enterprises Ltd., D.L. Blair, Inc., Elite Model Management (Toronto) Inc. and their parents, affiliates, subsidiaries and all other agencies, entities and persons connected with the use, marketing or conduct of this Contest are not eligible to enter. Acceptance of any prize offered constitutes permission to use Entrants' and Models' names, essay submissions, photographs or other likenesses for the purposes of advertising, trade, publication and promotion on behalf of Harlequin Enterprises Ltd., its parent, affiliates, subsidiaries, assigns and other authorized entities involved in the judging and promotion of the contest without further compensation to any Entrant or Model, unless prohibited by law.

5. Finalists will be determined no later than October 30, 2003. Prize Winners will be determined no later than January 31, 2004. Grand Prize Winners (consisting of winning Entrant and Model) will be required to sign and return Affidavit of Eligibility/Release of Liability and Model Release forms within thirty (30) days of notification. Non-compliance with this requirement and within the specified time period will result in disqualification and an alternate will be selected. Any prize notification returned as undeliverable will result in the awarding of the prize to an alternate set of winners. All travelers (or parent/legal guardian of a minor) must execute the Affidavit of Eligibility/Release of Liability prior to ticketing and must possess required travel documents (e.g. valid photo ID) where applicable. Travel dates specified by Sponsor but no later than May 30, 2004.

6. Prizes: One (1) Grand Prize—the opportunity for the Model to appear on the cover of a paperback book from the Harlequin Blaze series, and a 3 day/2 night trip for two (Entrant and Model) to New York, NY for the photo shoot of Model which includes round-trip coach air transportation from the commercial airport nearest the winning Entrant's home to New York, NY, (or, in lieu of air transportation, $100 cash payable to Entrant and Model, if the winning Entrant's home is within 250 miles of New York, NY), hotel accommodations (double occupancy) at the Plaza Hotel and $500 cash spending money payable to Entrant and Model, (approximate prize value: $8,000), and one (1) Runner-up Prize of $200 cash payable to Entrant and Model for a romantic dinner for two (approximate prize value: $200). Prizes are valued in U.S. currency. Prizes consist of only those items listed as part of the prize. No substitution of prize(s) permitted by winners. All prizes are awarded jointly to the Entrant and Model of the winning entries, and are not severable - prizes and obligations may not be assigned or transferred. Any change to the Entrant and/or Model of the winning entries will result in disqualification and an alternate will be selected. Taxes on prize are the sole responsibility of winners. Any and all expenses and/or items not specifically described as part of the prize are the sole responsibility of winners. Harlequin Enterprises Ltd. and D.L. Blair, Inc., their parents, affiliates, and subsidiaries are not responsible for errors in printing of Contest entries and/or game pieces. No responsibility is assumed for lost, stolen, late, illegible, incomplete, inaccurate, non-delivered, postage due or misdirected mail or entries. In the event of printing or other errors which may result in unintended prize values or duplication of prizes, all affected game pieces or entries shall be null and void.

7. Winners will be notified by mail. For winners' list (available after March 31, 2004), send a self-addressed, stamped envelope to: Harlequin Blaze Cover Model Search Contest 3569 Winners, P.O. Box 4200, Blair, NE 68009-4200, or refer to the Harlequin website (at www.blazecovermodel.com).

Contest sponsored by Harlequin Enterprises Ltd., P.O. Box 9042, Buffalo, NY 14269-9042.

HBCVRMODEL2

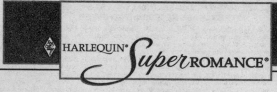

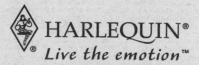